The Cheechakoes

ISBN: 1-4196-2783-X
ISBN-13: 978-1419627835

Visit www.booksurge.com to order additional copies.

BY GENE MADSEN

THE CHEECHAKOES

2007

The Cheechakoes

This Book Is Dedicated To My Wife Of Over 50 Years,
Geneva (Nin) Madsen. For All These Years She Has
Been A Great Wife, A Super Mother To Our Four Daughters
And A Great Companion

THE CHEECHAKOES by GENE MADSEN

BERT AND HANS MEET ON SEATTLE DOCK

CHAPTER 1

Hans stood on the grimy wharf in the port of Seattle. He was day dreaming about what might lay ahead for him. He had left his father's farm in northwest Iowa and also his girl friend Olive, to go to the Yukon. He worked on his father's farm all his working years, now he was twenty two and looking for a new adventure. The fog was coming in and the drizzle was getting heavier. As he turned to leave, he bumped into a fellow behind him.

"Damn, I'm sorry, I about knocked you over," Hans said.

The young man looked at Hans and gave him a smile, "Forget it."

"My name is Hans Hansen."

"Glad to meet you, my name is Bert Thompson."

"You don't look like a man who belongs on the docks here in Seattle".

Hans answered, "I'll tell you Bert, I'm one of those gold crazy farm boys from Iowa, looking to find some gold up in that Yukon country."

Bert gave Hans a smile and said, "Well I guess you're talking to another farm boy from Idaho way, going north looking for the same gold."

They shook hands; and both gave each other the grip test, to show the other guy he wasn't a wimp.

Bert said, "Hell, let's go find some place where we can sit down where it's dry and drink a beer".

As they meandered down the street, it was apparent the city of Seattle was full of other characters with the same idea. The two found a so-called bar or pub, or whatever it was called. They saw a sign showing a glass of beer, which was all that mattered. The main room was full of men dressed in heavy dark clothes, most had beards. It appeared the majority were puffing on pipes; the blue haze was so heavy it was hard to see where they might find some place to sit. They walked to the far end of the room and found a table not in use.

The bartender walked up, he was a skinny fellow with a hooked nose and a complexion that looked like old leather. He had one of those handle bar mustaches, which almost looked like a bird's wing. He leaned over the table and with squinted dark eyes said, "I sees we have some more of dose gold prospectors in our fine town."

Bert didn't know if this guy was a wise ass or just making talk but he gave the bartender a smile and said, "We're contracted to take twelve whores to the Dawson gold fields."

The skinny bartender's jaw dropped enough so you could see his grimy lower teeth.

He said "No shit, damn, that's the kind of job I want. I get along good with all women, skinny or fat, beautiful or ugly.... Say, the boss is looking, what do you guys want?"

Hans said "Two beers."

When the skinny old fart walked away, they both started to laugh.

Bert said, "That was one hell of an answer. If we both plan on going to the land of gold nuggets, why don't we team up, and save on buying all that duplicate gear?"

"That's a great idea Bert. I hear tell that's the way to go north, find a buddy you can get along with and save on the gear."

After a couple more five cent beers, they left to find lodging for the night. In the morning they sat on the two beds, talking about the gear they would take to the Yukon. Hans had stopped at the closest supply outfitter to the docks. He had passed on a list of gear and supplies they should take north. They went through the list: flour, yeast, corn meal, rice, oatmeal, beans, candles, sugar, baking soda, bacon, salt, pepper, mustard, dried apples, peaches, apricots, plums, onions, potatoes, coffee, tea, condensed milk, bars of laundry soap, sixty boxes stick matches, dried vegetables, butter, small metal stove, gold pan, bucket, cups, plates, spoons, forks and knifes, frying pan, coffee pot, pick, shovel, axe, whip saw, hand saw, jack plane, braces and bits, mill file, hatchet, wet stone, draw knife, chisels, nails, one hundred fifty feet of half inch rope, pitch and oakum, canvas tent, several changes of clothing, socks and under wear, long johns, wool blankets, medicine kit, extra canvas for boat sails, extra rubber sheets, rivets, tape measure, compass, wash basin, baking powder, pack straps, pie and baking tins, towels, extra axe and shovel handles, and maybe a 30:30 rifle.

"Course, we'll have to have our own extra clothes. That seems like one hell of a lot of equipment, to take north to the Yukon."

According to the store outfitter, it would cost about five hundred dollars to equip each man going to the Yukon, so if they went together, it would be less than five hundred dollars each. This would lower the total amount they would have to haul to Dawson City. They packed up their gear and headed to Cooper and Levy, the local outfitter's store. This part of Seattle had trolley tracks, but also still had dirt streets.

Since the ship was leaving the following day and they each had their passage bought, they made a deal with Cooper to haul the supplies right to the wharf. Before they left the store Hans asked the store owner if he had any old orange crates he wanted to get rid of. The owner told him "Go to the back room and help yourself." Hans picked up about twenty of the thin 3" by 18" by 1/8" boards, and bought a bunch of string to hold them together.

Bert asked, "What in hell are you going to do with those little boards?"

Hans responded, "Bert, you'll find out soon enough."

They spent a little over eight hundred dollars for their gear and supplies, so they had some money left over. Bert suggested they get some kind of liquor to sip on after mining gold all day. They bought two cases of brandy which amounted to twenty-four bottles.

The next day was bright and sunny when they boarded the ship with their supplies. They made sure all of their gear was in one area. It was stashed in the rear of the ship; they covered everything with canvas and tied it up tight. The two had a small room with two wooden bunks with straw mattresses. Hans said, "What the hell, it's out of the weather and dry."

The ship backed out the next day and headed out of the harbor. As Bert and Hans looked around they couldn't believe all the animals on board this old ship. There were horses, sheep, and dogs. "Damn" Bert commented, "Did you think you would be heading north on the ark?"

The trip over the open waters after leaving Seattle was a little rough and it had a bad effect on both men and animals. After they pulled into the Inland Passage, it was smooth and the sickness among the people on board soon left. The first stop the ship made was at Juneau, Alaska.

Bert and Hans left the ship to walk around the small town. There was a four hour lay over, so they had plenty of time. They saw a local Indian selling what appeared to be sleds. The men walked up and asked the Indian how much for the sled?

The Indian held up his four fingers and thumb.

Bert said, "He wants 10 dollars for two sleds."

He shook his head up and down. He was short, with a bowl type hair cut and had very dirty hands. When he smiled, his teeth all looked black at the roots.

Hans said, "We give you eight dollars for two sleds."

The Indian put his stubby finger in his mouth and looked off to his right, like he was getting a sign from someone, but there wasn't anyone there.

He replied after a couple minutes, "Me make you a good buy, me give you two haulers for nine dollars."

The men looked at each other.

The Indian said," Sleds have no nails, all hide, never come apart, you get good buy."

They paid the Indian and carried the two, seven- foot by two foot sleds back to the boat. As the ship moved north through the Inland Passage, Bert and Hans couldn't believe the mountains and all the timber. Some places the passage was only about three hundred feet wide; they could see fish in toward shore and sea otters would come to the surface, lying on their backs. It was quite a sight! They would have a rock on their stomach and would take a clam shell in the other hand and break the clam shell on the rock. Hans thought that was one smart otter!

The next day Hans dug out his little boards and laid them on his lap. Bert sat there puffing on his pipe, but didn't say anything, he kept his eyes on the boards. Hans took out his large jack knife and started cutting a circle on one end of the board. He cut off a section about two inches square, and then proceeded to round off the corners. After he had the corners rounded off so it was a circle, he laid it on the board and marked off another the same size.

Bert said, "What the hell are you making Hans?"

"Money," he replied.

Hans was intent on what he was making. He told Bert, "You'll see soon enough what I'm making."

After Hans had the two circles, he proceeded in making a fine slit in the center of each circle. After that he made a hole in each side of the slit. When he had the holes finished, he tied a string in the holes to make a pair of glasses and put them on his face and looked at Bert. Bert sat there and stared at Hans.

"What are you, a Chinaman?" Bert laughed.

Hans replied, "These are going to make us some extra money, did you ever see glasses like these?"

"Nope, I never have, so tell me, what you're going to do with them?"

"Well, I'll tell you, these are snow glasses. When you get out in the bright snow, with the sun shining bright and if you keep looking at that bright snow, you can go snow blind."

Bert sat there and just looked at Hans, with a dumb look on his face.

"Are you shitting me?"

"No," replied Hans, "My uncle had a pair of these he used back in Iowa when he had to look at the bright snow when he went to town in the winter."

Bert took out his jack-knife and started making his own glasses. The traveling time from Seattle was about seventy two hours, so they spent their idle time making so-called snow glasses. As they moved north, there was less sun to see while moving through the inland waterways. Early one morning they came to a town called Haines, then the ship turned to the right and headed up the long bay. The captain said they were getting close to Dyea.

As Bert and Hans stood on the bow, Hans said,

"Well Bert today is August 31, 1897 and we are on our way to Dawson City, to bring back a ton of gold."

Bert lit up his pipe and stood there with a big grin on his face.

"The first thing we do in Dawson is get us a claim in that gold field. Hell maybe we should each get one, then we'll have twice as much gold."

CHAPTER 2

When the ship came closer to shore, they could see a long slope to the main land.

As they stood there, the captain walked by and commented to the two young husky fellows, "You boys appear to have the muscle to carry your goods to shore, but if you have some extra money, I would hire a wagon to haul your gear to high and dry land. When we go in to unload, it will be at low tide, and then as soon as the tide water goes past the ship, we unload on the beach. At this point we have about twelve hours to get the animals and gear off the beach."

"Son of a bitch," Bert said, "We had better try to hire a wagon to get us off the beach, if we loose this gear in the water we'll be in bad shape."

As soon as the water was low enough at the bow, Hans went over the side and headed through the mud flats toward the buildings, which was Dyea. He couldn't believe the distance from the ship to the buildings. Since the people on shore could see the ship approaching, it didn't take long for some people with wagons to head for the boat to make a dollar.

Hans asked the wagon master, "What would it cost to haul our goods to shore?"

The wagon master answered him, "How far up the Dyea do you want to go?" Hans asked, "How far can you haul us?"

The wagon master said, "We can take you about three to four miles, and the cost would be fifteen dollars."

Hans said, "Let's go."

So the wagon master headed toward the boat and Hans jumped on the back of the wagon. After they arrived at the ship, it took about a half hour for their goods to be unloaded. This didn't set too well with the wagon owner but he soon cooled off and they proceeded toward Dyea.

There was great confusion at the ship. They were unloading horses over the side and when they let the belly strap loose the horses wanted to take off for the unknown. Bert was extremely glad the captain gave them some good advice before the ship came ashore. On the way in from the ship, the fellow running the rig told the greenhorns that they should pick up some heavy duty canvas bags at the store in which to haul their gear.

When they came through the small town of Dyea, it consisted of five or six stores. In the past, most of the business was with the local Chilkat Indians. As they passed the general store of Healy and Wilson, Hans jumped off and went into the store to buy the canvas bags.

As he entered the store, the old owner said, "Ah, we have a new bunch of Cheechakoes in Dyea."

Hans had no idea what the man was talking about. To be on the safe side he bought fifteen bags at fifty cents each. After paying for the bags, he raced out of the store and after a hundred feet he caught the freight wagon and climbed aboard.

On the way past the high ground they saw piles of supplies. They asked the wagon man, "How come they still had freight on the beach?" The wagon man told them it seems some of these gold seekers hadn't made up their minds when they were going to move on.

After about three or four miles the wagon came to a halt and the fellow told them, "This is the end of the line."

Bert asked, "Can't you take us any farther?"

"Yep, but the cost goes up".

So they unloaded all their gear in a pile. They now came to realize it was up to them.

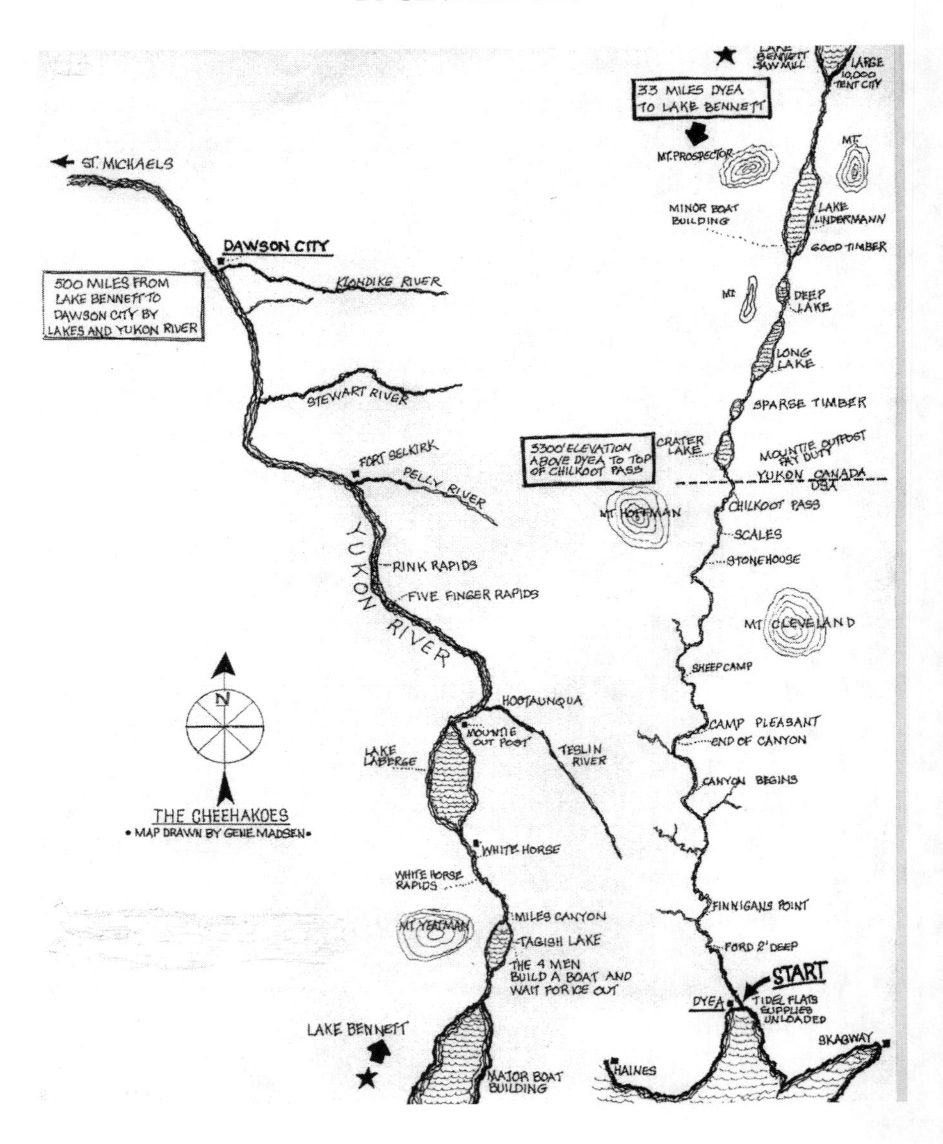

I guess this was the moment of truth. So far the two gold seekers had been along for the ride; at this point they had to figure how to get the gear up the trail. According to the wagon master, they had about thirty miles to Lake Bennett.

"First of all, we have to repack this stuff into the new bags we bought."

After re-packing their gear, they made an estimate. They had somewhere around sixteen hundred pounds of gear. If they could make this into fifty pound loads it would take them sixteen trips each to relay their gear.

Bert asked Hans, "How far should we carry this gear at one time? We have about ten miles to get to what the people show on the map as the Scales. I wish someone would have told us what the best distance might be for hauling. Why don't we try for a mile at a time, at least this will be a start."

Soon the men came to a small canyon on the trail. There were three men there waiting to pass their gear over the opening.

Bert asked the guy, "What's the deal?"

"Some other guys who were crossing when we arrived told us they call this a 'Jacobs Ladder.' That's all I know."

It was really a bridge over a crack in the ground. They each had to crawl across the so called bridge.

At first, they were a little reluctant to leave their gear along the trail unguarded, but soon they saw many piles along the way left unguarded. As they loaded up and took off up the rocky trail, they saw many large cottonwood trees. These trees were common in the prairie along the rivers, but they didn't think they would see trees this large in the north. The slippery rocks made the going hard. They now had the feeling that maybe they were not in as good shape as they thought they were to carry all this gear for many miles. This time of the year, the blood sucking bugs were out to get their nourishment. There were still many mosquitoes, black flies, or gnats as some guys called them, and then the no see-ums.

It was about eleven a.m. when they started their first relay. At around six p.m. they had made their one mile relay.

Bert said, "Let's fix supper and get an early start in the morning, I think I'm pooped."

Hans thought that would be a good way to end the first day in the north. The tent was set up for the first time. They had to cut a ridge pole and a couple of posts for up-rights. As soon as they got the stove set up, they put some water on for the beans. They thought maybe beans and bacon would hold them for the first night. Hans cooked some extra bacon for something to eat for the next noon meal; he was sure they would be too busy to cook the noon meal. The rubber tarp was laid on the ground, even though the ground was quite dry.

After the meal they laid down and lit their pipes. As they rested their tired muscles, they talked about how they forgot about their brandy. They agreed it wouldn't go to waste. The men were dead tired and before long both were sound asleep.

In the morning Hans figured he hadn't moved an inch all night long. His eyes slowly came open. As he lay there, he thought to himself, "Where the hell am I?"

Then, as his brain came out of the blackness, he heard something. It didn't dawn on him what was making the noise on the tent. Then he realized it was raining, "Oh shit" he said to himself.

"Since this day is off to a bad start, I'm going to make some flapjacks, maybe we'll need a good belly full to get us through this horse shit day."

Hans let Bert sleep until he had the extra bacon and pancakes about cooked. He almost had to roll Bert out of his blanket before he woke up. Bert sat there staring at the stove; then he heard the rain. He said "Is that rain I hear?" Hans replied, "It's not a cow pissing on a flat rock."

They couldn't believe how good the coffee smelled, boiling on the wood stove. Hans thought; if we were up at the gold fields now, this would be great. If we had a poke full of gold, we might even take the day off. They made extra pancakes to eat for dinner. Even though the rain was still coming down lightly, they packed up the gear, and started for the next relay point. They left the tent up, just in case they had to stay there this night.

The two headed up the trail. The rocks on the trail were hard to get around and the moss on the rocks made it difficult to get any traction. The trail was quite steep, making it hard to keep from falling down. As they came around the bend they saw some buildings. Then they could make out the names on the signs. Bert said, "I can see why they call this Canyon City."

CANYON CITY

The rain wasn't too bad, it was cool, about forty five degrees and they seemed to be getting in better shape to move the gear north. As Hans trudged along, he kept his eyes on the ground to pick his way through the sharp rocks. When you put fifty pounds on your back, you have to keep your head down and look at the ground. It also gives you time to think. I guess if I could think of something good, it would take my mind off this weight on my back. Then Hans started to think about moving their gear up the trail. We're about five miles north of Dyea, we have about twenty seven miles to get to Lake Bennett, and then it's about five hundred fifty miles from Bennett to Dawson City. Course, those last miles will all on water; just sit back and watch the trees go by. The two had no way of knowing that this was the easiest part of the trail. They were making good time now. It wasn't long before they came into Sheep Camp. They couldn't believe all the men on the trail; the closer they got to Sheep Camp, the more men they saw.

As Bert and Hans made their way into Sheep Camp they noticed there was gear piled all along the trail. This was the only part of the trail where the land was flat. It appeared many outfits were stopped here, maybe to rest to gather steam for the next haul.

Hans thought they should move on through the piles of supplies and get a little closer to the trail going out of the area. There were about three frame buildings in Sheep Camp, mostly for eating and sleeping. There were hundreds of people milling around so it made it difficult for the two men to pack their gear to their drop off point. The first stash they made was back off the trail, by a large spruce tree. They hurried back through the crowd to start their next relay. They noticed the rain they had in the morning had now turned to snow at this higher altitude. The snow made the trail very greasy in some areas; it seemed to be worse going down the hill. The men loaded up and took off behind some other packers. It was strange to see these long lines moving in unison; it gave the appearance of a large caterpillar, inching its way up the trail.

There wasn't much talk out of the men carrying these heavy loads. Some men had dogs carrying their gear, some had horses, and the horses appeared to be on a death march. It was amazing to walk up this trail and see so many piles of goods along the way. The saying along the trail was, "If someone would steal your goods, where would they take it?" No one seemed to worry about anyone stealing another man's goods.

Since the sun was so far north at this time of the year, it didn't get dark until around ten p.m. This gave the men extra time to move their gear. It was about seven in the evening when Bert and Hans got their last load to their pile. They cleared away the few inches of snow on the ground so they could set up their tent on dryer ground. With their small Swede saw, the men went into the woods to get some fire wood. Where the branches sheltered the ground better, they found some dryer wood. The dried spruce was hard as hell to break, but it would burn good.

When they brought back their first wood, they met their new neighbors. The older gentlemen told them, "It's not far up the trail where you run out of timber."

Bert spoke, "What do you mean; we will run out of timber?"

The old fellow took his pipe from his lips and pointed with the pipe up the mountain. "You see son, the tree line is up the trail a short distance, there just aren't any more trees. In fact, you'll have to get over the summit before you'll find more wood."

Bert threw down his wood and turned to Hans, "We not only have to carry all these supplies, now we have to carry fire wood. This little trip up north is getting worse all the time."

The younger guy with the old timer said, "If you talk to some of these guys who seem to know this neck of the woods, they can tell you some mighty big tales. One old guy we talked to said up on the Chilkoot you can get snow five feet at a time."

"How can a man carry this crap on his back through five feet of snow?" asked Bert.

The old guy lit up his pipe again, and looked down at the firewood. "You big guys won't have any problem carrying extra wood to cook your meals and keep your butts warm."

Bert and Hans went back into the woods to fetch more wood. Hans thought to himself, there sure are a lot of new things to learn on this little hike. Now we have to figure out how much firewood we need until the next time we get back into the timber. The spruce and hemlock in this area had a lot of moss on it, and one could see, with the clouds or fog so low, that everything had a tendency to be a little damp. Hans cut a few spruce bows to put under their beds while Bert started a fire in the stove. The men in the tent next door said you could get beans and bacon for seventy five cents at one of the frame buildings. That seemed pretty steep when back in the states men were getting around one dollar and fifty cents a day wages. Hans would have liked some good bread, but instead he thought about cooking some of the dried potatoes with the beans and bacon. A man on the trail gets a big empty spot in his stomach after a hard day packing. The guys next door told them that years ago this little cleared area was used as a sheep hunting camp, that's how it got its name. He also mentioned the trail rises one thousand feet the next two miles and then it's not too far to the Golden Stairs.

The men had some of their gear in the tent; they wanted to keep the flour as dry as possible. Somewhere along the trail, someone told them if the first one quarter inch of the flour gets wet and dries, this will protect the rest of the flour from getting wet in the bag. As the meal was cooking the men talked about the trail.

"What do you think he meant, when he talked about the Golden Stairs?"

Bert answered "I don't have the slightest idea, but I think we will find out soon enough."

The tent was still damp from the rain and snowfall. The sun was going down, so Bert lit a candle. The glow of the candle made it appear to be warmer in the tent than it really was. The stove didn't have a very large firebox, so with the small kindling they had to fire it regularly. They knew now that they would have to find some real dry wood and cut it into about four foot lengths. Later on it could be sawed off into one foot lengths. When the potatoes, beans and bacon were cooked, the food was dished out on their metal plates. The tin cups with the hot coffee could burn your lips if you got too anxious.

"Damn that hot food does wonders for a man's outlook on life."

"You are right there, friend. I hope some time in the future we can shoot an animal for a meal."

There wasn't much being said as the men proceeded to clean their plates. Bert took the plates and pans out and cleaned them with snow. Hans joked "Watch out for the yellow snow."

The nights now were getting down below freezing, but they didn't have to keep the fire going all night long. Both had put on long johns a couple days ago and they didn't have any intentions of taking them off real soon. As the stove started cracking and cooling, the men drifted into a heavy sleep.

They awoke when they heard noise from outside; their neighbors were talking and getting ready to start moving their gear.

"Damn" said Bert, "I guess we must have been pooped, we better get our asses in gear."

Even though it seemed like they had just eaten a meal, they lit the stove and cooked some so called flapjacks. One thing about flapjacks, you didn't have to be much of a cook to succeed. With some of the bacon from last night's meal wrapped up in the flapjacks, and coffee, they had breakfast. Since it had snowed last night, the sleds they had been carrying could now be put to use. Both cut a load of four foot firewood for one of the sleds; this should get them through to the next timber. Bert said, "I think we should leave the wood in the tent and bring that with the tent on the last load. We don't want to make this fire wood too tempting for any one."

The men took off up the trail with their first load. They decided to keep with their plan of making one mile relays.

Hans said, "That old fart was right, this is one very steep trail, my ass will be dragging tonight."

Pulling a sled through the packed snow trail wasn't as easy as they thought it was going to be, but when they rested they didn't have all that weight breaking their backs. The calves in their legs strained with pain after a hundred steps or so. Both men had to stop and rest, the incline was terrible. The only problem with stopping was, the men behind would say, "Buddy, get ta going or get off the trail."

So a man didn't have many choices. Part way up the trail, they came to a large glacier which was hanging over the edge of a large crevice in the mountain. The water was running off this glacier like a river, and the glacier was making a lot of noise. They both talked about how it looked like it was going to fall down any minute. It was frightening to look up and see that massive glob of ice, just waiting to come crashing down the mountain.

There was still snow coming down, so a man really had to lean over a long way to keep his balance and footing. The strain on the back was bad enough, but the calves in their legs felt like they were going to burst. Hans thought about the difference of carrying these fifty pounds up this steep slope or pulling a hundred or so pounds on the sled. At least we won't have to make as many trips with the sled.

This part of the trail had steep slopes going up on each side so there wasn't any place here to set a tent, and there wasn't a hell of a lot of room to stack your gear for the next relay. Hans thought he damn well better mark his pile very clearly; it would be hell coming back the next trip and not find the right gear. There weren't any trees here so it was hard to find a land mark. They finally found a pointed rock to stack it by.

The two men kept up the grueling work of moving the gear up the trail. Many men were met coming down the trail, going for their next load. Everyone seemed to be dressed in grey or black clothes; there wasn't much color on the trail. It was like looking at a photograph. If you weren't sweating; you were getting chilled by the cool air. The damn snow just kept coming down. Hans was used to snow in northwest Iowa, but it stopped once in a while. Here in this north country, it never stopped.

After a few days, the men had their gear up to the stone house, as they called it. There was a large square rock that looked like a building, so it was called "Stone House." Since it was taking longer than they thought to move the gear up the trail, they left the tent at Sheep Camp to be near the wood supply. Word coming down the mountain was that firewood cost one dollar a pound at the base of the Chilkoot Pass. This was a good reason for the men to keep their base at Sheep Camp as long as possible. It was four miles from Sheep Camp to the base of the Chilkoot Pass, known as the Scales. At this time they had all their gear about a mile or so from the Scales, so they thought they better move the tent up the trail first, along with their new wood supply. Having more time today, the men had mixed up some flour to make bread; they hadn't had any bread for more than two weeks. Hans dug out the little fold-up oven they bought in Seattle, set it on the stove to heat up. This was going to be the first bread either of them had ever baked. They really weren't concerned how it came out. Neither man had any experience in baking bread, though they had watched their mother do it, they weren't sure of the procedure.

EVENING IN THE TENT

Hans brought out a bottle of brandy to celebrate making it this far up the trail. Both knew they would have to conserve it, so they each had about one inch in their tin cup. They had forgotten how smoothly brandy goes into the body, how good it made them feel. It was very relaxing to sip this soothing drink. It was also a good time to do some talking.

Walking on the trail, a man has little time for conversation. On the trail a man was so winded, it was hard to talk to the man in front or behind him.

Hans asked, "What did you do before coming to Seattle?"

"Well, I spent most of my time making fence in eastern Idaho. I worked for a couple brothers who had over a thousand acres. To keep the neighbors cattle from coming in to feed on this guy's fine pasture land, we had to fence most of it. That wasn't the only job I had. You know when you're on the bottom of the totem pole you get all the shit jobs. We had to make fire wood, fix up buildings, just about anything going to hell around the spread we had to fix. One thing about working where they raise beef cattle, you eat damn well. Hans, give me some of your background."

"Well Bert, you weren't the only guy making fence. In north west Iowa we had more people then you had in Idaho, so we had to fence everything. My ma and pa had one section of land, which as you know is six hundred and forty acres. In Iowa, you just don't have cattle and let them run loose. We had corn, oats, pasture land and hay land, and we rotated the crops to help the land. My father was a smart farmer and he let you know it, off and on. What I hated most about the work was hitching up those big horses; damn they would make me so mad. Over night the harnesses would get stiff and it was hard to handle them. We had to work with a kerosene lantern and it wasn't much to work with. About the time you got the harness started, the big horse would lean toward you and squeeze you between him self and the wall. I use to cuss those sons bitches like you wouldn't believe. I always made damn sure pa wasn't within hearing distance; he didn't like cussing at all. He would get his buggy whip and give me a crack on the butt. It didn't bother him that I was as big as him; he just didn't like to hear a person cuss. Bert, I think that is enough talking for a while, the brandy in the cup is gone and we have a special meal with all that wonderful bread to eat."

Eat they did, there wasn't much said during this time. The hot food was a real treat, after climbing up and down that trail all day, one time overheated and the next feeling the sweat start to cool you down. They stoked the fire and crawled between the blankets.

They woke in the morning at first light to see their tent interior covered with hoar frost. Everyday there was something new on the trail, everything to make the going more difficult. It seemed like it would be a long time before they would get the tent dried out. It was now getting into late October and the snow was piling up. From the time they set up the tent at Sheep Camp, until now, when they were going to break camp, they had received over two feet of snow. All they had to pull up to their supply pile was the tent and firewood.

The fire wood was getting more important every day. They didn't have the extra money to buy firewood for one dollar a pound. Firewood was piled on the two sleds along with the tent. Hans dug out the steel clamps for their boots. The store owner at Dyea had talked them into buying these clamps for their boots. He told them with the thousands of men walking the trail on fresh snow; it would be hard to walk with regular boots.

They took off up the trail; it was still snowing and now the wind was blowing like crazy. The wind bit like the devil on the face. The beards helped, but the nose caught hell. The dripping from the running noses froze on their beards. Their warm moist breath caused frost to also gather on their beards. On and on they dragged the sleds up the thirty five-degree hill, the hot frosty breath going down toward the ground, keeping in unison with their steps. Now the men were breathing deeply to keep their internal engines going.

At about noon, the men reached their gear pile. Next to their pile was another pile of supplies with two men standing along side of it.

After pulling their sleds out of the way and catching their breath, they walked over to the men. The men introduced each other by their first names. Hans extended his hand, "My name is Hans Hansen and this is my friend, Bert Thompson."

The taller fellow said, "My name is Tom Jorgensen and this is my friend, Richard Brown. We just got back from the Scales."

Hans asked, "What the devil is the Scales?"

"Well, the Scales is the place where the packers weigh the gear. They will charge you so much a pound. If the Indians carry your gear, it's one to one and a half cents a pound. Let's see—- for a seventy pound load, that would be about one dollar a trip."

"What's the big deal about this Chilkoot Pass?" Bert asked.

"I'll tell you my friend, about the Chilkoot Pass. It's what they call the Golden Stairs. There are twelve hundred steps you have to climb, at about a thirty degree incline. There are places you can stop and sit down, but you may never get back in the line, best to keep going. It's what you call a ball buster. It takes about a half hour wait in line before you get to the steps and all this time you have your pack on your back. It's really a sight to see. These gold miners are carrying everything up that hill except the kitchen sink. I've been told they carry everything over the pass, including wagons, saw mills, two hundred knock down canoes, steam boat crates of chickens and turkeys. It's crazy."

Hans said. "Do you have some of your gear up there?"

"Yea, it's off to one side, you don't have a hell of a lot of choices where to park."

Hans responded "We'll follow you guys up this trip; maybe we can find a place next to you."

"Sure enough" the guy said, "And there are a couple other things you should know. There are Canadian Mounties up on top of the Chilkoot collecting duty, and you have to have eleven hundred and fifty pounds of food each. There is no food in Dawson City."

"Are you guys shitting us?" they asked.

"Hell no."

Bert sat down on the pile of wood on his sled and said, "Where in hell are we going to buy this extra food, to keep them Mounties happy?"

The tall feller told Bert and Hans, "Let's get the hell out of the blowing snow; come into our tent. We have a little heat and we can talk about this over a hot cup of coffee."

The tent was rattling like the devil; the wind whistling down the steep hill had no mercy. Hans looked at the stove pipe moving in the wind. He couldn't figure how it stayed connected to the stove.

Bert asked, "What can we do about the supplies we are short on?"

The tall guy answered, "All those guys you saw going down the trail are not going for their supplies. They took one look at that Chilkoot Pass hill and said "To hell with this crazy idea."

"You mean these guys sold their gear at the base of the hill?"

"Yes they did, and at one big discount. Some say ten cents on the dollar. Most men have their eleven hundred and fifty pounds each. They heard about it at Dyea I guess."

"Well, if you guys hear about anyone wanting to sell out, let us know."

Bert and Hans headed up the trail toward the Scales. They didn't go very far when they got a glimpse of the Golden Stairs. It was an incredible sight! The Chilkoot Pass is on the left and the Peterson Pass on the right.

CHAPTER 3

The foursome made it to the Scales in mid afternoon. Bert and Hans had to get their tent set up as soon as possible.

After they removed the three feet of snow, they then had to figure out a way to make the tent secure. The four foot logs worked well to hold down the side of the tent, the wood was also used to tie down the side ropes. The wind died down some and Hans could hear this loud noise, almost like a dog howling. He stepped out of the tent and looked up at the steady line of men going up the Chilkoot. He called to Bert, "Come out here!"

He did and they stood there staring at the mass of humanity trudging up the twelve hundred steps on the Golden Stairs. The noise was coming from these seven hundred or so men carrying their fifty to seventy pound packs up to the top. Hans thought to himself, I'll never forget this sight. Is this the greed in a man that drives him though this misery and punish his body for the sake of gold?

Both men stood there watching this spectacle, it was almost beyond belief. The groaning noise from the climbers echoed down the canyon.

They put the wood inside the tent and headed down the trail to get another load.

The men coming up the trail had icicles hanging on their beards; some had white noses which appeared to be frozen. Many of the men had either a scarf over their face or some kind of mask.

Hans thought to himself, the people on this trail don't really look like human beings and there's no sound except for the groaning and heavy breathing.

This would be the last load for the day, so they made it a good load. Bert suggested they carry about fifty pounds on their backs to give them more traction in the snow to pull the sleds. With heads bent low and the ropes tied around their waists, they made their way up the trail. Their hearts were beating hard. Now they could feel the pounding throughout their bodies, in their eyeballs, in their ears, this steady pounding, boom,

boom, boom. After a while, everything worked together, the heart, the breathing, the pounding of the feet. When they got to the tent, their friends had brought up their last load, and there was a fire going.

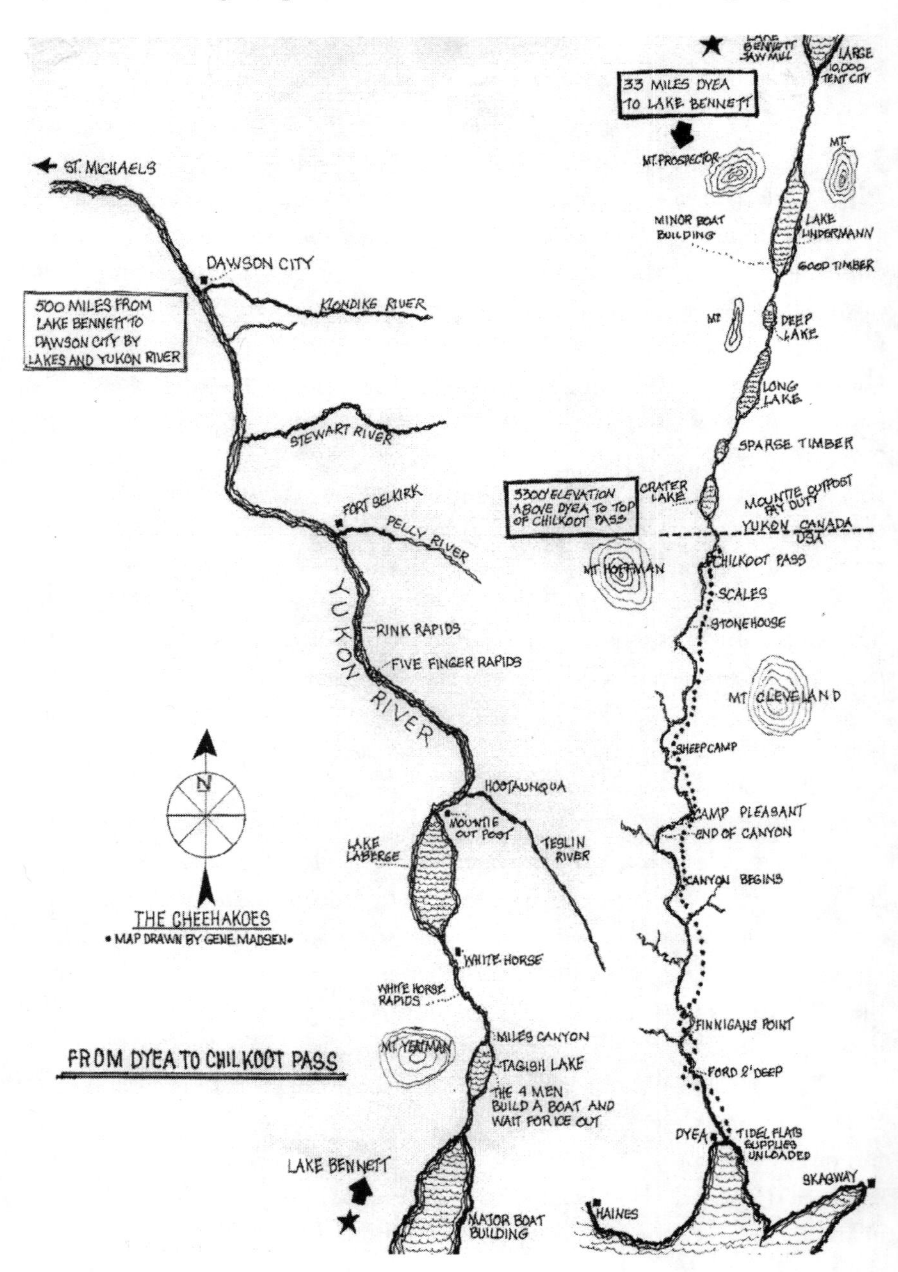

After Bert and Hans got their own fire going and the tent arranged, they went to their friend's tent close by. Tom poured the coffee and the men sat there with their hands around the tin cups to warm their cold fingers. The fire crackled from the dried spruce and the chimney chimed in with it's own tin snapping noise as it expanded. The talk got around to what was happening up here at the pass.

Tom told the boys, "It seems the average fee at the Mounties check point is thirty dollars and I guess they go through everything, to make sure you're not bringing in any whiskey."

This brought a sharp reply from Bert, "What right do the Canadians have charging a fee to go across Alaska?"

Tom said, "Bert, that's the same thing we thought. But after some of these big wigs started making a survey, they found the British Colombia border is just beyond the summit."

Bert looked down at the stove, "We've had nothing but surprises since we headed up this trail, and I suppose we're going to get some more. Maybe its best we don't know what's ahead or we might turn back right now."

The talk then turned to the news they had heard today on the trail. Seems that a couple men froze to death up on the summit a few days ago. The Mounties loaded their stiff bodies on a sled and took them down to Dyea. They have a cemetery down there and will bury them in the spring. Another tale they heard was about some 'dumb head', who had brought some pack dogs up here to haul his gear. One of the dogs was a greyhound. On a recent night, when it got down below zero, he left the dog outside figuring the dog had enough hair to keep him warm. Well, the next morning, this guy goes out to feed his dogs and his greyhound is frozen stiff. He's standing there like he's alive, on all fours, but the dog is dead. They had a good laugh when Bert imitated this dog standing there, frozen like a rock. They also talked about the number of people who had died on the trail from some disease called 'spinal meningitis.' They heard there had been about ten men over on the Skagway Trail who died of this disease recently.

Bert commented again, "Like I said, what's going to happen next?"

After three more days, they had all their gear at the Scales. Now it was time to move it up to the summit.

Bert and Hans still hadn't found anyone wanting to sell out their supplies. They walked to the base of the Chilkoot Pass. As they stood looking at the men going up the steps, an Indian about five feet tall walked up. "You Cheechakoes want hire good packer to haul gear up pass?"

Bert looked toward Hans and shook his head no.

For two days the winds blew fifty miles an hour and there wasn't anyone on the Golden Stairs. Thank God they had brought along plenty of wood for the stove. Each day they heard of men freezing to death on the trail. When the temperature was well below zero and the wind blowing like hell, no one could stand the climb. It was now into November and the men were getting anxious to move the gear toward Lake Bennet, which was about fourteen miles and would be half way. At Lake Bennet, they would build their boat and float down the Yukon River to Dawson City. On the morning of November 15, when they awoke, the tent was still and so bright that it hurt their eyes.

Bert said, "Hans you old sourdough, wake up. We have a new day and we're heading up those old Golden Stairs."

Hans came back, "This is the day Bert and Hans are going into the 'snow blind glass business', by Joe. We need some money and we're going to make some."

They heard their friends next door cooking something, so they went over to visit. Hans and Bert found a place to sit in the crowded tent.

Tom said, "I see you two hayseeds have your tin cups along, are you looking for something hot?"

"Yep," answered Hans, and continued, "Did you fellows ever see anything like this?"

He pulled out his snow blind glasses.

The quiet one, Richard said, "Say I saw something like that one time in some newspaper. I believe they used to wear them when the snow is bright, so you don't get blinded by the snow."

"You got that right, Richard. Bert and me are going into business today." Tom said.

"What do you two fancy business men charge for these so called snow blind glasses? Maybe the fellers who buy these are already snow blind."

Hans answered, "They're on the market for one dollar a pair."

Tom said, "Maybe we better get a couple, I heard tell when a man gets snow blind, he's laid up for some time. It's like getting your eyeballs sunburned."

"Tell you what boys, since we might need each other down the way, I'll give you each a pair." Hans handed over the glasses and each one tried them on. "Boy now we really look like Chinese." They all had a good laugh. Hans said, "We have to get our butts in gear and get something to put in our bellies."

After a hearty breakfast, the men walked out to look things over. The first guy on the big stairs was about three fourths of the way to the top and others were stacked up tight behind him. One guy appeared to be carrying a box about seven feet long. What a sight, Hans thought. The sun was so bright, they could hardly look anywhere without squinting their eyes almost shut.

Hans told Bert, "Let's meander up over to that long line waiting to head up the stairs, we'll test our salesmanship."

Bert gave a smile and a nod of the head. When they got to the line, a few feet from the stairs, Hans pulled out a pair of his glasses and put them on. He also had a pair in his hand. He stopped along side a fellow with a hefty, bulky load.

"Mister," he said "Did you ever hear about men getting snow-blind and having to lay up for a week before they can see again?" The young fellow answered, "Nope."

The older guy behind him spoke up, "You damn tooten I have. Are you selling those snow blind glasses?"

Hans came back, "Yes, I am, and they're one dollar a pair."

"Here's your buck, give me a pair."

All the others in line who heard the conversation joined in on the buying spree. Before they knew it Bert and Hans had sold thirty pair.

Hans called Bert aside and said, "I think we have these damn glasses priced too low."

They walked away from the line so they could talk.

Hans said, "Bert, we started with sixty three pair and we gave two to our friends, and we just sold thirty so we have thirty one pair left. Let's let the line move on a ways so we can make a new sales pitch. I don't want to hold these guys up, but we have something they really need so we should make as much as possible."

Bert said "If we charge two dollars a pair and if they buy them, we would have about sixty two dollars. That would take care of the duty and help pay for the extra food we need."

So they agreed. They headed back to the long line of men heading for the stairs. Hans pulled out his glasses and gave the first man the sales pitch. It was the same as the last time. Before they knew it, the glasses were all gone and it was only about ten a.m.

"Hans, you had one hell of an idea about those sunglasses. Let's go to the tent, we'll have to get a load and get in line."

Back at the tent they cooked some bacon to go along with their hot cakes. As they sat eating, they looked at each other and each knew what the other was thinking. They both started laughing.

Hans said, "Bert we had a gold mine and we didn't know it. Some say there will be twenty thousand people coming through here this winter. We could have sat right here and made our fortune. Who knows how much some of these people would have paid for these glasses? We could stay here for two months, and go back home with ten thousand dollars each."

"Isn't that something? Back in the states a laborer gets one dollar and fifty cents a day if he's lucky. I hope we have the same luck finding the gold."

They both loaded up about fifty pounds on their backs and headed for the line. This was the worst part, standing there waiting in the long line, waiting to start up the stairs. After a half hour or so they came to the stairs. At that point a guy was charging fifty cents for each person going up.

Hans asked the guy ahead of him, "What's going on?"

The guy said, "These are the men who cut the steps into the snow, so they feel they are entitled to a fee."

"I guess you can't argue with that."

Hans and Bert paid their fee and the guy said, "This is for all day, and tomorrow you pay another fifty cents."

They both started up the twelve hundred steps. Hans thought to himself, a man doesn't have much of a chance to look around going up these stairs. You have to watch where you're going. When the man's foot leaves the step in front of you, you're right behind him. The steps seemed to be higher than normal steps to Hans, or else Alaskan steps are bigger than the ones in Iowa. He could now hear the heavy breathing and the constant groaning vibrating through the pass.

Hans left a girl friend back in Iowa, her name was Olive. 'I wonder what she is doing now; maybe I shouldn't have gone on this wild goose chase. By the time I get back home, she might find a new guy.' He was about one fourth of the way up the hill and his legs were getting tired. He thought to himself, I can't go out on one of these by pass areas. I will look like some young guy that can't keep up with some of these old farts. I know some of these guys are over sixty years old, hell, they just keep trudging along. About every forty steps or so, they had made an area where a person could get out of the line and sit on the snow bank. You didn't see any smiles on these men's faces. They were looking down to the ground with a death stare. On and on the line moved up the hill. My dad used to say, 'A farting horse never tires, a farting man is the man to hire.' I think there is a lot of farting going on in this line. In fact, the men made no desire in keeping the farts silent. Step after step, the men climbed these five hundred feet to a total elevation of thirty five hundred feet. It was sad to see the older men, totally out of shape, staggering to get out of line to sit down to rest their aching muscles. There was a good chance the man may not get back in line for some time, as the line never stopped. The only chance was if, for some reason, a gap appeared. The line moved as fast as the slowest person in the line.

As the men were moving up the line, Hans could see off to his right, men coming back down the hill. Some would walk down on a crude stairway to the right. Next to the main steps, there were runways of some sort, to slide on. What took well over an hour to climb up, took only a few minutes for people to slide down. They sat on their butts or shoes. Some carried a thick material to use for sliding to the bottom. It looked like some of these men sliding downhill were having a hell of a lot of fun.

Now and then you would see a woman in the line or sliding down the hill. I guess whoever gets this gold fever, it drives them to their limits. After an hour and a half, Bert and Hans were at the summit. It wasn't as large as they thought it might be. It appeared to be about one hundred yards square with steep rock walls. Now the first thing they had to do was find a place to start stacking their supplies. It looked like one hell of a mess. Here at the summit, there were piles all over. Tom suggested picking a spot where the wind blows through, to keep the pile from drifting over with snow. They found a place at one side and it looked okay. They would park their gear in this spot, and mark it good with one of their seven foot sleds.

The four walked back to the edge of the summit. On this clear day you could see Dyea to the south and Lake Lindemann off to the north. It was beautiful; none of the men had ever seen a sight like this. Now it was time to head down the Chilkoot Pass. It was either walk or slide down.

Bert sat down on his butt and shoes and started down the hill, with Hans close behind. What started out as being fun soon got a little frightening. They were going like the devil. They didn't have long to think about the hill. Before they knew it, they were plowing into the loose snow at the base. Both men stood up and shook off the loose snow, then headed back to get their sleds.

Again they got back in line with their sleds. Since these sleds were seven and a half feet long and sixteen inches wide they had to be careful how they carried them on their backs up the hill. If a man would knock another guy along side of his head with the sled, he might not think too kindly of that. The two got to the stairs and proceeded up the ice steps. The man collecting the toll must have had a good memory for faces; he didn't ask Hans or Bert for a toll fee. The sleds were awkward, but not that hard to carry. Maybe it was good they had started out on the light side to build up their legs. After putting their sleds in an upright position along the side of their goods, they walked to the edge. Looking back to the north, they could see the Canadian Union Jack flag whipping in the wind on the small Mounties shack.

The summit was usually in some sort of a blizzard; the wind was always blowing and the snow was always drifting. To the north, the land sloped up for a short distance then it was all down hill to Lake Lindemann. They went to the edge and knelt down to get ready to slide. They could see some commotion about two thirds of the way down the stairs. They took off and could see a couple men were carrying a person down the steps. When they reached the bottom, Hans cornered a guy and asked him what had happened.

He said, "Some ass hole let his sled free fall down the hill and it hit this older man in the legs, breaking both of them. They're going to put him on a sled, then head down the trail to find a doctor toward Dyea."

Hans thought to himself, what a hell of a bad break for that guy, just because some idiot didn't use his head. I guess a man better be on the look out on the steps.

It was middle afternoon. Hans and Bert thought they should try one more load. This time they raised the weight to around seventy pounds. Many of these little packers carry one hundred pounds and they were only about five feet tall. By now the sun was getting lower in the sky and the temperature was going down. While standing in line for the stairs, a man's feet and hands started getting very cold. Many of the men were stomping their feet together to try to increase the circulation; the old trick of moving your arms back and forth across your body was hard to do when you had a pack on. Hans saw a big brute going up the stairs with a small piano on his back. Damn, he thought, how could one man carry that much? When standing in line there was idle talk with one another, most of the conversation was about, 'Where you from?' 'When did you start up the trail?' 'How many trips up the hill so far?' Also talk of the local news, about who got hurt, who got killed, and who froze to death recently. It made good conversation when you were in a warm tent at night.

Going up the stairs with the fifty to seventy pounds wasn't as bad as they had anticipated, it wasn't easy, but it was bearable. The sun was going down. From the top you could see the glow of the tents down the trail, even a candle in a tent was quite bright. They could see the same number of men in the waiting line. Down the long hill to the south, there was a steady line of packers. Hans could see a number of horses standing around. They had been abandoned by their owners. Having hauled their supplies this far, was as far as horses could be used. Even the Peterson Pass to the east side of the Chilkoot was poor for horses. It was a damn shame to bring these poor animals up here and turn them loose. Knowing a horse, if he has enough strength left in his body, he will go back in the direction he came.

Time was wasting; better get down the hill before my feet freeze. On this slide, Bert took a tumble and plowed head first into the snow. He was all white when he got up. They hurried to their tent. When they arrived, there was smoke coming out of the stove pipe. When they entered, it was quite warm. Damn this was nice; our neighbors must have done us a favor.

Hans told Bert, "Let's grab the bottle of brandy and go visit our good neighbors at the next tent."

Hans asked "Anybody home?"

Tom answered, "Come on in."

They opened the tent flap and entered the candle lit tent.

"This looks cozy." Bert said.

The men found a place to sit on the gear. Hans said, "Would you fellows like a little body warmer?"

It didn't take long for Richard and Tom to find their tin cups.

Bert said, "Thanks for starting a fire for us, it really fells good."

"No problem," Tom answered.

Hans poured a couple of inches in all their cups. All four leaned back and took a sip.

Tom said, "I just love the smell of brandy and it tastes so dang good too." He took a sip, "A man can go through a lot during a day if he has something like this to end his day. Have a brandy, sit around and talk, then a big meal and off to bed."

Hans asked, "Any news on the trail today?"

"Well, some lady brought up a stove. She was serving warm food to the back packers. Says she keeps it going every day."

Bert thought; wonder how she will get the stove up over the hill; is she young and good looking?

"A women young and good looking shouldn't be making money with a hot stove."

They all laughed.

"Heard on the stairs today about a place on the Skagway Trail they call Dead Horse Gulch. I guess it's just a terrible place to get through and by the time the horses get this far, they're so damn tired they just give up and die. I talked to someone today; he told me there was a horse in the same area, and when he got to a sharp drop off, he went over and jumped off. They said the horse committed suicide rather than go on. I wonder if that is true."

"Say Tom," Bert asked, "Have you guys seen anyone wanting to sell their gear?" Tom came back, "No, I haven't really talked to that many people. We'll all have to keep our ears open tomorrow."

Hans started toward the door, "Did you fellows ever hear the word Cheechakoes?"

Tom started laughing, "That's what Tlingit Indians call greenhorns."

Bert said, "Oh shit, well anyway we're going to get a good night sleep, we'll meet you tomorrow at the Golden Stairs. Give us a call when you get up, in case we oversleep."

Tom said, "See you guys tomorrow."

Bert and Hans walked to their tent; the stars were out now and there was some moon light coming from behind the mountain. Bert said, "It's going to be a cold bugger tonight. I'm glad we don't have a thermometer to see how cold it is. I'm sure we'll hear it from someone tomorrow."

They looked over toward the stairs. There were still men climbing but they couldn't see anyone in line. They guessed it was slowing down.

Hans said, "Maybe this would be the best time to climb. Hell, there aren't as many people around soyou wouldn't have to wait in line. One problem, it might be colder but there shouldn't be much wind. When the moon gets brighter, maybe we should give it a thought."

They entered the tent, the fire had died down somewhat, but it was still nice. The fire was stoked up and the evening meal was started. The floor was muddy. They had a tarp along but didn't think about putting it down; maybe the floor will dry soon.

Hans took out a pencil and some paper.

Bert asked, "What are you figuring?"

"Just trying to get an idea how many trips we will have to make up the hill to get all our gear to the Summit."

"What did you come up with?"

"With our short load, it came to around twenty one trips with seventy pound loads. We've already made six so, we have about fifteen to go".

"Lets give her hell tomorrow."

Tonight's meal was beans and bacon which could be called bean soup. They had a hell of a lot of beans to eat, so they had to find different ways to fix them. It was strange, with so many men camped in this area, there was hardly a sound at night. Many a night when Hans had to go out of the tent to take a pee, he would look up at the Big Dipper and wonder if Olive saw the Big Dipper at the same time he did. It would be some way of keeping in touch. He thought, it's a good thing this ground is all rocky, with all this peeing around here.

He went back inside and crawled back into his blankets. They both had their boots hanging above the stove to dry out. At night they would put on a dry pair of socks and hang the wet ones above the stove. Hans thought to himself, I wonder what it's like to be rich. If we find a bunch of gold, then we could go back home first class and maybe I could buy my own farm. Olive and me could get married and raise a family. By golly, that sounds good.

Hans and Bert woke the next morning to a howling blizzard. The wind must have been blowing fifty miles an hour or more, it was crazy to think about going out in this weather. They stoked the fire and crawled back in their blankets. On a day like this, you might as well conserve as much energy as possible. They kept the wood consumption as low as possible as there wasn't any firewood for seven miles. They were sure some of the men camped below the summit were either out of wood or had a very low supply. This was a miserable situation; the storm was raging day and night.

Wait they did. It was four days before the weather took a turn for the better.

The morning it broke, Hans woke up at around four a.m. and got Bert out of bed to get up on the pass before it became crowded. They woke up their friends. With their first load they didn't have to wait in any line. It was cold as hell; it must have been down around twenty below that morning. The guys left the tent without eating anything. They figured after a couple climbs they would cook something to eat. The wind came up about the time they were half way up the pass with their second load. The wind was so damn bitter they had to wrap their faces with a scarf they always carried along.

Their eyes watered profusely, the forehead above the nose ached from the cold, and their noses were running down on their beards and freezing instantly. Their hands were used to keep the load level on their backs. It was hard to take one hand, inside a mitten, to cover their face to shield the wind. Hans thought to himself; how the devil can a man be so dumb, to come to this God forsaken country? Here we are at the main pass and we're short of supplies. We can't get through Canadian Customs unless we can pick up about another two thousand pounds of food. Will we sit here until spring before we find someone to sell us their grub? Maybe I should have stayed in Iowa instead of coming on this wild goose chase.

By this time Hans was at the top again. They took their gear to their stash area, which by this time was getting snow covered.

Bert said, "Let's get the sled out and put it on top, so we can find this place next time."

After returning to the bottom of the hill, they returned to their tent to have something to eat. While they were fixing their meal, Tom and his buddy came over into Bert and Han's tent. Hans gave them coffee.

Tom said, "I think I have good news for you guys. The last time we were at the top, we ran into a guy who had some problems. After they had taken their last load up to the summit, the guy came down sick as a dog. His buddy hired some one to take him back to Dyea".

The partner said, 'I've had enough, this is a place for stupid, ignorant people, chasing something they will never find. I'm selling out. My so called partner can stick his supplies up his ass. I'm heading south.'

"He said he would sell for twenty five cents on the dollar. I have his name and where his base tent is located. The best part of this deal is he already has his gear up on the summit."

Hans jumped up, "Where is his tent located?"

They went out side and Tom pointed to a darker tent next to a wooden building, not too far from the base of the steps. Bert and Hans took off for the tent and made the deal. They couldn't believe that they picked up his food supplies for one hundred dollars and the best part; they didn't have to carry them up those damn twelve hundred steps. On the next trip up, the owner said he would show them where his goods were stacked. That evening it was time to celebrate. They invited their friends over and dug out the brandy. It just so happened that Tom and his buddy were finished packing over the pass, except for their tent. Bert and Hans were in the same situation.

"Hell, this will work out great." said Hans, and continued, "We can both head up the old Chilkoot tomorrow for the last time and get a move on toward Lake Bennett."

Tom brought his tin cup to his lips, "Ah, some days are better than others. Tomorrow, weather permitting, we'll get the hell out of this hole and find a new place to pitch our tents, down toward Lake Lindemann."

This would hopefully be the last night at the Scales and from here on it should be mostly down hill with the sled. The fire was stoked up good; the stove was talking with its snapping tin noise. The Stampeders of 1897 were feeling good. This damn stairway to the summit was just about behind them, and the hot brandy was warming their insides.

Tom sat up and said, "Say, did you guys hear about the three so-called thieves?"

Bert and Hans shook their heads. "Well, it seems there were these three guys, Wellington, Hanson and I forget the other guy's name. They stole some guy's sled and supplies at the Sheep Camp and brought it up to the scales. Well, the owner had burned his name into the wooden sled runner. In the mean time, it got iced up so you couldn't see the name. These three dudes stole the sled all loaded, and brought it to the Scales. On the way up there, the ice on the runners get chipped off and the name showed plain as day. The owner comes looking for his sled, and when he sees it, he finds some of his friends up there and they confront the three. They tie them up and take them to Sheep Camp for a trial."

In one of the restaurants the owner tells that story. There's a big crowd, the room is filled with smoke. When the guy tells his story, it's so quiet you could hear a pin drop. One of the guys, I didn't get his name, is let off free. He didn't really have anything to do with the sled stealing. This Wellington draws a gun and makes a wild shot and takes off down the trail. Of course, a bunch of pissed off men take after him. He runs about two hundred yards. I think he sees all these guys chasing him. He puts the gun to his head, bang! He's blows his brains out. They drag him off the trail and go back to see what Hanson gets.

After a trial of some sort, the so called, self-installed judge gave Hanson fifty lashes. They tied this guy to a pole, took his shirt off. A big bruiser took a whip of some sort, and gave it all he had. Whack, across the back. The crowd is out for blood, Whack!

The guy with the whip says, "I don't really like to do this, but we have to have justice in this wilderness."

After fifteen lashes some one says, "That's enough, turn him loose."

They do, and then they write on a piece of paper, "THIEF", then put it on his back, and send him down the trail to Dyea, and tell him to never return."

Hans and Bert sat there totally engrossed in the story.

Bert said, "That's a hell of a story, Tom. This really is a strange country. Kind of like the old cowboy west of fifty years ago."

Tom also mentioned, "I heard there are quite a few guys dying on the trail. You know, some of these guys don't ever get a warm meal and what they eat comes off dirty plates. As you guys know, when the hell does person take a bath? We all live like pigs. Sometime up the trail, we'll have to break out the dried fruits or sure as hell we'll get the scurvy.

And that's bad news. Your hair falls out, you get scabs all over your body and you get sick as hell."

Hans said, "By the way, the guy we bought the supplies from up on the summit said he had some vinegar in his gear, for this purpose. He said if you take like a teaspoon every other day, you won't get the scurvy."

Tom asked Hans, "Where did you get the wood to make those snow blind glasses?"

Hans pulled the glasses from his shirt pocket. "Back in Seattle, where we were buying supplies, I asked the store owner if he had any old orange crates. He told me he had a bunch in the back room and I could help myself. I remember seeing these crates in Iowa, and thought they would be great for these glasses."

Bert said. "Yea, he's smarter than he looks." They all laughed.

Hans stood up and made a gesture with his hand pointing up the hill. "Tomorrow, we have to make sure we take the right gear to Lake Lindemann. Its nine miles from the summit to the lake and good timber. We should take some firewood with us in case we hit a big storm. Then we have to have enough food for five or six days for the same reason. It's about all down the hill, so we can take a pretty good load. We've been busting our butts going up the hill, so going down should be a breeze."

"Sounds good," Tom said, as he got up, "I'm heading for a good night's sleep."

Early the next morning, Bert and Hans broke down their camp. Their friends next door followed. They were to meet the owner of the supplies on the summit by the steps at six a.m. Their tent and some food supplies were left at the base of the pass. When they arrived at the steps, their man was waiting. They paid their fee for the last time and headed up the steps.

It was cold this morning and the snow under foot squeaked and creaked quite loudly. It's hard to believe all these men are heading for the same place. How many have come through here, is hard to figure. The line of men never seems to stop, all the daylight hours the endless line continues. They got to the summit. For some reason it's rather calm, the wind had died down. The guy selling his outfit finds his pile. Bert and Hans go through to make sure all the items are there that they bought. It's hard to tell the weight for sure, but it certainly appears to be over eleven hundred pounds. The men line up at the Canadian check point, it is very busy. Since the weather turned out so nice the activity is heavy. For some reason the Mounties don't appear to be looking through the men's gear. It seems at this time, the Mounties are more interested in the food than the brandy. Bert and Hans couldn't believe how fast both groups passed through customs. The cost for both of them came to seventy dollars. The profit from the snow blind glasses just about paid their bill.

"Thank God we sold the glasses, or we might have been short on money later on." commented Bert. After both outfits had passed the Canadians customs, they had a short meeting to decide where to leave their gear before heading to Lake Lindemann. It was figured there was no way they could make more than one trip a day. Today when they make Lake Lindemann, they will have made nine miles. By the time they set up their tent, they wouldn't have time to make another 18 miles up and back

This trip, they really loaded the sleds to the maximum, it was down hill and they were only going to make one trip. This was the best day they had for a long time. You could see for miles, the snow was extremely bright, even with the snow glasses it seemed bright. Going down the hill they figured they must have around two hundred fifty to three hundred pounds on each sled. It was learned from the old timers at the Scales, to have your sled pull easier through the hard packed snow, put some water in your mouth, warm it up, then spit it on the cold wood runners. As soon as the water hit the wood, it freezes instantly. Then the sled would glide through the hard packed snow. Another thing they learned about water and cold temperatures; when the outside temperature is around 40 below zero, heat a pan of hot boiling water, take it outside the tent, and toss it in the air and it looks like it turns to steam. Puff, it's all gone, and no water falls to the ground. This weather up in the North Country is strange!

After five hours of keeping the sled on the move, the men came in sight of the timber and now looked for the best place to camp. The four wanted to find a good shelter in the trees, close to some good dry firewood. The wood they had gathered at the Sheep Camp was just about gone. Since there was more timber in this area, the many men on the trail had scattered when hitting the timber to collect their fire wood.

Tom told the guys, "I saw some dried tamarack when we were coming down the trail. This is some of the best wood you can find for a camp fire, it burns hotter than hell. Be careful not to load the stove up too high, this wood burns so hot it might burn up your stove."

They had to shovel about three feet of snow to get to the ground. Well, one thing, it would help to keep the wind out of the tent. After the tents were set up, Tom led the other three into the woods to show them the dried tamarack. The wood was about four inches in diameter, just about perfect for the stove. They each cut two sleds full, about four feet in length. Back in camp, the wood could be cut to one foot lengths to fit the stove.

It was only five in the evening, but they decided to quit for the day. There really wasn't much else they could do. The tents had a musty odor from being damp much of the time; this came from having hoar-frost on the tent each morning.

Tom and his buddy brought out the brandy that evening. The fire had warmed up the tent so it was quite comfortable. The men had enough supplies and wood inside to provide places to sit. It seemed like the farther north they traveled, the colder the weather. In the evening when the sun started down below the horizon, it really cooled off in a hurry. Neither camp had a thermometer, so they really didn't know the exact temperature, which probably was best for all.

As the four men sat in the tent, they had the appearance of how men going to the Klondike must look. All were getting heavy beards and their faces were very tan and most of them had signs of frost bite. When this happens, the skin dies on the surface and in time will peel away, just like a bad sunburn. During the day, when they were hauling gear, they didn't have much time to smoke their pipes. So at a time like this, sitting around the tent, soaking up the heat, as a rule it was one pipe full after another. The smoke haze became quite intense in the tent. If there was a draft coming into the tent from outside it was very noticeable.

The men started talking about the next part of their plan, moving supplies from the summit to their new camp.

"I feel a hell of a lot better since we got our supplies over that God forsaken Chilkoot Pass and up to the summit," acknowledged Hans.

Seldom heard Richard chimed in, "I can't wait until we start down on those nice flat smooth lakes. I heard some guys say you can put a sail on your sled if the wind's in the right direction. By golly you could fasten two sleds together and it would be just like a boat."

"Well," commented Tom, "How the devil would you steer a sled, and what the hell would happen when it picked up speed? I'm afraid you and the sled would go flying across the lake."

Richard pointed his pipe toward Tom, "Every time I come up with an idea you think it's a horse shit idea. Can't I have a good idea sometime?"

"Yeah, Richard, it was a good idea; maybe I was just kidding you. We should try to figure how many trips we'll have to make back to the summit."

Hans took a sip of his brandy and continued, "Each camp has about twenty five pounds of food and about another five hundred pounds of other supplies. We each brought down five to six hundred pounds on our first trip, so we can average five hundred pounds on two sleds. This means we have about six more trips each, if we can haul that much at a time. I keep hearing it's damn hard to pull more than your own weight."

For the first time during this conversation, Bert piped in "I have an idea. You guys remember the first mile leaving the summit? It's up hill until you get to Crater Lake. We should haul all our gear in lighter loads to Crater Lake. Then when we've moved all the gear to Crater Lake, we can increase the load amount coming down hill for the eight miles."

"That's a good idea, Bert. I knew we brought you along on this trip for some reason."

The men had a good laugh. By this time a candle had been lit in the tent; the men felt good; they had a little brandy in the stomach, and they felt very relaxed. The brandy made the food taste better. I'm not sure it tasted any better, but it made them more hungry. How many ways can you fix beans and bacon, to improve the taste? Tonight they had spruce bows to sleep on, and to give them some insulation from the cold.

They awoke in the morning to what sounded like a calm day. They both went outside to relieve themselves. While standing in the snow the air bit at their lungs, and there were great clouds of steam coming from their noses. It didn't take long for the cold chill to soak into the body. Hans thought it must be well below zero this morning; he could see smoke coming out of their friend's chimney next door. As he stared at the smoke, it rose straight up in the air about one hundred feet, then went horizontal, like it had hit an imaginary ceiling, then moved off to the north. By this time Hans' hands were starting to get cold. He went into the tent and stood by the metal stove rubbing his hands, to get a little warmth in them.

After breakfast they put on their heavy parkas and headed outside to meet Richard and Tom. All four men would be pulling sleds.

They left their tent area and walked up hill toward the summit. Each man had the rope from his sled tied around his waist, to leave his arms free. The mountain on each side of the trail rose up five hundred feet or so. They were all snow covered and there weren't many rocks showing. The trail was quite well packed. Each step the men took, the snow let out high pitched squeaks. You could tell when all four had their steps in unison, for there was the constant squeak, squeak, squeak. When anyone started to get out of step, there were double squeak and triple squeaks. This was about all that was heard for the next two hours.

The wind wasn't bad and there were a few clouds gathering to the southeast. There is an old saying for this type of clouds by the old timers. They were called, 'Mare's tails and Mackerel scales.' With a little imagination when viewing these clouds, you could see the tails and scales.

At the summit there was a mass of supplies piled all over, the distance between the stacks looked like trails, maybe six feet wide. There was drifted snow covering or partially covering these piles. At first the men just stood there trying to get their bearings. The sun was still shining, so the cast shadows made it easier to see the piles of supplies.

Hans asked Bert, "Can you see our pile? Before we had our sleds sticking out of the snow to mark the spot, did we leave a mark the last time?"

"I don't think we did, but we had the pile on the south side of the sharp protruding rock."

Since they had their gear together, they all looked for the sharp rock.

Finally Tom spoke, "Hey you guys follow me, I think I have that rock spotted."

All followed Tom to the northwest part of the flat area. Tom found what he surely thought was the right rock. He said, "Let's dig out some of this snow." After about five minutes Bert hit something, it was the tarp they had over the pile.

"It's a good thing we piled our stuff by this rock, if we would have had it out in the middle, how the devil could we have found it?"

The four started loading their sleds with a good one hundred and fifty pounds of supplies. It was hard getting out of the entanglement of piles, it was like going down a crooked street, and you had to watch ahead to make sure the street wasn't blocked by some men loading their sleds. When they came up out of the little valley of piles, they met the wind in their faces. Their foreheads ached with the burning cold, now their eyes started running, as well as their noses. Hans stopped and pulled the string on his parka hood tighter to keep out the wind.

In about twenty minutes they had reached Crater Lake. When they hit the part of the trail that started down hill, they looked for a place to make their new piles. Along the way Tom had picked up a pole lying along the trail. Tom rammed the pole into the ground by their piles; it went in three feet before it something solid. Now they started their relay back to the summit. Going back, it wasn't bad; they had their backs to the wind.

Hans thought to himself, 'No wonder a horse has enough sense to face his butt into the wind'.

Back at the summit there was a great amount of activity. Men were still hauling gear up from the scales, and some were loading sleds and back packs to start their way toward Lake Lindemann. By three p.m. both outfits had moved all their gear to the new staging area by Crater Lake.

Hans called the guys together, "We have at least a three to four hour walk to get back to our tents, its eight miles down hill, so we will have to get loaded right away and get our butts moving."

It wasn't long before they were stretched out along the trail. By this time the sun was being covered by a heavy overcast sky. After about three miles it started snowing lightly, and wind was picking up. After about another mile, when Tom was leading the pack, he stopped. By now the snow was coming down very heavily and the wind was blowing harder.

Hans came up along side of Tom, "What's the matter Tom?"

"I can't see the guy ahead who I was following, and now I can't see any trail or sled prints."

Bert came in, "Hell, I can't even see any of the mountains on either side of the trail; we're going to get our asses lost."

It was now about five thirty p.m., the four of them stood on the trail looking for something to get their bearings. The wind was whipping up the snow so bad; there was nothing to be seen. They looked at each other, their beards were crusted below their nostrils, and much of their faces had frost and icicles hanging from their beards.

LOST./ HANS USES KNIFE BLADE ON FINGERNAIL TO SEE SHADOW FROM SUN

"What the hell are we going to do now?" shouted Richard.

Hans answered, "Let's stand here a bit and wait for the snow to settle down a little."

"Does anyone have a compass with them?" Tom asked, from under his hooded parka. They all stood there looking at one another; no one had a compass. Hans asked, "Who has a knife?" Bert pulled a knife from his pocket and gave it to Hans, asking, "What the hell do you want a knife for?"

Hans opened the knife and put the point on his thumbnail, he stood there looking intently at the nail, his eyes focused on the knife blade on the nail. Bert stared intently at the thumbnail. The wind was howling so it was hard to hear one another.

"Hans, what the hell are you looking for?"

He looked up at Bert, "A shadow."

"What the hell do you mean a shadow?"

"Years ago when I was a kid, I went hunting one day with the neighbor's kid. It was cloudy and we got lost in the woods. The kid took out a knife and put the point on his finger nail to get a shadow from the sun. It was in the after noon and when he saw the cast shadow on his fingernail, he knew where north was, we walked right out of the woods."

"Can you see a shadow?"

"Think I can, when the snow stops blowing I can see something. Yeah, there's a shadow, I'll mark it with my foot. There, the sun is in the southwest, so that's north." Hans pointed, and made a mark in the snow with his boot.

Tom looked at Hans, "Hans, I don't believe it. I never saw a man find where the hell north was located with a jackknife."

They all huddled together. Hans explained to the others, "Let's line up in a straight line, about ten feet apart. Maybe if the last guy keeps the rest of us in line, we will keep on a northerly direction."

They took off, Hans staying in the rear, trying to keep the others in some kind of line. It was snowing heavily and the wind just about made it impossible to find any trail. They kept up an even pace.

After about thirty minutes, Hans called the men to a halt. Again he took out the knife to see if the sun would give him a clue to its location. Nothing, the sun must be too low on the horizon to make a shadow. He called the group together. They put their heads close to one another, so they could hear. Hans told them, "I have no idea where north is, but we have to get the hell out of this open area. It looks like we might have to spend this night outside of the tent, so we better find some kind of cover."

They all looked at one another. Tom said, "Hans you take the lead, you seem to have a way with directions."

Hans kept the wind in the same direction where he found the sun the last time. At that time the wind was out of the northeast, so it was off his right side. He moved on, bracing against the cold biting wind, some of his toes felt numb. That wasn't unusual. Every day at some time, his feet got cold and numb. On they trudged, with their heads down against the wind, daylight now was leaving them. Hans told himself, we have to keep walking until we find cover, and if we don't find firewood, we could well freeze to death.

It was now getting quite dark and hard to see where they were walking. Hans had his head down, when all of a sudden his head hit something. It almost knocked him out, and caused him to fall down into the snow.

Hans said, "What the hell was that?" as he stood feeling out in front of himself.

Bert came up along side, "What happened, Hans?"

"I ran into something."

They both felt in front of them, and then Hans' mitten hit something.

"It's a tree branch," hollered Hans.

They all gathered together.

Hans said, "Let's get into the thick of these trees. We'll find a big spruce; get under the lower branches and cut out enough of these branches to make a place for us to get out of the wind. We can pile some branches on top of the lower ones to make a shelter."

All four men worked to get their shelter prepared in which to spend the night. Between the two outfits they had food and pans to cook some food. It was a good hour before they had their rubber tarp behind and over themselves for weather protection. Most of the wood for the fire was cut off of old mature spruce trees. The lower branches had long since died, making excellent dry firewood. The fire was made, and soon it was giving off some welcome heat for the cold stiff fingers.

Hans took out his pipe and tobacco. His hands were stiff with cold, it was almost impossible to work his fingers to pack his pipe. When he finally got the stick match from the box, he couldn't hold it with his stiff fingers so he had to call upon Bert to light his match.

The men were talking about what horrible weather this country had. No wonder so many of the men heading north were dying on the trail. Many of the poor souls wouldn't be found until spring when the snow melts.

As they were huddled around the fire, trying to get some of the heat back into their bodies, they heard:

"Yo."

They looked into the darkness; but with the wind howling through the trees, they couldn't make out the sound.

Again they heard: "Yo."

This time they could make out snow covered faces coming out of the darkness. Hans hollered, "Come in."

The snow-covered man said, "Thank you mister."

The ragged man continued, "Damn, we got lost and were near frozen to death. Would it be possible to soak up some of your heat?"

The two men had pulled their light loads with them, close to the fire.

Bert told the men, "Get in here, we have plenty of heat for you."

Now they had the fire almost surrounded. They both appeared to have frost bitten noses. In the glowing firelight their noses had a strange appearance. One of the man's teeth were chattering so badly, he couldn't talk.

The older of the two stuck his hands closer to the fire and said, "Thank God you men had this fire going. If we hadn't come across this glow in the dark, we would have been dead by morning. I really think I was about to give up before I saw the fire. In fact, I didn't know what the devil I was seeing. First I thought it might be Christ making that glow. You know like 'Moses and the burning bush.' All I know is, when I saw that glow, I felt a burst of heat go through my body."

Now the younger of the two finally started getting out a few words. "You...you guys, saved our lives, my hands and feet are numb. I thought about lying down in the snow and going to sleep. If it hadn't been for my father here, pulling me along, I'd be dead. I really want to thank you again."

Bert looked at the two sad human beings, and said, "We're just fixing to make us some kind of supper, would you care for some?"

"God, I think I'm with a bunch of angels. We haven't had a bite since this morning; all we were hauling to Lindemann was flour on our sleds. We didn't foresee this storm. We would be deeply indebted for some kind of meal."

Hans started pulling some things from his pack and said, "Maybe the easiest thing to fix would be some hot cakes and bacon."

The older fellow said, "We could furnish the flour," and that they did.

As Hans was melting snow to mix with the flour to make the cakes, Bert was filling a coffee pot for the second time. He looked up at the older guy and said, "What's your name?"

The guy came back with, "My name's Roger Blankenship, and this is my son, Gerald."

Bert went around the circle and introduced the two crews.

He continued, "You heading up to look for gold?"

"No, I 'm a writer and I was sent to cover this gold rush by my newspaper, the L.A. Times"

"By golly, we have a real writer here sitting around the fire with us. So you're going to write about what you see going to Dawson, is that right?"

"I guess that's what the people back in the states want to hear about."

The bacon was cooking along side of the wood fire; the coffee with its strong aroma was drifting around the camp fire, and these men were dead serious about putting away a large amount of food.

Hans cut the bacon about one quarter of an inch thick, in order to get more meat in the pan. Now the fire was giving off good heat. When the large snowflakes came into the fire and hit any hot metal, it made a hissing sound. The men were well protected from the wind, and this made a big difference in their comfort. Bert took some of the bacon grease to start cooking the hot cakes. The bacon was done enough, so as soon as a hot cake was cooked, the first guy could start eating. Bert gave the first cake to the young fellow. He told him to put the bacon inside the hotcake, and make a sandwich, and he did so. As the hot cakes were cooked, they were passed to the next guy in line.

You could tell the men were about starved; they were stuffing themselves and not saying a word. The only sound you heard was the slurping of the hot coffee from their tin cups. Bert went around the circle twice before the bacon was starting to show the bottom of the pan. Soon there were a number of comments coming from around the campfire. "Damn that was good," "That really hit the spot," "That filled up my empty spot real good." Now everyone felt much better. The men still had some cold spots on their bodies, but it was tolerable.

Roger Blankenship looked across the fire and into the eyes of the four men. "My son and I are deeply indebted to you men. As I said before, if I hadn't seen your fire, we both would have frozen this night. To show my gratitude, when I get to Dawson, I'm going to have my newspaper get some money for you. There will be one hundred dollars there for the four of you, twenty five dollars each. Each of you give me your name and I'll make sure that in the spring or summer the money will be there."

They all looked at one another.

Hans said, "Mr. Blankenship, we sure didn't do anything to deserve that kind of money, all we did was have a fire going and you walked into our camp."

"That's right, but you were here, and that was the main thing. We saw your fire and that saved our life. Maybe you can put the money to good use."

During the process of Hans lighting his pipe, he commented, "That's very kind of you, and I think I can speak for the other three men here, thank you very much."

Most of the men around the campfire were either smoking a pipe or lighting one up. The black rubber tarp soaked up the heat, and gave off good heat. They had a nice pile of wood next to the fire.

Hans looked at the men, "We'll have to keep this fire stoked up pretty good. Whoever wakes up, make sure you put some wood on the fire."

The men all pulled their hoods up around their faces. Some of them with loose coats, pulled their arms out of their sleeves to get them next to their body to retain more heat, and it was much easier to keep their hands warm. Through most of the night the wind howled through the trees, sounding like a train engine coming through the woods.

Hans woke up in a few hours; the fire was down some, so he threw a few sticks on. He then looked around the fire, and most of the men had a layer of snow on them so they almost looked like they were dead.

Hans thought to himself, 'What a hell of a country and what a man doesn't do to look for gold. I hope this gold I'm going after is worth all this misery.'

CHAPTER 4

Before Bert awoke, he was dreaming about riding a horse through belly high grass, on a sunny day, in the rolling hills of Idaho. The first thing Bert heard was—- no wind. He opened his eyes. It was clear and the sun was just hitting the top of a snow-covered mountain to the west. He brushed the snow off his clothes, stoked up the fire, and started adding snow to the coffee pot. Soon all the men were up and heading in different directions to relieve themselves. They came back and all stood by the fire moving their arms to get their circulation going again.

Bert suggested, "That was such a good meal last night, let's try it again."

The coffee was done first. They were all holding the cups in both hands, to get most of the heat into their hands. Around the fire it was, slurp, slurp, as the steam from the hot coffee rolled into their faces. It was hard to keep from shivering, all their muscles were jumping.

Soon the bacon and hot cakes were being passed around the fire; it wasn't long before the cakes and bacon were gone. Each man had a stained sleeve from wiping the food from his beard.

As the men were finishing their repeat meal, Hans told the others, "We should melt some snow in the coffee pot to use to put water on our sled runners; we'll need all the easy going through this new snow we can get."

Bert took the pot and packed it full of snow. By this time the pot was about all black, from setting on the edge of the fire. Tom was stomping his feet while standing by the fire, "I'll be damn glad when I don't have cold feet anymore, it seems like I always have numb toes."

"You better watch those toes, Tom, and make damn sure they don't get frozen or you'll be burying those toes along this trail. Course if they fall off, some fox or wolf will pick them up." Richard injected his little humor.

Everything was loaded back on the sleds. They headed to the west, for the trail had to be west of the woods. They hadn't walked far before

Hans saw some familiar surroundings. Soon they saw men on the trail heading north and their trail made the heavy sleds pull easier through the snow. It was going to be a good day, anyway the sun was out. There were a few clouds coming in from the south coast, down Dyea way. Soon all six men were back on the main trail. The wind had blown hard and the snow was packed like a rock. The sleds pulled along very easily.

After a short distance, Hans stopped and looked intensely to the northwest.

Bert came up along side of him, "What's up Hans?"

"You see that tall spruce over there with the top broken off?"

"Ya, I sure do."

"Well that's the location of our tent."

"You mean to tell me we were only about a quarter of a mile or so from our tent when we slept outside last night?"

"Sure as hell looks like it."

"Son-a-gun," Bert replied. They all continued down the trail keeping the old snag spruce in their sight. It wasn't long before they were about two hundred feet directly west of their tent. They all stopped. Hans asked, "Mr. Blankenship, where is your tent from this point?"

"I do believe we are about another mile down the trail, closer to Lake Lindemann."

"If you have anymore problems getting back to your tent some time, stop in; the coffee is usually hot"

"You can be sure I'll keep that big tree as a guide for safe haven and a place where I can find friends. If I don't see you men again, you stop by that American Bank in Dawson and collect your money."

The men bid them farewell.

Hans hollered, "Don't forget, when the weather looks bad, take along your cooking utensils and some grub when you're hauling."

The four men walked in the direction of their tents.

Tom said, "It's a damn good thing we used some of these large spruce trees for our tent cover. We must have a couple more feet of snow; all that snow could have collapsed our tents as flat as a pancake."

After shoveling out the tent doorways, they unloaded the sleds.

Hans walked over to Bert, "It's about eight; I think we should take advantage of the clear weather and head back to Crater Lake right away. With the hard snow we should be able to make good time both ways."

Bert said, "OK", and an "OK" was heard from Tom.

They didn't bother starting a fire, knowing in eight hours or so, it would be long since out, and would be just a waste of wood.

Off the four men trudged with their sleds behind them. The sun was extremely bright so they donned their homemade snow glasses. At about noon the men came to the area of their supply stash. At first they were a little disorientated with the new snow. They stood there looking, and then Richard pointed to the northeast, "There's our stick, it's about covered with snow."

Bert said, "Without the stick, we would never have found the supplies. We have to make damn sure we do this in the future. Son-a-bitch, it must have snowed two feet here over night. Look at all the piles that use to be in the opening, they're all covered up."

Hans replied, "Lets get our stuff loaded and get the hell back to Lindemann."

They all went to work loading their seven foot sleds. Again they made sure they had bacon and flour along, in case they had to sleep outside over night. At about one p.m. their supplies were covered and the sleds were headed north.

Before they loaded their sleds, those that could, took a leak on the sled runners. The warm pee would make fast ice on the runners.

Tom and Richard were sitting on top of the stacked up supplies when they heard the crunch of the snow, "Come on in" hollered Tom.

He untied the flap and let the two in. "You guys have this tent all nice and warm. As I've said before, this is the best part of the day. Wouldn't it be great if we were at the gold claim, had just dug up a pile of gold, and sat down for the evening to relax and have a little brandy?"

Bert jumped up, "Lets drink to the first gold we find up north, and may we all get rich as kings."

This was a good time for them. If there were four men that would succeed, it should be this crew. They all came from hard working backgrounds. Hans did farm work all his life, his father drove him hard, so he knew what a day's work was all about. He was close to five foot ten inches, built very stocky, had big fingers for a man his size. They looked like sausages. Maybe this was the reason he hardly ever had cold hands. He also had a full thick beard, piercing steel blue eyes, and a good smile.

Bert was about six foot one, lean, but not skinny. A lot of his work on the ranch was done on a horse, but when he made fence, it was hard work. His hair was darker, and his beard was darker brown, he had widely spaced teeth and when he smiled, it was obvious. Tom was taller that Bert, in fact when you saw the four of them, Tom stood out by himself. Richard was about five foot eight, and just a little on the stocky side. His hair was a little on the rust-colored side, and his beard was more of a red rust color, the kind of beard most men would be happy with. Sometimes you see a guy with brown hair and his beard is reddish brown, something that always catches your eye. Each man had his tin cup with a couple fingers of brandy. Now it was time to just sit and relax. Bert asked Tom what he did before heading up north.

Tom answered, "Well, I did many things in my twenty years. I guess what I did most was pound nails. I worked for a guy in southern California, mostly building houses. About six months ago I was hired on to work on an oil rig; the money was a hell of a lot better. We worked like hell for three months, about sixteen hours a day. That's when I saved some money to head north."

Bert looked at Richard, "If I don't come back rich, I don't know what will be next, how about you?"

"Do you guys know what a Gandy Dancer is? If you don't, I'll tell you. I worked on the railroad, mostly laying track. I guess I was kind of a foreman. We had many Chinese doing the spiking. They were pretty good. Two guys at a time swinging the spiking mauls, and it wasn't long before the spike was set. Most of those guys had pigtails; they were kidded a lot by the white guys. It was really a horse shit job, living in tents all the time, poor food, and not very good pay. I know this guy won't be going back to working on the railroad."

Hans had his pencil out doing some figuring, "I don't know where you guys stand, but Bert and me should have about four more trips to make. If the trail stays hard and we can get those runners iced up real good we'll be okay."

Tom looked at Hans, "If you guys have about four more loads, we should be close to the same amount, we're kind of running the same pace."

Richard set his tin cup down and walked over to the stove, closed the draft, opened the door, chucked in a couple pieces of wood, closed the door, opened the draft a little, and walked back to his seat. All this time, nothing was said. All eyes were on Richard.

Bert said, "Richard, you should have been a firemen on the railroad, you do a good job stoking that fire." They all laughed. Tom made like he was pulling the whistle rope on a train, and made a "woo, woo, woo."

They all laughed again. Tom got up and poured them all about another shot of brandy. They had an idea. Any brandy up around Dawson City would cost many dollars, so now was the time to conserve. Tom pulled out a map he had in his coat pocket. It showed the trail from Dyea to Lake Lindemann; Lake Bennett on to Tagish Lake. "I wonder where the best place is to build a boat for the trip down the Yukon."

Hans moved his boots a little closer to the wood stove and said, "I'm quite sure a person wouldn't want to build a boat by Lake Lindemann. According to the map, you have to come down through bad rapids. I sure as hell don't want any more rapids than necessary. According to the Mounties at the Summit, most of the boat building is taking place on the south shore of Lake Bennett."

Tom studying the map, made an interesting comment, "Do you guys think it would be better to make a larger type raft, or make two boats?"

"That's an interesting idea, hmm, we'll have to give that some thought. It might be hell of a lot easier for four men to build one boat than two. Tell you what, by the time we get to Lake Bennett, we'll have to give that some serious thought."

Bert lit his pipe, made some strong puffs to get the coals going, crossed his legs, and said, "I don't know shit about how to build a fancy type boat, but I think it wouldn't be hard to build some kind of a barge. One good thing about a barge, we could set one tent on the deck to sleep in. I've heard once you get started down the Yukon it takes about twelve days to make the trip. In the spring, we know we're going to get some rain. We could also keep the supplies, you know, like the flour, or anything else the rain might screw up, dry in the tent."

Richard, quiet up to this time, "I wonder if we could catch any fish in the river, while we're floating along. I can see myself now, sitting on the boat, watching the woods go by. Hell, maybe we can shoot a deer, maybe a moose. By golly this sounds better all the time."

Bert stood up, stretched his arms out wide, gave a grunt, and said, "Hans, I think we should head for home and fix us a meal. I'm so hungry; my stomach thinks my throat's been cut."

Tom said, "You look like it's been cut."

The fire was stoked up and men started cooking. The next morning after they did their morning duties; they grabbed their sleds and headed south, toward the summit. In a way, it was hard to tell if they crossed Long Lake and Deep Lake making their trips to and from the summit. Today the sky was a deep blue in north and kind of hazy toward Dyea, probably because of the influence of the water in the bay.

The day went without incident; the men made two more trips and arrived back at their north camp around seven p.m. After the long grueling day, all they wanted to do was cook a good hot meal and get between the blankets. Both were getting sick of beans and bacon. If they had a permanent camp, they could bake some bread and maybe make a decent meal. They fixed hot cakes and bacon, it was fast and filling. After the pans were wiped clean with snow, they prepared to get some sleep. Bert was down to his long johns. Instead of being all the same tone of white, the dirty spots were showing up very well. The neck on his long johns was a dark grey, the same with the end of his selves. They say a skunk can't smell his own hole, but Bert could smell the rancid odor coming from his arm pits.

He thought to himself, 'Soon Bert, you'll have to get a bath.'

The men hadn't had their long johns off since they left Dyea.

It was pee time, so Bert headed outside, in his boots and long johns. It was moonlight and almost like daylight. He stood there peeing away, gazing into the distance. He saw something moving in the woods. Damn, it was hard to make it out, it had a strange shape. He kept staring at this object. 'Son-a-bitch, it's a damn snowshoe rabbit.'

He tore into the tent, "Hans, where the hell is the 30:30? I see a damn rabbit out there."

Hans reached behind some supplies, pulled out the rifle, and said,

"Pump the lever, and she'll be ready to fire."

Bert tore out of the tent, after being in the candle lit tent; it took a bit before his eyes adjusted to the moon light. Damn, he thought, where the hell is that bunny? He stared, and then about sixty feet away in the thick timber, he saw a movement. He leaned against a tree, set the front sight on the largest part of the rabbit, brought up the rear part of the sight, so the front sight was cradled in the back saddle. He squeezed the stock and the trigger. He didn't really hear the gun go off, but he heard the echo traveling between the hills.

"Son-a-bitch," Bert hollered.

From Tom's tent came, "What the hells going on out there, are you two guys breaking up your partnership?"

At that time, Tom met Bert coming out of the thick timber carrying two rabbits. "I heard one shot, and here you're carrying two rabbits, how did you do it?"

"When I pulled up and shot at one rabbit, the other one must have been behind the first one. You talk about a rabbit being in the wrong place at the wrong time, course, maybe it was his girl friend."

Tom said, "I want to get some more clothes on and then I'll show you a fast way to skin these two."

They both went into their tents for some warm clothes.

Tom met Bert back by the rabbits, He said, "Here, hold the rabbit by the front and hind feet." Tom took out his knife, cut the skin around the rabbit's belly. He then took hold of the skin on each side, and pulled in the opposite direction. Swish! The rabbit was skinned. Tom had to pull the front legs out before it was finished.

"Son-a-bitch," Bert cried, "I never saw a rabbit get skinned so fast in all my life. Now that I know you're a big time skinner, I'm going to find some more animals to shoot."

Hans came out to check on the progress. When he saw the two rabbits all skinned and butchered, he said, "How about tomorrow night we have some rabbit stew?"

Tom replied, "That makes my mouth water, damn that would taste good. I'll tell you what, we'll furnish the vegetables. We have a bunch of them all dried out."

Bert stuck the rabbits into the snow, and covered them good with loose snow; that would keep them from freezing.

Bert went into the tent, and closed the flap. He sat down beside the stove to warm his hands. Hans had a good fire going; the base of the chimney was red and giving off a little glow in the dark. Bert opened his hands to the stove, and then rubbed them to get the numbness out of his fingers. When his fingers were warm enough so he could bend them and make them do what he wanted, he took out his pipe. After loading the pipe, he struck a match on the hot stove; the match exploded and lit up the tent for a second. After a few puffs, he had the tobacco glowing in the pipe. As he sat there, he heard Hans snoring. Bert thought to himself, I've never heard Hans snore before; I must have gone to sleep too fast to hear him. When the pipe died out, Bert stoked the fire with some green wood and crawled into his wool blankets.

In the morning before heading south to haul more of their supplies, their breakfast was the same old bacon and hot cakes topped off with hot coffee. There was a theory in the north, the more fat in your diet, the more warmth to the body. If this was true, they should have kept quite warm. The four headed south toward Crater Lake. If luck was with them, two more trips should complete getting all the supplies to the tent area.

As they moved south against the bitter cold, they met men on the trail heading north. Due to the lack of good food and the terrible winter conditions, many of the men on the trail looked 'like death warmed over.' When they met, there was a "hello" or "hi" or most likely a nod of the head. This really wasn't the time for conversation. For all of the people traveling this trail, most had never been in conditions like these.

The open area from the summit to Lake Lindemann was hell on earth for these travelers. Snow blindness was rampant, frost bitten body parts showed up on almost everyone. When the body part is frost bitten, it doesn't hurt, but when it thaws out it burns and hurts like hell, the worst thing is a lot of heat.

Before they left the supply area, the spot was marked with a shovel sticking straight up. All four urinated on the runners. With practice, they were getting better, and it appeared Richard was the straightest shooter. About the time they saw the big spruce snag by their camp, the wind picked up out of the south, they all knew there was a good storm coming. They were damn glad they had their camp in view.

The sleds were unloaded; it appeared this would be the last load they would haul today. The next thing to take care of was the fire in the stove. It was starting to snow in earnest; the south wind was whipping it up. If there were any men were on the trail at this time, they couldn't be seen from their tents. Bert and Hans talked over the plan for the remaining part of the day. It was agreed they would cut up the rabbits, remove all the meat and start making the stew. Hans started getting the flour and yeast ready for the bread making. Since they would have plenty of time, it was decided to bake up extra loaves of bread for the next few days.

While Hans was mixing the flour, he turned to Bert, "What do you think about making our next stop at the south end of Lake Lindemann? Then we can move our supplies seven miles across to the north end of the lake."

"That sounds good to me; we'll run it by the other guys tonight when we have supper."

Tom took the vegetables he had soaking to add to the stew. On through the afternoon the weather continued its blizzard conditions. Bert and Hans were really upset that they still had one load left at the summit. They both agreed to head out early the next morning to retrieve the last load. It was getting dark.

Hans asked Bert if he would get their friends next door to come to their tent. The three came up, stomped their feet to remove the snow, came in and found a place to sit. By this time Hans had two loaves of bread baked, setting on a box next to the stove. "That bread sure smells good, it's been quite a spell since we've had fresh bread." "The same with me Tom," Hans answered.

Tom continued, "As soon as I came through the tent flap, I got a whiff of that stew you're cooking. Right away my stomach started growling; boy does that ever smell good."

Bert brought out the brandy bottle to celebrate this festive occasion and started pouring a good shot in each of their tin cups. "Like I've said before, a man can put up with a lot of shit, as long as he has a little reward in the evening. We've made quite a few miles so far, and everything is going along pretty good. We're making good time, and we'll be at the boat building area in good time to build out boats."

Richard came into the conversation, "Do you think we should try some sails going across Lake Lindemann?"

His buddy Tom answered, "Let's wait until we see what the other guys are doing, if it works for them, hell lets give it a try."

Hans asked the others, "How are your feet doing? I think mine need a good soaking in warm water to get the crust off of them."

Tom said. "I'm not going to look now and make you guys sick but if this weather doesn't break, I think I'm taking a bath tomorrow. It might also be a good time to change underwear."

The pipe smoke was circling around the tent, following the drafts. It was like a river looking for the correct drainage. By this time, the pan with the rabbit stew had a little fat slick on top of the water; it was looking and smelling better as time went on. The one lone candle gave the tent interior a very nice warm glow; even the four men's skin had a warm glow. They were also getting a warm glow on the inside from the brandy.

Hans dipped a large spoon into the stew and carefully brought it to his lips. He ever so carefully took a small sip, looking back at the boys with a big grin on his face, "It's ready."

Over the next half hour there was very little said. They had butter on the fresh bread and many cups of the rabbit stew. The sound effects told the story, the rattle of the spoon in the tin cup, the slurping of the stew passing from spoon to mouth, and the sipping of the hot coffee. Once in a while there would be a burp from eating too fast. When the men were full, the rabbit stew was gone, as well as the three loaves of new bread.

At this time they all had one thing on their minds, a warm bed and sleep. When Tom and Richard walked to their tent, they could see the wind blowing down the trail. Tom thought about Roger Blankenship and his son, he hoped they weren't on the trail again getting lost.

The next day when they awoke, the tent was still whipping with the wind. Bert got up and stoked the fire, opened the flap, and took a look outside. "Son-a-bitch," Bert said, "The damn wind is blowing like hell, we can't head up to Crater Lake, not with this wind."

He decided to crawl back into the warm blankets.

Both Bert and Hans stayed in their warm beds until about ten a.m. when hunger forced them to get up. After they had their meal, they lay in their beds reading books. This was the first time since Dyea the men had any spare time. The wind kept up all day and the next one also. Hans was getting very irritated, being cooped up in the tent.

For two days Bert and Hans hung out in the tent, in and out of the beds. Sleeping was the best way to pass the time while waiting for the wind to die down. Off and on they would visit their friends next door; it wasn't a good time for the four men. When there is a job to be done, they didn't want to waste this time sitting in a tent.

On the morning of the third day, both woke up at daylight. It was calm, they checked the outdoors, and it was bright and calm.

Off the four went for their last load at Crater Lake. It was smooth going; the wind had made the trail hard as a rock. They met men moving north. This morning it seemed as if everyone was in a good mood. Being holed up for a couple days, gave the men new found energy.

When they arrived at the supply base, the only part of the shovel showing was the top foot of the handle. As the men stood by the pile of snow covering the goods, they looked around. It was amazing how the depth of the snow had increased. They dug out their supplies, loaded them on the sleds and headed north. It was easy going. By the squeak of the snow under their boots, they could tell it was well below zero. They all made good time getting back to the camp.

It was decided by the two camps to go to Lake Lindemann for their next camp site. Hans suggested to the other men to take one tent with them and leave one set up here. They could set up one tent by Lake Lindemann. This way, if the weather got bad, they would have a place to sleep at each end. This was agreed by all. The men had the sleds all loaded so they headed toward the main trail.

Hans was in the lead; all of a sudden he tripped over something in the snow, and fell flat on his face. The three guys, who were following, started laughing at his expense. It really was something to see, Hans' nose diving into the snow. Bert walked up to where Hans was getting up out of the snow, "Sorry about the big laugh, but you really took a nose dive into the snow. What the hell did you fall over?"

Hans brushed the snow from his clothes, "Beats the hell out of me, it was almost like someone tripped me."

Tom walked over and made a kick at the object in the snow and knelt down, and with his mitten, brushed the snow some more. "Hey you guys come here and take a look."

Bert looked down, "Son-a-bitch, it's a human being, and he's froze like a rock. Damn, what a way to end it all. Better if this poor soul had died before having to haul all his goods over the Chilkoot Pass."

As the men stood looking at this poor guy, they were talking about what to do next. Hans suggested telling the Mounties at Lake Lindemann about this man and let them take care of the matter. Death on the trail wasn't uncommon, but this hit a little close to the four men. Bert looked over the guy lying in the snow, "If we leave him where he's lying, he'll just get covered with snow again, maybe a stick would show his location."

Tom spoke up, "I have a better idea."

Tom walked to over the frozen man, took hold of one arm and dragged him over to a dead snag tree about twenty feet away. The other three men stood there not knowing what he had in mind. Tom raised the stiff body to an upright position and leaned him against the dead tree.

"This way the Mounties won't have much trouble finding this fellow."

THE FOUR SAY GOODBY TO THEIR NEW FOUND FRIEND

The other three men stood there for a moment, and then all three started laughing. The man had frozen with one hand over his head. It looked like he was waving to someone. The four men started pulling their sleds. Each gave a wave to their frozen counterpart leaning against the tree. Back on the trail again, they set out for Lake Lindemann.

As they headed down the trail to the north, the weather wasn't bad, the sky was overcast and there was a slight wind from the south. Even though they had over five hundred miles to go before they would reach Dawson City, maybe, just maybe, the worst was behind them.

Hans was in the lead pulling his sled. At a time like this, a person's mind has a tendency to wander. It seemed the farther he traveled north, the more he wondered what really brought him here. Was it the drive for finding gold, to get rich, or to prove to himself and other people that he could succeed?

The Mounties figured there might be ten to fifteen thousand people around the Bennet Lake area before the ice went out. Where in hell would all these people find enough trees to build all the boats they would need? Damn, the more he thought about this, the crazier it sounded. Maybe he made a big mistake going on this crazy venture. He could have stayed on dad's farm in Iowa. At least he would have always had a warm bed, plenty to eat, and then there was Olive. Olive had a more intense feeling for him than he had for her.

By this time the tents on the south side of Lake Lindemann came into view. There must have been a hundred or more. The smoke from all the wood fires cast a massive white haze over the area. The four men wove their way through the many tents and piles of supplies.

Until they were close to the lake, the other men or women in this tent city didn't pay much attention to them. As they came in among the tents they saw where a lady named Mary had set up a tent restaurant.

After unloading the first load and setting up one tent, they headed back for their last stash. As they came by Mary's restaurant, Bert stopped to read the dinner list, for what it amounted to. The four were standing as a group. Bert, the closest to the menu read: "Ham, beans, potatoes and coffee for 50 cents. Damn that's kind of high, but it sure would be fast and the longer I look at that sign, the more my mouth waters."

Tom piped up, "Since this is a democracy, I say we should take a vote." It was unanimous that they go in. Mary had a bench and table set up inside, and by golly, it was warm as well. She served large helpings. The four dug in and there wasn't much said until the tin plates were wiped clean.

When Mary came over to pick up the plates, she said to them, "I have peach pie for ten cents a wedge; here I'll show you one of the pies."

She passed the pie pan in front of each one of them. She was a good salesman, even though she used very little verbal persuasion. They all responded, yes, as if one person spoke. The pie was still hot and the aroma was just about overwhelming. The final mouthful was washed down with very hot coffee. After all all four had finished, they just sat on the chairs, as if they couldn't move.

Finally, Hans got up and started toward the door, "Come on boys, there are four sleds waiting for us outside."

All the remainder of the day light hours the men moved their gear the short distance to the shore of Lake Lindemann. At about the last light of day, the remaining tent was set up and the fires were started. The men were all very tired. After a stable meal, they bedded down for the night.

Early the next morning, the all met by Tom's tent

"How about the four of us looking around for a while? I guess we can spare an hour or so. Maybe we can get some ideas about boat building."

As the men walked through the camp they could hear the sound of the whip saws cutting the trees into boards for the boats. They stopped to look at the men sawing a twenty foot tree into boards. The log was up on a platform about six feet high. The log was fastened to the stand, so it wouldn't move while being sawed. The saw would whip up and down, the saw dust filtering down into the man's face below. "God damn it, Pete, will you quit riding that son of bitching saw!"

"You're full of shit. I'm not riding the saw. It's getting so I can't hardly pull this ass hole saw above the log."

"Pete, everyday you piss and moan about this same bull shit."

The four onlookers were standing in an area where the two who were sawing couldn't see them.

The future boat makers were enjoying the scene.

"Jake, how come I have to push this damn saw up when you're supposed to pull the son of a bitch?"

"Shut your God damn mouth Pete, and saw. You're getting to be a pain in the ass."

At this time Hans motioned the others to move on and follow him. After they were out of hearing distance from the two sawyers, Tom said, "Son-a bitch, did you guys hear those two guys trying to saw boards for their boat? Along the way someone told me, 'Two angels couldn't get along sawing boards like that.'"

"That looks like one job I'm not looking forward to," replied Richard.

Bert spoke up, "I wonder how you decide who saws from the bottom. All that saw dust falling down your neck. Damn, that would be terrible. I can just feel all that shit going down my neck."

The four strolled through the tent city, taking advantage of this little time away from their sled pulling. Up on a hill to the west, they could see a steam engine puffing away. In this cold weather the steam from the exhaust cylinder made large clouds of white vapors. In the valley the engine had a unique sound, puff——puff——puff——puff.

They could tell by the shrill noise, off and on, that it was a saw mill. "That would be the easy way to cut those damn logs." commented Hans. "I wonder what they get for cutting the trees into boards. Maybe we can find one of these yokels."

They meandered back toward their tent. As they stood at the tent opening, Hans started the conversation, "This lake is seven miles long. It should be a good trail, and we know damn well that it's flat. So down and back is fourteen miles. If we take a full load down, set up the tent, then return, it should take us no more than eight hours. What do you guys think?"

I guess there wasn't much to say, they all shrugged their shoulders. "Okay, let's get our butts in gear and make some tracks north."

It was still early morning when they headed north. The walk down the lake wasn't bad at all. If the wind was blowing it would be rough. So far this day it wasn't bad. It appeared the farther they moved north from the pass, the less the wind blew. They made good time pulling the sleds.

It took about three and a half hours. Now the problem was where to set up the other tent. By this time the men were gaining knowledge where the best place was for a tent, mainly to get some wind protection. There was about fifty or sixty tents in this area, they didn't want to stray too far from the trail. They found a site about a hundred yards from the lake edge. In forty five minutes the men were ready to head back south. It was easy going and they arrived back in three hours. They figured one trip a day was enough. They knew all the trips down and back wouldn't always be this smooth. They had to lay in some firewood before dark. There was a lot of scrap wood lying around on the ground, but they couldn't decide if it belonged to anyone. They decided to go into the woods, find some dead trees, and be done. No use pissing someone off over scrap wood.

After a quiet evening and a restful night, they all were up and on the trail at an early hour the next morning. As they made their way up to their north tent and back, a light snow had fallen. The men made it back to the south shore in good time.

As they grabbed a bite to eat, Bert looked up from his metal plate, "Hans, we should make another trip to the north tent and stay there over night."

"I never thought of that. All we have to take along is our bedding; make sure we have food and utensils on each end. Hell, that's a good idea."

The all agreed, so soon they had their sleds loaded; all the runners pissed up, and headed north. Making the extra seven miles, took a little out of the men. The group arrived about a half hour before dark, unloaded their loads and started a fire. They all headed out to find some firewood. With the buck saw, after a half hour, they had a couple of loads. Making sure you had plenty of fire wood in this cold country was number one on the list. I guess it was a job most men really didn't mind doing; it meant a warm butt and hot food.

This night they had a roaring fire, the base of the chimney glowed red, and the old stove was giving off plenty of heat. They had their boots hanging above the stove, their stocking feet on a log near the stove. Soon the numbness would be out of their toes.

Early in the morning, when they headed north to the end of Lake Lindemann, it was overcast and very foggy. The seven miles to the north end of the lake took about two and a half hours. They unloaded and headed back south. In eight hours they were back to the north end, having made two good trips. Twenty-one miles or so a day, was good traveling. After a hardy meal the men went right to bed.

Early the next day they were headed south. Along the way the sun was out bright, the sky was very blue. Hans noticed he could see 'sun dogs' on each side of the sun. He knew that when he was living in Iowa this meant cold weather and probably a change in the weather. It was good weather all the way back to the north end. After loading, they headed south again for another load. On the return trip back to the south end of the lake, it started snowing. It wasn't hard following the trail; the line of men making their way back and forth, helped them to keep their bearings. The line of men and their supplies looked like a row of fence posts.

About half way back the snow increased in intensity. The men started getting further apart, and soon there weren't any to be seen. The four stopped and listened, all they felt and heard was the wind blowing across their faces.

Hans pulled his compass out of his shirt pocket. "One good thing about being on a lake, you sure as hell can't get lost for long."

Tom pulled out his pipe, "This here lake runs pretty much north and south. Hans, you take a heading and we'll follow you."

Off they went single file. The four had traveled about ten minutes, when they ran into two men pulling sleds north.

"You guys know where the hell you're headed?"

Hans replied, "I have a compass, so we'll hit the south end of the lake some time and somewhere."

"Ya, mind if we tag along behind you?"

"Okay by us, it shouldn't be more than a couple miles back to the south end".

About a half hour later, the group hit the shore line. Hans figured it had to be the south end. Now which way should they go, to the right or to the left?

Bert said, "I don't see any trees cut down for boat wood. I bet we should head to the left."

For a spell, the men stood and looked around at the trees. The compass read about due south as Hans put the compass back into his pocket, "Aw shit, lets go left, maybe Bert knows where he's going."

The six men walked in single file along the shoreline, After about fifteen minutes, they heard the puff—puff—puff of the steam engine.

"I told you hay seeds I knew what I was talking about."

They found their tents. As Bert walked up to his tent, he saw foot prints in the newly fallen snow. The tracks went into their tent and came out. "What the hell is going on here, we got someone snooping around our tent?"

Hans came over to the door of the tent. "I wonder what the guy was after. He's got big feet, and the track of his boot shows bars on his soles."

The two went in the tent to look around.

Bert picked up a tarp, "Some two bit ass hole done walked off with a half bottle of our brandy. I had that bottle under this tarp; I know that for damn sure."

Hans was piling wood in the stove, "Let's get this fire going, then we'll take a look at that track outside before the snow covers it up. The two headed out of the tent. Bert was leading on the tracks, "Don't step on the track Hans, we might have to prove to some jackass where he was walking."

They hadn't gone a hundred feet when they saw the footprints entering a tent.

"Yo," Bert made a call to the people in the tent. "Ya," came a reply.

"Can we come into your tent?"

"You got something you want to talk about?"

"Ya, we got something very serious to discuss."

"We're very busy."

"If you don't open this tent, I'm going to open it with my knife."

Bert and Hans heard someone walking to the tent flap. A husky middle aged man opened the tent flap. "What the hell is your problem?"

Bert looked the beard faced man in the eyes, "One of you jaybirds came to our tent, and now we're missing a half bottle of brandy."

Bert could see a bottle on the ground between two skuzzy looking stampeders.

"That bottle between those two guys looks like my bottle."

"Why don't you get your big ass out of here and leave us alone."

That was all Bert needed to set off his fuse. He grabbed the fellow in the doorway by the shirt collar, and gave him a shove backwards. The guy landed on some flour bags. Hans came into the tent; he reached down and grabbed the brandy bottle. Raising up the bottle to eye level, he turned the bottle in his fingers,

"Ah, there, you ass holes, see this B.T. on the bottle that stands for Bert Thompson."

The two guys by the stove were half in the bag, and didn't appear that they wanted to argue with Hans. Bert pushed the big fellow to the ground. He got up and came back toward Bert.

"Listen buster, if you want to get knocked on your ass; keep a coming toward me. I'm in no mood for bullshit. You ass holes stole my brandy, and you can keep the empty bottle. If any of you shit heads come close to our tent in the future, my friend and I will kick the shit out of all of you."

The big fellow stood in front of Bert, his face was making some kind of gyrations like he was trying to say something, but nothing came out. Bert and Hans walked out of the tent.

"I wish one of those piss heads would have came toward me, Hans. I was mad as hell. On this trail you meet all kinds, some the best in the world, and some, the scum of the earth. That big boy wanted to start something, but he didn't have the guts."

They went back to their tent to settle down. It was still snowing and was now dark.

When making their next moves, they made sure any brandy was well out of sight. After eight days the four men had all their gear on the north end on Lake Lindemann. The next move was to the shore of Bennett Lake. This should be the end of the hauling supplies by sled, for from here they could build a boat and sit on their butts and watch the trees go by.

CHAPTER 5

As they came into view of Lake Bennett, they stood and couldn't believe the sight. All they could see were the white tents surrounding the south end of the lake. There must have been over three thousand tents; it looked like someone started a new town.

Hans pointed toward the east side of the lake and said, "I think we should get the hell away from the main tent area. Off to the east, up the lake a ways, find a place to camp away from the crowd."

They hauled their first load with their tent to the new home site. It wasn't long before they were headed back for more supplies. The entire area was busy with boat building. There were boats setting all over the area. All the boards had been freshly sawn; they looked brand new, with their seams lines all black with pitch. This was a busy place. Every where they looked they could see the men with their platforms sawing the boat boards.

As the men stop to look around the area, Hans said, "There sure will be a pile of boats leaving here in the spring. I wonder how they will get across the lake in one piece. I sure would like to know which way the wind blows here in the spring."

Tom looked at Hans, "You know, Hans, I never met a guy like you always thinking two months ahead. I guess you might have given us something to think about."

The four moved their supplies from the north shore of Lake Lindemann to the east shore of Bennett Lake in three days. Now all were sitting in Hans and Tom's tent having a brandy. This was the first drink they had for over a week. This was a well deserved break in the action. They started talking about the big 'brandy heist.' Tom pointed his tin cup partially filled with brandy, toward Bert, "Bert, it sounds like you were out for blood when that hombre stole your bottle of brandy."

"I'll tell you Tom, that feller got under my skin in a hurry. First he wouldn't let us in the tent, and then when I saw the bottle by the stove, I got a little upset."

Hans got into the conversation, "Can you imagine this guy being so damn dumb to come into out tent, leaving tracks, big as life? That feller wasn't too swift in the head."

The men were getting to look more ragged all the time. Their hair was getting longer, their beards were covering more of their faces, and bathing wasn't very high on the list of things to do. Hans suggested they look over the boat building in the area in the morning. It was important that they find a model to copy for the trip to Dawson City.

The next morning after a hot meal of oatmeal, the men left their tents to look over the boat building. The river flowing north out of Lake Lindemann came into Lake Bennett, on its south west corner. The shoreline of the lake meandered around to the east. In this area of Lake Bennett the shoreline was quite level, the entire south end was dotted with white tents.

The area west of the river inlet was also covered with many tents. Lake Bennett was surrounded by mountains, the largest lying to the west. With all the snow on the ground, the tents were hard to define. There had to be two to three thousand tents, most of them putting out wood smoke after the morning meal.

The four men started their boat inspection trip. It was amazing all the different types of boats they saw scattered along the lakeshore. It was surprising how well constructed the boats appeared. Most were about twenty feet long and six feet wide and had high bows and sterns with a bulge in the middle. The larger flat bottom types were all pretty much along the water's edge.

They walked inland a ways to see where the boards were being cut. Most of the teams cutting from their platforms were quite silent, except for the hum and twang of the saw. It appeared some of these sawyers were more experienced than others. They had lines drawn on both top and bottom. The guy on top tried to follow his line and the same with the guy on the bottom. The saws were extremely sharp; someone had a talent in sharpening these whip saws. They finished sawing one board, one inch by about twenty feet.

Tom walked up to the guy on the bottom, "Mind if we ask you and your partner a few questions?"

The fellow sawing on the bottom carefully laid the saw on top of some wood. "It's time for a smoke, friend, we can sit down over here. We'll try to answer your questions; course when I start cooling off; I'm going back to sawing."

Tom bent down and felt the saw tooth, pulling back a cut finger tip, "Who the devil sharpens your saw?"

"There's an old fellow that stops by once a day, he charges fifty cents to sharpen and to set."

"I just hardly touched that saw tooth and it drew blood."

The fellow who had been sawing on top climbed down and lit his pipe.

"You fellows all traveling together?"

"Yep" came the reply from Bert.

"I think it's best to make one boat for the four of you. The easiest boats to build are the flat bottom type. You guys would have space for your supplies, and you could have one tent set up, to keep out of the weather when it rains, and a place to sleep."

"I think we heard that someplace before," replied Tom.

The older guy went on, "Since these boats will probably get some pounding, I would suggest you overlap the sides, just like a regular boat. That way you can still pitch the seams or use tar to seal the boards. When you get out into the rough water, hit some rocks or whatever, you better have that boat well sealed."

Hans stepped closer to the two guys, "Do you think it would be helpful to have a sail on this boat?"

The old timer, taking his pipe from his mouth said, "It doesn't take much to make a post for a sail, course you have to have a couple cross arms to hold the tarp. It's over five hundred miles down to Dawson City. That sail, along with some wind, might be your best friend; beats the hell out of rowing."

Both of the sawyers stood up, getting ready to go back to work. "Another thing you have to keep in mind. Most likely you will spend next winter up some creek by Dawson City. When fall comes, it would be nice to have some boards for your living quarters; you'll freeze your butts off in a tent at seventy below."

All four stepped up and shook the men's hands. "Thanks a lot for the information."

They walked away from the saw stand, and soon the whine of the saw going through the spruce broke the silence. They saw many other men sawing their logs into boards, the white puffs of warm breath into the cold air looked like small steams engines.

"I think Richard, being the shortest, will make a good sawyer on the bottom." Tom said, giving Richard a poke.

"Bull shit," was the reply from Richard.

The four continued their route through the boat building area. Now they could hear the saws, planes and hammers constructing the boats. It wasn't pleasant work in this cold weather. Trying to hammer nails with mittens on was a finger busting job. They soon found that the cost of nails, tar and oakum was at a premium. If you bent a nail, you better save it to be used later.

They could see that sawing was the hardest part of this boat building, and the way the conversations were going, the hardest on friendships and partnerships.

In the distance the men saw the Canadian flag flying high on a pole. Hans suggested they go talk to the mounted police to find out what water lies north of Lake Bennet.

At the tent the men met Sgt. McPherson, a broad shouldered northwest mounted policeman. He stood at least six feet, and appeared to be a man in control. They introduced themselves to the sergeant. Stepping into the sergeant's tent, Hans asked the officer, "I understand this Lake Bennett is about twenty -six miles long. When the ice goes out in the spring, which way is the prevailing wind?"

The sergeant looked at Hans, "Well sir, the wind doesn't do much right at ice out, but just as soon as the lake is clear, it seems the wind comes out of nowhere from the north. You can take my word for it, sometimes it can rile up this lake pretty good."

Tom stepped up to the officer, "Would it be a good idea to move on by foot to the north end and build a boat?"

"Sir, that's a good question. There is a lake beyond Bennett Lake called Tagish Lake. If you went to Tagish Lake, you would be in some good timber country and you wouldn't have to worry about the wind on Lake Bennett. Are you gentlemen figuring on building a boat someplace?

I'll have to give you a number. By the way, will you have two boats or one boat between the four of you?"

The four men looked back and forth at each other. Hans said, "Let's go with what the old timer told us, we'll build one large enough for the four of us."

The officer commented, "That's a good idea. Makes a lot less work and the four of you will get the job done better and faster."

Hans took the officers hand, "Thank you sir, you were a great help."

Each man stepped up and shook his hand. The officer handed Hans a piece of paper, the large numbers read, '1932'.

"Now you take this paper. When you gentlemen complete your boat, paint this number on both sides of the bow. This will give the Canadian government a chance to keep track of all these boats heading north."

"What's the charge?" Bert asked.

"No charge sir," replied the officer.

The four walked out of the tent and headed back toward their camp area.

Tom started, "We have to sit down and figure out what we intend to do. I think we have some serious decisions to make."

Hans stoked up the fire; they all moved close to soak up some heat.

"Okay, we're here on the south end of Lake Bennett. It is twenty six miles to the north end, and a couple of miles or so to Lake Tagish. If we build our boat on Tagish Lake, we'll have to pull all this gear by sled to that lake. Damn, I hate to think of pulling all this gear on that ball busting sled."

Now it was time for Richard to get into the conversation, "If we build a boat here on the south end of this lake, and we get the boat all loaded; the wind blows like hell for a week. Here we sit, while the guys at Tagish Lake are on their way."

Bert gave his two cents worth, "By gad, the more you guys talk, the more sense you make."

Hans let out a big puff of smoke from his pipe. "One other thing boys, if we take the time now to haul all our gear to Tagish, when spring comes, and the ice goes out, which guys are going to be in front of all these guys on Lake Bennett?"

After another few minutes of discussion, the decision was made to have the last camp at Tagish Lake.

Tom was standing by his upright sled, taking a leak on the wood runners. "Why don't we keep on pulling these damn sleds all the way to Dawson City? Hell, by the time we get another thirty miles we'll be half way there."

Bert tied the sled rope to his waist, "Take off Tom, we'll follow you to Dawson."

At least the men were in a good mood at the start of the twenty six mile walk to Tagish Lake.

The men made good time heading north on Lake Bennett. They could average three miles per hour on the lake, so they would have a good idea of the time it would take to make ten miles.

They stopped when they had been on the trail for five hours. At this point the bank along the lake had easy access, and there was plenty of firewood. While two men set up the tent, Tom and Richard went for firewood.

Within the hour they were headed back to the south end of the lake. By the time they could see all the smoke from the tent city; the temperature was dropping.

By this time the boat builders had put away their saws and hammers and their attention was toward a hot meal. In a tent city like Lake Bennett, the men had one thing in common, the 'Gold', at Dawson City.

In the evening the men had a great time visiting other men. They didn't know it, but this was the largest tent city in North America. When a group of people are on the same venture, friendships are not hard to make. All have a common thread for conversation, where you're from, packing, boat building, health and what they're cooking for meals. Since the four knew the packing would be at an end soon, tonight they would have a little brandy.

Sipping brandy became the favorite time of the evening; it gave time to vent their ideas, and if someone had something to complain about, the others were all ears. It was getting close to the first of March. The weather was getting better, the snow was wetter and it was packing better.

Tom poked a stick into the fire to light his pipe, "We're making good time getting our gear north. I think the last thing we want to do is start slacking off. I think we should bust our butts and get to the boat site."

"Anybody have any idea how many more days it will take to get where we'll build the boat?" asked Richard.

Bert took out his old lead pencil, "By gad, we sure can give it a wild guess."

Both Bert and Hans got their heads together, trying to figure the loads and miles to Tagish Lake. About that time, they heard a ruckus a short distance from their tent. They all put on their coats and went to take a look. About eight tents to the west of them, there were two men fighting. Cups in hand, the four went to take a look. When they got closer they could see these guys were mad as hell at each other. They didn't have coats on, so they must have come out of a tent to fight. They were cussing each other right and left, "You pain in the ass son of a bitch. I'm going to knock your block off." "You couldn't knock the block off a piss ant." Both men had blood running from their noses, their hats were on the ground; snow was all over their clothes.

Hans stepped up to the men, "Hey boys, what the hell's going on here? Let's take a breather and talk things over before one of you guys gets killed."

Tom stepped up with Hans and got between the two men. "What the hell are you guys fighting about?"

The two were standing face to face breathing very heavily, in fact; they could hardly speak.

The tall guy said, "This miserable ass hole ate the rest of the bacon, when I went out to take a piss."

"Listen, you tall hunk of shit. Who cooked the bacon? I did. If you wanted more, you could have cooked more."

Hans stepped close to the two men, "In this god forsaken country, sometimes it's hard to keep things on an even keel, but we all have to get along. In this harsh weather, you have to count on one another, if you don't have a buddy, you won't make it. You see too many dead men along this trail that didn't have a buddy to watch out for each other. Shake hands and put this bull shit behind you."

Tom put up his hand on the tall guy's shoulder, "Hey what the hell is a little fight between friends? It takes a man to get over something like this. Now shake hands like Hans suggested."

While they were shaking hands, Hans said, "We should get back late tomorrow night. If you guys are still alive, we'll have you over for a shot of brandy. What do you say?"

The two fighters looked at the four and gently nodded their heads up and down.

The peace makers returned to their tent for another sip of brandy.

Bert raised his tin cup for a toast, "Here's for peace in the valley." A good laugh followed.

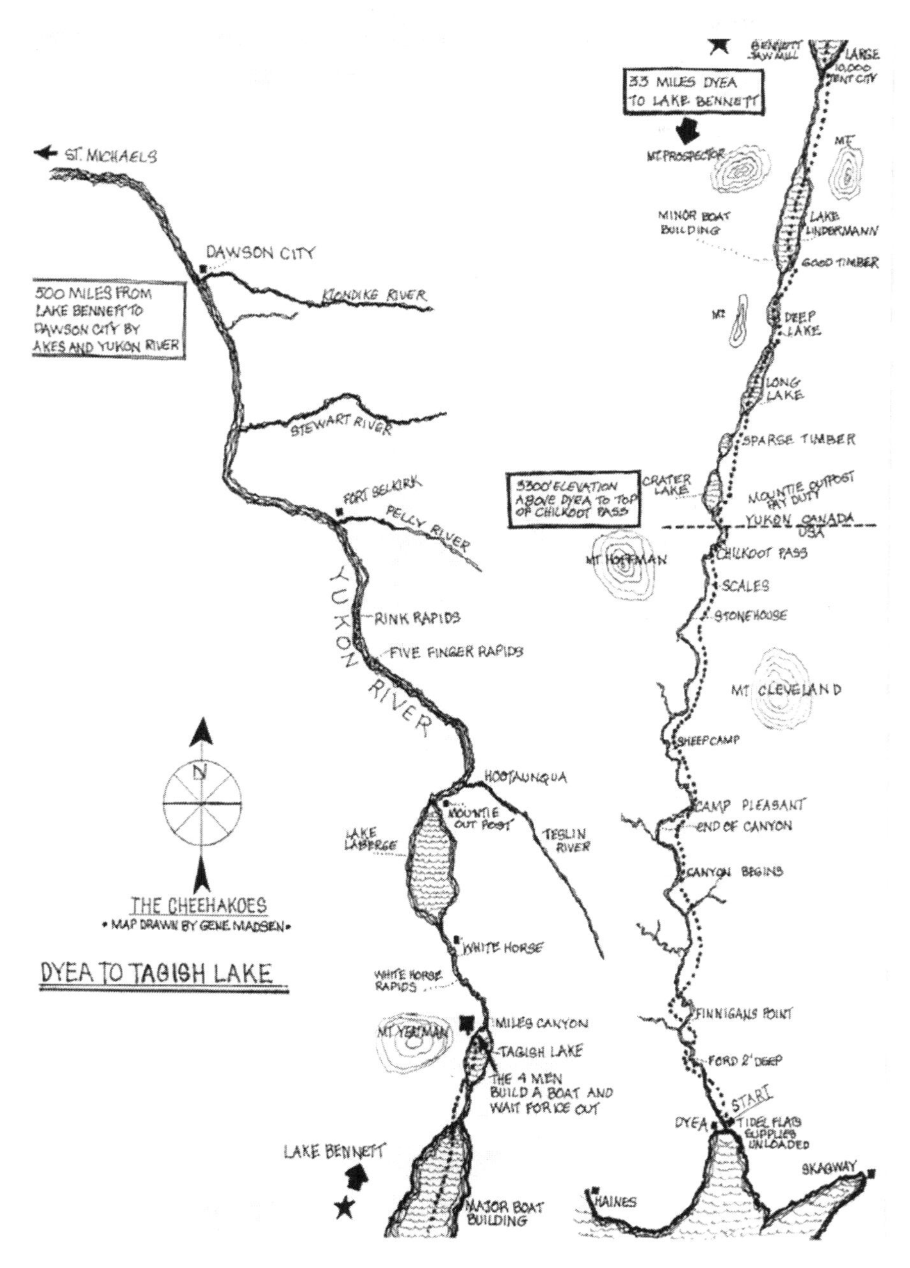

This latest movement of supplies was set to make one trip a day, and then bring the sled back for a load the next day. Hans kept his word to the two fighters. They returned the next evening toward dark. The six men had a good talk and had a couple drinks each. During the conversation, Hans told their guests their plan on going to Tagish Lake to beat the crowd. Before the evening was out, the two strangers decided to tag along with the two groups.

By the end of March, the four had all their gear at the head of Tagish Lake; both tents were set up close together. This was the first evening at the lake; it was a time to celebrate. From here on, the supplies would travel by boat; this was the best news they had heard for most of five months. According to the Mounties, if you hauled your fifteen hundred pounds of supplies all the way to Lake Bennett, you would travel well over three thousand miles. Making the extra miles from Bennett Lake to Tagish Lake, they most likely added another three hundred miles.

At this time in their lives, they were in the best physical shape they had ever been in. There wasn't an ounce of fat on any of these men. Months ago, they stepped off the ship in Dyea. Now months later, with over thirty five hundred miles behind them, they felt like they had been set free.

Their new found friends were still working on moving their supplies from Lake Bennett. They would watch out for them upon their arrival.

Bert set his stocking feet on the log by the stove, "Damn I haven't felt this good for years, this is the first time in my life I really feel like I've accomplished something."

"I think we all feel the same way," added Hans, "It was a great experience so far, but I sure as hell wouldn't do it again. A man doesn't know what a day's work is all about, until you made your forty trips up the Golden Stairs."

Tom took a slow sip of brandy; and let the tin cup slide down his lower lip, "Making our camp off of Bennett Lake was a great idea. Some day I would like to give that Sergeant Mountie a gold nugget. I can't believe there's only ten or twelve tents set up here on this Tagish Lake. Tomorrow we'll have to find four trees the right distance from each other, to make our saw platform."

They talked about the boat size, and it was agreed to make the boat twenty six feet long and twelve feet wide. The size might be changed before it is finished.

Hans sat there looking into his tin cup, giving the brandy a little swirl, "The first break I get in the action, I'm gunna bake me up about a half dozen loaves of bread. Shit, we haven't had any fresh bread for over a week. The hot cake bread fills the gap in the stomach, but it's about like eating sawdust."

"Amen brother" said Bert.

"I heard tell from one of the neighbors that there is a herd of caribou about two miles east of here. I think maybe tomorrow might be a good time for a couple of us to take a walk. Two guys could take a sled and a rifle and take a look in the morning. If we could find the herd, maybe shoot a couple. If they were de-boned, we could haul two easy."

Hans took his compass out of his pocket, "Whoever goes hunting, make damn sure you take this along. I sure would hate to have you get lost in this country and end up in the belly of some hungry wolf."

Bert took the compass from Hans' outstretched hand, "Let me have that, maybe Tom and I could go shoot a couple of them caribou. By the way, what the hell do they look like?"

Richard spoke up, "Bert give me your pencil. I'll draw you a picture of this animal you're going to hunt. I would hate to see you come back with a stray burro someone let loose."

After he finished the drawing the other three got up and came to look over Bert's shoulder. "Son a bitch, that's a goofy looking animal. Hell, it won't be hard to find some of these guys; they ought to show up like a pee hole in the snow."

Hans pointed to Richard, "You and I will find the trees for the saw stand. Is that okay with you, young feller?"

"Don't make me no difference Hans, beats the hell out of walking over some mountain chasing those caribou."

CHAPTER 6

Early in the morning, Tom and Bert headed to the east looking for the caribou. As soon as they started inland, the snow became deeper away from the lake. Where the wind blew intensely, the snow stayed hard and easy to walk on. When getting into the trees, the snow became softer and much harder to make much headway.

They hadn't gone far when Tom told Bert, "We might as well drag a log behind us, instead of these sleds. The deep snow makes these sleds worthless. I think we should go back to the camp and get our back packs."

Bert agreed, so they returned to the tents. Soon they were back on the trail heading inland looking for caribou.

After bucking the wind and snow, the men came over a hog's back with a great view to the east. As the men stood and looked over the valley, the wind made their eyes tear. It was hard to focus on things in the distance. To the north they could see a heavy spruce swamp. "By God, Bert, there appears to be something moving at the edge of that far swamp." They both stared and strained their eyes to make out the movement. Tom motioned with his right hand that they should move to the north. "If we circle up to the north and get into that finger of timber, we just might be a in a good position to get a shot at a caribou."

"Are you sure we're looking at caribou?"

"Well, maybe it's something to eat."

The two men pressed on against the wind and soon they reached the swamp. The timber was thick, and the ground had a heavy cover of moss. Every step the men sunk in about two feet. "I can see why these animals are in here feeding, they're feeding on this moss."

Bert was in front with the 30:30 and Tom was right behind. They checked the wind; it was still in their favor, so slowly they worked their way to the east. Bert held up his hand to his mouth, indicating to be quite. Both men froze in their tracks. Bert crouched down to the ground, Tom did likewise.

Now Tom could see the movement in the conifers. The animals were feeding into the wind. If the caribou didn't get their scent or see them, they would come within a hundred feet of the two men.

Bert could feel his heart beat increasing as they waited, he could even feel the beat in his eyes. He thought to himself, take it easy Bert, don't get buck fever, settle down, and take some deep breaths so your body slows down. They agreed ahead of time; try for a couple young females if possible. A half dozen of the caribou passed before Bert saw a good sized female, in fact, there were two of them quite close together. He pulled up on the first one's neck, right behind the head. He squeezed the trigger, the timber exploded with the shot. For a second the animals froze, not knowing what happened. In the instant Bert shot, he ejected the shell and ran a new cartridge into the chamber. The animals didn't move, they looked like they were in a trance. The next minute they started feeding again like nothing happened.

The caribou Bert shot stood as if he had missed it. Then the front legs collapsed, the head went into the snow, the rear legs buckled, and it fell to the ground. Bert pulled up on the other doe, since the first shot was so successful. He tried another shot in the neck just behind the head. Again the explosion, ringing through the timber. After this shot, the caribou trotted off like show horses with their heads held high; it looked like they were prancing. The second animal Bert shot ran about ten steps and sank into the moss.

"Son a bitch, Bert that was the damndest thing I think I ever saw. I don't think those animals know a human being from a tree. Gol damn Bert, you made two great shots. That's going to be some damn fine cheap meat, two five cent shells, and two nice fat caribou."

The men moved over to the animals. They had bitten their tongues, so they knew they were dead. Before heading back to camp they field dressed the animals, cut out the heart and liver, and deboned all the meat. This hunt they felt would give them between one hundred to hundred twenty pounds of meat for each man to carry back to camp. As the men were packing the meat into the bags, they saw a movement to the south.

"Another bunch of caribou," Tom said. "Hell, we can't shoot any more; I think we have a load with these two."

It was quiet in the heavy timber. They were just about finished deboning the meat when Tom looked back toward the south where he had seen the movement in the trees. Now the animals were no where to be seen. As he looked back at the hind quarter he was finishing up, Tom saw a movement to the east of him. He stared through the low hanging branches on the conifers. It was amazing how all of a sudden things came into focus.

"Son a bitch" said Tom,

"What is it, Tom?"

"It looks like some kind of wolves, make damn sure the gun is full of shells."

"It's full up."

Tom finished packing the meat into the cloth bags, while Bert kept an eye on the wolves.

"Tom, do you think I should fire a shot at them, maybe scare them off?"

"Shit, I don't know what the hell we should do."

At that time, three of the wolves started creeping toward them. The lead wolf now had its head down low, walking very slowly.

"Watch them Bert. Shoot one of those bastards and maybe they'll stop coming."

The shot echoed through the valley, the lead wolf dropped like a rock, the others ran back a ways and took up a defensive position.

"Let's get the hell out of here Tom. You go first, and I'll stay in back here with the gun in case they follow us."

They cleared the timber and walked back along the hog's back. After covering most of a mile, they hadn't seen any wolves come out of the timber. The men moved over the hog's back, now they could see the camp area about a mile away.

Tom stopped, looked back at Bert, "What the hell is that noise?"

They both stood looking at each other. Tom pulled his ear flaps up off his ears. At about that time, seven or eight large, grey wolves came racing over the hogs' back. In a split second, the wolves raced to within about twenty-five feet and stopped.

"Goddamn, look at those sons' a bitches," cried Tom.

"They're going to eat our ass sure as hell."

Tom had pulled his knife out of the sheath, standing ready for the charge. A few seconds passed. Bert thought his heart was about ready to bust out of his chest. Tom had seen mean dogs back down if you showed aggression toward them.

"Bert, keep the gun handy and start toward them, maybe they'll back off."

"If you want me to walk toward them, you come up beside me; we'll both go toward them."

Tom moved up, knife in hand, they crouched over, started toward the wolves. The first two steps the wolves held their ground. The next step, the wolves backed up a step, then another. Then the wolves turned.

Tom said, "Holler loud as hell," "Aahaaahoooow."

The wolves took off like scared rabbits.

"Son a bitch, I wonder if I have any crap in my pants. Damn I was scared. Those guys back at camp will never believe this bull shit."

"Damn, my legs feel like they're made out of rubber, I don't want any more wolf stand offs."

They headed for camp. Bert turned around about every ten steps for about a quarter mile. Each time he expected to see wolves ready to bite him in the butt. About noon the men arrived back at their camp. Both Hans and Richard were fixing something to eat. When they spotted the back packs with fresh meat, their mouths turned into large grins.

Hans took the pack off of Bert's back, "You guys had a hell of a hunt, maybe we'll have to stock up more meat. Looks like an easy place to shoot these so called caribou."

"Ya Hans, it's like going into a hog pen and shooting a couple pigs, really nothing to it. This evening over a hot brandy, we'll tell you about the easy hunt."

The men grabbed their tin plates and made quick work of the beans and bacon.

Hans and Richard told the other two about their tree search. Not too far away they found four trees that would make a good platform. They also spotted some good straight saw trees.

The next afternoon was spent making the saw platform. The four trees were cut off about six and a half feet above the ground. A platform was built to stand on, and the men braced the four stumps to make sure they stood upright. They made a ramp out of logs to roll the saw logs up onto the platform. The sun was going down over the hill and it was cooling off fast so the four headed for their tents to soak up some heat, and make plans for their meal.

That evening when the men returned to the tents, the wind was whipping up and the temperature was below zero. Tom suggested the other two come to their tent for a hot brandy.

As the men gathered close to the stove to soak up the heat, their appearances was something to behold. Their new clothes had become tattered, some patches showed, and the dark clothes showed many miles of dirt and stain. Their appearances were of older men, not the youths who started the three-month journey from the ship. Their hair was uncut, their beards were straggly, and they had smeared charcoal on their faces to keep their skin from getting sunburned. In essence, they looked rough and tough.

Bert grasped the tin cup with the hot brandy in both hands to warm his fingers. He took a sip, "Ah, this is the nectar of the gods; I can feel this all the way to my toes. Tonight we will have caribou for supper. Tom and I should tell you about our little hunt."

Both men went into great detail telling about the hunt. When it came to the part about the pursuing wolves, Tom and Bert stood up and acted out the entire wolf encounter. Hans and Richard were laughing so hard they had tears in their eyes. That evening they cooked their supper together. It was the first time they had fresh meat in over three months. The aroma from the fresh meat cooking was overwhelming. They ate meat and potatoes until they were stuffed.

After cleaning the plates in the snow, Bert and Hans went to their tent. They stoked the wood stove, and crawled into their make shift beds. Since they would be here for some time, the beds were built up with many spruce boughs, and covered with a rubber tarp to keep the cold away from their blankets.

Early the next morning they headed to work with their tools. It was only about two hundred feet to the sawing site, and this site was only fifty feet from the water's edge. They built their platform with smaller trees. In order to get the saw logs up on the platform, two logs twenty-feet long were angled from the top of the platform to the ground. The saw logs could be rolled up these logs to the platform top.

It had been decided to make the boat twenty- four feet long and twelve- feet wide. The men rigged up a two man carrying handle at one end of the log, with a rope loop under the log, to carry the twenty four-foot log. The log was about fourteen inches in diameter on the butt, and a little less on the other end. It was very heavy and the men strained to carry it to the saw site. The log was rolled up the slanted logs to the top of the platform.

First they had to remove the bark. It wasn't bad, for all the sap was in the roots in the winter, so the peeling was quite clean. The log was then fastened to the platform, and then a snap line was stretched for the first cut. It was first cut into a block, and then marked off in one inch increments. The two man rip saws were very sharp and the logs were green. It wasn't bad, but it took a lot of effort to keep the saw blade on the line.

Both the top man and the bottom man had a hard job. The bottom man had to push the weight of the saw up for the next stroke, and when the blade came down the fairly dry sawdust blew everywhere. The man on top had to pull the saw up and also use much effort to push the saw down for the main cut. It's easier to pull the saw, than to push it. When you're pulling and the man on the other end puts weight down on the saw, it's called 'Riding the Saw.' This part of sawing causes the most arguments, hence, 'Quit riding the damn saw.' Since this was a four-man crew, it wasn't bad. After each two man crew sawed their tree length log, they could sit and smoke their pipes while their partners did their tree length. As the man on top made the cut through the log, he would pound in wooden wedges to keep the saw from binding. It would take about one hour or so to make the twenty four foot cut. Spruce was good wood for the boat's interior. It showed little evidence of knots. One log gave them seven or eight boards, about nine to ten inches long by one inch thick. The first day the four men cut up one log. They stacked the boards to keep them straight. The best way to saw logs on a good windy day is to have the wind blow the sawdust away from the person on the bottom. The bottom man had all his clothes buttoned tight to keep out the sawdust. About anything was better than back packing supplies.

By the end of the day, all the men were extremely aggravated with one another about the sawing. It seems there never was a good cut, either one or the other couldn't stay on the line or the other party was accused of 'Riding the damn saw'. This six- foot saw was truly a beast, even though the top man traded places with the down man, it was a miserable job. Soon, it came to where during the cut, no one talked. It seemed the best when the saw men were at work, to get away and let them be by themselves.

That night as they sat in the tent, they all talked about how many trees would have to be cut. It was estimated it would take about thirty-six boards to make the barge type boat. Hans suggested cutting extra, they could always sell the boards to the neighbors if they didn't use them.

During the night a storm came up and lasted for two days. The wind was fierce and the snow drifted high by the tents. In a way, this kept some of the wind off the tents. During the next two weeks the four man crews had all the logs cut and they were still partners, though at times it wasn't easy. It was now the first part of April. There were some twenty -five tents in their area. All of the men here were eager, as each group wanted to get the jump on the others. In the evenings the men visited all the other tents in the area. Over this time, some very good friendships were made with the other men.

When the men started planning their boat, it was determined they needed more boards for the basic structure. Four more trees were cut for two-by-fours and two-by-sixes. The frame was laid out on a flat spot close to the water; soon the frame was completed. Even though none of them had built any boats, most were quite handy with their hands. After the frame was completed, it was tipped over; the bottom boards were nailed to the frame.

To ensure a tight fit, most of the boards had to be planed for a straight edge. The two ends were at about a forty-five degree angle, and the sides had a slight angle to make the boat more stable.

As a kid, Hans had built a small boat for use on the farm pond. He made the sides straight up and down, but it was so tippy, he dared not move while in it.

When the bottom was attached to the frame, oakum was stuck into the seams to make it more water proof.

Hans told the men, "The time we spend now making this boat water proof, might save us much grief later on."

The men didn't mind this kind of work; in fact it was a pleasure, compared to carrying the gear 3000 miles. The weather was getting better; it was staying in the thirties in the daytime. Compared to forty below, it felt like spring. After the bottom and ends of the boat were in place, it was flipped over and the side boards were attached. It had also been decided to make a mast for a sail.

The extra tent would make a good sail. Hans suggested they have an oar on each end of the boat, to maneuver the boat through the rapids. Two of the men were put to work with draw knives making the oars.

THE BOAT IS FINISHED AND ON THE ICE

In two weeks the boat was just about finished. A trap door was made in the floor for access to either store goods or for bailing. The day the last nail was driven, they all sat down and all looked intently at their work.

Hans sat crossed legged, with pipe in hand, "By God, she looks great. I can't believe the four of us could have built such a beautiful boat."

"I hope the old girl floats." said Richard.

Tom walked over to the new boat and laid a hand on the deck, "I hope in the next month or so she dries out a bit. Wouldn't it be the shits if the 'old girl', as Richards put it, sinks to the bottom?"

Bert ended the conversation with, "Let's celebrate this day with a drink and more caribou steaks."

They all gathered in one of the tents. Today was really a day to be happy. They had conquered the Golden Stairs, pulled their sleds through some of the worst weather on earth, pulled the sleds across forty miles of frozen lakes, built a magnificent boat to carry them north, and now they had nothing to do but wait. The relief on their faces was obvious. The elusive gold was now five hundred miles to the north, the next venture to undertake.

It was the end of April, the weather was improving every day. The snow was starting to melt and the water was running into the lake. Their boat, the 'Dawson Special', was on peeled spruce timbers, along the water's edge waiting for the ice to go out. During the last week, the four men had taken turns hunting any game that they could take north to the Yukon. Since there was still snow on the ground, they could use their sleds to haul back the meat. They had shot three more caribou, with no more wolf problems. Two of the caribou were made into jerky. Wooden racks were made near the outside camp fire and the heat and the smoke helped to dry out the meat. They all knew any meat they could take north as a food supply, would come in handy this summer. Meat would be the one thing that would be in short supply.

Two of the late comers to the Tagish Lake area were guys from Minnesota. Since they were the last ones to head down Lake Bennett, some of the local boys helped them with their boat. They were two Swedes by the name of Johnson and Olson, that's the only names we knew them by. They both had quite an accent and were hard to understand. We helped them cut their lumber, using our old platform. After the day's work we invited them to Hans' tent. To show their appreciation, they brought along a bottle of brandy. After we poured the first drink, we started asking what was going on down the trail.

Hans asked, "What does it look like at the south end of Lake Bennett?" Johnson spoke up, "Vell I tell you, dar must be ten tousand tents on da sout end. My Got, dey build da boats night und day. I tell Olson, ve got to get are ass out of here. Ven all des boats head nort, dare won't be enough vater, to float dem."

Olson couldn't keep quite any longer, "Ven ve come into dot tent city, I tells Yonson, ver da hells are ve? Ve must hav took da wrong turn, ve are in a big city. Da smoke vas so tic it looked like da whole voods vas on fire."

Needless to say, the four were getting a charge out of their guests, when one stopped talking, the other took over.

"Da Mounties told us dar might be seven tousand boats heading nort in da spring. I thought, he mus be full of da shit, you get seven tousand boats on dis dam lake un it vill be full from end to end."

The two Swedes told the group about all the men that had died along the trail, mostly after the Chilkoot Trail Pass. After a couple of brandies and much conversation, all left for their own tents.

Days came and went; this was the easy time here on the shore of Tagish Lake. It was getting toward the end of May. After sitting around for most of a month, the men were anxious to head toward Dawson.

CHAPTER 7

On the morning of June 1, 1898, the four awoke to a loud crunching sound coming from the lake. The wind was in the south and the ice was moving!

All day long the men sat along the lake watching the ice flowing down the river. This was the day that had been so long in coming. Wild flowers were poking their heads out of the mossy grass, you could smell spring was in the air, and Dawson City here we come! That evening, men were sitting outside their tents, enjoying the spring evening. The pipes were lit, some had their sleeves rolled up to their elbows, and their dirty long johns were hanging loosely on their arms. It was peaceful night. All of a sudden the men stopped talking, looked at one another, and cocked their ears to the south.

Tom said, "What the hell is that noise? By God, it's singing coming down the lake. Listen, you can make out the words a little. It's Old Susanna," he cried.

Soon the men on Tagish Lake joined their fellow singers from down the lake. For the next hour and a half, they sang Old Black Joe, Old Folks At Home, My Old Kentucky Home, plus many more. Many of the songs the men knew quite well. Within ear shot, some men with great robust voices could be heard. The last song was I Dream of Jeanne with the Light Brown Hair. This brought many a tear to this tattered and torn group of men. Many had left a girl friend or a wife, to head north into the unknown, to find their fortunes. When Hans lay in his bed that night he thought about Olive, his parents and friends he had left behind.

It was the morning of June 3, 1898 and Lake Tagish never looked better. It was five a.m. and the ice flowing down the lake was getting less and less.

Hans hollered at the other three, "Let's get these tents down, and start our dash toward Dawson. We didn't carry all this gear twenty- six miles down Bennet Lake to be last in line."

On this historic day seven thousand one hundred and twenty four home made boats started their five hundred mile float down through terrible rapids and dangerous canyons on their way to Dawson City. This was the greatest armada of boats assembled in one place that the world had ever seen.

The four of them took the tents down and hauled them to the boat. Next came all the supplies. Everything was stacked on the shore next to the boat. All the other men along the lake had the same idea; everyone was rushing to get their boats floating down the Yukon. The four pushed the boat away from shore where it had settled after the ice went out. They loaded all the gear onto the boat. Tom pushed the boat out into the lake; the guys on shore gave a cheer. This was about the fifth boat to get into the water on Tagish Lake.

Tom and Bert were on the side paddles. They were anxious to get the boat into the lake, headed toward the river. Hans was in the back using the back oar as a rudder. In a couple of hours the boat was in the river.

Hans told the men to gather around him.

"When we head down through some of these rapids, we have to work together and fast. If we crash this boat into one rock and the boat tips over, we'll loose everything, and you know what that means. We'll have to work out some maneuvers, so each person knows what to do. I'll do the calling, so we'll have less confusion. When I holler front left, Tom you pull the oar so the front goes left and so on. Richard and I will stay on the sides."

Hans told Richard, "I'll tell you to pull front or back, got that Richard?"

"Yup."

"We'll have a little practice, now, you all get set."

Hans barked, "Front left, back left; and they did so. Then he hollered front right, back right, left side back."

The boat swung just as Hans wanted. After another fifteen minutes of practice; the men had the maneuvers down real good. The first part of the river that started to look bad was what they called Miles Canyon. The walls of this canyon were about one hundred feet high. The boat started speeding up,

Hans hollered, “Keep the boat straight.”

The sound of the rushing water was deafening. The white water was spraying high in the air, and the waves looked to be about five- feet high. The boat was riding the waves in good shape, when all of a sudden the boat started toward the left side of the canyon.

Hans hollered, “Tom pull hard right; Richard pull forward; Bert, you pull right.”

The boat came right back into the middle.

Just ahead, Hans could see where the canyons narrowed down to about thirty feet. Hans hollered at Richard, “Take your oar loose, in case you have to push against the canyon wall.” The four men worked to get the boat in line with the river. They were moving along at a very fast clip. The boat was very stable, the three to five foot waves didn’t seem to bother it.

Hans, looking ahead, saw a smaller boat stuck in a whirlpool. He thought to himself, those poor devils. In an instant he hollered over the roar of the rapids, "Bert, grab the rope on the deck and make about a two foot coil."

At that time as their boat was angling toward the whirlpool, the men in the smaller boat looked horrified.

Hans hollered above the roar, "Front and back pull hard to the left."

Frantically, the men pulled on their oars with all their might. The boat started to move to the left. At this time they were approaching the whirlpool. The men in the smaller boat looked horrified to see the larger boat coming toward them. In a couple of seconds it would be all over for the two boats. The thrown rope had missed by a couple of feet.

"Bert, throw the rope to the other boat."

Bert put his oar on the deck, grabbed the coil of rope, and gave it a hefty toss across to the other boat.

Bert hollered at the two men, "Cinch the rope around something strong."

One of the men wrapped the rope around part of the boat and braced himself. By this time the boat was turning, and the men were jumping around getting away from the slack rope. All of a sudden the rope went taut. The big boat almost came to a stop, and then there was a mighty jerk on the rope. Suddenly the big boat started turning sideways in the strong rapids. In haste, Bert forgot the rope was tied to the front of the boat, and that it was hung up on the side oar mount.

Hans hollered as loud as he could to the men in the small boat, "Untie the rope from your boat."

About the same time as he yelled, the man in the front untied the rope and gave it a toss. There wasn't time for the men in the large boat to worry about the rope dragging behind them. They had other things to worry about. Hans again hollered instructions to the men. First they had to rotate the boat back in line with the flow of the river. With little time to spare the boat turned, missing the wall by inches.

"Son a bitch," Tom shouted, "I don't ever want to go through something like that again. Everything happened so fast, I thought for sure we were all going to drown. Maybe Saint Peter was looking out for this boat."

"Amen," said Richard.

As their boat passed through the rapids and started into the smoother waters, they could see wrecked boats on shore. They came around a slight bend and saw a number of boats pulled up on shore.

They came through the first rapids without a scrape. The crew hadn't expected these terrifying rapids.

The next part of the river was easy, until they heard the roar of the White Horse Rapids.

Hans yelled at the men, "Before we head into the White Horse Rapids, we'll dock the boat and take a look at the rocks we have to dodge."

They pulled into the shore, among about twelve other boats, and pulled the boat up on a bar. Hans told Richard to grab the rope and keep the boat into shore. The other three went up over on the west side. The rapids, where they saw the most white water, appeared to be about half mile long. As they walked along, a number of small boats were heading into the white water. One of them was going side ways.

Bert said, "Those damn fools better get that boat straight, there's a rock ahead of them." All four watched as the two men tried to get the boat in line with the current. Then it stopped in the middle of the rapids, the down stream side hung up on a large rock; only about one foot was above the water. The up stream side of the boat started to rise in the water. It was just about ready to tip over when one end swung around and freed it from the rock.

Bert said, "Son a bitch, I bet there's some shit in a couple guys' pants down there."

They ran into a Mountie along the side of the rapids. Hans asked him, "Are all the boats getting through okay?"

The officer pulled his broad brim hat down to shield his eyes from the sun. "There's been twenty- three boats come through, one broke in two and one tipped over and floated down the river. Most of the trouble you'll find on the right side, watch the whirlpool over there."

As the Mounties pointed to the east side of the rapids, they said, "Not far from the beginning, you'll see a large rock. You want to stay clear of that area. Many a boat has hit that rock, some were okay, and some broke in half."

The boats they saw coming through the rapids were moving at a very fast rate; it seems like the men on them had very little time to maintain control.

"I think we are in for a wild ride boys," Hans said to the other two.

Tom pointed to the large rock on the left side, "We have to make damn sure we bear to the right. Damn, I didn't think these rapids would be this bad. When you hear tell about the White Horse Rapids, that is one thing; then when you take a look at it, it's something different."

The three walked back the half mile to their boat.

Tom said to Richard, "Do you know any prayers for people going through rapids?"

Richard coiling the rope around his arm said, "I think I could make one up to fit the occasion. In fact when we start down the river, I'll work on it." The four men climbed onto the boat.

Hans said, "Let's wait until the boat ahead of us gets down the rapids a ways, before we head out."

They watched, so when that boat was about one hundred yards down stream, Hans hollered, "Okay boys, lets get the hell through the rapids."

The four men lined the boat up in the middle of the river. Now their first concern was to dodge the rocks sticking out of the water.

They hadn't traveled very far when they saw a boat sideways on the rock on the side of the river.

Hans hollered, "Tom grab the rope on the deck; coil it up so you can throw a line to those guys stuck on the rock."

By this time they were heading right into the large rock.

Hans hollered, "Front and back pull hard to the left."

The boat started to move to the left. At this time the boat was approaching the large rock. The men in the small boat looked scared to death at the larger boat coming toward them. The large boat hit the corner of the small one, and one of the men in the small one about flew over the side.

"Tom, throw the rope to them."

Tom grabbed the coil of rope, gave it a toss. He hollered at the man in the small boat, "Tie the rope to the boat."

Instead he held onto the rope and braced himself. When the slack went out he just about flew out of the boat. Hans hollered as loud as he could, "Throw the rope from your boat. We want to get the hell out of these rapids. Every time we come through we have to drag some boat out of the danger."

As the men and boat traveled down the river toward Lake Laberge, they saw more rigs on shore. It appeared they were having problems with their leaking boats. They assumed some had stopped to make some adjustments. It was late afternoon when the men decided to put up one tent on the deck. There were ice chunks on the river; more ice seemed to be coming out of the streams flowing into the Yukon. As soon as the tent was up, they started a fire in the stove to cook a meal. In all the anxiety coming down the river, the men hadn't had anything to eat since breakfast.

It was estimated it would take them about a week to get to Dawson City, which was about five hundred miles from Lake Bennett. The weather was overcast and there was a stiff wind out of the north. Along toward evening, the wind seemed to pick up. They were about a half mile from what they thought was Lake Laberge; anyway it looked like a large lake. Hans and Bert stood on the front of the boat, looking intently down the river.

Hans told the others, "We better put to shore; I can see large whitecaps on the lake ahead. If we get on that lake with this head wind, we will have a hard time making any head way."

Bert said, "I agree with Hans, let's pull into shore and tie up."

Tom pointed toward the left shore, "Hey boys, there appears to be a point over there we could get behind."

The men put their oars to work, two men on the left and two on the right. Hans was running the rear oar as a rudder. Richard was getting the ropes rigged up on each end. Now there was a light rain coming down, the wind blowing up the river was making it hard to keep the boat going straight toward the left shore. Just as the boat came into the dirt shoreline it started raining like the devil. The men tied up the front and back of the boat to old snag trees.

They had all their gear covered with their rubber tarp and the flour was in the tent. The men rushed to get out of the rain into the tent.

Tom bent over to put some more wood into the fire. "Damn, did you ever see a storm come up so fast? Thank God we didn't get onto the lake very far. Laberge is about forty miles long, we could have all drowned."

No sooner had Tom made the statement, when the men heard the loud roar of the wind. Tom standing now, holding on to the tent post, "I think we better say a prayer tonight, the good Lord did us a favor."

Where the boat was docked, it had some shelter from the wind. The men were starting to relax. Bert suggested they have a drink of brandy the first night on water. Each man sat and stared at the stove. What the hell would man do without fire? The wool clothes they had on dried out fast. Soon the men started talking about their day's adventure.

Richard started off, "If seven thousand boats started down out of Lake Bennett, I wonder how many crashed in the rapids? Some of those boats we saw in Tagish Lake were really loaded."

Hans put the heavy cast iron frying pan on the stove, pulled out the heavily wrapped caribou steaks and flopped them into the pan.

"Tonight boys we eat good."

The meat sizzled in the heavy pan, and rain was leaking into the tent where the stove pipe passed through the tent. The rain drops hit the hot stove and made a sharp hissing sound. Some drops landed in the grease from the meat, where they danced around until they evaporated. The smell of wet, dirty, wool clothes filled the tent. By this time the men had accustomed themselves to many odd smells coming from their bodies; one of these days it would be bath time. They had a candle lit in the tent which gave it a warm glow from the outside. This must have been the beacon the two men in the small boat saw from a distance. Their boat had taken water, and they were trying to get out of the wind when they saw the glow. When their boat bumped into the Dawson Special, all four men in the tent jumped to their feet.

Tom said, "What the hell?"

They all hurried outside. By this time, two men were holding onto the side of the larger boat.

"We're taking on water; can we tie up by your boat?"

"Sure, but tie the boat along the shore by itself. The waves might beat both boats all to hell. When you're finished, come into the tent and get warm, we have a fire going in there."

It wasn't long before the two came into the tent.

They stood looking at the others. Nothing was said for a moment, and then the shorter of the two walked toward the stove to soak up some heat.

"By Jesus, you're the four guys that saved our ass in that whirlpool. When we came out of that damn whirlpool, we were so damn confused from all that spinning. I bet we were in there for 15 minutes. I was about to throw up."

The other fellow then spoke up, "Boy, did you ever get us out of one horseshit mess. We tried to miss that damn whirlpool, but it just sucked our butts in."

Tom offered the two a place to sit on a tarp, "You two sure as hell did look a little funny going round and round."

The short fellow stood up and said, "I better tell you guys what we're called. After all, you did save our butts. My name is Chris and my tall partner is Everett. He hates the name, so we call him Slim."

After that Bert told the two strangers their first names.

"Now it looks like you kind of saved our butts again. We were about drowned out there, and we see this glow in the dark. We pretty much had the things covered in the boat that the rain could hurt, but we should have headed somewhere to get out of the rain. Our boat isn't made for a tent on deck."

"Tell you what, boys," Hans told the two, "If you can find a place to park, after we make our nest, you can stay in this tent tonight."

Chris putting his hand out to Hans, "We're much obliged mister. A night's sleep out of the rain would be much appreciated. In fact, we smuggled some extra whiskey past the Mounties in our stove. I'm going to grab a bottle, and we'll have an ass saving drink."

They all had a couple good drinks from the Jack Daniels bottle. After a couple hours of telling stories about their coming over the Chilkoot Pass and down to Bennett Lake, Hans invited them to share their caribou steaks. He also cooked some dried potatoes. When the candle was blown out, it was still raining lightly; it wasn't long before the tent abounded with wild snoring. With the whiskey and a large meal, the men were all in a dead sleep.

Bert was the first one up. He scooped some water out of the river with the coffee pot, set it on the stove and added a few scoops of coffee. He also mixed some flour with the river water to make flap jacks. The men sat around eating them like bread. The jacks and coffee would hold them untill supper. By the time they had finished eating, the rain had stopped, and to their luck, the wind had switched around from the south.

Chris and Slim bailed the water out of their boat and shoved off. "You guys keep the rest of the Jack Daniels, the way it's going, you'll be saving our asses again."

The four waved them off and readied their boat to depart. It wasn't long before their boat was out in the main current. After they were in the middle of the river, Hans suggested they try the sail. They had a hard time getting the tent set up on the cross arm and fastening it to the bottom pole. Along with their tent and new sail, the wind really gave the boat a boost. The sky cleared, the sun was shining, and Lake Laberge looked beautiful. The waves running with them were about two feet high. Tom was on the tiller; the others sat and stared at the country.

Bert lit his pipe, "When I get my share of gold back to America, I'm going to buy me a big boat. By golly, I really like this sailing."

Richard looked at him, "Doesn't this beat the hell out of carrying all this shit 30 miles through hell's half acre?"

"This is a great way to travel to Dawson City; this is what they call 'First Class'."

Hans listening to the two, "Are you two dining on deck this evening?"

Bert came back, "Hans, you cook it and we'll serve it on the top deck."

Richard was staring across the lake, when he poked Bert sitting close by. "Take a look where I'm pointing, is that a boat out there?"

Bert cupping his eyes, "I don't see anything except water."

Richard looked back and forth, "Ya, there it is, it looks like one of those whaler types. Look where my finger is pointing."

"Oh shit, now I see it." Tom headed the boat in that direction. After about twenty minutes, the whaler boat was about 500 feet from the Dawson Special. Tom hollered, "Drop the top of the sail down, so we slow down a bit." Bert and Richard grabbed the boat, and Richard grabbed the rope, "I wonder what the hell happened to the owner, or owners?"

THE FOUR FIND AN EMPTY BOAT ON LAKE LABERGE

The boat was pulled along side. The four men looked intently at it, looking for some clue why it wasn't occupied. "By the size of the boat and the gear, there must have been two owners."

Hans pointed to the rear and said, "Look there, isn't that blood on the inside?"

Bert got down on his hands and knees to get a closer look, "By God Hans, it does look like blood. What the hell should we do with the boat?"

Hans said, "Tie it to the rear of our boat, and we'll haul her along. When we see a Mounties Post, we'll stop, drop if off and tell them how we found it."

Tom walked over to Hans, "By dragging this damn boat until we find a Mountie, won't that make our trip a lot longer? You know we're in a race to get to Dawson before all the rest of those yokels."

"Hell, I don't know Tom. We can't just leave all these supplies out here to drift around. Maybe the Mountie will give us the gear, and it would make our supply situation a lot better. We'll load all the gear onto our boat, that will make pulling it easier."

The crew loaded all the gear onto their boat, two thousand pounds plus, making their boat sink a little lower in the water.

Tom looking over the side of the boat, "If we get off this big lake we'll be okay."

It took the Dawson Special about eight hours to cross Lake Laberge. It was about forty miles across the lake; they figured they were making about five miles an hour.

Hans told the men, "If we keep this tail wind the remainder of the day, we should make Hootalinqua before its dark."

The tent sail was doing a good job moving the large boat. They all took turns running the rudder. The temperature they figured, was about forty degrees. When not on the tiller the other three were taking it easy on the deck; a good time to catch a nap. Throughout the day the men could see many boats behind them. A couple of small boats with sails passed them while crossing Lake Laberge. The men kept their eyes open for the missing boat men; there was no sign of them. They did see some pieces of boats drifting on the lake; they had no idea where they came from.

At about seven in the evening the boat pulled into Hootalinqua. There were a number of gold rush boats tied up there. A few tents were scattered about, some were very different, maybe Indians. By the time the boat was tied up at the dock, a half dozen Indians came over.

One small dirty looking Indian with long hair, and white man's cloths came to the front. He was carrying boots made from animal skins. He held out the knee high boots, "We trade for tobacco."

The four stood looking at the five foot Indian; he looked about as dirty as the others looking on.

Hans pointing to his shirt pocket, "We have no tobacco to trade, we no smoke tobacco."

The front Indian waving his finger back and forth said, "Aaahhh", with a big grin on his face.

Tom asked, "What the hell does that mean?"

Hans shrugged his shoulders, "Who knows? I should ask him if there is a Mountie Post here."

The Indian, hearing the word Mountie, turned and pointed toward the tents.

Bert looking at the Indians, said, "Someone better stay by the boat to keep these Indians honest. I'll stay. I don't think they believed us about the tobacco."

Bert sat down on the deck, the other men headed toward the tents. It wasn't long before the Indians took off toward the tents. As the men got closer, they could see the Union Jack flying over a small log building. Hans knocked on the door.

Soon a short stocky Mountie in a brown uniform opened the door.

"Come in gentlemen."

The three entered; all had to duck when entering the low doorway. On a crude wooden table there was a glowing kerosene lamp.

"What can I do for you gentlemen?" asked the Mountie sitting there.

Hans proceeded to tell the story about the storm on Lake Laberge the night before and how they found the empty boat. The Mountie started to write down all the information on his yellow pad.

The sergeant said, "By the way, my name is Sergeant Allan Heighten."

Hans introduced himself and the other men.

The sergeant said, "Let's take a look at the boat."

Hans led the way.

The men walked down to the boat. Bert was sitting on top of two sleds that were latched to the deck. He stood and walked toward the men. The sergeant climbed up on the deck and walked to the rear of the large boat, where the smaller boat was tied. They all stood looking at the boat. Hans jumped in first to show the sergeant where they had seen the blood. The sergeant followed behind and knelt down where Hans was pointing.

"It does look like some kind of blood" said the sergeant.

"Did you men see anything else with blood on it?"

Hans looked up at the sergeant. "That's the only blood we saw. Course we never saw hide nor hair of the people owning the boat. We figured after that hell of a storm we had the night before, somehow they fell overboard and drowned."

"Where did you find this boat in the lake, south, north, in the middle?"

Hans pulled on his chin whiskers, "I would venture to say, around the middle of the lake."

The sergeant climbed out of the boat, "Would you please show me their gear?"

The sergeant was led to the large pile of gear on the front of the deck. It was still covered with the tarp. The Mountie looked through each item, looking for names of the men or any other identification. "It's getting too dark for me to go through all this gear. If you men could stick around until daylight, it might be worth your while."

The Mountie took down the number of the orphan boat, "Can you men wait till daylight tomorrow?"

After a quick discussion, they all agreed. "Yes sir, we'll wait till morning."

The sergeant walked toward his cabin. The four men stood looking at each other. Bert took his pipe from his pocket, "What the hell did he mean; 'it might be worth our while'?"

"I think he might give us the gear. You know if we hadn't loaded the gear on our boat, most likely it would be at the bottom of the lake. Let's get the stove going, and get something to eat."

That night the meal was bacon, beans and some small pan fried flap jacks. At this time of the day, they wanted to get some sleep. They all decided to make a bed using their wooden sleds, it was better than on the deck.

Soon after daylight the Mountie came down to the boat. The men were getting a fire started for breakfast. "Hello there, are you up?" asked the Mountie.

Hans answered, "Yep, we're ready to go, come on up."

The Mountie went back to the pile of goods belonging to the lost crew of the boat. The sergeant took all the items that had any information about the crew and put them in a pouch. He then took the names of all four men and got the number off the front of their boat.

The Mountie standing erect in front of the men, said, "You men should be commended for bringing this boat and gear to my post. You could have taken the gear and headed for Dawson. If you hadn't bothered to bring the gear here, most likely, it would have been lost for good. You leave the boat here for evidence, and you take the found gear. I want to thank you again. Maybe sometime in the future we might find out what happened, and if we do, maybe we can let you know in Dawson."

"Thank you for your kind words, sir," replied Hans.

They passed the smaller boat over to the sergeant and headed out into the river. By this time there weren't any other miner's boats tied to the shore.

While Hans fixed breakfast, two men at a time worked the oars on each side of the boat. After they got their boat on the Yukon River, north of the Teslin River, the river current really picked up. Even without the sails up, they were clipping right along. They gathered in the tent to eat. The flaps were tied back so they could see the river ahead. "Boys, we lucked out, with this new gear; if nothing else, we can sell it to some Dawson miners."

As the Dawson Special headed down river, there was a steady line of boats coming from the south, headed north.

The men on the 'Dawson Special' were making good time on the Yukon River. They were surprised at all the holes some birds had made in the high river bluffs. There must have been thousands of white and black birds coming and going to these holes. Later on when the men reached Dawson City they found out these were insect eating Purple Martins.

There wasn't much of a description about the so called rapids ahead, except, there was a notation about some islands. For some reason they were called The Five Fingers Rapids. It wasn't long before they were approaching the islands.

Tom standing in front of the boat, hollered, "Keep it right between the two islands ahead."

"Okay," answered Hans, who then told Bert and Richard on the side oars, "Pull to the middle."

In the confusion, Richard pulled the wrong way on the oar.

Tom about fell off the front of the boat. "Richard, you horse's ass, pull the other way."

Richard seeing his mistake, started pushing on the oar, and the boat was again headed down the river. "Tom you don't have to call me a horse's ass."

"How about a horse's pecker?"

"Oh go to hell, Tom."

Not too far past the islands, they came to the Pink Rapids. After the White Horse Rapids, most other rapids looked quite harmless. With the moon out bright, the Dawson Special traveled through the night. Bert and Hans slept while the other two guided the boat downstream. The candles were put out to keep the hordes of mosquitoes away.

Bert and Hans were getting exited about the goldfields near Dawson City.

"I can't wait until we can make our way to the goldfields and make our claim."

Hans came back, "As long as we have been together this long, I think we should work a claim together. Hell, we could get two claims next to each other and work them both."

"If we stick together, we should take this boat apart and share the wood with Tom and Richard. If we are in the gold fields next winter, we'll have to build a shack."

For the next few hours until daylight, Hans and Bert made plans for their landing at Dawson City. On the boat traveled, down the Yukon River, running night and day to keep ahead of the other stampeders. They passed Fort Selkirk one evening. It was amazing to travel for hours and not see any people in the wilderness. They would have enjoyed a time off the boat, but now they felt like they were in a race to get to Dawson City. They passed Stewart in the evening, now they had about sixty five miles to Dawson City. At this time there was only one thing on their minds; getting the hell off this boat and get into the gold fields.

That night they sat in the tent in the dark, eating their last supper on the river.

"I think Bert and me are going to stick together," Hans said, then continued, "It's going to take a couple of guys working together, to get the job done, and there's a hell of lot we don't know about prospecting. Maybe we can watch our neighbors."

On through the star studded night, the Dawson Special made its way down the fast flowing Yukon River. In the minds of these four men were fame and fortune.

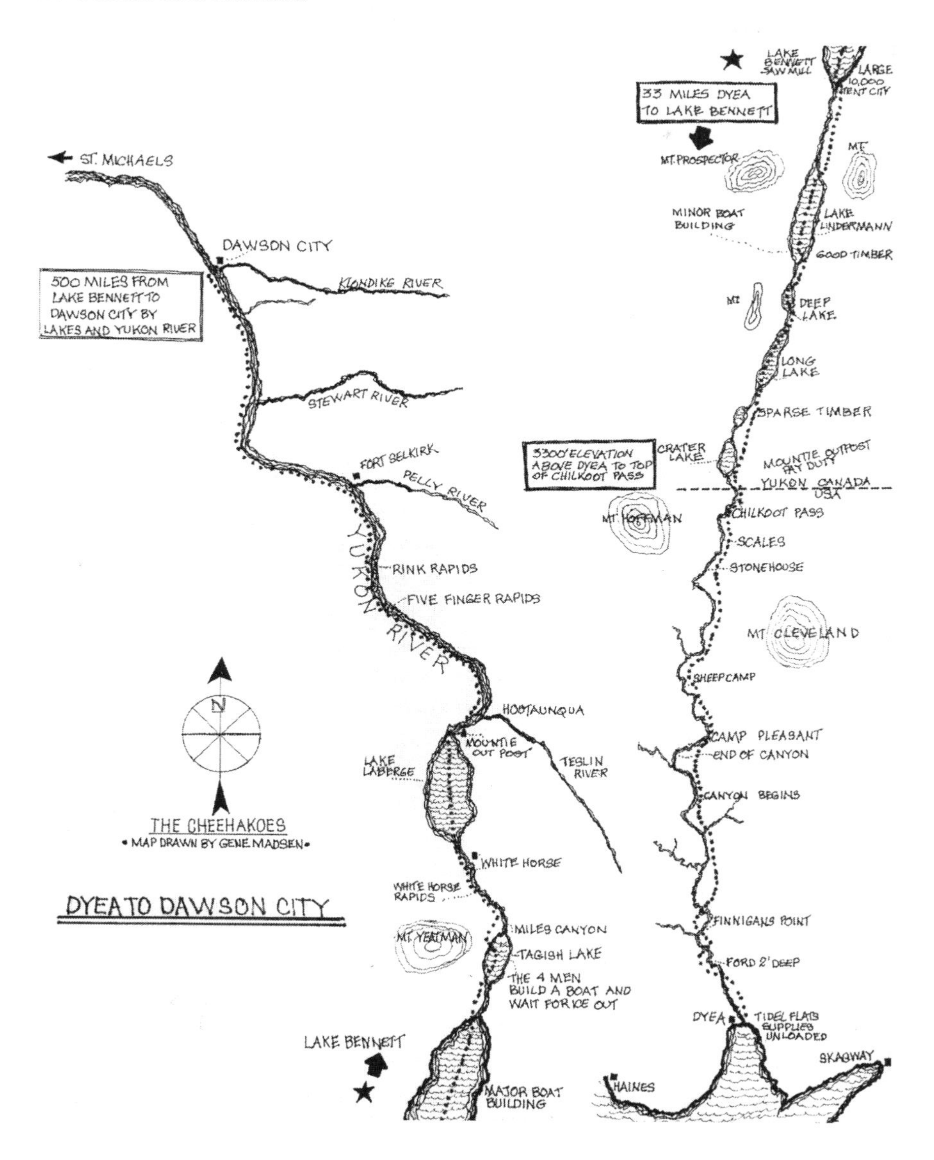

CHAPTER 8

They had two shifts during the night so each man would be wide awake when they pulled into Dawson. This far north, it was light around three a.m. From a long straight stretch in the river, the men could see what appeared to be a town.

"Yahooo," hollowed Tom, "Son a bitch boys, we made it to Dawson. I wouldn't make that trip again from Dyea for one thousand dollars, but, by God it was one hell of a trip."

"What a story we can tell our grand kids some day" replied Hans.

Richard looking at the three standing by the tent, "We look like we dragged ourselves out of hell; our clothes are all tattered, dirty, full of odd looking patches, and our faces look like cave men."

As the boat moved down the river, under the overcast clouds, the men started looking for a place to come to shore. They saw two men on shore by a boat, one man in the front and the other standing on shore.

"Let's pull in by that boat."

They rowed the boat toward shore, and when they were about four feet out, they hit bottom. All four jumped into the water, to pull the boat up on the shore. Bert tied the rope to a stump. All walked over to the two men by the boat, "What's up boys, did you file a claim already?"

The tall fellow on shore pulled his pipe from his mouth, "You boys are in for one hell of a surprise. We just got back from the Mounties office, and all the gold claims in this area are taken."

The four new arrivals stood there stunned. Tom looked right at the tall fellow, "Mister, you isn't bull shiting us, are you?"

"Listen friend, I feel just as bad as you do. We busted our asses to get here, same as you, so you don't feel any worse than we do."

Tom threw his hat on the ground, "Son a bitch...son a bitch, what a kick in the ass! What in hell are we going to do now?"

The four sat down on a log; they all felt like they had the wind knocked out of them.

The tall fellow came over to the men, "If it will make you feel any better, the Mountie said the miners up on Bonanza Creek and Eldorado Creek are short on hands and are paying fourteen dollars a day."

"Shit, now we have to go work for some other guy and make him rich. Boy what a bunch of horseshit." Bert replied.

They sat on the log for about a half hour venting their anger.

"I think this is the lowest day in my life," commented Hans, "Damn, I've been looking forward to this day for a year, now I have my ass stuck in the gold fields, and I can't get a claim. If that damn Yukon River would take me back to Dyea, I would head out today."

He continued, "This isn't the only set back we have had in the past few months. Maybe we should all take a walk into town to see what we busted our butts for. I'm sure our friends are telling the truth. What the hell, let's take a look for our selves."

They tied the boat up good to the shore and went into Dawson City.

They trudged into Dawson City. It really didn't look like much. The buildings were mostly in poor shape. Some of them were new with green lumber. The streets were a mess with mud and water standing everywhere. They saw a horse and wagon stuck at the end of the main street. The horse would need a great amount of help to get the wagon out of the mud. It would be best to unhook the wagon and lead the horse away. After a brief walk they headed back to their boat.

Richard and Bert talked to the two men next to them, found out they were from Utah, and had sold every thing they had to get to this spot They were in a damn poor mood as well.

Richard said, "What the hell are the thirty thousand guys coming behind us going to do? The beach will look like there was a flood with all the boats piled up on shore. Well, we have to get some grub."

A fire was built, nothing was said. Both were thinking the same thing…no gold claims.

Hans spoke, "It's just like these guys told us, these claims were filled last fall, but I sure wish someone would have told us before we left Seattle. Maybe those merchants knew it, but wanted to sell more gear."

"I think we best get our boat settled after we eat and head up Bonanza Creek." Richard commented. "There are thirty thousand people coming down the Yukon River. If we want to get a job in the gold fields, we better get our asses going."

They all looked at Richard.

Hans spoke up first, "I think Richard has a good idea, maybe we'll get a break and get into a claim somehow."

The men ate their breakfast and pulled the boat up on shore as far as they could. The Mounties had given Hans directions to the Bonanza Gold fields. It was still overcast and looked a little like rain.

CHAPTER 9

They didn't see as much activity as they expected. It appeared many of the men working on the claims were by themselves. Hans and Bert headed toward Bonanza Creek to look things over.

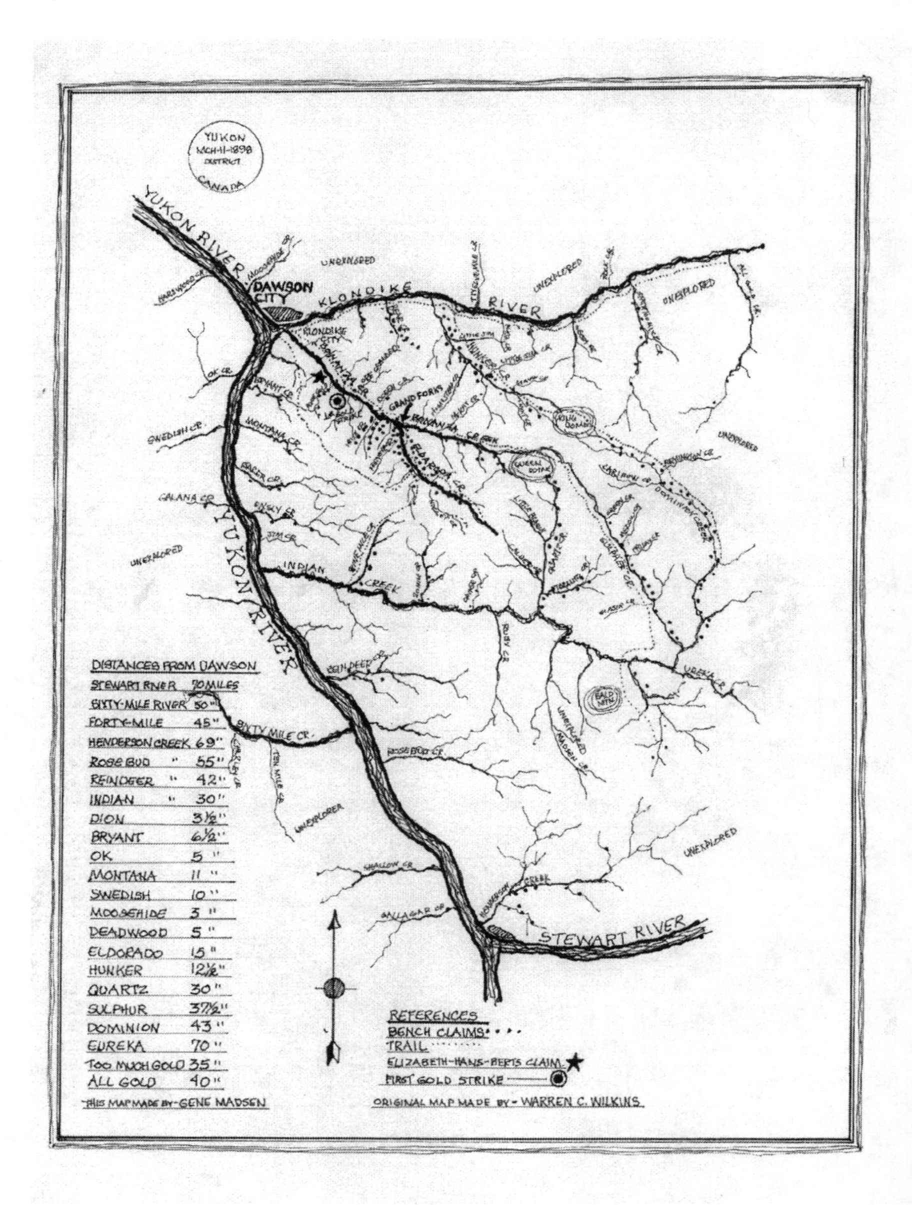

The area by the creek had wooden water ways running all through the different claims. Soon Hans and Bert found a single, older fellow working a claim by himself. Hans walked up to the man shoveling dirt into a sluiceway.

"Sir, we just landed our boat near Dawson and found out that all the claims are taken. We heard miners are looking for help."

The old crusty guy stuck his shovel into the dirt, pulled out his pipe, and filled it up. Took a match from his pocket; after a few puffs he tossed the match aside. "You must be the first of all those crazy people coming here to get rich. Tell you what; you boys are big, look strong. I'll pay you ten dollars a day, and that's a ten hour day."

Bert jumped right in, "The Mounties said you miners were paying fourteen dollars a day."

"Well, well, are the Mounties paying you? No, I don't think so. Tell you what I'll do for you boys, now listen carefully. Since, I'm the fellow paying you; I think I should say how much I'll pay you per day. Now don't that make some sense to you?"

Han's took off his cap to scratch his head, "You got a point their mister, but I want to remind you, we are two hard working fellows. If you point our noses toward gold, and show us how to get it out of the ground, you won't be sorry."

The old man stood looking at Hans. His arms crossed, he removed the pipe from his wrinkled mouth. "I think I'm getting a message here from you boys, it sounds like you two have some crust on you. I'm going to pay you twelve dollars a day for a week. If after a week, you both show me some gumption, I'm going to make you a deal, and I'll give you a choice. You can work for fourteen dollars a day or, I'll keep your pay at ten dollars a day, plus you get 10% of the gold we dig."

Bert said, "There's a possibility we may never see any gold money off this claim."

"Son, this is gambling country; you made a hell of a gamble just coming up here. Take a little time and think it over."

Bert and Hans walked off a ways from the old fellow.

Bert spoke first, "That guy might be making us one hell of an offer. He looks like he knows how to find gold. It seems like we could walk all over this area and may never get a better deal."

"Well Bert, I think you and I are thinking the same way. First we should ask if we could bring our tent up here so we'll be close to our job. I'm also going to ask him about the boat material."

"Okay Hans, let's give it a try"

They both walked back to the old fellow; he hadn't gone back to work, and they first wanted to know if he had some help.

Hans spoke for the two, "If you think after a week, we're worth keeping on, we would like to go on the 10% offer. Would it be possible for us to set our tent up here, so we can be close to our work? We also want to dismantle our boat and stack the lumber by the tent. Do we have a deal?"

The old fellow walked closer, held out his hand, "We've got a deal. My name is Jeb Stark."

Bert and Hans both introduced themselves.

Jeb pointed toward the river, "Maybe you two should go get your tent and supplies, get your camp set up. If you get all set up, and get some work in today, that's fine with me."

"Thanks again, mister," Hans told the old fellow as they walked off.

This was just what the two needed to get back on track; they didn't waste any time getting back to the boat. Their tent wasn't the one set up on the deck; they had theirs covering their supplies. Soon they were hauling their first load to their new home site. From the boat to the claim, where they would be working, it was about one and a half miles.

On the way to the claim, Bert commented, "Maybe we lucked out; we might have tied up with the meanest bastard in the valley. He was the first single guy working a claim, when we came through here. I guess we'll find out soon."

It took them a little over a half hour to go one way. They found some high ground out of the way. They leveled off an area, set up their tent and then laid down the rubber tarp in one end, to keep the flour and dried goods dry. They hurried off, waved at Jeb, set off for the boat in a hurry. Throughout the passing day, the two transported load after load to their new home.

"I think if we keep going through the day, we might get our original gear to our new camp today. It will be light until at least ten, or so. It would be great for us to get our stuff to the work site."

On the last trip to the boat they met Tom and Richard. They had both found work farther up Bonanza Creek.

Bert told them, "The next trip we make we should go together, and then we'll know where you two are working. After we get the job going, we can come visiting. The first chance we get, we should divide the community gear we found on Laberge. Since it stays light so damn long up here, let's come back this evening."

The four agreed and took off up Bonanza Creek. Most of the men in the claims were still hard at work. It was getting close to six when they arrived at their tent; Jeb was still working.

As the four stopped at Hans and Bert's tent, they dropped the gear to the ground. Tom pointed to the left side of the creek, up past a knoll, "Just pass that knoll where I'm pointing is our job site. I reckon it might be half mile up there."

Bert said, "We'll meet you two back at the boat to divide the other gear."

After everything was unpacked, they went over where Jeb was working.

"Jeb," said Tom, "Where do we go to get firewood?"

"Well, you'll have to get up over the hill; none of that high ground has any claims, too far from the creek."

So Bert and Hans took their Swede saw and axe, and headed up the hill. They cut one small tree, and then cut the tree into four foot lengths.

Each man carried two lengths on their shoulders and headed back to camp. They cut the wood into one foot lengths and stacked it beside the tent to be split. Tom and Richard came by; the four headed for the boat. Since the new found gear was picked up on Lake Laberge, none of the four had really looked to see what it included. To their surprise they found a kerosene lamp, three gallons of kerosene, and three bottles of cognac. None of these fellows had ever drunk any cognac, so they didn't know what to expect. The remainder could pretty well be divided equally in two piles. The only problem they had was with the brandy and lamp. Also included in their new gear were two sets of playing cards.

Tom took one deck, "Well boys, since we are the big gold gamblers, let's cut high card for the lamp and the extra bottle of brandy."

Tom shuffled the cards, told Bert to cut them, then fantailed them to give Bert or Hans the first draw. Bert started to pick a card from the deck, he said, "Let me get this straight, the highest card gets their choice, the other gets what's left."

"Yup," Tom said. Bert pulled the card from the deck. "Aah, shit, look what I drew Hans, a damn five spot. Boy, what luck."

Richard looked at the fan tailed deck for a few seconds, pulled a card out toward the end, turned it over for all to see. "I'll be a son of a bitch, look what the hell I drew, a damn three of hearts."

Tom replied, "I hope you have more luck finding gold, then finding high cards."

The four men had a good laugh.

Bert and Hans decided to take the brandy. "We have plenty of candles for light," Hans told the other two. "It will now be a problem keeping you fellers away from the brandy."

Tom and Richard walked away with their kerosene lamp.

Hans pulled a little book out of his pocket, "Think today is the eleventh of June; Thursday, if I'm right. We should meet back here on Sunday to take this boat apart. I heard tell they don't work the claims on Sunday; enforced by the Mounties."

They all loaded up and headed south toward the tents. Bert and Hans worked until ten that evening hauling gear. To their surprise it was still daylight. They rustled up some grub, keeping it simple; they were both dead tired. Hans remembered the vinegar; this was to prevent scurvy. It was said a teaspoon a day would keep you from getting sick. They still had plenty of dried fruit left, so they were not in any danger. For some time they hadn't had the chance to do much with the dried fruit. They crawled between their blankets.

Hans lying on his back; looked up toward the still lit tent, "Bert it was a long trip, but by God we made it. There were times when I had my doubts. Our dream of having our own claim sure got shot in the ass, but I guess we can get part of a claim. I think when we get that boat pulled apart, we better make some beds, and we also will need a couple chairs and a table. After being on the move since last fall, it sure is nice to settle down to a permanent place."

The night went by so fast they couldn't believe it. Of course, in the morning, it was just as light as when they went to sleep. Pancakes, bacon and coffee were their breakfast as they filled the empty spot in their stomachs. Both put their knee boots on for the first time, grabbed their shovels, and headed to find Jeb.

Jeb had been burning wood to thaw out the ground, so they could make a shaft.

The first shaft he had sunk yielded some gold, but he thought he should move more to the south about fifty feet for a new shaft. Jeb, pointed to his wood supply, "Today, I want you boys to get me some wood, I'm just about out. I think we have about six more feet to go to bedrock."

THAWING THE GROUND ON JEB'S CLAIM

Bert and Hans headed up the hill. In the morning the ground might have a little frost on the surface; so they might try the sleds then. On top of the hill the two stared down the valley to the north. Just about every camp had a fire going to thaw out the ground. It was a rare sight; the many fires with their orange glow. The smoke hung over the valley, as if it couldn't escape. The sun was up early, with only six hours of darkness; it was always near by in the summer. They carried two four foot logs on the first trip.

Bert said, "I feel like a damn horse again."

Until noon, the two new miners hauled and carried wood down the hill; they didn't like this way of mining. The last trip was at noon, and then they walked over to Jeb.

Hans asked, "What's the story here Jeb, since we don't know much about this type of mining, would you explain it to us?"

Jeb pointed toward the burning wood, "Years ago the gold was higher in the ground, since the gold is nine times heavier than water, it sinks faster into the ground, then even a stone of the same size. Over a million years, it sinks down to bedrock, that's where we are headed. Most of the time when you get within a foot a so from bedrock, you hit the dark colored magnetic dirt That's when digging for gold gets very interesting."

Bert stood there, staring at the fire, "I can see you're about eight feet down, how much farther to go? Do you have any idea?"

"If I had to take a wild guess, I think bedrock will be found at about twelve to fourteen feet. We might get there today."

"How about starting another fire in another spot, maybe we should check other parts of your claim? By the way Jeb, how far down does the permanent frost go?"

"As a rule, you can find it down all the way to bedrock, hell; it could be twenty feet as well. Go ahead and start some more fires here."

Bert asked, "Is it bean time?"

Jeb replied, "Start another fire first, then we can eat while it's burning."

A half hour later, Bert and Hans were getting their camp fire going.

"Bert, what do you think so far?"

"I don't know what the hell I think. First of all, I thought all you had to do to get the gold was dig a hole and just keep digging. Now we have to keep fires going to thaw out the ground. I guess we'll have to hang around and see how this mining works."

These hurry up meals didn't amount to much variety; same old bacon, beans and flapjacks. They weren't as good as bread, but it didn't take long to fix and they filled the stomach.

Hans was finishing off his coffee, "Bert, one of these Sundays we will have to take some time and bake some bread. We haven't had any fresh bread since we were camped on Tagish Lake."

The remainder of the day, they were either hauling wood or keeping the fires going. When the fire would die down, they would shovel out the ashes and coals, and then remove the dirt as far as it was thawed; it went about a foot at a time. The top three or four feet was frozen muck; it was hard to thaw. The ground below was mostly gravel, this thawed much faster. Most of these holes in the ground were about four feet wide. If they got too narrow, it was difficult to remove the dirt. They kept working the fire and removing the dirt throughout the day. About seven in the evening, the dirt turned black. Bert was in the hole.

"Jeb," Bert hollered, "I'm getting into some darker dirt, hand me down the pick with the shorter handle, maybe it will come faster than building another fire."

He was about twelve feet down the hole. He shoveled the black dirt into a pail and Hans pulled it up to the surface with a rope. The black dirt was dumped near the hole. For the next hour this process was repeated until there were about two bushels of dirt on the surface.

To end their day, another fire was started in the hole; hoping this fire would take them to bedrock. Jeb thought by morning the pile of black magnetic dirt would be thawed out. It was hard to leave the black dirt on the surface set until morning. The two wanted to see gold in a pan.

Tonight Bert and Hans had bacon, flapjacks and oatmeal for supper. The oatmeal had been packed deep in the gear; it was a well needed change. The two sat not far from the stove. In the Yukon, the evenings cooled off very quickly and the heat felt good.

Bert said, "We'll have to get back on the caribou soon."

He asked Hans, "Do you think about home?"

"I'll tell you Bert, some times I think a lot about my ma and pa, and I just hope everything is going along fine on the farm. With the rest of the family, they have plenty of help to keep the farm going. Sometimes I feel a little guilty about leaving them, not knowing how they're doing. I often think about the girl on the farm down the road. Her name is Olive. I think I told you about her before. I get to a point, where I can't remember what she looks like. I know that sounds crazy, but it's true. How about you, Bert?"

"I've been away from home so long, I can't recollect much about my folks. My old man passed on a few years ago, my mom still lives in a small town in Montana. My brother has been taking care of her for years. I guess I should be doing my share, but I haven't. If I go back with some riches, I'll take good care of her."

Bert was trying to get his bed arranged so he would have a level place to sleep, "We have to get some beds made soon. This damn so called bed is ruining my back."

As both men lay in their make-shift beds, they listened to the noises in the Bonanza Valley. It was still daylight. They could hear the squeaking noise, the windlasses used to haul the dirt from bedrock to the surface. It was wood upon wood. The longer they were in use, the higher the squeaking pitch. The men thought maybe some excess bacon grease on the wood would silence the squeaking. The voices in the valley were seldom heard, unless a miner hit his thumb with a hammer, then some low pitch cursing came drifting down the valley. The wood smoke from the hundreds of fires was always in the air.

Hans lay on his back, looking at the tent peak, "Bert, one of these first nights, when we get through with Jeb, let's go into Dawson, and look around. We should go to one of those salty saloons and have a drink. Hell, we have a job now, so we can go have a little fun. I hear tell they have some good looking women in Dawson City."

"Shit, Hans, I'm not sure I want to get too close to a woman. I might get a little horny, like one of those Montana bulls. When they get a mind to go after the girls, they'll go right through the fence. Hell, I might be the same way. I better get that shit out of my head."

The next morning while breakfast was cooking, they could hear voices outside. They both went out through the flap to take a look. They saw about twenty men walking up the creek. Bert and Hans stood by their tent with their hands on their hips, watching the men approach.

Bert commented, "Looks like they're out to lynch someone."

"Damn if it doesn't."

Hans said, "Hi boys, where you off to?"

The guy nearest, walked over to Hans and Bert. "You men have claims here you're working?"

"No" said Hans, "We hired on here to help the guy who owns the claim."

The stranger folded his arms across his chest, "Well, we're looking for work, we all came in last night on the river, we found out all the good claims along the creek have been taken." Hans replied. "We came in about three days ago and found out the same thing. We hired on here the first day. You can ask the older fellow up there working on the windlass, he's the boss." "Thanks a heap, partner." The men walked toward Jeb.

Bert grabbed the tent flap, "Let's get to eating, old Jeb will be on our ass soon. We might have some competition for our jobs. Looks like there will be hundreds of men coming through here looking for a job."

The two found Jeb working on a windlass to get the dirt up from bedrock. He was talking to himself something awful, rambling on about something they couldn't understand.

"Jeb, who are you arguing with?"

Jeb looked up at the two, "Oh, shut up you two hayseeds." Jeb stood up slowly; looking like his back had a permanent bend to it. "You fellers grab your virgin gold pans; we're taking this black dirt to the creek to wash it out."

They carried the two pails of dirt to the creek. Jeb took a pan, filled it about half full, and stepped into the creek so the water would flow through the pan. He held the front of the pan down into the water. The water swirled around; the black dirt flowed over the edge. The three men gazed intently at the pan. Soon, all the black dirt was gone.

Old Jeb, with his tobacco juice running down his chin whiskers, said, "Look at that boys, see the glitter in the bottom of the pan. We got some gold." When Jeb pulled up the pan, there was just a small amount of magnetic dirt in the pan with about twenty flakes of gold and one pea size nugget.

Jeb did a little jig. "Hot dog boys, we have some gold down that hole, maybe you two hayseeds are good luck."

The fire they had down the hole was now out; the dirt had thawed down to bedrock. Bert and Hans worked the hole, hauling the dirt out, hand over hand with a rope and pail. About that time, Jeb was getting ready to set up the windlass. The windlass consisted of a crib made of three to four inch logs, about four feet square. A log was placed on top, with a crank at one end. The rope was wound around this pole; the rope with a bucket attached was lowered down the hole. When the bucket was full, the man on top turned the crank attached to the pole, the rope wound around the pole, and up came the bucket, with black pay dirt.

Now Bert and Hans had a new interest in digging once they saw the gold flakes in the pan. The digging became more interesting instead of grueling hard work. In this claim, the rush was on, they didn't even take time for dinner, and in fact none of the three even mentioned eating. Throughout the day, they dug and washed the dirt pile and the dirt piled up along the creek. About seven in the evening, someone mentioned they were getting hunger pangs in their stomach.

Jeb came over to Bert and Hans, "Reckon you fellers want to quit for the day. We aren't going to get the gold out of this claim in one day. I'll meet you over at your tent in a minute. I'll bring over the gold we processed today."

The two walked back to their tent, the mud was getting slimly and greasy. When they lifted their boots, it made a sucking sound.

"Damn it, Hans," Bert said, "We got a good day's work in and we should have made some money from the gold if we passed the test. I hope that old fart, Jeb, keeps us on. We can make some money and learn how to be gold miners."

Hans opened the tent flap, "I'll get a fire going, so it will be a little more comfortable when Jeb gets here. Maybe we should offer Jeb a drink of brandy. I guess we're some kind of partners here in the Yukon."

In a short time Jeb came to the tent. Hans could hear the slurping sound of his boots coming through the mud.

"Come on in Jeb," hollered Hans.

Jeb sat down on a butt end of a log; and pulled a small leather pouch out of his pocket.

"From now on boys, what we find together, I'll keep in a separate place." He held up the pouch, "This is the start of our partnership."

Jeb grabbed a tin plate by the stove and dumped the contents out of the pouch. Bert and Hans leaned over and stared at the pan.

"Son of a bitch," Bert said, "Look at that beautiful gold."

There appeared to be over a table spoon of gold in the pan. Old Jeb had separated all the magnetic dirt from the gold. It lay in the bottom of the tin plate. Bert stuck his finger into the little pile of gold, moving it around and around.

"Hans, I do believe the trip was worth it."

Bert pulled his hand back from the pan, looking at Jeb.

"Jeb, you just said this was the start of our poke. When we hired on you said we would have to wait a week to see if we were worth a shit."
"I'll tell you boys, it didn't take me long to see you two knew how to do a day's work. Also the fact that you set up your tent on the claim, meant another thing to me. Most men would have set their tents up close to Dawson so they could go chasing, if they got in heat. You boys are in, from the first day you started work."

Bert and Hans both had big grins on their faces, "Thanks Jeb, what you just said means a lot to us. We won't let you down."

Jeb put the gold back in his poke, stood up, was just about ready to leave.

"Boys, do you know tomorrow is Sunday and the Mounties say we can't work on the Lord's Day. I'll see you bright and early on Monday."

Early in the morning Hans said, "So, today is Sunday. I guess we should get our butts down to the boat and start taking it apart before someone else beats us to it."

"Maybe our friends will have the same idea. Later we'll take a walk around Dawson, see what's there."

When the men left the tent about six a.m. it was a little overcast. There was a little noise coming down the valley, but they couldn't see anyone working. The Mounties must mean what they say about keeping Sunday a holy day. They just started toward their boat on the Yukon when they heard someone holler, "Hans." They stopped, looked around and saw Tom and Richard coming down the valley.

Tom raced up, "You sourdoughs going to the boat?"

Bert grabbed Tom by the neck, "Yea, you horse's butt. We want to get the boat apart. We're in a hurry to move the lumber." Tom replied. "We saw you guys had some working tools in your hands so we didn't think you were looking for girl friends." When the four got close to the river, they stopped and looked in disbelief. There were hundreds of boats pulled up along the shore, as far as they could see.

"Son a bitch," Tom said, "We've been seeing many guys heading up the valley looking for work, but shit, there must be thousands of guys here some place."

Richard cupped his hands over his eyes, "I hope we can find our boat.

Damn, they all look alike. Well, we know the number we painted on the side of the boat for the Mounties. What the hell was our number?"

Richard hollered back, "Nineteen hundred and thirty two." Many of the boats were being used as homes for the new arrivals. Some had smoke coming out of the chimneys; many of the men were staring up the creek, and the boys had a good idea what they were thinking.

Tom and Richard found the boat toward Dawson. They hollered at Bert and Hans. They all started pulling the nails out of the boat; it wasn't long before some other men gathered around.

One short heavy set fellow with hair all over his face, walked up, "What the hell are you boys up to?"

"Can't you see we're taking this boat apart?" "That's what I mean. Is this boat that you're taking apart yours? We've been here for three days; you fellers haven't been around here during that time."

Tom walked over to the fellow who was asking all the questions, "We four boys built this old girl on the shore of Tagish Lake, about two months ago. Another thing my friend, it ain't any of your damn business, you understand?" The short guy backed up a couple paces, in case Tom was going to take a swing at him.

"Hey big fellow, we were just keeping an eye out for the owners of this boat; we didn't mean to rile you guys up."

Another guy walked up, and asked Tom, "What are you fixing to use the wood for?"

Tom laid his hammer and crow bar down, "Well boys, we might have to spend the winter in this country, and we sure as hell don't intend to live in our tent."

The guy came back with, "You four guys have a claim up the creeks?"

"No, when we arrived here a few days ago, all the claims on the creeks were staked. We heard the men owning the claims were hiring help to get out the gold. The first miners we talked to gave us a job. They say the going rate is ten dollars to fifteen dollars a day. You won't make any money sitting here on your boats feeling sorry for your selves."

"You think there are jobs to be had?"

"Sure as hell, you men head up Bonanza Creek, I think you'll find work."

"There is a law here no work on Sunday."

Fat boy says, "Who says I can't work on Sunday?"

Tom looked down at the short fellow, "There is a Sergeant Mountie in Dawson that says so. Anyone violating their law just might end up chopping fire wood for the Mounties, and they might need a lot of wood for next winter."

The four went back to work, pulling the nails from the boards. Richard looked over at Hans, "I wonder if the Mounties call this work, what we're doing."

"They didn't say what kind of work was against the law." "Damn," Tom said, "If we got pinched for tearing this boat apart on Sunday, our friends who are watching would laugh like hell. I think we should work a little faster, get this done before some Mounties walk up."

The four worked without stopping. The sixteen by twenty four foot boat came apart a lot faster then when it was built five hundred miles upstream. In five hours it was all in pieces. The boards were set out according to length. The men made two equal piles and were now ready to haul the boards to camp.

"I think these boards soaked up little water coming down river," Bert said as he lifted a couple to his shoulder. "I think I'll carry two of the long boards along with the tools and head back."

The others loaded up and also headed back to camp.

At noon it must have been eighty degrees and the mosquitoes were out in force. It was hell keeping the bugs off your face and arms while carrying the boards and tools. For the next five hours they carried boards back to their camps. It was a little less than a mile from the river to their camp. When they made the last trip with the boards, they stopped off at Hans and Bert's tent.

As Bert piled his last boards along side the tent he asked, "Boys, what do you say we head to Dawson for a drink?"

"Ah crap," Tom said, "Today is Sunday; everything will be closed up tighter than a drum."

Bert grabbed Tom by the shoulder, "Tom let's have a drink in our tent."

"Now you're talking my friend, I would like to try some of that cognac. We'll be there real soon."

It was about seven in the evening when Tom and Richard made

their return. It had cooled off a bit so Hans made a small fire. Out came the tin cups, Tom poured about an inch in each cup. Each man was very quiet while he sipped this new drink. Tom said, "By golly this is one hell of a drink."

The four settled back and started telling what they had heard the past few days Tom told the boys the story he heard about some fellow up on Eldorado Creek.

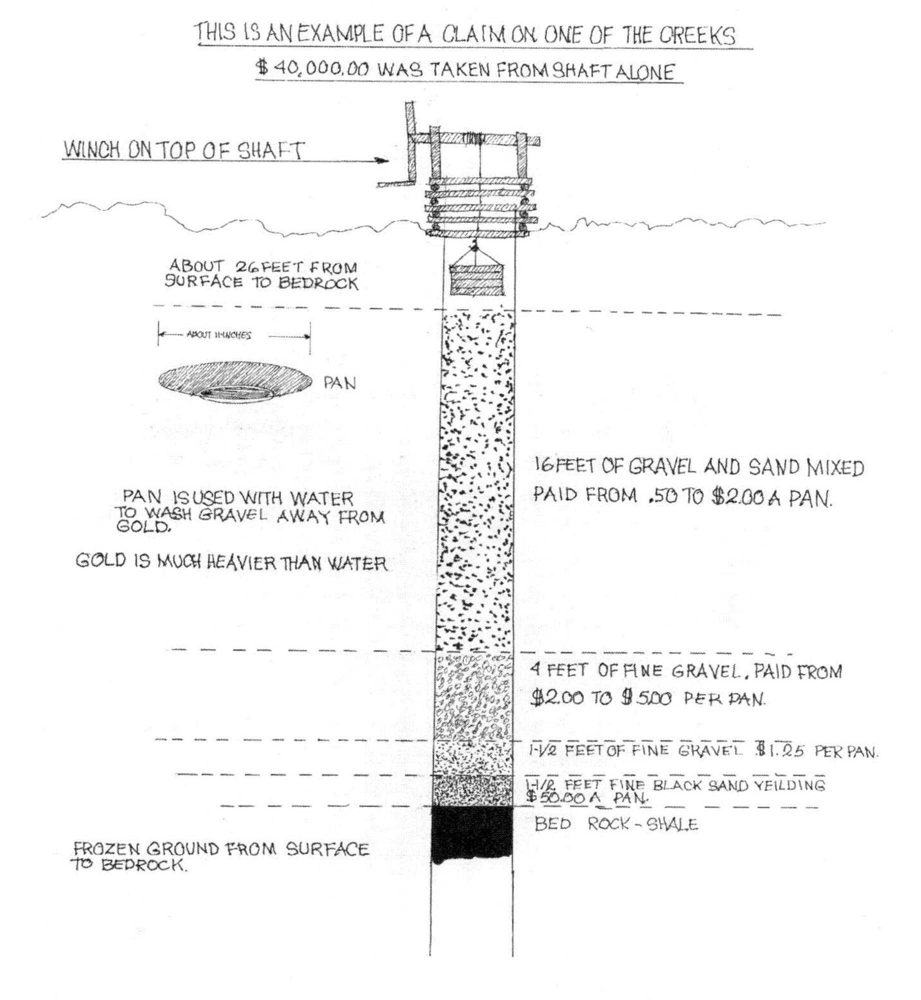

"This fellow and his buddy dug a shaft, about fifteen feet down to bedrock. By the time they hit bedrock, they had made $40,000. Damn, how some people can be so lucky."

Bert took a sip, "Say, this German juice is good, by golly it really warms up the belly. Getting back to this shaft, do you think that story is true?"

Tom answered Bert, "Well, the guy that stopped by to tell us, said it was 'God's truth', so I guess you have to believe the guy."

Richard told the boys, "We also heard that some of these guys washing dirt were getting three hundred dollar pans. Can you imagine making that much money from one pan of dirt? How are we ever going to get our hands on some of that gold?"

Hans leaned over, "The old guy we're working for said if we work for ten dollars a day, he would give us 10% of the gold he finds. I guess he figures he's saving some money and getting more work out of us"

"Shit that sounds like a good thing for you guys" said Tom. "If you were working for the guy that dug the forty thousand dollars shaft, you two would have made four thousand dollars. Say, that's a hell of a deal."

Richard told Tom, "Tomorrow, we'll ask our boss about a percent deal, if we take less per day."

By this time the bottle was taking a beating.

Tom suggested, "We should save this for another night; we're going to have many nights ahead of us."

Tom and Richard were heading out the tent flap as Tom said, "What do you two think about heading into Dawson tomorrow evening? We could be by here around seven. I haven't had a good look at a female for months."

"Okay," Bert said as the other two headed up Bonanza Creek.

Hans and Bert sat by the stove cooking a big supper. Hans was stirring the bacon in the heated pan, "Tom must not have seen the lady and the guy in the claim next to us. We'll have to have Jeb introduce us to them."

"Yah" answered Bert, "You sure don't see them working the claim very hard, and in fact I've only seen them out there working a half dozen times. Maybe they're rich and don't need the gold."

"Yah, it is a little strange. I sure wish we had a claim. I guess we have ten percent of one. Bert, I think I'll mix up some bread dough, and let it raise a couple times. Maybe I can get some bread baked tomorrow morning."

Hans was up early baking bread. This was the first fresh bread since

Tagish Lake. The aroma of fresh bread in the tent was overwhelming; it brought back thoughts about Han's mom baking bread on the farm. To show Jeb their appreciation, Hans set aside a half loaf for him.

Bert and Hans met Jeb at the hole at six in the morning.

Jeb said, "Thank yee for the bread son, it will make my dinner like home cooking."

The hole was down to bedrock. Now Jeb had to make a decision which way to go; down hill would head for the creek, up would go away. Jeb stood leaning on his shovel with one hand, wiping the tobacco juice off his chin with the other. "It makes sense gold would go to the lower ground, so let's head toward the creek."

Hans and Bert took turns working in the dirt hole. The mosquitoes liked the shady damp ground; they hung in droves looking for blood. The ground was still frozen at this level, but not like on the surface.

One of the men would fill the box; the guys on the surface would crank the wooden pulley until the box full of dirt was high enough to grab by the handle. The top man emptied the box on the pile and lowered it back down the hole. The two men on the surface took the bucket to the creek to wash it out with the pan to look for gold.

When the man underground hit the bedrock, he would have to dig horizontal along this bedrock. When the miner dug this way it was called a 'drift'. This drift had to be at least four feet high to dig the dirt. It was back breaking work. Though it was warm or hot on the surface, it was cool in the hole. The farther they went toward the creek the less gold they were finding.

Walking back from the creek, Jeb was looking intently into the pan, "What hell is going on here? The first time we hit bedrock we made money, now we get shit for our work. This damn gold prospecting is about to drive me nuts."

Hans walking along side of Jeb didn't really want to offer any suggestions. About this time four men walked up to Jeb. Hans looked at them and then he thought to himself; that's the fat guy that Tom almost took a swing at.

"Hey mister, we're looking for work, could you use some help on your claim?" Jeb didn't appear to be in any conversational mood, he walked up to the short fellow, "So, you men are looking for work. It appears to me, I might have two more men than I need right now. We've been digging our asses off all day, and might have made fifty cents. So I sure as hell don't need any more men standing around."

"Say old timer, you don't have to get on our ass, it ain't our fault if they can't find any gold down that hole."

Jeb pulled down his hat tight over his head, "Move on boys, we got work to do here, this talk is costing me money."

Hans and Jeb were waiting for Bert to fill the box down in the hole; both men were leaning against the windlass. "That's the crew we had a little run-in by our boat."

Hans told Jeb the story.

When he was finished, Jeb said, "Well we're going to have all kinds of jackasses here this summer. I heard a rumor that there might be thirty thousand new people in this part of the Yukon. I don't know where the hell they're going to live. If they stay around this winter, they'll be freezing to death like dog turds."

CHAPTER 10

Hans knew once Jeb started talking, it would be a while before he stopped.

"Say Jeb," Hans started with, "What do you know about the people in the claim next to you? I sure don't see them working the claim, are they just here for the hell of it?"

"It appears to be kind of a sad story. This guy's name is Dick Larson. He worked for a long time with a surveyor name William Ogilvie. They surveyed this whole damn valley. For some reason there was a measurement mistake on one of the claims, so when everything was corrected, there was this one piece left over, seventy five feet at the widest. The surveyor talked Larson into taking the claim. He tried to sell it for nine hundred dollars, but no one was interested. So he kept the claim. Now the poor guy has come down sick with something. He's got a wife named Elizabeth, she's a damn fine woman, hard worker, but she can't mine the worthless claim by herself."

Throughout the remaining part of the day they dug and washed. It didn't get any better. It was hard to dig up this earth and not find your pot of gold. Every man with a claim knew his neighbors were piling up gold dust by the bag full. Damn this earth, they thought, I wish I knew where the hell to dig.

That evening around seven, Tom and Richard showed up at the boy's tent. "Are you dudes ready to hit Dawson City?" Tom called as they were close to the tent. "You better keep those mud slopping boots on; I heard main street in Dawson has mud ass deep on a midget."

To town they headed, Tom and Richard were in the lead, they were setting the pace. Since they hadn't been to town for over six months, Bert and Hans were having a hard time keeping up.

After about an hour's walk, Dawson City came into view. All around the town were hundreds of tents, maybe thousands. Where the hell did all these people come from? The sun was behind the big dome mountain. Dawson was giving off its own glow. The four men couldn't believe all the noise. The activity was unbelievable, there were horses pulling wagons through the muddy main street, the dogs were barking, and piano music was coming from an adjacent bar.

Tom said, "What the hell boys, how about hitting this whiskey house? Like my pa use to say, 'Any port in the storm'."

The boys stomped the mud from their boots the best they could. They meandered up to the bar. Tom said, "Watch out for the slivers boys, this home made bar wasn't built by a first class carpenter."

The bartender walked over to the four. He was over six feet, had a large black mustache, his hair was slicked down, the lantern light gave it a yellow shine.

"What will you gents have?"

Bert standing on the end looked down the row, "Whiskey okay for you boys?" Each guy gave a nod. "I guess we'll have four shots. By the way sir, how much is a shot?"

The big guy said, "Fifty cents a shot, total bill, two dollars."

"Holy shit," replied Bert.

The bartender scratched his chin, "Mister, you're lucky it isn't a dollar a shot. That's what it cost last winter. The boat just came up the river with this load yesterday. If you pay with cash, I'll knock off twenty-five cents; gold is great, but it's harder to use for purchases."

Bert laid two dollars on the counter. The bartender gave Bert his change.

They all turned their backs to the bar and started gawking around. All the wood in the bar room appeared to look like it was cut yesterday. The ceiling was about ten feet high, and there was a fancy kerosene lamp hanging in the middle of the room. The heavy smoke from the pipes swirled around the heat of the lamp. The only person in the bar room with a white shirt, was the bartender. All the patrons had grey or black clothes on; needless to say there wasn't much color. For this reason the hefty female with the red hair piled high on her head, illuminated the room.

It appeared she had attention of everyone in the building.

Bert said, "What do you think Hans?"

Hans was leaning against the bar, "I think the longer I look, the better she looks. She's not the most beautiful woman I've ever seen, but I don't think she is the most unattractive women I ever saw, but by golly, you know she is a woman. In this part of the country, the men out number the women about a thousand to one."

They all stood looking at the big red head.

Bert stoked up his pipe, "If she was walking down main street in my home town, I don't think she would get a second look, but here in Dawson she is a one hundred fifty pound queen."

At the end of the bar, the bartender was weighing out some gold for a miner. Bert motioned to the boys to take a look, the old miner had a gold poke in a little cloth bag. The bag was about two inches in diameter and about five inches long. The rule was that a teaspoon was about one ounce; that would be about sixteen dollars. These goings on fascinated the four. The bartender gave the old timer a piece of paper; he must have given him credit.

"I think the bartender has his own gold mine; he wears a white shirt, and doesn't have to crawl around a muddy hole." Tom said with a smile.

Richard leaned over, "We could start our own bar out there in the diggings. Hell, about every bottle we sold we would take in sixteen dollars, you know that's more than a days work."

"Are you going to go back down the Chilkoot, and sneak over some more whiskey?"

"Awe, shut up Tom, you know I was just bullshitting."

The men sipped the whiskey to make it last longer. For straight whiskey, it didn't have a very dark appearance; most likely it was watered down a bit. The place was about half packed; they figured this wasn't the hot spot.

Tom suggested, "We should look for another bar where we can get some bar space, something to lean against."

So they decided to leave and walked on down the street to see what they could find.

Richard stopped the men in the middle of the street, "Would you believe all the new building going on? The first boat into Dawson must have brought in a bunch of rich people."

Richard pointed to a hardware store, a laundry building, and there was a bank. They couldn't believe their eyes.

Bert said, "Why the hell didn't we take the boat up the Yukon, instead of busting our butts coming over the inland pass?"

Hans told the boys, "Look there, that sign says its Diamond Tooth Gertie's, I say we check out that bar."

As they passed the window on the wooden sidewalk, they could see the place was packed. The four stood looking in the window. To their surprise they saw a number of females hanging around the tables.

Tom headed toward the door, "Hell boys, let's get our feet wet."

The front part was packed with men from the diggings having a hell of a time. Each guy was trying to out shout the other. They all looked like they came off the same boat; most had beards, dark coats, and boots of some kind. The floor looked like the inside of a barn; the chunks of clay and mud were everywhere. They made their way to the back side of the room; there was only enough space at the bar for one person.

Bert said, "I'll get four glasses, you can pay me later."

They got their drinks, same price as before. The boys could see some poker games going on, it looked very serious; the money was piled heavy on the table. Tom meandered over toward the table; he wanted to see how the game was going.

There were five men around the table; all had drinks setting on the table. Tom thought if one of these guys was a shark, the appearance had him fooled. They were playing Five Card Stud. There was one card down and two up. It seems when men play poker, the puffing on the pipes increased with the action. There wasn't much light by the table in the first place, so all the smoke looked like the sun was going down.

Tom looked at the cards around the table, sure didn't see anything to brag about.

They took turns betting on a new card as they were dealt. It was the third man's turn to bet, no one had a face card up. The guy bet ten dollars, the first guy says;" I "I call." It went all the way around to the dealer.

The dealer took a peak at his hole card, and said, "I'll raise you ten big ones."

All the other players stayed. The dealer dealt out another round of face up cards. Tom looked around the table, still no damn face cards up. He thought to himself, everyone must have a high face card in the hole. There were no pairs showing, the dealer had three hearts showing on the table. The other players didn't have any pairs up or any face cards showing.

Tom did see a number of hearts up around the table.

The forth man called.

The dealer was the next man up to bet, "Boys, the price of poker is going up, this time it will cost you twenty dollars to hang around."

The first guy called. Each man in succession did the same. The dealer's hearts had the others very interested; they thought they would pay twenty -five dollars to keep the dealer honest.

By this time, Tom was about to take the last of his whiskey. He was getting nervous himself, the dealer dealt around the table. The first card was a king, no pairs showing, the second player got a queen, no pairs up, the third man got a three, now he had a pair of threes, the fourth man picked up a six spot, no pairs up. The dealer gave himself a big red heart, now he had four hearts up. The dealer, a little short guy with a weasel like look in his eyes, had a big smile on his face. Tom had a thought this guy was really in the drivers' seat, the way he bet from the beginning.

The first player said, "Call."

Second player says, "Call."

And the third man with a pair of threes bet five dollars. The fourth man with a hidden pair of sixes said, "I'll stay," and put in his five dollars.

The dealer took a swig from his whiskey glass. He started rubbing his hands like he was about to make some easy money. He bet the maximum fifty dollars.

The guy with the pair of threes said, "I'm out, I don't know why the hell I stayed in the first place."

The first guy threw his cards in, the second man pulled his hole card from beneath the others, and without a word, threw his cards into the middle of the table. The third guy had already thrown his cards in, out of order.

The fourth guy appeared to be a little on the drunk side, as were many of his buddies in the saloon. He had a hidden pair of sixes down; he had a feeling the dealer didn't have a heart in the hole. The man took a sip of his whiskey, to drag out his bet. During the hand he had counted eight hearts up on the board with the five players, so with the dealer's four hearts up, that made twelve hearts up. He looked at his hole card again; it was the six of hearts. About that time he had an explosion go off in his head, the damn dealer can't have a heart in the hole; they're all gone.

The fourth guy then says, "I'll call and raise you fifty dollars."

The guys at the table and the men standing watching couldn't believe this guy raised into the heart flush showing. Tom thought the old fart, half drunk, must be out of his mind. The dealer was more surprised than anyone, he didn't want to look at his hole card again, this would cast doubt on his having his heart flush, and he knew his hole card was the ace of spades. The dealer was steaming mad now; that little fart is trying to bluff the bluffer. Sure as hell he has a high card in the hole, the guy never did bet or raise during the entire game.

"Okay, little man. I'm upping the pot another fifty dollars."

Now the little guy knew he had the weasel dealer beat, but he was down to his last sixty dollars. He put fifty in the pot, and said, "Well dealer man, I call you. Now I guess its show time."

The little man pulled out his hole card and laid it on top of the others, "I have a pair of sixes."

The dealer had fire in his eyes, "You're a stupid ass card player, you bet into my hearts like a damn fool."

The little man raking in the greenbacks said, "I might be a fool, but you see, this six of hearts I had in the hole, was the thirteenth heart of the deck, so maybe I'm not the only fool here."

The dealer man stood up, he appeared he was about to take a swing at the little man; instead he stormed through the crowd and out to the street.

Tom said, "I'll be a son a bitch, that little half drunk fart stuck it to the big shot with the so called flush."

Tom turned around to find his friends standing close behind him.

"Did you guys see that game? The little guy had me fooled. I thought he was so drunk he didn't see the guy had the heart flush."

Hans holding his empty whiskey glass, "I guess that's the reason I don't play the game of poker. I never could keep track of all the cards that have been played."

About that time in the back of the saloon, Diamond Tooth Gertie stepped up on a platform about two feet high. It was fairly dark in the area, except for two kerosene lamps hanging from the rafters, one on each side of her.

Richard told the boys, "Give me your glasses, I'll get another round, the Queen of Dawson City is about to sing us a song."

The four stood off to one side so they could get a good side view of Diamond Tooth. She stood on the platform with her hands on her hips; a good portion of her breasts were showing above her dress. She was really quite attractive. Her hair was long and blond, she had it piled high on her head, and her red lips matched her dress. When she started talking, the saloon became as quiet as a funeral parlor; all eyes were centered on the five foot four blond. She had a husky voice, probably too many cigarettes and too much whiskey.

"I want to sing a song for all you handsome men. You're the reason I came north to Dawson City. I knew you men would be lonesome, so I came north to keep you company."

Every man in the saloon took the bait; hook, line and sinker and each thought she was singing this song for him. *"I dream of Jeannie with the light brown hair..."* When Diamond Tooth Gertie finished the song, there wasn't a dry eye in the house.

She hollered out above the tremendous applause, "Get another drink, and I'll sing you another song."

The rounds of drinks were making Diamond Tooth over one hundred dollars a song. She knew how to milk the boys. For an hour she sang to her sweethearts; they all loved her.

After she sang a few songs, they could see where she got the name. Both of her eye teeth were gold, and when this blond sang a song, even in the dim kerosene lamp light, the gold teeth sparkled. After a half dozen whiskeys apiece the boys thought they should get their butts back to the gold fields. It was around eleven at night and it was still light enough to see where they were walking. Needless to say, with all the mud and whiskey, it was hard for them to maintain a straight course. The four talked about the great time they had in town. The three dollars each spent on whiskey hurt their pocketbooks; that was two day's wages down in the states.

It was getting toward the end of the June, the weather was unbelievably hot, and with the heat came the damn bugs. The mosquitoes, gnats and no see-ums were everywhere; it was even hard to keep them out of the tent. On Jeb's claim, they were still drifting along bedrock in both of the holes. They were getting five to six teaspoons a day. Due to the heat and the bugs, Jeb cut the work day down to eight hours.

On Sunday, Jeb took the boys up to a creek, about two miles, where the humpback salmon were running. They made spears from willow sticks to catch the fish. It didn't take them long before they had all they could carry back to camp. They cut off the salmon's head, removed the entails, cut it down the middle to the tail. This way the salmon would hang on a long pole. Bert and Hans had two long poles between the two of them, they carried a good load. Jeb carried one good size pole.

Back at camp they had to dry the fish in the sun. The problem was getting it high enough off the ground so the loose dogs wouldn't eat it. They did come around, but Bert and Hans chased them away with their shovels.

The two sat in the tent talking about their neighbor, Dick Larson. They had heard he was quite sick and discussed what would happen if he died. What would his wife, Elizabeth, do with the claim? Hans had a thought, "Bert maybe we should try to buy the claim from her, she sure can't work the claim by herself."

"Yah, it's kind of a gruesome thing to talk about, but, you know, it could happen, and we have to look out for our interest. We didn't work our butts off coming up here to make someone else rich."

"Well, we'll see what happens," replied Hans.

About a week later while they were working Jeb's claim, Elizabeth came running over to tell them she thought Dick had died. The three dropped their pans and shovels, and rushed to the Larson's tent. Hans felt for a pulse on Dick's neck; he felt none. Bert checked for a pulse on his wrist; nothing. Elizabeth wiped away the tears running down her cheeks but she was taking it well. Hans thought to himself, this is a strong woman; otherwise she wouldn't be up here with her husband in this God forsaken place, digging for gold.

In the past week a funeral parlor had opened in Dawson City. With fifty thousand people; there would be many dying from living under such harsh conditions. Hans and Bert offered to go into Dawson to fetch the undertaker. The undertaker had a horse and wagon to haul the corpse. The problem was getting around through all the claims; since the land was all torn up.

Mr. Larson was hauled into town. Elizabeth rode along to take care of matters, and she asked Bert and Hans to accompany her. After all the burial details were covered, the three headed back to the claim. The boys admired Elizabeth. She was strong and dressed like a man, rubber boots and all.

The three were about halfway back when Hans started talking,

"Elizabeth, did you ever consider what you would do if your husband died? I guess he had been very sick for some time."

"Well Hans, I have been thinking some about that problem. My first thought was to sell the claim and get the hell out of here. Dick came here in ninety seven; I came here this year, on the first boat from St Michaels. Now he's gone, and I just don't know what to do."

"Bert and I would certainly like to buy the claim. Jeb said you offered this small claim to him for five hundred dollars, I think we might be able to find that much somewhere."

"I'll have to think that over. I like the challenge of being in this vast gold field. The thought of finding a fortune, really intrigues me. I also want to tell you about my relationship with my husband. The past couple of years, Dick spent most of his time here in the Yukon, and I was living by myself in Oregon. We more or less drifted apart, so, for this reason when Dick died, I was surely sorry, but it wasn't like losing someone you were madly in love with. Can you two men understand what I'm talking about?"

Hans was the first to answer, "I've never been married but I do have a girl friend back in the states. I guess there aren't any plans on getting married, so I guess I do understand."

Bert said, "All I have had are girl friends, with no thought of marriage."

When they arrived at Elizabeth's tent, the three stopped outside. Elizabeth extended her hand to Hans,

"I want to thank you two for your help in my time of need. I'll think about this claim. You stop by on Sunday, we'll talk things over."

Bert and Hans went back to Jeb's claim.

The remainder of the day was spent drifting and washing. Jeb was doing most of the washing for gold. He decided to make a sluice box to separate the gold from the pay dirt that they were removing from the shaft. Jeb made the box about six feet long and about two feet wide. He had seen sluice boxes on other claims; they all had groves in the bottom to catch the different size rocks. The groves in the first section of the box were about one eighth inch apart. The next section they were about one quarter inch apart, the last section was about one half inch apart. At the end of each section there was a stop to keep the rocks or gold from going out the end.

The weather was remaining very hot; men from the northern midwest part of the states couldn't believe it could be so hot this far north. Through the remaining part of the week the drifting continued along the bedrock. To their good fortune, the amount of gold that came from the sluice was picking up.

When they finished on Saturday, Jeb invited the boys to stop by and he would pay them for their work so far. A claim owner with plenty of gold in the bank could pay his men each week. Since Jeb was just getting the claim going, it was a little 'hand to mouth' situation. He had constructed a twelve by twelve foot log and frame building in which to spend the coming winter. This was the first time Bert and Hans had seen the inside.

Looking things over Bert commented, "Jeb, this is nice, it sure beats the hell out of those tents. You have a good looking bed, even a table and a couple chairs. I like your windows made from quart canning jars."

Jeb answered, "Thanks Bert, it's going to feel real nice this winter. Sit down boys, so we can settle up. Would you like a shot of good whiskey?"

They both replied, "Sounds good."

Jeb poured each one a couple ounces in some small cans he had saved. "One thing you learn in this country, don't throw anything away. If you keep everything, some day you'll find a use for it."

Jeb was sitting on the bunk, Bert and Hans at the table. After the drink was poured, the three lit up their pipes.

Jeb took out his note book, "Well, you two have ten days work coming, at ten dollars a day, that would be one hundred dollars each."

Jeb counted out the money for each one.

"Now I have to settle up on the gold we mined in those ten days. It comes to one hundred ten ounces. Ten percent would be eleven ounces, and this means you each get five and one half ounces. I'll pay you in gold, at sixteen dollars an ounce. You each made eighty-eight dollars for the gold."

Bert pushed the pouch over toward Hans, "Here Hans, you keep the gold pouch; we can will split it up later."

The three sat around the table, in the dimly lit cabin talking about the gold fields. There were boundless stories passing through the camps, about all the extravagant claims of finding gold. Some of these stories were hard to believe, as were stories about men on some claims not finding any gold.

Jeb's little cabin in the gold fields was quite cool, even though it was very hot outdoors. Jeb had followed the plan many men used in the Yukon. He put sod on the roof, and this really kept the heat out of the little cabin. When the whiskey was finished, Bert and Hans told Jeb they had better get back to their camp and get some supper. Since it was late when they arrived back at their camp, they made a small simple meal. After the meal they sat talking about their future.

Bert was the first to speak, "It looks like we might get into some good money with Jeb. So far we haven't gotten into any heavy gold. If we did, the ten percent would add up fast. There is a saying I've heard my dad say many times, 'a bird in the hand is worth two in the bush.' When we go talk to Elizabeth tomorrow, we'll have to make a hard decision. We might pay her five hundred dollars for her small claim, and get nothing or very little."

Hans replied, "You're right Bert; we're making good money working for Jeb. We made eighteen dollars a day the past ten days. Back in the states, we would be getting a dollar and a half a day."

"Well Hans, let's wait until we talk to Elizabeth tomorrow."

They woke up Sunday morning to a light drizzle coming down on the tent. This morning they had flapjacks and coffee; this would be an easy work day. After they talked to Elizabeth, maybe they would walk into Dawson to look around. Around eight, they headed for Elizabeth's tent; the drizzle was still coming down. The frozen ground below let loose with more moisture, and it was as slick as oil.

When they arrived at Elizabeth's tent, Hans gave a knock on the tent pole, and told her it was Hans and Bert. She told them to come in. The floor of her tent was just starting to dry up some, the perma frost in this ground was horrible to live on; it took forever to dry out.

Elizabeth had a table and two chairs in her tent. They were crude, but they served the purpose.

She spoke first, “You fellows want a cup of coffee?”

They both nodded their heads; yes. After Hans had cautiously sipped his hot coffee, he looked at Elizabeth.

“Elizabeth, did you come to a decision about selling your claim?”

“Hans, since I last talked to you two, I have been doing some heavy thinking. In fact, I was awake half of the night trying to figure out what I should do. If I was one of those pussy foot females, I would probably sell out and head south on the next boat. Then I got to thinking, what might be under this ground? All my life I have lived hand to mouth. So, I think I'm going to stay right here in the Yukon. Now you know, I'm a big strong girl, and can pull my share of the weight, but by God, I can't do it all. This is where you two boys come into the picture. I'm thinking about making you two a deal. Now you don't have to tell me this morning what decision is, but I would like to know soon. Here is how I figure the situation. I know you two for what you are, you appear to be honest and hard working, and Jeb thinks you two are the greatest. Instead of having you working for me, I want to make you partners. I get fifty percent and you two get fifty percent of any and all gold we dig out of this ground.”

Bert and Hans sat there looking at Elizabeth and didn't say a word. It was like they were both in a daze.

After about thirty seconds, she said, “Hey you two, did you hear me?”

Bert looked at Hans; they still had this glazed look.

Hans said, “I” I think Bert and I will have to go to our tent and talk this over. Would you be willing to sign over half of this claim when we start working the ground?”

Elizabeth spoke right up, “I guess that would be the fair way to do the deal. We would have to have a clause, if either of the parties leaves Dawson City, that person's share will go to the ones left in camp.”

Bert stood up, facing Elizabeth, “I think you're a very fair person, and I think we would make a good team. I know that if we go into a partnership with you, Jeb is going to be upset with us. Then again, if we are helping you he might understand.”

After saying 'so long' to Elizabeth, they headed for their tent.

"Hot damn," said Bert. "We'd have part of a claim; it isn't the biggest one in the valley, but by God, it's a claim. What do you think Hans? Should we gamble on having our own claim or stay with Jeb?"

"Don't forget this claim is the smallest one on Bonanza Creek, being only seventy five feet wide at the widest."

"I say half of a small claim is better than no claim. I say we go find Jeb and talk it over with him, see what he thinks."

As they walked toward Jeb's claim, the drizzle stopped and the sun started peaking out from under the clouds.

"Hans, what do you think Jeb will say, about you and me leaving him high and dry?"

"Shit Bert, I don't know what he might say, he will either be pissed to the high heavens, or he might say, you boys are doing the lady a good deed. I know when we get face to face; I'll be wishing I was someplace else."

The two approached Jeb's cabin and knocked on the door. There was no answer, and they were just about to leave, when around the corner came Tom and Richard.

Bert saw them first, "Hey, what the hell are you guys up to, where you heading?"

Tom walked up to Bert, "Well, we were just moseying around; thought we would stop by and see our old buddies. Say, did you guys hear there's a new hotel going up at the junction of Bonanza Creek and Eldorado Creek. They call it the Grand Forks Hotel, and they even have a restaurant."

Bert answered Tom, "By golly, we'll have to take a hike up there one of these days and look things over. Let's head back to our tent and have a little talk."

The four went into the tent and Hans said, "When you saw us at Jeb's tent, we wanted to talk to him about a business offer we had."

As they sat there, Bert and Hans explained all the details about taking over half of the Larson claim.

Hans asked the boys, "What do you think of the offer?"

Richard replied, "It seems like you have a good deal with Jeb. Then again, if you can hit it good on the small claim, who knows? Dang, I don't know for sure what I would do."

Now Hans had a very serious look on his face, "If we take the offer from Elizabeth, would you two guys have any interest in working for Jeb?"

"You guys never did say what kind of an arrangement you had with your boss," Tom said.

"As we told you, we get ten dollars a day plus ten percent of all the gold that comes out of the ground. In the past ten days we just about doubled our wages, and we really haven't hit that much gold. Jeb has a big claim. He might hit the big mother lode and take thousands of dollars off his claim. Are you guys interested in working with Jeb?"

Tom answered, "Hans, you're asking us a shit load of questions. For the record, we get fourteen dollars a day, and no percent of the gold. What do you think Richard, do you think we should change claims if the old guy will have us?" "I think, for myself, I would prefer making more money if I work harder. You know we won't be up in this country very long, and when the gold runs out, it will be a ghost town. I say if Jeb will hire us on, lets make the change."

Bert poked around in the tent and brought out a bottle of whiskey.

"I think this might call for a drink, we might be giving Tom and Richard a great job, and Hans and I might get into something very good. Anyway it's worth a drink."

Over the past few months the four had become very good friends. They enjoyed just sitting around and shooting the breeze. There was always plenty of gossip to talk about. Some of the most interesting stories in the gold fields were about some of the courageous women that came north. Most men thought they would never see a female come north to the Yukon by themselves, but quite a few did. Tom told the story about a lady called Belinda Mulroney. She was a coal miner's daughter out of Pennsylvania who came north on her own. When she first came to Dawson she had a small restaurant and hotel, called the Magnet. After being in Dawson for a time, she sold it and decided to move to the Grand Forks. You know the junction of Eldorado Creek and Bonanza Creek; she built a new hotel there called the Grand Forks Hotel.

Bert said, "I want to meet this lady called Belinda; she sounds like my type of woman."

After a couple more hours, Bert saw Jeb heading toward his cabin.

"Hans, we should go talk to Jeb. Damn, I hate to break the news to Jeb. Hell, he might take a swing at me."

Tom replied "I think Richard and I'll wait here for you guys to return. If things go well, we'll talk things over with Jeb; maybe we can change bosses today. Our boss has six guys working for him. He won't miss us that much."

Bert and Hans walked up to Jeb's claim. When they got up on the hill, they could see Jeb going into his cabin.

"Hey Jeb," hollered Bert, "Can we talk to you for a bit?"

"Come in boys and make yourselves at home."

Hans opened the conversation.

"Jeb you know we helped Elizabeth take her deceased husband into the undertaker. When we were walking back from town, we asked Elizabeth what she intended doing with her claim. Well, after a couple of days thinking about her situation, we thought she might want to sell her claim. Instead, she wants to make us half partners. Jeb, we really like working for you, but this might be the only chance we have to get a claim of our own. If we take her offer, I sure hope you won't be mad at us."

"Boys, if you didn't take her offer, I would think there was something wrong with you. This country is like the roll of the dice; you won't be here long, and the big money won't be here long. So I say, get what you can, when you can. I hope you two make a ton of money. There are many men around the gold fields looking for work, so I won't have a problem finding some hired hands."

Hans leaned over the table, "Jeb we have two buddies that came down the Yukon River with us. They're good guys and I'm sure good workers. We told them about you today, and the deal you made us on the percentage. They told us they would like to talk to you if you're interested."

"Well boys, if you say they're good workers, I would like to have a talk with them. When can you send them over?"

"If you'd like to talk to them now; they're in our tent; we can send them right over right away. Jeb was stroking his chin," Hell "Hell, send them over."

Bert and Hans headed back to their tent. The sun was passing down below the hills and this time of evening the mosquitoes came out in earnest. They went into their tent.

Hans explained their talk with Jeb. "If I were you guys, I would hightail it over to Jeb's tent right away; you two are the first in line."

As Bert and Hans sat in the tent; nothing was said for a time.

Bert was the first to speak, "I hope we didn't shoot ourselves in the foot with this new venture. We might dig that entire seventy eight feet and just find gravel. Tom and Richard might make a ton of money with old Jeb". Bert replied, "Yah that thought crossed my mind a few times in the past hour. Sometimes a man can jump into something before he gets his full brain in gear. I guess we made the deal, so we'll have to live with it."

After about an hour they could hear footsteps approaching the tent; they knew it was Tom and Richard by their voices.

Bert told them, "Come" Come on in you two. What did Jeb have to say?"

The quiet one, Richard, was the first to speak, "Hell, we hit it off with the old timer. He's a hell of a nice guy, and I couldn't believe how good we got along. He told us he would make us the same deal he had with you two, so tomorrow morning, or this evening, we'll have to let our boss know what's going on."

Bert dug into a bag and pulled out one of the bottles of brandy.

"By golly, I really think this is another time to celebrate. I guess we never run out of reasons to have a drink. Of course, in this country, what is there besides having a drink and working? If we have a drink in this tent, it's a lot cheaper than drinking in one of those Dawson saloons."

Tom replied, "I" I hear tell, there are still many boats coming down the Yukon from Bennet Lake. When they pull into Dawson and see all those damn boats and people, they're ready to sell their gear just to get passage down the river. With twenty thousand people in Dawson, most newcomers don't even bother going into the goldfields. There will be full boats heading to St. Michaels this summer."

"Tom," Bert said, "Do you know the first boat into Dawson was five days behind us fellers coming over that Chilkoot trail?"

"Damn, don't remind me."

Just then they could hear the sloshing of boots in the mud outside.

"Ya got room for one more in there?"

Hans hollered, "Come on in Jeb, did you bring your cup along?"

"I sur did."

Jeb found himself a place to sit, "Say, did you fellers ever hear the story about George Carmack?"

He crossed his legs and said, "Settle back boys, this might take a bit. The story goes something like this. Robert Henderson, a long time prospector in the north had found some color on Gold Bottom Creek, near present day Bonanza Creek; which at that time was called Rabbit Creek. He met George Carmack, a white man who had married an Indian, and adopted the Indian ways. He adopted two of his Indian relatives named Skookum Jim and Tagish Charley. The four of them met at the mouth of Klondike River. As was the custom with prospectors in the area, Henderson told Carmack about his discovery of gold on Gold Bottom Creek. He asked George to come by himself and stake a claim. Henderson had no time for Indians and didn't want anything to do with Skookum Jim and Tagish Charley. George told Henderson they would spend some time on Rabbit Creek.

The three trudged up Rabbit Creek for days looking for gold. Then on the sixteenth of August they found some gold. It seemed to be a good quantity, so they decided to stake their claim. After the claim was all staked, they headed to Forty Mile to record the claim.

As a rule, if you found gold, you would tell your friends, so he could get his claim. No one knows for sure why George never told Henderson about his find. Most people think it was because Henderson had such a dislike of Indians. So they never told him, this most likely cost Henderson a pile of money. The three went to Forty Mile and recorded their claims. With some money in their pocket they went into the only saloon in Forty Mile to have a whiskey to celebrate. They were proud of their new found gold. They told the men in the saloon about their new strike. No one would believe Indians could find gold. If a white man couldn't find gold, how could Indians find any?

After hours of no one believing them, they showed the locals some of the nuggets. It finely sunk in; these three guys were telling the truth. It wasn't long before Forty Mile was deserted.

At this time, the biggest gold rush in the world was on. All up and down the Yukon River, men were heading for Bonanza Creek, the new name for Rabbit Creek. By the time Robert Henderson found out about the new strike, the creeks had all been staked. Needless to say, Henderson was mad as hell at George. So far George and his two relatives had taken thousands of dollars from their claims; you know it's just up the creek where Eldorado meets the Bonanza."

"You better have a little more brandy, after that long story." replied Bert. "Do you know Carmack?"

Jeb took a little sip from the tin cup, "Yah, I see him around once in a while, he has other men working his claim, and George doesn't need much money."

Jeb stuck a chew into his mouth, and then started talking again.

"Did you fellers know in ninety six the entire area, which is now Dawson City, was under water, because of the spring flood? That's the reason it's such a soup hole now."

Tom spoke up, "By golly Jeb, it's interesting to hear you tell about this area."

"By gum, I just thought of something I heard today," Jeb said raising his finger in the air.

"You fellers heard about that young gal Belinda Mulroney? She has a pet donkey she brought north with her. This damn animal has taken a liking to whiskey and it gets half drunk. At first the boys got a big kick out of this animal, but now it's getting to be a pest. It goes right into the bar and won't leave until it gets a drink."

The boys all started laughing so hard they couldn't stop.

"Jeb, are you telling us a wild story?" Bert said with tears in his eyes. Hans looked at Jeb, "Say Jeb, are you going to stay in the gold fields this winter?"

"It kind of depends on what comes out of the ground. If the gold Gods are real good to me, I might head south for the winter; it all depends. I think once I leave here, I won't have any big desire to return. This is miserable country to live in; if it ain't the damn bugs, it's the long cold winter. You won't find many places where the summer is any shorter than here.

When September comes, the leaves will start turning, then here comes winter. For about three months it's as dark as the inside of a cow."

That statement drew more laughter from the boys.

The way Jeb was talking, he was starting to feel the brandy, and he wanted to talk all the time.

He continued. "Do you know that the fourth of July will be here in about three more days? By Jove, that's right, and I hear tell there will be some boys celebrating. I think all of us should go into Dawson to join the birthday party. What do you boys think about that?"

Bert was the first to answer, "What day of the week does that fall on?" Richard pulled a book from his pocket, "Just a minute, I have a little calendar here in my pocket. The fourth will be on a Tuesday, so whiskey will be flowing in Dawson that day. We might see some of the old friends we met on the trail."

It was getting around eight in the evening. Jeb was the first one to leave. He told the boys he had to go cook up something to eat. Soon after, Tom and Richard headed to their tent.

Bert and Hans cooked up some grub. It was decided that this coming Sunday, they would bake some bread. Sunday was chore day, washing clothes and sometimes taking a bath.

Bert was just finishing up his plate, wiping the juices with his last piece of flapjack, "I just remembered about our agreement with Elizabeth, we should walk over tonight and let her know everything is all set, and we'll have to start moving our gear to the new site".

Hans answered, "I think we better also start making plans to get a winter cabin going soon. We want to have the cabin all ready to go by the middle of September at the latest. How are the three of us going to live together?"

"Dang, I never thought about living area for the three of us. If we make two separate cabins, we'll have to have double the firewood. Maybe we could somehow make a double cabin and have a curtain between us and Elizabeth."

"We'll have to bring this up soon with our new partner."

Bert and Hans walked over to Elizabeth's tent, "This is Bert and Hans, are you here?"

Elizabeth answered, "Yes, please come in." They both entered.

"Sit down boys. Well, how did my friend Jeb take the news?"

Hans answered, "Jeb thinks a lot of you, and he had nothing but good things to say about our working with you, so I guess all three of us are off on a new venture."

Elizabeth replied, "I thought he would agree with you boys, he told me you two are very good workers and easy to get along with. After you left, I started thinking about how the three of us will live in the diggings this winter. I think we better plan on spending the winter. Dick had plans to dig throughout the winter. Once we get down to bedrock and start a drift, we won't have to worry about the ground caving in, as it's all frozen. You fellows told me you have lumber from your boat. I have some here also. I think it would be best to make a little larger log building so we can all three live together. What do you fellows think?"

"We were talking about the same thing," replied Hans. "In the morning, we'll start a fire to thaw the ground, and then head for the timber to get cabin logs, firewood and wood to melt the frozen ground. That way we won't waste time later on."

"We should get an early start in the morning." said Bert.

"After you fellows have your breakfast, do you want to start moving all your gear over to this site?"

"Sounds good, we'll see you in the morning."

As they walked back to their tent, Bert was the first to speak, "That woman has good common sense. I think she will be easy to work for. I sure hope so; it might get to be a long winter if she becomes a terror. Dang that would be bad for us."

The next morning Bert and Hans started their exodus to their new claim; by noon all of the gear was on the new claim. Elizabeth had a good fire burning in the hole to thaw the ground.

At noon she told the two, "Come inside, I have fixed a meal for us."

She dished out a plate full for each man. They sat and ate in silence. In the surrounding area, they could hear the pounding of hammers working on claims. In the distance they could hear the whine of the large circular saw blades slicing through the spruce trees, making slabs of lumber. Hans thought to himself, this is the same food we have been eating, but now it tastes so much better; it must be a woman's touch. Things were looking better the first day.

Bert and Hans set up their tent close to Elizabeth's; they would have to use these tents, until the new cabin was constructed. The three decided that Bert and Hans would keep hauling trees for the cabin and Elizabeth would keep the fire going in the hole. All through the day they worked. After a short meal at noontime, they continued working the remainder of the day.

By the evening of the third of July, the men had a good stack of log poles for the cabin. These spruce logs were about six inches on the butt end and four inches on the tip. Before the day's work was finished, they had a row of logs on the ground for their new home.

That night, both men were awakened by numerous gunshots bounding through the valleys.

Bert sat up like a shot, "What the hell is all the shooting about, are we being attacked by some renegades?"

Hans was also sitting up in his bed, "Oh shit, it's the fourth of July gunfire."

They sat there listening to the rumble of the gunshots. Sometimes someone must have used a charge of gunpowder, and there would be a loud booming noise, along with the cheers of men.

Both Hans and Bert laid back down on their beds, taking in all the celebration. Off in the distance there was a roar coming from the direction of Dawson City. Hans had his head on his moss pillow, his eyes closed, enjoying all the noise.

In the morning, they awoke to more gunshots, it sounded like the July fourth celebration was going to go through the day. They could smell the aroma of fresh cooked coffee coming from Elizabeth's tent.

About the time they approached the tent; the flap came open, and out came Elizabeth, "Ready for some breakfast boys?"

While eating their breakfast, Hans asked, "Should we take the morning off to see what's going on in Dawson? I think we should, I bet there will be people building to building, hell, the streets will be packed"

Bert wiped his mouth on his sleeve, "We have many hard days ahead, let's take a break; it's our country's birthday."

All three lifted their coffee cups at arm's length, the cups clanged together. Elizabeth stood up and said, "Let's head for Dawson to celebrate this birthday."

They did chores and headed to town. It was a bright sunny day; the puffy white clouds were drifting to the southeast. All around the valley they could see bodies moving in their same direction. After a few hot windy days, the ground was drying up, the walking wasn't too bad.

As they made their way around the mountain and through the thousands of tents, the sight of all these men clad in their dark clothes, was an eerie sight. There was little color to be seen, aside from the garish signs hanging in front of the buildings. The bars seemed to be packed and overflowing, most of the miners were in the bars. Even at this early hour, the drunken miners could be seen staggering along the street.

It was a festive occasion; everyone seemed to be in a good mood. Out of town the rifle and pistol shots could be heard echoing down the valleys. The three enjoyed walking around town, just looking at all the other people. Scattered here and there were a few women, most were dressed in drab clothing. There was an occasional woman, walking on the board walk, with her bright colorful dress. These girls didn't work in the gold fields; their work was all performed in town, mostly in Louse Town.

Bert stood up and said, "We should have a drink to celebrate this birthday. Let's go into this bar. I know Hans can handle whiskey, how about you Elizabeth, would you like a drink?"

"Yes, I would Bert; please have the bartender fill the top half with water."

"You know Elizabeth; there already is water in this Dawson whiskey."

"Yes I know, but I still need to dilute it."

As the three partners sat on the boardwalk, they had a great time talking about all the different characters walking past. It was a great day; here they were in Canada with about thirty thousand fellow Americans. It was like a Little America in the heart of Canada.

All of a sudden Hans hollered out, "Hey Johnson, come over here."

For a second Bert couldn't recognize who Hans was hollering at. The two men walked over.

"By golly its da guys ve saw on der Tagish Lake."

"Da las time ve saw you, you boys ver heading down da river, you must have made good time getting to dis Dawson City."

Bert stuck out his hand, "Hey, it's good to see you two Swedes."

"By golly, ve had von hell of time getting tru dose damn rapids. Ve got hung up on da damn rock, had von hell of time to get off. How about you boy's trip through dot damn vater?"

"I guess the four of us had more luck than brains. Say boys, this lady's name is Elizabeth Larson."

"Nice to meet you Elizabeth, my name is Arns Johnson, and my friend is Olaf Olson. Ve come nort from nortern Minnesota."

Elizabeth shook hands with the boys and said, "Bert and Hans are my partners, and we're working claim far up on Bonanza Creek. You're welcome to stop by sometime and visit."

"Tank you very much, you very kind lady, to invite us to your camp."

The next hour was spent talking about their travels down the Yukon River, their trials and tribulations in keeping the boat between the banks. They told the three partners about the four men who drowned at White Horse Rapids. None could swim, and by the time they could get them out of the water, they were dead.

They parted company as the two Swedes went into a bar.

"Let's take a walk and look over the town."

As the three meandered through the crowded mud streets, they were amazed at all the new stores going up in Dawson. They stopped and stared at the buildings on the south side of the street.

Elizabeth was talking, "Would you believe there's an attorney's office, a dentist, meat market, a hardware store, laundry, hotel, bars, tailor, and the stores went on and on. My God, where did all these people come from?"

Hans said, "I can see two banks from here; we don't have two banks in our town back in Iowa."

"Hans, I just thought about the money we're supposed to pick up at a bank here in Dawson. What was that guy's name?"

"Gee, let me think a minute, he was going to deposit twenty five dollars for each of the four of us. Hell, he probably died or forgot about the money. I think his name was Blankenship."

"By golly Hans, you got it. That was his name. He also had a son, he was a newspaper writer. Let's take a walk over to this Bank of Dawson on the corner."

They stepped up onto the muddy boardwalk and went inside. They were quite surprised to see a nice wooden interior. The counter had four grated windows with vertical bars. Three of the windows were occupied, the empty one had a very tall thin man with slicked down hair and a thin mustache. He looked more like a crook than a banker.

He leaned toward the brass vertical bars, "Sir, what may I do for you?"

Hans looked up toward the tellers face, "A Mr. Blankenship was supposed to deposit some money for me and my partner at a bank in Dawson; we thought this might be the bank."

"Sir, if you will excuse me, I'll check the deposits."

Hans turned toward the two, "Hell, I bet that little feller we saved had a short memory, and probably drank up the money himself."

As Hans stood waiting, he found himself staring at Elizabeth. She had on bib over-alls, a blue work shirt, and her deep brown hair was up on the back of her head with a red bandana tied above her forehead. She had high cheek bones, and very pretty green eyes, a very attractive woman. Then he thought to himself, 'all women look attractive here in the gold fields.'

"Sir, I have checked my deposit records, I can't find anything deposited by a Mr. Blankenship. I'm sorry."

Hans said, "Thank you for your time."

As the three stepped onto the street, Bert said, "I knew this was too good to be true."

While they walked down the street, Hans told Elizabeth the story about Mr. Blankenship, stumbling in to their camp past the Chilkoot trail.

Soon Elizabeth stopped and looked up in the sky toward the sun, "Boys, I think it's getting toward noontime, we should probably head back to camp. We're not going to find any gold here in Dawson."

As they continued on, they saw four Husky dogs pulling a sled down the street, with a long box on the sled.

"Hell, that looks like a coffin." said Bert. "Damn what a strange town."

"Hans, let's stop at that Canadian Bank on the corner."

"Yah, we can stop into this bank. It won't take long to see if we have a deposit here."

The three walked into the Canadian Bank of Commerce, it looked very official, with a very large vault behind the counter. For some reason this bank wasn't as busy. Hans walked up to the counter; the lady behind the counter had a longer neck than normal, with a nose that had a slight hook to it. She really wasn't very attractive, so she must have obtained this job because she knew what she was doing.

With a rather high pitched voice she leaned toward Hans from behind the metal bars. "May I help you sir?"

"Uhh, a Mr. Blankenship said he would deposit some money here for my friend and me."

The teller raised her glasses a little higher on her nose, "One minute while I check the accounts."

Bert walked over to where Hans was standing, "Here we go again. Blankenship most likely died on the trail, he wasn't the hayseed with the most brains I ever saw. I can't really believe he would give us twenty five dollars each, that's a month's work back home."

The tall stately lady walked up to the counter, she picked up a pencil from the counter, pulled a piece of blank paper from the drawer, "I will have to have both of your names, the first name and the last name, so we can verify you're the correct recipients."

Both Hans and Bert stood there, surprised to hear this lady acknowledge that the money must be in the vault. First Hans printed his full name and Bert did the same. The lady teller looked at the names, as if she were trying to find something incorrect. She made out a receipt for each to sign, and then removed from the drawer a bundle of five dollar bills. She counted out five for Hans and five for Bert. Both men were grinning from ear to ear.

Hans said, "Thank you mam. You were very helpful."

She added, "By the way, when you see the other two men on this list, and I can't give you their names, tell them to stop in."

When the three stepped onto the street, they all stopped.

"Good old Mr. Blankenship, you are our friend, you have renewed my faith in human being," Hans said as he put the money into his little pouch.

"It's very tempting to take this money and do the town. Maybe some time later on, when we need a break in the diggings, and if we have any money left, we'll celebrate."

As they passed the many tents scattered on the edge of Dawson, it was plain to see the tenters were having a good time. Drunken men were lying on the ground, some in the tents and some that didn't quite make it inside. Some of the areas stunk from the human waste; some men couldn't care less where they went to the toilet. One man would be peeing upstream and farther down another man would be taking water out for cooking.

It was shortly after noon when they arrived back at camp. The fire was smoldering in the four foot wide hole. Bert grabbed a shovel and started to remove the coals.

Elizabeth hollered at Bert, "Bert, I'll work on the hole, you two work on the cabin."

The remainder of the day they worked on the cabin. They decided to make the cabin twelve feet wide, so they could fit in two six- foot bunks, end to end. Since there would have to be some kind of separation for Elizabeth, they decided to make the cabin eighteen feet long.

Elizabeth would have her bunk in the opposite end, the stove and kitchen and would be in one end. The men proceeded with the cabin and Elizabeth worked on thawing the hole.

Another five days dragged on, the four foot square hole was down twenty feet and the placer gold was running light. It was running about a teaspoon a day, about an ounce, or sixteen dollars.

The cabin walls were up and most of the roof boards were on. Both men agreed to put the canvas tent on the underside of the roof boards in case the roof leaked. By this time in the summer, the frost had gone out of the sod for about four to six inches. The center of the roof was braced good to hold the weight of the sod. The cracks between the logs were filled with sphagnum moss. The new home was starting to look great. After living in a grungy tent for eight months, the new log home would be a great improvement.

The next evening, Tom and Richard stopped by the cabin for a visit. As the two entered the cabin, Richard sat down at their new table.

"This cabin looks great; I wouldn't mind spending a winter here. Where did you get the glass window?"

"Elizabeth's husband had this window stashed for a year; he intended to use it in his cabin." Hans answered.

Elizabeth took a pie pan off the shelf, "How would you boys like a piece of peach pie and some coffee?"

"We haven't had any pie since we hit Lake Bennett last winter," commented Tom. "It sure looks great, and I can smell the peaches."

"These are some of those dried peaches the boys brought over the Chilkoot. I guess with all the work, they didn't have time to eat them."

It started to rain; though the rain couldn't be heard on the sod roof; the raindrops could be seen running down the four windows.

Tom was finishing up the last bite of pie, "Elizabeth you are one great cook, I can't remember when I have ever had a better piece of pie. I suppose everything you cook tastes great."

"Well Tom, thanks for the compliment. I figure the better I feed these two guys, maybe the more work they will do."

"Did you hear that Hans? That's why she feeds us so good; she wants us to find more gold for her."

That drew a loud laugh from the four men. Hans thought to himself. With a woman in the cabin with the men, everyone seems more at ease and they seem much happier. If we have to stay through the winter, Elizabeth will make the long dull days more enjoyable.

Bert asked the visitors, "How are you guys doing with the diggings?"

Tom was first to answer, "In the past week we have hit some pay dirt. Jeb figures we dug out twelve thousand dollars worth of gold; it was just like picking up coins lying in the dirt. You wouldn't believe it; it sure makes a man look at life a little differently."

Bert leaned forward, "Damn, you guys did hit it good, so each one of you picked up six hundred dollars in gold. I can't even imagine that much money. I suppose if you guys keep making that much money; you'll head out before winter sets in?"

Richard replied, "We haven't even talked about leaving the gold fields, course if it keeps rolling in like last week, we might head for Frisco to spend some money. How are you doing on this claim?"

Hans had been sitting on his bunk, "About all we have been making is wages, we can't find the damn bedrock. We must be down twenty one feet by now; all we're picking up is the small stuff. We have a lot of faith, but you guys know what faith buys in Dawson."

Tom and Richard stood up, "We better get back. Jeb is working the heck out of us, so we need to rest up for tomorrow. Let's get together on Sunday."

Hans said, "Okay, we'll see you on Sunday."

Hans and Bert were sitting at the table having a cup of coffee, kind of staring off into one of the cabin corners. Elizabeth pulled up the third chair and lit a candle to give them a little light. The candle gleamed off the beardless faces.

"I know what you two are thinking about. You jumped off the good ship and came aboard a poor ship. I have to say, it does sound that way. That's about the best strike I have heard of so far. Maybe Jeb is sitting on the mother lode. Keep in mind boys, we're just below Jeb by about five hundred feet; with some luck we might hit the lode also."

Hans was the first to talk, "Yah, I guess it's hard to take. We could have had the six hundred dollars each. Maybe we'll have to increase the work, to get to bedrock sooner. Maybe the bedrock is fifty feet below the surface."

Bert set his cup down, "Hans, don't even talk like that. If we are only half way down to bedrock, I don't even want to think about it." He added "We may not have as much gold as our friends, but, by golly, we have a better cook."

All three had a good laugh. "Dang, I forgot to tell Tom and Richard about the money in the bank from Blankenship. We'll have to make sure we tell them on Sunday."

Hans asked, "Do you think they have the post office open on Sundays? The Mounties don't allow any work on the Lord's Day, but maybe they would pass out the mail. I should have a letter from home one of these days."

CHAPTER 11

On the morning of the twenty fifth of July the three partners were having breakfast. The talk as usual, got around to the hole.

Elizabeth started the conversation. "Maybe we should have been working on a number of shaft holes at the same time, instead of just working on one. I can understand that you fellows don't have a great deal of faith in our present shaft. You both became my partners and we can't even get the main hole down to bedrock; maybe there is no bedrock. I guess there doesn't have to be bedrock under this ground."

"Well, replied Hans, "Let's give the hole another week. Like you said, maybe we're sitting on a hole where bedrock is a hundred feet below the surface. Maybe we should start another hole a good distance away from our present hole."

Bert was just finishing up his breakfast, wiping the plate with a piece of bread. "Maybe this small pie shaped piece was by passed because someone or others knew this ground was dead; no gold. Here we have a cabin built for winter, and no gold in the ground. We will be the joke of the Klondike."

Hans stood up, "The fire we had in the hole last night must be out by now, I'll go start to dig out the unfrozen ground."

"Okay, I'm right behind you. I'll gather some more wood for the next fire in the hole."

Elizabeth cleaned up the utensils and walked outside. The sun was just coming over the hill, it was a crisp morning, and in fact she could see some frost on the vegetation. She thought to herself, just about the first of August and we have a frost. I hope it killed off all the mosquitoes and no-see-ums. At this time, Hans gave out a yell in the hole. Elizabeth's first thought was that there was a cave in down the hole.

She ran to the hole, leaned over the edge of the crib. "Hans, are you okay? Can you hear me?"

Hans hollered, "Stay right there, Elizabeth."

She stared intently down the dark hole. Soon she could see Hans' cap appear in the darkness. "What's the matter?"

Hans climbed over the cribbing, reached his hand into his pocket and pulled out gold nuggets the size of marbles and larger. He was so excited he could hardly talk.

"Elizabeth, you wouldn't believe all the gold down that hole. As soon as I hit the black magnetic sand, it was full of beautiful gold. Here, feel how heavy it is. Oh, thank you, Lord. You did lead us to the right place, and Sunday I'm going to church to give my thanks."

About that time Bert came up with a load of firewood, "Hey, what's all the noise about?"

Elizabeth grabbed Bert's hand, "Here, look at this, we hit gold. Hans says it's like picking up rocks."

Bert stood there staring at the nuggets in his hand, "My God, it's gold and I was beginning to think this was the jinxed claim in the valley of rich mines."

The three man crew worked throughout the day, with no stopping for noon dinner. By six in the evening, the partners were dead tired. They had all the gold dug that day in an old flour sack. During the day when they had a pan full, they would bring the gold into the tent and dump it in the flour sack. Elizabeth was the first to enter the cabin. She lit a candle, placed it on the table, walked over to the gold flour sack, grabbed it by one hand.

"Goodness gracious, this sack is heavy. I sure would like to know how much it weighs. Here Hans, give me your opinion"

The partners celebrated for well over an hour; having nothing to eat since early morning, the three were very relaxed.

Elizabeth said, "Do you men know how long it's been since we had something to eat? I'm going to cook something. I sure wish we had some good big steaks to eat. I hope we can get some fresh meat one of these days. This bacon is looking a little green but I guess it will hold out for a while."

As tired as they were, and under the influence of the brandy, there was no lack of appetite. While they ate, the talk kept coming back to the gold. This was truly a great day for the three stampeders.

Bert said, "I wonder now if they will still call us Cheechakoes."

It wasn't long before they were all in their bunks, sound asleep. The cabin was quite dark when the door was closed. The window let in enough light to make your way around. The cabin remained quite cool during the hot, ninety degree heat of the day. In the evening and during the sleeping hours, it was very cool.

The next day they were up at five and excited to get back down the hole to explore for gold. Today Bert took his turn in the hole, though the work was hard. It was about sixty degrees, so it wasn't all bad.

Through the hot August day, the three toiled at the digging and running the crank on the windlass. To rid the windlass of the eternal squeaking, they poured the excess bacon grease on the friction areas, so then it was a lot easier to crank up the wooden box full of dirt. They had diverted water from the next claim through this claim by means of a wooden trough. After they finished with the water; it was passed on to the next claim.

They had a sluice box about eight feet long, with a number of riffles to catch the small pieces of gold. Some gold flakes were the size of a match head. Since gold was nineteen times heavier than water, the gold in time would be caught on a riffle. When the bucket was dumped on the up side of the sluice, the larger pieces of gold were picked out first, and the remainder washed down through the riffles.

SLUICING THE PAYDIRT FOR GOLD

After a couple of buckets were dumped into the sluice box, they would divert the water, to bypass the sluice box so they could clean out the gold. When the miners watched the water flowing through the sluice box, they could see when the gold was piling up on the riffles.

This was truly a labor of love, when you see gold coming out of the mine in nugget form; they never tired. Today was Saturday, so tomorrow would be a day of rest. In a way, the miners were glad the Royal Mounties made Sunday a day of rest, otherwise, these miners would be working seven days a week.

They worked again until six in the evening; again the amount of gold coming out of the hole was unbelievable. The gold was carried to the cabin and put into anything that wouldn't let it leak out. They devised a way to measure the weight of the gold. They took a board, made a hole in the middle; a rope was tied to this hole, and hung from the cabin ceiling. On one end they tied some tins amounting to ten pounds; as close as they could determine. On the other end was tied a small bag. When enough gold was put into the bag, to balance the board so it was horizontal, they dumped the bag of gold into the larger flour bag and continued.

This day the weight of the gold was estimated at around thirty-five pounds. Elizabeth would take out her little book and record each weighing. She calculated the weight of the gold, times sixteen ounces, then times the sixteen-dollar value per ounce.

"Wow" she said, "Today's gold, comes to over eight thousand nine hundred and sixty dollars. Oh, I can't believe we've been this lucky! When your wealth starts to accumulate, it sure makes a person feel differently. It takes some of the worry out of life. We know for sure, we won't starve this winter as long as they keep bringing the food into Dawson."

Hans dug out the bottle again, "Think we have to celebrate again; maybe it brings us good luck the next day, who knows?"

After the drinks were poured, the three partners just sat there and looked at each other. Then they all started laughing, it was contagious. When one would slow down, someone else would start

"I haven't laughed like this since I was a kid," giggled Elizabeth.

It was Sunday morning, six a.m. The sound of Bert firing up the wood heater woke Elizabeth and Hans.

Hans rose up on one elbow and looked at Bert, "One day that we can sleep in and someone has to make all kinds of noise."

"Well, we have to take full advantage of this day of rest. You know, soon someone will be complaining about where's the coffee?"

This morning they all had flapjacks, oatmeal and coffee.

Elizabeth came out of her draped off area, "Today, when I have time, I'm going to do some high class baking. As long as I have to fire up the stove, I might as well fill up the oven."

The three were sitting around the crude table, wolfing down the flapjacks.

Elizabeth asked Hans, "Last night, you said we should go to church today to give the Lord some thanks. Did you mean that?"

"I sure did at the time, since then, I haven't really thought much about the matter."

Elizabeth looked straight into his eyes, "I think we should go. We went from the bottom to the top of success in a short time."

After breakfast, they were sitting around, talking and relaxing.

"Say," Elizabeth said. "Did you fellows ever hear about the Confederate Prison, down in Andersonville, Georgia?"

Both men nodded their head, "Yes."

"Well, I read a book about that place. The south or Confederates had this prison for Union troops, out in this large open field. They had a tall wooden fence made out of about twenty foot logs, stuck in the ground. This fence covered about forty acres. In the center was a valley with a small creek flowing through. I guess it was about three feet wide. From this small creek, the forty five thousand Union troops had to get all their drinking water. In late summer the creek was flowing less and less, the men were getting very short on water; in fact it looked like many would die of thirst. One day a storm came up and by an old stump along the creek, a mighty lighting bolt struck and made a large hole in the ground. After the dirt fell back to earth from this fireball, water gushed out of the ground from a new spring, giving the men plenty of drinking water."

"Are you making this up Elizabeth?" asked Bert.

"No, I remember reading this in a history book."

"By golly, that is some story, it really makes a person think. Who knows, maybe the good Lord did have a hand in our finding the gold."

Hans, taking the last sip from his coffee cup, "I think it would be very appropriate, if we would find a church in Dawson, and say our thanks."

Elizabeth stood up; looking at the clothes she had on, "I sure don't have any fancy clothes, to wear to town. I guess I do have an old black dress. I'll have to wear it with these big mud boots. Let's leave here about seven thirty. We'll be there in a half hour, maybe catch a nine o'clock service."

Bert said, "I'll go tell Richard and Tom we'll be heading for town at seven thirty. We know they want to tag along."

Soon Bert came back to the cabin. "They'll be here before seven thirty. I told them, maybe they should dress up a might, we intend on making a visit to one of the local churches. "

Later the five headed for Dawson. This Sunday morning was one of those Canadian low overcast days. The clouds were hanging on top of the hills, and it appeared as if they were stuck there; there was no wind to move them along. Along the way were many men with the same idea, all were anxious to get out of the claim and go to town. Some had been very successful the past week and some were still trying to find their first gold.

As they came around the large hill with the big scar, they saw a sea of white tents; it was a sight to behold. The report was that this was the largest tent city in North America; in fact, it was the largest city in western Canada. The tents were laid out to resemble streets of some sort; at least a person could make their way through them to get to downtown Dawson.

The first church they came to was a Lutheran Church, but the first service was at ten a.m. The streets were very crowded, even now at about eight thirty. Two blocks down the street, they came to the Holy Name Catholic Church; the sign said there would be a mass at nine a.m. The five looked at one another.

Tom was the first to speak, "I don't know, I've heard some odd things about the Catholic Church, they have some strange carrying on. Will we have to go into the confession box? And if we don't tell the truth, will they lock us up?"

Hans said, "Tom maybe you should be locked up.... someplace."

As the five stood looking at one another, Elizabeth spoke up, "This appears to be the only church open for business in Dawson at this time. I say we give it a try."

She turned and started toward the front door, the four men followed. To their surprise there must have been twenty five or so people in the church, mostly men. They took the first seats they came to toward the back. They sat and waited. They noticed some people were praying with rosaries, kneeling and leaning against the chair in front of them. Soon the priest came out in his colorful vestments.

The mass proceeded. Through the priest's homely, the message was about giving back to God, as he has given to you. If you think God has been generous to you, then you should be generous to God. The priest made it clear he wasn't talking about money, but your good things in life and your spiritual rewards.

In another half hour the mass was over. The priest walked down the isle first. When the people left the church they had to pass in front of him.

To each stranger the priest introduced himself, "My name is Father McGarry, what is your name?"

Each introduced themselves to the priest and had a few kind words. They left the church and headed down the street.

"Well Tom, what did you think about that?" Bert asked.

"By golly it was all right. I hadn't been inside a church since I was a kid. You get a lot of exercise in that church, they stand up, then they sit down, then they do it again and again."

Hans said with a laugh, "I think they do that for guys like you, to keep you awake."

"Tom, I think I saw you get heavy eyelids a couple times," said Richard.

"By the way Tom, did you put money in the collection box or did you take it out?"

Tom answered, "This week I put money in, and next week I take some out." As they walked down the street, Hans said, "We have to look around for the post office, maybe since this is a Canadian city, we'll have to look for the Mounties Station."

The sun was out now and it was becoming a very pleasant day. The streets were packed with strangers. At this time in Dawson's history, there were close to thirty thousand people in the city.

On Sundays most of them came to town to see what was going on. It was a great chance to look for friends they had made on the trail from Dyea to Lake Bennett. It was great, just to walk around and look at all the new businesses in Dawson.

Elizabeth saw a marketplace and stopped the group, "I want to see if I can find some canned fruit to make pies."

Tom said, "If you can find some canned fruit Elizabeth, I'll buy it, if you make the pies."

"Okay, let's look for the fruit."

By the time they left the store, they were carrying four large cans of fruit that cost two dollars each. In Seattle, they would cost twenty- five cents a can. They all walked into the new hardware store. The men were fascinated with all the items for sale. Hans and Tom each bought a box of twenty-four candles for three dollars. Elizabeth bought herself some new work gloves and a new work hat.

After another half hour walking around the store, they headed out into the muddy street. There were a few horses pulling wagons through the muddy streets. A number of wild-eyed dogs were running through and around the people.

Hans said, "I have to find the post office."

After asking a few people they found where the building was located. It was in the office of Sergeant Steel, the head of Mounties in Dawson. It appeared there must have been a hundred men outside, waiting to get into the building.

Hans asked a guy waiting, "How does this mail delivery work?"

The older fellow said, "They go by the first letter of your name, they're on 'F' now. When the guy comes out and says the next letter, then all the people with the last name starting with 'G' will go in and get their mail."

Hans told the others, "Hey, I lucked out, only a few more letters and I'll go inside and check on my mail."

The others also decided to check for their mail. They waited their turn outside. After two hours, they all had their chance to check on their mail. Three of them had mail, Elizabeth, Hans and Richard.

The five friends stood outside the post office. Elizabeth had the attention of the other four.

"Since this is the first letter I have had in months, I would like to read it back at the cabin. I think this would be a good day for us to have a little Sunday gathering at our cabin. Maybe we could cook something a little special for this beautiful day. What do you fellows think?"

They all spoke at the same time, thinking it was a good idea, so they gave their approval.

Elizabeth said, "First I think we should take a walk through the rest of Dawson, to look at the other new stores."

The streets were totally crowded; it was hard to walk very far in a straight line without running into someone. On Front Street, bordering the Yukon River, they could see many boats parked along the shore. These were the boats from the Lake Bennett area. Many of the men making this trip soon headed down river in paddle wheel boats when they found out all the creeks had been claimed.

It was also the opinion of many that scores of men made the trip for an adventure and they really had no intentions of working in the gold fields. Many travelers coming north went into business. They could see money could be made from many different ventures. One man brought kittens for the miners, to keep them company. Some brought chickens, others brought eggs to sell. One person had month old newspapers, one man made an excellent profit on brooms. One rugged group packed a small paddle wheel boat over the Chilkoot Pass. The stories go on and on, the more you hang around Dawson, the more endless stories you hear.

Bert spotted a meat market, "I'll be darned. I never knew there was a meat market in Dawson. Maybe we can find something in there for our Sunday dinner."

Much of the meat was lying on slabs of marble, with cold water underneath to keep it cool. Hans saw a roast of some kind on the counter,

"Say mister what kind of roast do you have there?" he asked, pointing to a large piece of meat on the marble slab.

"That, my friend, is a choice moose roast, just brought into the market yesterday."

Hans leaned over and took a sniff of the meat, "Smells fresh to me, how about it boys? This would be a great piece of meat for our Sunday celebration."

Tom and Richard said, "We'll pay for half of the meat."

Hans told the butcher, "Wrap up that moose roast, we'll take it."

They all left the store and headed down Front Street. Along the way, they could see many men fishing for salmon.

Tom said, "Why don't we try to get some of these salmon and smoke them for eating later on this winter."

"One of these first Sundays we'll do that," Hans told Tom.

They passed through tent city on their way to the diggings. Across the river in this area, was what was called Louse town. This was the part of town where the whores made their homes. Small one room cabins in this area rented for one hundred dollars a month. With thirty thousand men in Dawson, and very few females, the women of the evening could well afford the rent. These women were in high demand and they knew it; they had a certain attitude about them. I guess you couldn't blame them.

Along the way back to their cabin, they met many miners heading for town. On Sunday, the men doing the hard work in the claims were, as a rule, in a very good mood. They knew the day was theirs, and they wanted to enjoy it as much as possible. The mud was drying up, though with the perma frost a few inches below the surface, the ground was drying up too.

When they arrived at the cabin, Tom said. "I still have a full bottle of that cognac over in our tent. I'll go pick it up, and we'll have little party before we eat."

Richard said, "I think I'll tag along with you, I want to sit down and read my letter from home."

The other three went into their cabin. The door had been closed, which kept the log cabin quite cool.

"This has been a very nice day so far, I want to thank you men for taking me along."

Hans said, "Elizabeth, you don't have to thank us for taking you along. You're one of the group, having a lady along is something special for us.

Don't forget, we're partners, and partners have to stick together."

They sat in silence in the one room cabin. Hans and Elizabeth were reading their letters.

All of a sudden Hans said, "Well, I'll be gosh darned! My girl friend is coming north to visit me. Wonder what made her leave the farm and come north looking for me. It says here, she should be here some time in August."

"Did she say how long she plans on staying in Dawson?" Bert asked.

"No, she just says I want to come visit you; you may never come back to the farm."

Elizabeth was listening to the conversation, "Hans, it's not really any of my business, but are you two serious? Have you talked about getting married?"

"Elizabeth, as you ask me that question, I don't know how serious we are. We were together quite a bit back on the farm. I guess we were kind of serious."

Bert was sitting on his bed listening to the conversation. "I guess the first thing we'll have to do is check on the boats coming up from St. Michaels. You'll have to run in and meet each boat coming up the river the rest of the month."

"You better not miss her boat coming into Dawson; she would be lost without someone meeting her." replied Elizabeth.

Hans asked her, "What did you hear in your letter?"

"Oh, it was a letter from Dick's parents. They wanted to console me, give me word of encouragement. They asked me, if I needed some money to return to California. It was a very nice letter. Now, if we plan on having a Sunday dinner, I'd better get busy. If you boys want some fresh bread for today and next week, maybe you can give me a hand."

The three went to work. Soon there was bread dough rising. Bert got the fire going to roast the moose meat.

While Elizabeth was doing her chores, getting the kitchen area in order, Bert and Hans sat at the table.

"We'll have to make a list of things we have to get finished, or started, before too late in the fall." Hans commented.

"Yah, I have been thinking, we should try to get some meat in when we get the first snow. We could take the sled and a pack; head south for a couple days. There should be some moose or caribou within a few miles. Of course, there will be other men out looking for the same thing. It might be a waste of time but I don't want to count on the markets in town having meat all winter."

"I heard last winter many of the people in the area almost starved. We might be sitting on a good gold streak, but we sure as hell don't want to starve this winter."

"Okay, when we have a good snow fall, we'll head out and look for wild game. In the meantime we should get this camp ready for winter. We should lay in plenty of firewood. We should start taking some days to just haul wood; one thing we have to do is keep our butts warm."

Soon they could hear the sloshing of mud outside the cabin; Richard and Tom were at the door.

"Come on in boys," hollered Bert, "Did you bring the cognac along? We haven't had a taste of that, for a long time."

Tom replied, "We wouldn't forget our Yukon friends. How's the best cook in the gold diggings doing?"

Elizabeth wiped her brow with a rag, "I think I have all the cooking under control. The moose roast is now in the oven. Before the moose, I baked a number of loaves of bread so if I can keep you men under control; I think everything will be fine. Are you ready to pour me a little drink of the French cognac?"

Bert took her metal cup and poured her an inch drink, "Here you are my friend. In fact, since we all have a drink in hand, we should have a toast."

The five friends raised their tin cups toward the ceiling. In the dim cabin their tin cups touched.

"It's a fine day, when strangers a short time ago, can meet and enjoy each others company, so dearly," commented Hans.

This was truly a friendly group. From the time they first met they had enjoyed each other's company.

The cabin door was kept closed to keep out the pesky insects. A candle was lit on the table and its light gave the cabin a warm glow; it was a fitting setting for the friends of the north. The conversation, as always, revolved around the gold fields.

Three of the group sat at the table, Bert and Tom sat on the bunks. The talk was mostly about the five in the cabin. Each one got great enjoyment in making some kind of fun about their fellow friends. Hans asked Tom and Richard about their winter plans.

Tom responded, "Well, I guess Jeb thinks we ought to start making plans to go through this winter. Hell, it doesn't make me much difference. I'm here to grub up some money and I want to take as much back to the states as possible. It would be my dream to make enough to set my self up on a ranch or some kind of business."

Hans was in the process of lighting his pipe, and after a couple puffs, said, "Did you and Richard ever stop by the Canadian Bank and pick up your money from that Mr. Blankenship?"

Richard answered, "As a matter of fact, we did stop in there like you told us. The twenty five dollars was there and waiting. We plan to save that money for a special occasion, if we can hold out that long. I sure would like to see that feller again. You remember when he staggered into our camp, up there on the Chilkoot, he and his son weren't far from dead."

The four hashed over the night the two strangers found their camp, and that they most likely saved their lives.

Bert asked Tom, "Do you guys plan on building a cabin like your boss has, or are you planning on spending the winter in your tent?"

"Jeb told us we better get our butts in gear and get the cabin built if we plan on spending the winter. It appears next week we have to go drag out some timber, from the non claims. I sure as hell don't relish chasing around the woods, hauling timbers out for a building."

At that time Richard saw the chance where he could get his opinion into the conversation, "I'll be so damn glad to get the hell out of that tent. It seems like I was born in that canvas building. I would like to be inside, where the wind doesn't rattle the building, and when it gets cold, you can make a fire and warm up fast. Last winter I about froze my butt off; no more. I want heat this winter and a warm bed to sleep in. I envy you, Bert and Hans, you have a good warm cabin set up, and most of all you have a woman for company. Just being in the same room with a woman makes everything feel more comfortable and much warmer. Just seeing a woman up close makes me feel good."

Elizabeth sitting at the table, taking in all the men's conversation, felt she should speak up at this time, "Richard, you are a very kind and thoughtful person. Most times I hear very little from you, but when you speak, you say some profound words. I really appreciate what you say about my company. I only hope I can bring comfort and good company to my friends. I truly feel I have been blessed in making friends with you four men, who have really helped me through my ordeal. If I had been left here, on my own, with no friends to help me, it would have been terrible. I hope in the future we can remain friends. Time does strange things to friends; small things can bring large division between some friends. I say we make a toast."

They all gathered together over the candle lit table.

Elizabeth led the toast, "We are gathered here in the Yukon. Months ago we were all strangers; today we are friends. Let us remain friends from now on."

They all touched their tin cups together and said a word of confirmation. The group sat down in silence. The toast by Elizabeth had touched all of them, thinking about what she had just said.

She broke the silence, "I think it is time we tasted this fine moose roast. Get your plates boys, here comes the food."

This was really a very special day. Fresh meat in the Yukon was a rarity. All that many men in the gold fields had to eat was good and bad bacon for months. It isn't hard to tell when the food is good. At that time, no one talks, and their primary interest is on the plate in front of them. Elizabeth had made gravy from the moose meat; it was soaked up with the fresh bread.

Tom said, "Life doesn't get much better than this. I think the good Lord might be looking out for us; we might have to return to the church and tell him thanks."

During the evening meal, a thunderstorm erupted out of the southwest. This was a rarity here in the Yukon.

Hans said, "The rumbling thunder reminds me of Iowa in the summer time. When you have a thunderstorm come through northwest Iowa in August, there is no mistaking it as you hear it rumble through the plains. Many a night I have laid in bed, scared to death. I knew I was going to be struck by lighting before morning. It really was terrifying."

"Listen to that thunder, it sounds different here in the north," replied Richard.

The dinner lasted a better part of an hour, the big eaters in the group, couldn't stop eating the moose roast.

Tom wiped his plate clean with the heel of the bread, "Elizabeth, if you can make a moose roast taste this good, what could you do with a beef roast?"

She was sitting with her elbows on the table, and her head cradled in her hands, "Well, Tom, I sure wish I had a chance to fix you guys a beef roast. Maybe some time soon we'll get lucky and have that chance."

The get-together lasted about another hour, and then Tom suggested they head back to their tent, so the party broke up. During the night the thunder storm subsided and in the morning the sky was clear.

Throughout the morning the partners retrieved tailings from the hole in the ground. The dirt at bedrock was barely frozen, so, the digging was going faster than usual. Rather than spend time washing, the three kept on digging. Around noon they stopped to eat. Soon after, Hans headed to town to check on the boats coming up from St. Michaels.

Before he left, Elizabeth asked him to check on some sugar.

She and Bert were now by themselves in the cabin. Strangely, this was one of the few times they had been by themselves. Elizabeth was lying on her bunk, resting after the noon dinner.

Bert pulled up the crude chair a few feet from her, "Elizabeth, do you think about your husband a lot?"

"It's strange, Bert. Just now I was lying here thinking about Dick. I try to think what he looks like, and it's hard for me to see his face. In my mind it gets kind of blurred. It seems the more I try to recall what he looked like, the harder time I have remembering his face. After I met him in Dawson this year, something changed. He wasn't the same man I married three years ago."

Bert moved his chair a little closer to Elizabeth's bunk, "You are a very pretty woman. Maybe I shouldn't be telling you this, but I have become very fond of you since we became partners. It's so nice to be living in the same cabin. It makes every day so much easier to take, living here in this God forsaken country."

Elizabeth was lying on the bunk with her work clothes on; her hair was up in a bandana. Even though Bert couldn't see her pretty brown hair, her sparkling eyes and bright smile were a strong attraction to him.

"Elizabeth, I just wanted you to know, you make my day's work on this claim much easier since you are part of it."

"I like to hear you enjoy having me around. Many times people are close, but they never express their feelings; thanks again Bert."

He got up from the chair, "I guess that gold in the ground is waiting for us to come find it."

As Elizabeth left the cabin, she said, "It will be interesting to hear what Hans found out about his girl friend."

They stood by the hole in the ground. They could hear the sound of squeaking winches, bringing the tailings to the surface. The sound drifted down through the valley. The sluice boxes and cradles were making their own separate noises. It was the sound of the diggings; men trying to out- do their neighbors, to find the mother lode.

As Elizabeth stood gazing at this once in a lifetime spectacle, she looked in awe. This was the largest gold strike in history!

Bert was digging in the hole. They now had a twenty foot drift, running parallel to the creek. The vein looked good, they knew they couldn't run the drift too far; this was the smallest claim in the valley. When he came out of the hole around six o'clock Elizabeth had sacked up another ten pounds of gold, mostly nuggets. She intended to pan the smaller gold flecks later on.

"Nice sack of gold," Bert said as he came into the cabin. "We'll have to measure how far we are toward our claim line; though I hate to stop on a good vein. I wonder what's keeping Hans; he must have found his lady friend by now"

CHAPTER 12

Bert was washing up and Elizabeth was fixing supper when they heard voices outside the cabin. The door opened, Hans and his girl friend came into the cabin.

"Hans you made it back. This must be Olive from Iowa." Bert said.

Hans taking off his cap, "Olive, I would like you to meet my very good friends, Elizabeth Larson and Bert Thompson. This is Olive Rutan from northwest Iowa. She came up the Yukon on the Yukon Belle and just arrived today at three."

Elizabeth extended her hand, "I'm very pleased to meet you. Hans has mentioned you to us many times. I'll bet you are very tired after the long trip. I'm about to fix supper. I'm sure you're starved."

Bert came over, "Olive, I'm really glad to meet you. On the trail north Hans told me about you both living on farms in northwest Iowa. I hope we can make you comfortable here."

Hans then spoke up, "Olive won't be staying here at the cabin. She met a nice lady on the boat coming up from St. Michaels, who told her she could stay with her in Dawson, as she thought it might be too crowded here in our small cabin."

Olive was about five foot three, long dark hair, with dark eyes and a wide smile. At twenty three, she was a very attractive young lady. As a rule, a young lady this attractive, living in the farm country would be married by this time.

Bert gave her his chair at the table, "Olive, tell us about your trip from Iowa."

She told the group about the long grueling trip, the train to the west coast, the long boat ride to St. Michaels, the paddle wheel boat up the Yukon. "We had to make a number of stops to pick up fire wood for their steam boilers. One of the boat people told me it took one hundred cords to make the trip up the swift river."

Hans asked her, "How was the food on the Yukon?"

"If you like beans it would be great. The worst thing on the trip was that the bugs were bad."

They all enjoyed the tale about the trip. Here in the north an interesting story was a great pleasure. With scarcely anything to read, the only basic enjoyment was hearing someone tell an interesting story.

The four sat around talking the better part of an hour, and then Elizabeth served the supper meal. This was a good time, friends sitting down to a good warm meal. The conversation around the table was very entertaining.

Later on, Hans told Elizabeth and Bert he was taking Olive into Dawson. He wanted to make sure he had plenty of daylight to find the right cabin.

They all said goodbye and the two headed toward town. Bert was helping Elizabeth clean up after the supper meal. "What do you think of Olive?"

"She's a very attractive girl. I sure wouldn't think she was born and raised on a farm, to me she looks like a city girl. It seems like farm girls always look a little differently. Do you know what I mean Bert?"

"Now that you mention it, she does look a little citified. Course I never spent much time around any farm girls, so maybe you're asking the wrong person. Like you said, she is a good looking woman. Old Hans will have his hands full with her."

As the two lay in their separate beds, it was relaxing to carry on some kind of a conversation.

Elizabeth said, "I can't believe it's getting close to September, and we'll have to start making plans for fall."

Bert replied, "I've been thinking about winter coming on and what we should do to prepare. I think we should start another hole just west of the cabin. If we can get that one started and get some depth to it, we could then use our extra tent to put over the hole. With the extra stove, we could have a little heat in there to keep things from freezing up."

"We should really give that some serious thought. If we have two holes to drift, we'll get about twice the amount of pay dirt come next spring."

"Tomorrow at breakfast we can talk over this idea. We'll also have some more winter plans. Snow balls will be coming before we know it."

"I think one of the biggest pains will be getting six months of firewood stacked up."

The cabin came alive about six in the morning. Elizabeth was busy fixing oatmeal and had sliced some bread to make toast on top of the stove. The three were sitting around the table having their first cup of coffee.

Hans said, "Did you hear me come in last night?"

Both shook their heads, 'No'.

"Well, it must have been about eleven when I crawled into my bunk. You wouldn't believe the mosquitoes on the way home. They about drove me nuts. I had a hard time breathing, keeping the little fellers out of my nose."

Elizabeth brought the oatmeal over to the table along with the toasted bread.

"Last night Bert and I were discussing some of the things we should get completed before fall gets here. Bert suggested we make a new hole close to the building. Maybe we could put the extra tent next to the building and let a little heat go in there, to make the work easier. What do you think, Hans? "

"I think the new hole would be a good idea. We could work both holes through the winter. Having the area over the hole covered would certainly help make the work more tolerable, especially when the temperature hits fifty below zero."

"Then we agree we should start another hole. We'll have to start thawing the ground when we hit the perma frost. We should decide today where we make the new hole," Bert replied.

The work progressed. They decided to make the hole adjacent to the west wall. If they used the extra stove they had stashed, they could use the same stove pipe. Bert opened the hole until he hit frozen ground, and then Elizabeth kept the fire going to thaw the dirt.

One day turned into the next. Hans made the trip to Dawson after the evening meal. Olive was working at one of the popular bars; it was called the Golden Nugget. In fact it was one of the nicer bars in Dawson. To Hans' surprise, Olive was singing at this bar. He knew she sang in the church choir, but didn't think she would like singing in a bar. During the noon and evening meals Hans would talk about Olive. The way he was talking, Olive's new singing job at the Golden Nugget bothered him.

One day he invited Elizabeth and Bert to tag along with him to hear her sing. They arrived at the Golden Nugget at around eight o'clock. The place was packed, as were most of the bars in Dawson providing entertainment. There wasn't a seat to be had in the house; it took them a while to find a spot where they could see the little stage.

"Are we having a drink, boys?" asked Elizabeth.

Bert coming back with one of his witty sayings, "Does a porcupine shit in the woods?"

They took the money out of the partnership pouch to pay for the drinks. Then they moved away from the noisy bar; also to get away from some of the stinking old miners. Some men didn't bother to buy any soap, or to use any. Many of the miners had certain priorities; digging for gold, eating and drinking. For some reason, men working in the gold fields had a strong desire for whiskey. Some would come to Dawson after spending a couple weeks in the diggings. When they arrived in Dawson, they would stay drunk for three or four days before heading back to their prospecting.

Before Olive came on the stage, a large robust man, wearing a white shirt, stepped up on a box behind the bar. He was a fat, rough looking man, his black hair parted in the middle; and a wide handle bar mustache highlighted his pocked face.

OLIVE SING AT THE GOLDEN NUGGET

"May I have your attention? We have coming on stage, the Yukon Queen. Her name is Lily Lateral, and she came all the way from San Francisco to sing for you. Now let's give Lily a big hand."

The crowd roared; the building seemed to shake with all the

clapping, feet stomping and hollering. Elizabeth could see in Hans' face that he was somewhat embarrassed by all the big to-do, about Olive , put on by the bartender. She also had the feeling that he was in the process of losing his hometown girl friend. Elizabeth had been around many situations such as this between Hans and Olive, and knew Hans would soon have much competition for her hand.

As Olive started to sing, the large crowd quieted down to almost a whisper. One drunk in the far corner didn't seem to notice the quietness of the bar room; and he was soon silenced by a poke on the head. Olive's beautiful clear voice bounced off the ceiling and walls like a clear bell ringing through the valley. It was truly amazing how quiet a bunch of rowdy drunks can be when the need arises.

Olive was standing on a raised platform, with a fancy kerosene lamp hanging on each side of her. The other lamps were turned low to give her the most light. The heavy smoke from the many pipes filled the air. The heat from the kerosene lamps drew the smoke to each side of Olive, giving her a mysterious appearance. After two songs she stopped so the bar could sell more drinks, and drinks they sold!

Since Olive started singing at the Golden Nugget the business had increased greatly and the owner had taken a strong fancy to her. Mike McDougal had won the bar in one of those notorious poker games which had taken place in Dawson City. Mike was a handsome fellow with a good personality. Elizabeth saw this when Olive introduced the three partners to him. He was clean shaven, except for a mustache. He was a rugged looking individual and this made him stand out from the crowd. His dark eyes and dark hair gave him a very rugged appearance.

That night the drinks were on Mike, and needless to say, the three partners had a drink in their hands throughout the night.

About nine thirty, Olive finished singing her final two songs. She came over to Hans, Bert and Elizabeth and told them she had a long day, and was going to try to get to bed early. At this point, Hans, who had about one drink too many, was just a little bit unsteady. He offered to walk her home to her cabin.

She said, "Thanks, Hans, but Mike is going right by my cabin and he said he would walk me home." Hans Hans didn't really know what to say, so he just said "Okay."

The others headed for their cabin on Bonanza Creek. The straight line they had walked on the way to the Golden Nugget, was now a very wandering line on the way back.

As Hans walked back to the cabin, his thoughts were on Olive. He had a gut feeling she was no longer his girl friend; maybe she never was. Maybe she just used Hans to get off the farm. Most farm girls wanted to get away before they were tied up with one the neighbor boys, and the next thing was marriage and a family. I'll bet she was glad I came to the Yukon; this gave her a chance to go see the world. I don't think she had heard from me before she headed north. Hans thought, maybe you're a dumb head.

The three staggered along, swatting mosquitoes with a leafy branch from one of the bushes, it was a constant battle to keep them off their faces. These pesky bugs made people very irritable and gave them short tempers. It was about dark when they got to the cabin. It was plain to see the days were getting shorter. When they entered the cabin, there wasn't much said. The whiskey had a numbing effect on all of them; soon they were all snoring.

As they entered September, the trees gave the appearance of fall being in the air. In the north, you can just about tell the seasons by the smell. Each season has a distinct aroma, spring being the most prominent. Spring has that sweet smell, like walking through a bunch of blossoms. Now the aspens were turning yellow, the tag alders were turning a deep purple, the tamaracks started their turn toward their mustard hew.

Elizabeth stood by the windlass, staring down the valley. Working men could be seen scattered all the way to Grand Forks. It was strange, the trees had color, but the men working the claims were in most part, in tones of grey and black. Here and there she could see a miner with faded red long johns, giving off a little color. Grand Forks had sprung up at the junction of Eldorado Creek and Bonanza Creek in a matter of weeks. Belinda Mulroney was the prime mover in this new little town. She started the town with a small eating place; soon she built a number of small cabins, now she had a good sized hotel.

As Elizabeth stood looking around the valley, she saw the trees were being cut at a very high rate. She thought soon there wouldn't be any trees to be seen from her cabin. Every one is getting wood cut for the coming winter and we too, had better get busy.

Early one morning there was a light skiff of snow, so they all decided to spend the day bringing in firewood. They brought the wood down to the cabin in four foot lengths, and then they cut it in one foot lengths. As a rule, the wood was all split at least once, in order for it to dry it out.

The first hole they dug seemed to be running out of gold; the amount being washed was getting less and less. For the time being, they all decided to concentrate on the new hole, so they kept a fire going in the hole night and day.

About the end of September, Bert and Hans decided to go hunting. Elizabeth could keep the fire going in the second hole. They had about three inches of new snow as they headed southeast where there was an old caribou crossing. The herd had passed there for many years according to the old timers around Dawson. The hunters in camp said the herd hadn't yet passed as of this date.

Bert and Hans took one sled; they also took one of their tarps along to keep warm and dry at night. So far the temperature hadn't been much below freezing. They took enough food to last at least five to six days. The two headed up on the ridge to get away from the mining area as soon as possible. The sluiceways were everywhere; they wanted to pick the easiest route out of the claims.

CHAPTER 13

It took them two days to arrive at the large lake due southeast of Dawson. Jeb had given them this direction; it was supposed to be the migration route for the Caribou. This part of the country was void of heavy timber; it appeared to be mostly stunted black spruce. The trees were about three inches in diameter and about eight feet tall. They set up their tarp a couple of hundred yards off a valley where they thought the caribou might pass. In the distance they could see some other hunters; this was a long valley with the lake in the center.

After camp was made, the two took the 30:30 and walked down to the lake. It was crystal clear. As they stood looking into the water, they could see fish moving by.

Bert looked at Hans, "Get your knife out, we'll make a couple spears. Maybe we can spear some fish."

They found some young saplings, sharpened one end to a point, and then they made an arrow at the tip. The two wings on the arrow would keep the fish from coming off the spear. They found that if they stood still and threw some small pieces of wood into the lake that this would attract the fish, and then it was easier to get a good shot. The water gave a false impression. When they made a lunge to spear the fish they were always below the fish. Driving the spear into the water, above the fish, gave quick results.

That night they cooked some bacon, to get some grease for the fish, and then filled the pan with fish. They sat around the fire drinking coffee and enjoying their fresh cooked salmon.

"This fish is finger licking good," said Bert. "I think we should keep spearing, maybe we could make a rack and start drying some, and we'll haul back as much as we can stack on the sled."

Hans was lighting his pipe, "How long do you reckon we should stick around, waiting for the caribou herd?"

"I'll tell you what I think. Why don't we keep fishing, if after a couple days, we have a bunch of fish to take back to camp, we'll forget about the caribou."

"I think that would be a good plan, food is food, we can live on fish as well as meat. Of course, I sure would like to pack some steaks back to camp."

The stunted spruce made good firewood; they kept a fire burning most of the night. Through out the next two days, the two men speared salmon.

Bert commented to Hans, "This is almost too easy. I can't believe it's this easy to spear these buggers."

By now, they had a number of racks around their camp with fish drying. That night when Hans got up to relieve himself; he was amazed at the northern lights. It was a light show he had never seen before; most of the light rays were pink, and dancing all over the sky. It seemed he could hear them crackle. Hans went back under the tarp, after stoking the fire.

Bert raised his head, "What's up?"

"You should come out and look at these weird northern lights; they're jumping all over the sky."

Bert crawled out from under his blankets and went out side. The two men stood there in awe, the bright northern lights were all around them. As they stood gaping at the bright lights, they heard a strange grunting sound. They couldn't make out what was making the sound. The two men looked at each other, not knowing what to make of the strange noise. Bert shielded his eyes from the fire, looking intently in the distance. In the darkness of the night, he could see something moving in the brush.

"What do you see Bert, is it a wolf?"

Bert turned and started his way back toward the fire, "Hans, there is something out there; it might be wolves."

They both returned to the fire. Bert threw in a few sticks to get the fire going. About that time they heard the loud growl.

"Son of a bitch," Bert said, "Look at those green eyes shinning, it's a damn bear, stoke up the fire, grab me some more shells."

They both peered into the darkness. All of a sudden the bear came out of the darkness. He was charging at the two men, Bert pulled up the 30:30 and started shooting; it was Bang, Bang, Bang! Bert got off three shots. The bear came to a halt not ten feet from the two.

As they looked at the large bear in absolute silence, it stood on its hind legs and took a quick lunge at Hans. The four inch long toe nails just caught the front of his coat. It popped off most of the buttons. At the same moment, Bert lunged toward the bear with the 30:30 and put the barrel next to the big bear's left ear. Crack, went the gun. The large bear did a cart wheel, and landed on top of the fire. Both men stood waiting for it to get up and start a new charge. It lay on the fire, his fur sizzling, and making strange puffs in the fire.

Bert started jumping up and down, "Did you see that big damn bear keel over like a ton of shit, into that fire. I must have shot that bugger bear right in the brain through his ear."

Hans looked down at his coat; the bear had done an excellent job of peeling it open. "I thought I was a goner, that bear was so damn close, a couple more inches, he would have ripped open my chest."

Both men stood looking at it.

"We better get the damn thing out of the fire. I guess we'll have some bear meat this winter instead of caribou," said Bert.

They gutted the bear and removed the hide. This would let the bear cool down during the remainder of the night. After an hour, they returned to their blankets.

Both men had a hard time getting to sleep. This encounter with the bear was a close call; both of them could have been ripped up good by this big fellow.

Early the next morning, they deboned the bear. They would now have plenty of meat for a while. Thank God, they had snow on the ground. The bear dressed out at over two hundred pounds of meat that they wanted to keep. They also had thirty- five pounds of fish to haul back.

They loaded up the meat and the fish. They each carried about sixty pounds of meat in their back packs; the remainder was hauled on the sled. They made a double hitch on the sled, so they both could pull the load. They took their time; their main goal now, was to get this large supply of meat and fish back to camp. This amount of meat and fish would go a long way in getting the three partners through the winter. It was a damn fool who counted on someone else to provide food through these Yukon winters. It took them one and a half days to arrive back at their humble log cabin on Bonanza Creek. When they pulled the sled down the hill toward the cabin, they were met by a jubilant Elizabeth. She rushed out to meet the two.

"Oh, I'm so happy to see you guys. After being a little late I thought you must have run into some problems. Did you get two caribou? Looks like you have a lot of meat on the sled."

"Elizabeth, we had a trip you wouldn't believe. We want to get this meat unloaded and then we'll tell you the story."

They set the meat and fish in the tent next to the log cabin where the new shaft was located. They hung the meat on racks so it could cool down and eventually freeze. After the fish and meat were in place, the men went into the cabin to relax.

"Would you boys like me to pour you a drink?"

They sat down at the candle lit table.

Hans told Elizabeth, "We are ready for a relaxing drink of brandy. The hunt was really full of many surprises."

Bert sat down and stretched out his legs, filled his pipe and struck a match, "I think I'm going to give up hunting, before I get killed. You should have seen the tussle we had with this damn eight foot bear; it's only by the grace of God we made it back to camp."

Hans raised his tin cup to his lips, took a long sip of the brandy, and set the cup on the wooden table.

"That brandy is sure relaxing. Now I feel like the long walk wasn't that bad."

Elizabeth pulled a chair up to the table. "Now boys, tell me about the big hunt"

Hans crossed his legs, took a couple puffs on the pipe, and started telling her all about it. The story went on for more than half an hour.

Elizabeth said, "You're lucky the bear didn't ripe off all of your clothes. By the way, did you find the buttons the bear tore off?"

"Ya, I picked them up after things quieted down a bit."

They sat around the table, talking about the hunting trip.

After that Elizabeth gained the floor. "When you two were gone I had some time to think about this Yukon Country. I was thinking about all these people, mostly men, who braved the winter trail over the Chilkoot trail in the winter of ninety seven and eight. It's hard to believe what really possessed these forty or fifty thousand men to take this crazy venture across this wilderness."

She took another shot of the brandy in her tin cup. These were the times in the cabin when stories were being told, that she really enjoyed.

Elizabeth got a big kick out of sitting around with Bert and Hans, talking about anything. Just talking and telling a story was their entertainment. The three partners were now very relaxed; the brandy had done its job. The work in the Yukon is hard and dirty. After a couple drinks, things seemed easier; it was well worth the effort.

Elizabeth said, "Let's cut some bear steaks and have a feed. I'm about starved. We'll cook some of the dried potatoes. Along with the bread we should have a big meal to celebrate the big successful caribou hunt. It's funny in a way, you two go hunting for caribou, and you return with bear and fish. I wonder what you would bring back if you went hunting for moose."

Now the days in the Yukon were getting shorter; by seven it was dark, the long dark winter was coming to the north country. As they sat in the small log cabin, the single candle gave out a warm comforting light. While Elizabeth was cooking the meat, the happy partners kept up their robust conversation. It was good times in this Yukon camp. What more could three Cheechakoes ask for? The gold was coming out of the ground at a good rate; they had meat and fish for the winter; the log cabin was just about ready for winter and there was enough wood cut to last the long winter. Life was good.

As they sat around nursing their tin cup of brandy, the conversation turned to Tom and Richard.

Bert commented, "I wonder where our friends have been hanging out? Even though they're not too far away, we haven't seen hide nor hair of them for a couple weeks."

"Maybe we should take a walk up the Bonanza and see what's going on in Jeb's camp." Hans said.

Elizabeth turning the bear steaks in the pan, "Maybe we could head up there tomorrow after supper. This has been a long day for all concerned, so I think tonight is out."

She took the steaks out of the frying pan; each plate had a large slab. She put some of the new baked bread on the stove to make toast.

Bert cut a slice off the steak, and gently put the hot meat in his mouth, "Elizabeth, you sure can make any steak taste great. I can't believe how tender this meat is. Hell, I never had bear meat before. I guess I didn't know what I was missing."

As they sat around the candle lit table, eating their meal, there wasn't much said. Bert was sitting across the table from Elizabeth. As he raised his fork to his mouth, he looked across the table toward her. She was looking at him. As their eyes locked on one another, Bert felt a strange sensation go through his body, and they looked at each other for a few seconds. It was a strange feeling for Bert, he always had a strong feeling for Elizabeth, but she had never shown any interest toward him, until this instant. He wondered if he was reading something into a long glance, that didn't really mean anything. The three worked to clean the tin plates and frying pan. Most times it worked well with a little sand and water. Now they used snow instead of water.

They played a few hands of rummy before going to bed.

Early the next morning they were out working the claim. They figured the hole by the cabin was a few feet from bedrock and the black sand. On the way down this new hole, the crew picked up a fair amount of gold. The gold was now stacked under all the bunks. The group really had no idea how many dollars they had accumulated in their gold bags. Bert was spending the most time down the hole; he liked digging with the anticipation of finding the gold nuggets, and many times during the day, he would come across a nugget and let out a war hoop.

Hans and Elizabeth didn't mind working the top. The two had a water sluice way running through their claim. The long sluice box was filled with gold bearing gravel. Then water was diverted from the main sluice into theirs. The water would wash away the gravel and dirt, leaving the rocks and gold nuggets in the riffles.

It was hard work, but the rewards some days were amazing. As time went on, they would take the dirt and gold flecks out of the riffles, clean and separate them in the gold pan. That night they had smoked salmon and bread. Elizabeth had made a fresh pie with their dried apples. Many supplies were running low; soon they would have to take some gold to the bank and get dollars.

While Bert was cleaning the last piece of pie from his tin plate he said, "Elizabeth, you will make some lucky man a fine wife."

"Oh Bert, you're so kind, maybe I'll find a new husband some time in the future. I want to make sure the next one has the same likes as I do. My last husband and I didn't seem to have the same interest in life."

At that time Bert wondered if he might be in her future. He sure had a strong affection for this attractive woman. She had high cheekbones, a strong chin, perfect white teeth, and her large eyes would melt a man's heart with one glance.

Elizabeth, picked up her jacket, "Well boys, I think it is time we went to visit our friends."

Off they trudged, up the creek. With the new snow and unfrozen ground, it was muddy and very slippery. Sometimes the muddy clay soil would create a great suction on the rubber boots. This would stop a person in their tracks. They would have to pull the boots up with their hands; it was really a sloppy mess.

Hans swatted his cheek, "I thought all these damn bugs were dead by now. The winter is hard to take in this country, but these damn mosquitoes, black flies and no see-ums, I think are worse."

"Ah Hans, the next thing you'll be complaining about will be your cold feet."

"Well at least you can put more socks on to keep your feet warm. There ain't a hell of a lot you can do about these damn bugs."

Soon they arrived at the new cabin of Richard and Tom.

Hans knocked on the door, and then gave a holler, "Tom, Richard, you guys inside?"

The three stood there wondering if maybe their friends had gone somewhere.

Elizabeth pulled out her pocket watch, "Well it's seven o'clock, I thought for sure they would be around at this time in the evening."

They stood looking at the cabin, it was crude, but it looked very sturdy.

Bert pointed to the roof, "Look at all the grass on the roof, they must have carried that sod a long piece. Hell, there ain't no sod around here".

"They sure didn't build a very large cabin, it can't be over twelve by twelve," commented Elizabeth.

"Well it won't take much wood to heat their cabin this winter. They sure have a large pile stacked on the other end of the cabin."

The three were just turning away from the cabin when they heard a shout.

"Hey you Cheechakoes, you looking to steal our gold?"

It was Tom's voice coming from just outside of Jeb's cabin, about one hundred feet away.

Elizabeth answered, "What do you mean, 'Cheechakoes?' We've been working these gold fields a long time partner."

"Richard and I will be down in just a minute, go in the cabin and have a chair."

They walked into the dark cabin, the open door sent light onto the table. There they saw a candle in an old coffee can lid. Hans struck a match; the candle lit up the one room. They sat down on the three chairs around the table.

"Smells like a couple bachelor's cabin to me boys," remarked Elizabeth.

She continued, "I wonder why they have three chairs, when there are only two of them. Maybe the two boys have a lady friend like you two fellows."

Soon footsteps could be heard outside the cabin. The door opened, and in walked Richard and Tom. The two had new winter beards. Having not seen them since they were bare faced, it took a while to get used to the new appearance.

Bert spoke first, "How's things going in this camp? You guys have gold piled under your beds?"

Tom answered, "By golly, we have done okay for ourselves. Old Jeb here picked a good piece of land to prospect. Old Jeb isn't doing too good; he seems to be pretty sick. I think living under ground like he has for so long mining the gold, has given him some lung problems."

Richard jumped into the conversation, "You know; there have been many men die throughout the summer. I think all this crapping and pissing in the area, gets into the water. Hell, it's a wonder we're not all sick. If more camps would dig a hole to crap in, it wouldn't run off so easy. You see guys pissing every where."

"Slow down Richard," Tom interjected, "Jeb's an old man. Course he doesn't eat like he should. Hell, we try to feed him every day, but he's a stubborn old German, he does what he wants."

Elizabeth asked. "How sick is Jeb? Could we do something for him?"

Tom told them, "I'll tell you, Jeb isn't in very good shape. He's lost a lot of weight, which he never had much to spare anyway. Now he has a fever. With all his blankets he says he's still freezing. Richard ran into town this afternoon to see if the doctor could make a trip out here to check on Jeb. He said he would get to our camp this evening."

Hans lit a new load of tobacco in his pipe, "What would happen if he should die on you fellows? Does he have any family? At least you should make some kind of agreement about his claim. You guys might get all the gold out of the ground and someone comes along and hauls it south."

Tom said, "You're right Hans. We thought about the same thing, so we talked this over with Jeb before he was real sick. He hasn't looked good for some time."

Tom pulled a bottle of whiskey out from under his bunk. "Did you remember to bring your tine cups along?"

He sat down on his bunk, took a sip of his drink, "I really think Jeb has a good idea he won't come through this illness, he looks real yellow and gaunt. We talked at length about what we should do with the claim if something should happen to him. He told us he has a sister living in a town called Dubuque, Iowa. He hadn't heard from her in more than a year, and she is the only relative he has. They both came over from Austria in eighteen seventy. The last Jeb knew, and she was a nun."

The friends sat listening intently to Tom's doings with Jeb.

"Jeb also told us he wants a good burial. He said he was christened a Catholic when he was born in Austria, but in recent years he didn't seem to have time to go to mass. He wants Olive to sing at the funeral. He heard her a couple times before he came down sick. He couldn't believe a little gal that small could have such a strong voice. We have to get him a tombstone; I guess the mortician got a new load in last week. They're a simple cross of some kind. Jeb's last request was something really different. He wants us to take five hundred dollars from his gold account and after the funeral; he wants a party at the Golden Nugget. He said he'd buy the drinks until the five hundred dollars has been used up. He also made a request we give Olive two hundred dollars to sing, until the bar money has been used up.

Bert was the first to speak up, "Damn, that old guy sure came up with some great requests. He must have been thinking about this for some time. Tom, do you guys think he has come to the end?"

Richard spoke up, "Old Jeb never has looked like he was healthy and so it's kind of hard to tell when he might be in bad shape. I think the doctor coming out tonight will have either good or bad news for us."

Elizabeth was pulling one of her curls out of her bandana with her finger, "If old Jeb should pass on next week or a month from now, what happens to the claim?"

Tom answered Elizabeth's question, "One evening we cornered Jeb after supper. This was a couple weeks ago, and he really wasn't looking good at that time. We asked him, if you come down real sick and can't work your claim, what will you do, would you sell it to someone?"

Jeb said, "I have a good idea what you boys are thinking about. You're wondering what will happen to the claim if I should die. The way I feel, I may not get out of this Yukon country alive. My pa died of a bad heart when he was around fifty years old. Hell, I'm ten years past that age, so maybe I'm getting on thin ice myself. I want to tell you boys something. You both have been damn good to me and I really appreciate this. I know I pay you boys a good wage, plus ten percent of the gold we mine. I see you busting your butts every day for me. Hell, I'm the one getting ninety percent of the gold. I really appreciate your hard work I want one of you to write up an agreement for me. We'll see if the local banker will keep the paper for us. Keep the damn thing simple.

If I should die, of course from health reasons, I don't want one of you boys getting any fancy ideas."

Jeb thought this was a big joke, and he had a good laugh. "On the day I die, you take this paper we signed to the banker and have the claim turned over to you two fellows. You take all the gold to the bank and convert it to cash, pay for my wishes, divide the cash in half. You two get half of this money, the other half goes to my sister living in Dubuque, Iowa. The last I knew she was still a nun. I'm sure she will find a good place for this money. Maybe it will help old Jeb get to the great beyond. If for some reason she has passed on herself, give the money to the church. You have to promise me you will try to find her and give her the money."

"So Richard and I sat down one evening and wrote out Jeb's request on some old brown paper we found. We took the paper to the bank in Dawson, we all signed the paper in front of the banker, and he also signed as a witness. So I guess every thing is in order."

"One hell of a story" replied Hans, "You two might end up owners of a rich claim. You came into this country with out a pot to pee in, now you might end up with a rich claim."

"Damn life is sure full of surprises." Richard took the brandy bottle, "Let's have a drink for Jeb, he's one of a kind. If he passes on, we'll surely miss him. Let's each of us say a little prayer for him."

After the group said a few silent words for Jeb, they sat in silence; each person had their own thoughts.

Tom broke the silence, "This is sure one hell of a place, we have people living like rats in so called cabins. Hell, they're nothing more than holes in the ground. We have miners living in this barren dug up country with many thousands of dollars in gold stashed in their cabins, and they're dying for the lack of decent food to keep them healthy. How long can people endure this kind of life, or live long enough to spend any of this money?"

Richard could hardly wait to give his thoughts, "You see my friends, we have a problem here in these God forsaken gold fields, and its called greed. Yes, my friends it's greed. What do you think drove the thousands of people that busted their butts coming over that Chilkoot Pass? It was greed in their souls to find this damn gold. Look around these gold fields, men live in terrible conditions, eat the same old meager food, day after day. Then by chance they find some gold, that's when the greed really starts to take hold. If their bodies would take it, they would work twenty fours hours a day and dig down through that black dirt, to find all those beautiful gold nuggets lying there just for the taking. If Jeb would die, and leave Tom and me the mine, would we stay here until we're both on death's doorstep? Would we have to get every last nugget or gold fleck out of the ground?"

"By golly Richard, you have been doing some heavy thinking," Bert commented.

Tom added "I think some of the things you mentioned are on many a miner's mind. It's true we do live under poor conditions and we sure don't always have much to choose from when we sit down at the table. If those assholes with the big boats bringing supplies up the river would be more concerned about food than bringing all the barrels of whiskey, we would have a better choice of food to choose from. I guess greed enters into the boatman's mind also. Since he can make more money hauling whiskey than he can flour, he hauls whiskey. You made a number of good points. If a man is working a claim, how long does he work it? Let's say he came up here with his shirt on his back and all his supplies; he hits pay dirt and through the winter he takes in fifty thousand dollars worth of gold. How much more gold is in the ground? Should he keep working the mine until he has all the ground dug up? When the hell does he stop and head south, while he has his health? Hell, he could always sell the claim for a good price. If he went south with say, seventy five-thousand dollars; that's more money than he could have earned back home during his entire life. You figure it out, a dollar and a half a day. If you worked every day of the year, you would have earned about five hundred and fifty dollars ."

Elizabeth hadn't said a word for some time, "I think what we are all worried about is what might happen to our friend Jeb, could just happen to us. Course, he didn't have a chance to head south this fall before freeze up. He still hadn't gotten to the good diggings at that time. I'll bet every miner that strikes it good, sits down one night and asks himself, how long do I keep working this claim? I've got a good chunk of money, why not head south to the good life and spend it. I think when a person comes to that time; he'll have to be honest with himself. What is best for me and my family? It wouldn't surprise me if fifty miners died this next long winter; bad health, accidents, killings and maybe some suicides."

Hans raised his cup toward his friends, "They're right. It's something to think about."

Just then Tom interrupted, "I can see a lantern coming down the hill toward Jeb's cabin. Richard and I should get over there to see what the doc can tell us about Jeb's condition."

"It's time we headed for our cabin, it's getting dark," Hans said. "I don't know if we have a moon out tonight or not. It could be damn dark out there. He looked out, "It's okay, we can see our way home."

They Theyall said so long and headed out. They picked their way back through the mud and slush to their cabin. Hans entered first, lit a match, then a candle.

"Think I'll start a little fire to take the chill off."

It wasn't long before the three were all in bed.

In the morning, Elizabeth, Hans and Bert were sitting at their primitive table having their coffee, when they heard footsteps coming through the wet ground.

About the time there was a knock on the door.

Bert hollered, "Come on in."

It was Tom. He looked quite solemn, there appeared to be grief on his face.

Elizabeth knew why he was there so she said, "It's about Jeb isn't it?"

"Yah," he said, "You know the doc came to visit last night. He gave old Jeb quite a check over; in fact he was there about half an hour. For a long time he said nothing. Jeb was kind of in a sleeping state. I think he knew the doc was there, but I wouldn't bet on it. He gave Jeb some pills to make him comfortable. When the doc left the cabin we followed him outside."

He said, "Jeb is in poor shape, his heart sounds very weak and his lungs have fluid in them. If he starts running a fever, he will probably come down with pneumonia. If that happens, it will be real serious."

"Is Richard with Jeb now?" asked Elizabeth.

"Yah, we figure we better keep someone with him all the time, case he needs something, or whatever."

"Tom, if we can be of any help, let us know."

Elizabeth asked, "Does Jeb have any appetite at all? I could make him some soup, he sure needs to eat something."

"That would be nice; the soup might perk him up."

Tom left the cabin and headed back to help look after Jeb. Elizabeth dug out some condensed milk, some potatoes and bacon. In the meantime, Bert and Hans went to the hole in the ground.

MAKING A DRIFT FROM THE MAIN SHAFT ON BEDROCK

Bert had stated a drift in the long direction of their claim; it was just large enough for the two of them to work side by side. The temperature in the hole stayed around fifty degrees. The candle provided very little light; one of the two was always working in the shadow of the other. It was grueling work; their knees were always on damp, hard ground or the rock bedrock. By the end of the day, the two could barely stand, and their knees were swollen.

It was as Richard had said, 'Greed drives these gold hungry men to the extremes.'

Late in the afternoon, Elizabeth took the pan of hot soup to Jeb's cabin. When she arrived, she found Richard looking after him. The door was ajar, so she walked in. Richard motioned her in, saying, "It's very warm in here, that's why the door is open, still Jeb keeps telling us he's freezing."

Elizabeth handed the hot pan to Richard, "Maybe he could try to eat some soup."

He checked the soup to see how hot it was, "That's great soup and if Jeb's hungry he should gobble this down."

He took a spoonful and raised it to Jeb's lips. His eyes were open slightly. Richard pushed the spoon between his lips, and tipped it up. The soup ran down his chin, there didn't seem to be any response at all. Elizabeth reached over and raised one of Jeb's eyelids; she could see the pupil of his eye had rolled to the top. She closed the eyelid.

"Richard, your friend is dead."

"Are you sure Elizabeth?"

She said, "Let me check his pulse in his neck." She put her finger on the left side of Jeb's neck.

"There isn't any pulse. We better get the doc to make sure. Richard, you run into Dawson, I'll go tell Tom."

When Elizabeth told Tom the news, he climbed out of the hole.

The first thing he said was, "This sure is a hell of a way to inherit a mine, have your good friend die…son a bitch."

Elizabeth made her way back to her cabin. Both Bert and Hans were on top of the ground, standing by the windlass. They were having a smoke from their pipes.

When she walked up, the first thing Hans said was, "Jeb's dead, isn't he?"

"Yes."

"I could see it on your face, a woman's face can tell many things."

She told the two the story about Richard and the soup.

"I really think Tom and Richard dearly loved the old man, it seems they are taking this very hard. I suppose he was about the age of their fathers and Jeb has been very nice to them. Tom told me, 'This is a hell of a way to inherit a mine.' Let's go over to see if they need any help."

The sky was a dull grey with dark clouds to the east. Hans thought, a fitting a day for death.

CHAPTER 14

When the three arrived at Jeb's cabin, Tom and Richard were standing over the old man. It was a sad day for the two men. They had met Jeb by chance, went to work for him, now they stood to inherit the entire mine. Hans led the three into the musty dark cabin. He looked at Jeb lying on his old rumpled bunk. The sphagnum moss he had for a mattress was indented where he had slept these many months. Hans thought, his bed is form fitting, he must have had a warm bed in the cold Yukon nights. At this time Richard left to fetch the undertaker, he wanted to get Jeb back to Dawson before dark.

Tom spoke up. "I'm going to miss that old guy, he was an ornery old fart sometimes, but I really think he had a heart of gold. He used to get on our butts in the beginning for not working hard enough, but, as time went on he thought we were doing okay and gave us praise for doing a good job."

They all sat down at the table, the coffee pot was perking on the stove, so Tom poured coffee for all. Even though the cabin was quite warm, the hot coffee warmed the bodies. Tom was staring at Bert and Hans; maybe it was time for reminiscing.

He set his cup on the table, "Do you guys remember when we met at that damn Chilkoot Pass? Damn, that was a sour time in my life. It was cold as hell, and we were each about half finished with our forty climbs over the God forsaken pass when we met you two guys. I think teaming up with you really helped us get our butts over the pass. I think at times you need some friends to talk to and bare your problems."

By this time Hans had finished his coffee. He set his cup on the table, took out his pipe and said, "I think you two helped us as much as we helped you. It was one damn poor day when we were working to get over that horrible pass. It's a good thing a man doesn't know what's ahead; otherwise he would turn back many times."

The four sat there talking about the year before, getting to Dawson City. Now it was more humorous; they could talk about the problems and laugh about the times. The door opened and Richard had the undertaker with him. The undertaker took matters into his hands and proceeded to get Jeb ready for moving. By this time Jeb was starting to get stiff so he had some problem getting his leg and arm bent back to where they belonged. It was a little gruesome to watch him force old Jeb's limbs back into the correct position.

"Would you fellers give me a hand loading this feller onto my wagon?"

The men jumped up and gave him a hand. By now, Jeb was wrapped up entirely in his blankets; they lowered him onto the wagon.

Richard told the undertaker, "We'll stop by in the morning to take care of the details."

When he came back into the cabin he told the group, "The undertaker said we could have the funeral the day after tomorrow, he said ten in the morning would be fine."

Soon they were sitting in Tom and Richard's dimly lit cabin. It smelled of sweaty clothes, pipe tobacco smoke and the sourdough working over the stove.

"What the hell," said Tom, "Let's have a drink. It's sad to say we lost a good friend and by a quirk of fate we gained a gold claim. Somehow I feel like we took advantage of our good friend, then again I don't know what the hell to think. Thank God we had the foresight to get something signed by Jeb. You know, you people suggested we do something like that, it's a good thing we took your advice. When you think about how we came to acquire this claim, it was because Hans and Bert recommended us to Jeb. I guess Richard and I should make a toast to our buddies that pointed our noses to this claim."

He dug up some containers to pour each one a couple shots of whiskey. Two of the drinkers had to drink out of tin cans.

All this time, Elizabeth hadn't said a word. She thought about what was going on between the four men and Jeb, and she didn't want to impose on them when they were sharing their old times.

She started off with, "I want to make a toast to all of you. I think I could have looked far and wide before I would have found four guys like you. You two were damn good to old Jeb, and Bert and Hans have been damn good to me. It's really a pleasure to raise this tin can and make a toast to all of you. Grab your drink boys. May we always be friends to the end. I have a fondness for all of you in my heart."

Bert was the first one to respond, "Elizabeth, you have meant a lot to all of us, and Hans and I have had the best of everything. We live in the same cabin, and we have your company almost twenty-four hours a day."

Hans raised his tin cup, "I want to make a toast. Here's to Elizabeth. She is a friend to all four of us; she brings sunlight into our day, even if the weather is miserable. She took Bert and me into her trust and made us her partners. Here's to a wonderful lady. All I want to say is thank you from my heart."

The men raised their cups and touched over the wooden table.

After a while Tom looked at Hans, "Do you get a chance to spend much time with Olive?"

He looked back at Tom, not really wanting to answer this question.

"Well Tom, as a matter of fact, I really haven't been with Olive that much. It seems we have kind of drifted apart. I think since she came to Dawson City, she's had hundreds of men trying to get her eye, and it's possible someone has."

"Gosh, Hans, I didn't mean to pry into your personal business. We've been to the Golden Nugget a few times ourselves; she does get a lot of attention. Course when you're that good looking and have a great voice, everyone wants to talk to you. She has been nice to Richard and me when she sees us in the room, most times she'll stop by to say hello."

"I guess I just feel a little awkward going to see her, since we used to be quite close, maybe I expect too much from her. I hate to say this, but, I think Olive and that Mike McDougal fellow have become real good friends. It appears he watches over her whenever she's in the Nugget. In fact, I've heard he has punched a few fellows out for getting too friendly with her."

Quiet Richard held up a finger, "Hans, it's kind of sad when your girl friend makes a trip all the way up here to see you, then things go sour. I'm sure it's hard for you to take. You're very lucky to have a woman's company in your cabin. If it wasn't for Elizabeth, you would miss Olive more. I think we better let Hans' personal life die right now, instead of thinking about troublesome things, let's have a good time."

The five of them sat around the crude wooden table making plans for Jeb's funeral. It was agreed they all meet at Elizabeth's cabin about eight in the morning. It was scheduled to take place at ten so that would give them plenty of time.

Tom and Richard went over tomorrow's arrangements. First they would take care of the undertaker, and then they would have to talk to Mike McDougal about the free drinks. Last they would have to talk to Olive about Jeb's singing request.

When Elizabeth, Hans and Bert headed for their cabin, a very heavy wet snow was coming down. The mud was very slippery, and after a few drinks, the footing was worse than usual. The three walked in single file, collars up, heads down, keeping an eye on the trail. There was a bright flash from a close bolt of lighting. They all stopped. The country side was lit up with bright tones, and then a loud crackling boom echoed through the sky. The ground shook with the rumble. They lowered their heads and hastened to their cabin.

During the night a storm brewed, the snow was about half rain, so the mud was worse than ever in the morning. The next day the digging went on. Bonanza Creek was still flowing, so they were still sluicing for gold. Soon the creek would freeze, at that time the pay dirt would have to be piled up and wait for the creek to open in the spring. It was agreed by most miners that a hard freeze would be welcomed. The sloppy mud would turn to frozen dirt; the many varieties of bugs would be gone, the work would be lessened, and there would be more time for visiting and relaxing. In the morning when Bert went outside to relieve himself in their little crude toilet, he had to pass by the pay dirt pile. Here and there in the pile he could see flashes of gold, the rain had washed some of the dirt away from the gold. He couldn't wait to get back into the cabin to show his friends the new found gold.

PILING UP PAY-DIRT IN THE WINTER

The long daylight days of the north meant more hours to work. Many men put in extremely long hours each day, searching for pay dirt, which eluded many a miner. With the winter heat, the sourdough would work better, and the cook would have to rely less on the yeast to make the bread and hot cakes. There was never any guarantee which supplies would be available throughout the winter; best to stock up early as possible.

Tom and Richard had gone to Dawson to take care of all the details for Jeb's funeral and the big celebration for him at the Golden Nugget.

The five close friends met at Elizabeth's cabin on the morning of the funeral before going to the Catholic Church. Tom and Richard were waiting outside the cabin.

As the two stood looking at each other, Tom said, "Richard, you and I don't really look like we're going to a funeral, our clothes really look terrible, but I suppose most of the people will be looking more or less like us."

By this time in late September all of the men's beards had become full, in anticipation of the oncoming cold winter. Elizabeth, Hans and Bert joined the two outside. Elizabeth had on a dark dress, with a heavy black coat, and her knee boots. Her small hat was kept on her head by a large stick pin.

She made a hand motion toward town, "Lead us on to the church, Richard."

The old priest had reserved some chairs in the front of the crude church for the five close friends of Jeb. Soon the church was packed with standing room only. Old Jeb had made many friends over the past three years while he had been in Dawson. The funeral mass lasted about forty-five minutes, then the pallbearers carried the wooden coffin down the aisle, through the front door, then onto a wagon.

It was a nice sunny day for the funeral. Soon there were a handful of men that had known Jeb, here in the north, walking behind the one horse wagon, making the slow trip to the new cemetery.

Even though this new cemetery was only two years old, there must have been more than fifty graves; all sites were marked with white wooden crosses. The priest said a few prayers, and then ended with the Our Father. Each person who passed by the grave, paused, took some dirt in his hand, and tossed it onto the top of the wooden casket.

At this time, Hans saw Olive with Mike McDougal. Since Hans was in the front of the line, and was waiting at the cemetery gate, she came right past him. She stopped and talked to him for a couple of minutes. Hans thought to himself, Olive sure has matured since she arrived in Dawson.

Soon the handful of miners were standing at the edge of the cemetery, lighting their pipes, and talking about their friend, old Jeb. Elizabeth and her four male friends decided to head down to the Golden Nugget. By the time they arrived at the door, the place was filling up. Word got around fast in Dawson, that there would be free drinks paid for by the deceased. It wasn't long before Olive had the crowd quieted down. It was amazing what a woman's voice will do to a bunch of lonesome men. If any man didn't stop talking, another man close by would give him a poke, he either shut-up or the next poke would be on his head.

It was really a sight to behold, most of these old and young miners hadn't been with a woman for many a month, some maybe a year. The ladies of the night that lived in Louse Town did a good job of taking care of many of the lonesome men, if they wanted to part with their money.

As soon as Olive finished a song, there would be a loud burst of applause.

Soon the roar of all these loud mouth men trying to out shout each other would fill this wooden frame room with a constant roar. After each song, Olive would take about a fifteen minute break. She knew she had a long day ahead of her. The whiskey flowed freely into Jeb's mourners. As the hours went by, a number of the over drinkers where helped outside to sober up. There was some pushing and shoving by the drunken miners; no one was hurt, so far.

For the past hour, Hans could see Mike McDougal, the bartender, eyeing their group. Most of the attention was given to Tom, since he was the tallest, he stood out the most. Hans didn't like the look on Big Mike's face, he also didn't like the fact that he appeared to be getting a little on the drunk side. Soon Hans saw Mike walking toward them.

Big Mike put his two large fists on the bar, "Well, how are Jeb's friends doing?"

Since Hans was the closest to him, he said, "We're having a fine time, the whiskey is good and so is Olive's singing."

"I really wasn't talking to you mister. I was talking to Jeb's two leeching buddies. At this time Hans could see trouble coming from this big blowhard.

Tom had overheard the comment. "Did I hear you say something about Jeb's two leeching buddies?"

"You heard me right, sourdough. I heard how old Jeb took you two hayseeds in, gave you a percent of his claim, and now you will own the claim after Jeb died for some reason."

Tom was getting bristled, "What the hell are you talking about? Are you saying we took advantage of our friend, and just maybe we did him in? You're as full of shit as a Christmas goose."

"Watch your talk sourdough or I'll punch you out. Another thing, Jeb promised me he would sell us his claim, now you two jackasses steal the claim out from underneath us."

By this time the crowd was getting quiet, they were hearing the talk between these two adversaries. Big Mike walked back behind the bar, but he didn't shut his mouth. Tom and the group walked over to the bar, looking into Mike's beefy face.

Tom said, "Where the hell did you get all this bullshit information? You probably tried to steal Jeb's claim, now you want some hide."

At that moment, Big Mike took a swing at Tom who could see it coming like in slow motion. He pulled back his head, and the extended right fist went past his head. That threw McDougal off balance with his weight over the bar. Tom plowed his right fist along the left side of McDougal's nose. Blood squirted from his nostril, and he fell to the floor like a large tree. The Golden Nugget became as quiet as a church. McDougal was lying on his back with crimson blood splattered on his white shirt. Hans looked around, he knew Mike McDougal had many friends standing around, most were in a daze. No one had ever thought of taking a swing at Big Mike. His friends stood off to one side, not saying anything.

Hans turned to his friends, "Let's get the hell out of here before there is more trouble, some of these drunks look mean and might want a piece of our hide."

They started walking toward the crowd. At that minute, Olive's crystal voice boomed off the wooden ceiling. Hans and his group came to the crowd, where they stopped a second. Soon the wall of men opened slowly to let them through. Elizabeth was third in line, it was apparent a woman in the group turned the men off from starting trouble. That, along with Olive's singing started bringing the men back to their previous mood.

Outside, they headed down the street. It was about three in the afternoon and the sun was below the hills.

Elizabeth was the first to speak as they walked.

"That Mike McDougal is a jackass. I couldn't believe he was accusing you two of stealing Jeb's claim, and you may not have heard the last of him. He most likely will try to get even."

Richard was walking along side of Tom. "You're one mean son of a bitch. I think you knocked him out colder than a turd. I'm going to keep on the good side of you."

They all laughed as they headed through the claims. The weather had changed since they went into the Golden Nugget; a light snow had fallen on top of the two inches they had on the ground.

CHAPTER 15

As they turned and headed toward Elizabeth's cabin, Tom and Richard turned off and headed toward theirs. When they got closer to their cabin, they could see horse tracks heading toward it.

Elizabeth commented, "Maybe the undertaker came looking for us, he's one of the few people we know who has a horse."

Soon they could see the tracks were going toward the door. As they arrived at the door, there were many horse tracks in one area, as if the horse had stood there for some time. They could see the tracks had left the cabin and headed easterly.

"I wonder who came a calling, must have seen we were gone and left." Hans said.

In the cabin, Bert lit a candle. It didn't take long to see that the room was somewhat torn up.

"Someone came in looking for something." Bert said, "Check the gold, everyone check under the bunks, see if any sacks are missing."

"Damn, some low life critter stole some of our gold," Bert said, as he was down on hands and knees looking under his bed. "I can't believe some scum head would come into our cabin and help himself to our gold. It looks like two bags are missing from here, how about you two?"

They both answered at about the same time, "Everything looks okay here."

The three were stunned; this was the last thing they ever expected. In the gold fields, the cabins were open. If a person needed a meal, they could help themselves, but no one ever had anything stolen. The three sat down at the table, both men were mad as hell.

Bert was the first to speak, "We have to go after this person who made off with our gold. I didn't bust my butt digging down that hole to give it to some good for nothing."

Hans responded, "I agree, but first we have to make a plan. We have fresh snow so we can track this person if he heads out of the area."

Elizabeth took her turn in the conversation, "I don't really think the thief headed back to Dawson. There's only one guy in Dawson who rents horses, this thief wouldn't go back there after he stole the gold. My bet is he's heading out of the area. If I were that person, I would most likely head for Skagway, then head for the states."

The men agreed with Elizabeth, but now they had to decide what to do to get their gold back.

Bert said. "I'm going out to see if this guy is leading his horse or riding."

He was back soon, "He's walking. This leads me to believe, he took a large quantity of our gold, and the guy is a big heavy person, or else he would be riding. That's good; this means he won't be moving very fast. My uncle told me one time, 'I can walk any horse into the ground; they just don't have that human desire to keep going.'"

Hans started piling some things on the table. "We'll need blankets, rubber tarp, matches, food and the Winchester, with plenty of shells. We can't let this person get away with our gold. Elizabeth, you let Tom and Richard know about our problem. If you need any help, you know you can count on them."

In about fifteen minutes they had their back packs loaded with their gear.

"Elizabeth, you come outside and watch where we head on this person's trail, so you'll know which direction we left the valley."

Bert and Hans put on their warmest clothes over their grey long johns and headed out the door.

Elizabeth stood in the doorway, "You two take care of yourselves and make sure you come back, the guy you're tracking might be a bad person."

As they rushed off, they both gave her a wave. It appeared they might have an hour of daylight left to track the gold thief.

Hans told Bert, "The one of us without the gun should watch the trail, and make sure we don't loose the tracks. The guy with the gun should keep a sharp eye ahead, to make sure this crook doesn't ambush us."

The tracks headed to the southeast; that was good. If the tracks went into Dawson they would have a hard time keeping on the horse tracks. Bonanza Creek was at the bottom of two large hills. The men kept up a strong pace. Daylight was diminishing rapidly. After an hour on the trail, it was getting dark.

Bert slid the pack from his back, "We must have made at least five miles, and we should check the wind. If the wind is in our favor, we should make a fire and get some food in our bellies. I can't remember if the moon is getting full or not. Let's eat, get a little sleep, and wait until the moon comes up. If we have some moon light, we can track the person through the night; the quicker we find the thief, the better."

Soon the two were wrapped up in their blankets with the rubber tarp over them. About eight, Hans woke up. The night was crisp, he could see his breath, it was deadly still, and there was nothing to be heard. He turned his head upward, looking for moonlight. The stars were shining bright, and as he looked at the brush next to him; no shadows. Even with the bright stars, it was very dark. He looked at their own tracks by the campsite; you could hardly make them out. Damn, we better not go stumbling around in the dark, wasting time and maybe losing the tracks.

The clear sky meant there wouldn't be any more snow tonight. Most likely the sky would be clear tomorrow. He laid his head back down on his arm and closed his eyes. It was warm in the blankets under the rubber tarp. He was warm, and he felt good; the two bodies under the tarp gave each other some heat.

About six a.m., Hans woke up, sat up, and looked around. He pulled his watch out of his pocket; ten to six. He poked Bert.

"What happened last night, why didn't you wake me up?"

"It was no use. It was as dark as the inside of a cow. I couldn't see anything three feet away, so I didn't bother to wake you up."

Hans crawled out of his wool blankets, stood up and looked around. The wind was still out of the southeast.

"What do you think Bert, should we fix some kind of a breakfast? The wind is in our favor, so the guy we're tracking won't smell the smoke."

"We have a little time before we can start tracking, so let's get our bellies full. It might be a long time before we get a chance to eat again."

Elizabeth had sent along some of the sourdough, so they had flapjacks and some bear meat. After they had finished their coffee, it was just about light; they stood up and lit their pipes. The fire was about out, now the horse tracks could be seen.

Soon everything was packed and loaded on their backs, and they were on their way. The horse tracks and walker followed an old Indian trail. After a couple of hours they saw an old prospector's cabin ahead through the spruce trees. Hans was in the lead, and he held up his hand to stop. He knelt down on one knee, Bert did the same.

In a low whisper, Hans said, "Look, there is smoke coming out of the stove pipe; maybe he's still in the cabin."

Hans made a motion to Bert to go around so he could see the back side of the cabin. "Take a look for the horse; he probably has him tied by the little clearing, along the side of the cabin."

Hans crept a little closer so he could get a good view of the front door. The sun was out bright, so the cabin was in good view. There was frost coming off the trees, filling the air with little sparkles. Hans kept his eye on the front door as Bert made his way around the back side of the cabin. He knelt down, and shook his head back and forth, indicating no sign of the horse. He sneaked up to the cabin, keeping at an angle to the only window. He crept alongside, then rose up to take a look in the window. It was dark inside; he couldn't see anybody.

Hans shrugged his shoulders. Bert motioned toward the front door. Hans had the rifle, so he went to the door, pushed up on the latch with the gun barrel, and then gave the door a push. The door creaked open. They stood waiting for something to happen; all they could hear were the Canadian Jays calling to each other. Hans stuck his hat on the tip of the barrel, stuck in slightly into the doorway; nothing happened. Soon they got up enough nerve to step in.

The cabin was about eight by ten with a small wood stove, a bed in one end, a table, and a box on the wall for a cupboard.

"Look here Bert; there are some supplies in the box. Either there are some miners working around here, or this guy had his route stocked for his get a way."

"I'll bet he had this gold stealing all planned out, he also knew he had some grass here for the horse. It's good for us. If we make it back this way, we know where we can stay in a warm cabin."

Hans said, "Let's get on the trail; we lost some time here farting around with an empty cabin."

There was about three or four inches of snow, so it was easy walking. The trail more or less followed the Yukon River. The trail was good; it had been used frequently, so there was very little brush or downed trees in the way. After about two hours, they noticed there were many tracks in one area.

"Hans, the guy mounted the horse; the big guy must be getting tired of walking."

"That's good, if he is a big man, and he has a good weight of gold, the horse will play out sooner."

When they left Dawson, they knew the Stewart River was about seventy miles from Dawson. They figured they had covered about a total of fifteen to eighteen miles, so it was still a long haul to Stewart River where they guessed the thief was heading. The trail kept to high ground, sometimes it would go around a bog, and this cost them tracking time.

If they would chance to see the trail ahead on a hill side, where it went around a black spruce bog, they would high tail it across the bog to meet up with the trail.

After a short distance Bert said, "There he is."

He was at the top of a long hill.

"We're getting close Hans, we'll catch him tomorrow, and I hope he doesn't look back."

They hurried along, wanting to get a closer look at the thief. Here they came across some more swampy part of the trail. The thief on horseback had to stay on high ground, so Bert and Hans, to save time cut through the low swamp area to gain time on the thief. The two now were trotting, wanting to get the part of hill where the thief had been spotted. A bend in the trail brought them to what they thought was the right part of the trail.

"Horseshit," Hans said, "Look here Bert, these are moose tracks over the thief's tracks. Damn, we sure got fooled there; I thought sure as hell we saw our man, I guess it was a Moose"."

Bert was looking intently at all the tracks, "The big guy is walking again, his horse must be playing out, and I bet we're making good time on this guy. He probably has no idea we are on his butt."

The trail was now passing through a large tamarack area. The two slowed down to a fast walk; there was just about total silence in this heavy timber.

"Hans did you hear that noise?"

"What was it? Sounds like a timber wolf starting its howl."

They both stopped. "There it is again, hey, now there are more joining in. Damn, there are a number howling now, must be going after something."

"Hans, do you remember the time Tom and Richard had the run-in with the timber wolves?"

He answered, "I sure do, and we don't want any part of them critters."

Hans stopped, raised his gun to his shoulder and said "Listen, there is something over in the woods, do you hear it? Maybe the thief is doubling back to ambush us."

They both spoke in a very low whisper.

"I can hear brush cracking; it's up the hill by the trail."

All of a sudden, five large timber wolves came out of the brush, and ran full speed down the trail away from the two men.

Hans lowered his gun, "Damn, I'm glad they took off the other way. They must've picked up the moose's scent."

Soon ahead of them and off to the right, brush was breaking continually, it was a hell of a racket.

"I think the wolves are closing in on the moose, I hope they don't pick up our scent."

Throughout the afternoon the men kept up their hot pursuit, they were making good time. Along toward evening, the trail came over a rock ridge. As they came over the crest; they froze in their tracks. There was the thief and his horse down the trail; he was about a half mile away and about to go over a high crest.

Bert said, "Let's hide behind these trees; he just might take a look back to see if anyone is following."

After the thief went over the crest, the two decided to wait a spell in case he waited to see if anyone was following.

After a few minutes they took off up the trail. When they came over the hill, they meandered into the woods for cover. They sneaked toward the old trail. He was gone. They moved down along the side of the trail, after another hour of tracking they could see some buildings in the distance.

Bert said, "By golly, it looks like an old mining site, see the sluice ways?

Now I can see more timbers down there, and it looks like it's been vacated some time ago. I bet this bird has another cabin down there, where he'll spend the night. He planned this little venture well; he probably has plans all the way to Whitehorse, and then he'll make his way down to Skagway and on to Seattle."

Hans checked the tube in his gun to make sure it was full of bullets. "Let's wait until it's dark. We should be able to make our way around and find his cabin, but we'll have to watch out for his damn horse."

In about an hour, they headed down the hill toward the old mining site. They knew the guy headed easterly when he hit the clearing.

Hans said, "Let's keep to the timber; we don't want this guy seeing us before we find him."

Now it was getting dark, they were still in the dark side of the moon. With the snow, they could make out the trees and brush in front of them. Still no sign of a cabin. At once, both men looked at each other; they both whispered the word 'smoke.' They could smell the smoke in the air. "It's wood smoke, he must have just started a fire, and he's getting ready to start supper."

The two kept going in the direction of the slight breeze coming from the east. All of a sudden to the right of them, they heard a low muffled whinny.

"Damn, it's the horse; he's going to give us away."

Now they saw a dim glow in the night, they could make out the shape of a window. The two moved closer, and knelt down at the edge of a clearing. Across the hundred feet clearing there was what appeared to be some kind of cabin. The lighted window was on the right side, the door was facing them.

The small log cabin was built a couple feet into the ground, to save cutting any more logs than they had to.

From the dark, came a loud shrill whinny from the horse, it started out high and went down to a very low tone.

"Shit," said Bert, "Now we're in trouble."

They hid in the trees and waited. There wasn't a sound to be heard. They could see the horse in the dim light looking at them. Then the creek of the low slung door started. The candle light made a dim beam in the cool night. Then a large, wide figure appeared in the open door light. When he stood up after the low bend, to get through the door, only the area from his chest down was silhouetted. They could see a revolver in the man's right hand. He just stood there. They couldn't see his head, so they couldn't tell where he was looking. Both men figured the light from the door must be showing them in some kind of light. The man's right hand with the revolver remained at his side. Both men had their eyes glued to his gun. The horse whinnied again, now the horse appeared to be looking at the man in the doorway.

In a loud, low voice the man said, "Who's out there? You trying to steal my horse? Come out in the open, you yellow bellied coward. I know you're out there."

Just then, the dead spruce branch Bert had his hand on snapped.

Instantly, the man in the candle light started bringing his gun up toward his waist. Bert and Hans made a movement to get behind some tree cover, in doing so they made more noise.

"I'll fix you horse thief sons a bitches."

He fired two quick shots in the men's direction. Both shots hit the tree trunk two or three feet above their heads. Just that fast the man ducked back into the cabin, and the light went out. Then came a sound of him latching or bracing the door.

"That no good son of a bitch, tried to kill us, he steals our gold and now he wants us both dead." Bert said as he rose up. "Now what the hell do we do? That really makes me mad."

Then Hans called out, "You're the asshole that stole our gold, we tracked you here from our cabin on Bonanza Creek."

From the cabin came, "Go to hell, if you want your gold, come and get it."

Hans cupped his hands to his mouth, "We're not leaving till we get our gold back."

Again from the cabin, "Go to hell you thieves."

In an instant Hans was boiling mad, he pulled up the rifle to his shoulder, and fired a shot into the door.

"You come out now or we'll do more shooting."

Bert told Hans, "We don't want to waste all our shells shooting through that door."

They waited; nothing from the cabin.

"He wants us to come to him. When we do, he'll shoot both of us."

Bert whispered, "I'm going to sneak around the back side of the cabin. That thing is so low in the ground, I can easily pack some sphagnum moss into his metal chimney, and then the smoke should drive him out."

"Good idea, I'll wait in front for him to come out."

Bert snuck around to the right; again the horse gave a low gravely whinny. He moved into the darkness of the black spruce swamp, where he gathered a bunch of moss. There was a good amount of smoke coming from the chimney. He took a large handful of the moss and stuck it into the chimney, and packed it tight. The smoke quit coming out.

He went around the other side of the small cabin, to make sure there weren't any other doors or windows. He made his way back to where Hans was standing in the trees.

He whispered, "Now all we have to do is wait for the fat ass to come out of the cabin."

After about ten minutes, they could see a little smoke drifting out the top of the door. Though it was dark, the white smoke in this crisp winter night really showed up. The two waited, there wasn't a sound. Another period of time went by, no noise or coughing from the man inside.

"Bert, are you damn sure there wasn't a door or opening on the back side of the cabin?"

"I'm damn sure. He can't get out, other than through the front door."

Now the smoke was pouring out from all the cracks.

Hans said, "He's gone. Somehow he got out. Pull the moss out of the chimney."

Bert ran over to the back side, pulled out what he could with his hands, and then took a stick to remove the rest. Both men waited, soon the smoke stopped coming out. They walked slowly toward the cabin.

Bert stood to one side and pulled open the low slung door. Nothing happened.

Hans said, "Get some of that dry moss; put it on a stick to make a torch."

Bert lit the dry moss, and stuck it into the small cabin. The big guy was flat on the floor; he was lying on his back, and had a hole in his forehead. His head was propped up against the log wall. Blood was running into his beard. His glassy eyes were staring toward the ceiling.

"Oh my God, I shot the guy right in the head," Hans cried, "I didn't think I would hit him, shooting so high. Damn, what do we do now? We'll have the Mounties on our butts."

Bert lit a match to get a better look at the dead man. "I think I've seen this guy around McDougal's place. You don't think Mike would have hired this guy to steal our gold?"

"I don't trust Mike McDougal and his buddy, Alex, any further than I can throw them. Let's pull this guy out of here; I'll light a candle to see what we're doing."

The guy weighed well over two hundred pounds; each man grabbed a leg and pulled. Within a short time they had him outside.

"We should pull him under those thick trees, that way he won't get covered with so much snow. We'll have to tell Sergeant Steel about this matter."

Hans emptied the thief's pockets, to take back to the Mounties.

He had an old billfold in his shirt pocket. There was a name inside; Jack McGraw, and he also had twenty dollars in gold coins. After the cabin was well-lighted, they saw two flour bags on the floor.

"Bert, we got our gold back. I wish he hadn't taken it; now he's dead and we might have our butts in trouble."

"Remember Hans, if he hadn't stolen our gold, he wouldn't be dead. He brought this on himself. Now we have to figure out what we're going to do next. I say we fix ourselves something to eat, get a good night's sleep, and then decide what to do tomorrow."

Both men dragged the thief outside to get him out of their sight.

The fire was stoked up. They found some bacon and beans the dead man had brought along. They ate until they were overfull, lay down on the warm bunks and fell asleep in a second.

They awoke early in the morning, and lay there thinking what their plans were for today. Hans got up first and made some coffee. Soon both men were eating some old stale bread with bacon, left over from the last night's meal.

Hans spoke first, "Here is what I thought we might do. If we turn the horse loose, over by the trail, he should head back to Dawson. You know they always go back the way they came. Then we should gather up some of the timbers around here to make a raft. We might be forty five miles or so from Dawson. With this strong current, we could be back to Dawson in two or three days."

"I guess that sounds okay to me. Let's go looking for timber and wood to make a raft. Let's not turn the horse loose until we've finished the raft."

They started looking around the old mining site for timbers. Bert, by chance, headed toward the river to see what he could find. He hadn't walked very far when he found an old boat turned upside down. He rolled the boat over to check the inside. It looked like it would float.

Bert gave a loud holler for Hans, "Come down to the river."

They dragged the boat to the water's edge, and then pushed it into the river to check for leaks.

"If it does have a few leaks, it will soak up and seal the cracks. Hell, we'll be on our way before we know it."

They walked back to the cabin, Hans untied the horse; gave it a whack on its butt and it took off down the trail. Hans thought to himself; the horse might be back to Dawson before we get there. The two carried the gold and their supplies to the boat, loaded up and shoved off. The two oars stashed under the boat would make navigating much easier.

CHAPTER 16

The clouds were low in the sky; the wind was out of the east; so it looked like a change in the weather. The temperature was around freezing; just sitting in the boat, it was hard to keep warm.

The men were hugging the south side of the river. About five miles down stream they spotted two figures standing along side of the river on a sand bar.

Hans said, "Let's head for the bar, maybe we can help the two fellows."

When they got closer, they could see they were Indians.

Bert said, "Now what the hell's going on, are we about to get ambushed by a bunch of Indians? There might be more of them back in the woods."

Hans replied, "We'd better stop and see what they want, they might be in real trouble."

As they drifted onto the sand bar Hans had the 30:30 ready to fire, in case the Indians were figuring on playing some kind of trick. Their boat came to an abrupt stop on the sand.

"We're going to Dawson City, can we help you?" Bert asked.

The Indian dressed in an assortment of white man's clothes said, "We go to Dawson to get strong drink of brown water, and we make some dollars in creeks. Our boat hit sharp stick and sink, we come to land. Now we need ride to Dawson town."

Bert told the Indians, "Get into the boat, we're going to Dawson, sit on bottom of boat."

They shoved the boat off into the swift current. They were now going down the north side of the Yukon; the current was taking them along at a very fast clip. About five miles down the river, the boat was pushed by the current toward shore. As it came around the corner, the Indian in the front made a quick motion with his arm toward shore. In the water up to its belly was a large cow moose. The Indian put his finger to his lips. There wasn't a sound as the boat drifted toward the moose.

It had its head under water pulling up roots. The boat was now going sideways. Hans was in the back; he was right in line with the moose. They were about a hundred feet out when the cow pulled its head up and looked toward them.

DOWN THE YUKON TO DAWSON CITY

Hans put the site on the right temple; a shot rumbled through the valley and on down the river. The large cow moose stood there for a second, then its back legs crumpled and she sat down on her hind end in the water. At that time it rolled over on its side. It half sank into the water, then came to the surface and stayed right where it was shot.

One of the Indians stood up and said. "Son a bitch, you good shooter, kill mama moose with one shot to head. We help you skin that son a bitch."

It wasn't long before the four men were hard at work pulling the moose up onto the shore. They cut it into quarters, and left the hide on. Half an hour later, they had the moose pretty well taken care of. All that remained on the gravel bar was the carcass. Hans motioned for the two Indians to get into the boat.

They were only about two hundred feet from shore when Bert said, "Look back there." A very large brown bear was hunched down by the moose carcass, eating up the remains. "Damn, that big guy could have jumped us when we were cutting up the moose. Let's not make any more stops."

Throughout the day, the four men rowed some, but mostly drifted down the Yukon. They were making good time. Toward dusk, they came to the area in the river which was due north of their claim.

The boat was pulled up on shore; and the meat was piled on boards on the gravel. The Indians wanted to help the men carry the meat to their claim. Hans told them, "No thanks, you take your gold to town, get money to eat and drink". Hans didn't want the two Indians to know where their cabin was located, he figured when they ran out of money, they would be knocking on their door.

Hans told the two Indians, "If you want to use this boat to get back across the river, go ahead."

The men loaded the gold into their back packs, carried their gear, along with some of the moose meat and headed for the cabin. When they came over the little knoll, they could see smoke coming from the chimney.

As they came around the end of the cabin, Bert gave a little shout, "Elizabeth, we made it back."

Soon the door opened, and Elizabeth came out. She had a grin on her face from ear to ear, "Damn, I'm glad to see you two."

She rushed up and gave Bert, who was in the lead, a big hug, and then she went to Hans, threw her arms around him, and hugged him tight.

"I was getting worried about you two; I guess I was thinking the worst. Last night I had a dream that you both got shot by a bunch of renegades."

Bert spoke up, "We have more meat down at the boat; we'll go get the remainder. Then we'll have plenty of time to sit and tell you the whole story."

They unloaded the meat into the back tent and headed to the boat for more. Within an hour, it was all in camp. They were very tired and ready to just sit down and relax.

The three of them were at the table, Elizabeth had a drink of brandy in her tin cup, she looked up at Hans, "Well boys, I sure would like to hear all about your trip during the last few days."

Hans pulled his pipe out of his shirt pocket, loaded it full, and after a few puffs, started the story.

When he got to the part about the shooting, Elizabeth became excited, "Did you try to kill that thief, or was it a wild shot?"

"Believe me, all I wanted to do was scare the guy, I didn't want to kill him."

"Are you going to tell Sergeant Steel about the accident?"

"I intend to go there the first thing in the morning, and give him all the details."

"Hans, the Mounties might put you in jail, you know it may not be called self defense."

All this time Bert sat and listened to the two talking. "Did anything new happen in Dawson or in the gold fields?"

"Up toward Grand Forks, a couple more miners died, I guess from poor health. Hell, I don't know, they're always dying along these creeks. This is not a country for people to grow old in. I heard there have been 45 who died so far this year."

Elizabeth was on her second inch of brandy, she was happy her men were home from their trip. She had become lonesome for the two. She didn't really know it before, but she had become very fond of these men.

In the dimly lit log cabin, the candle gave all three a glow on their faces. Though the cabin was small and crude, it was home for the partners.

They enjoyed the comfort and warmth that it provided.

"How about some nice moose steaks for supper? I made some bread while you were gone. I figured you boys would be hungry when you returned. I still have some dried potatoes; by golly, we'll have a coming home party."

It was good times for all, things were going their way and they enjoyed it.

"Have you heard anything from that McDougal guy, from the Golden Nugget?"

"No, I haven't heard a thing, course I haven't been to Dawson since you two left. One day I did see Olive walking in the direction of Tom and Richard's cabin, but I haven't talked to them since the day you left. I told them what happened, but I guess they're too busy mining."

This seemed to get Hans' attention. "So you think Olive and Tom are seeing each other? I knew as soon as she arrived here in the north, with all these men, I would soon loose her. Though I guess I can't really blame her. I guess I neglected her for too long, and maybe took her for granted."

The others didn't really want to talk about Hans' love life, so the subject was changed back to the chase of the crook. Soon Elizabeth had the large moose steaks frying on the stove; she always saved the bacon fat to use for cooking other meats.

"Damn, that moose smells great. I guess we haven't had a decent meal for better part of a week." Bert commented, "I think me and my bunk are going to get along very good tonight. The more I live in this country, the more I appreciate getting into a nice warm bed."

Hans went out side. While standing in the cool night he looked up toward the moon where he could see a circle shining around it. He thought to himself, snow is coming; we should get things in order around camp. After Hans closed the cabin door, he looked over toward the table. Elizabeth was looking very intently at Bert. He thought, I brought my girl friend, Olive up north and I think I'm loosing her. Now I've found someone in Elizabeth who could take her place and it looks like she has more affection for my partner, than for me.

He sat back down at the table, "I think I'll have another shot of brandy, it's been a long time and I need to warm my guts."

Soon Elizabeth placed the food on the table; the candle was in the center; the shadows jumped around the ceiling and walls. It was quiet; all that could be heard was the sound of metal knives on the metal plates, the occasional burp from the men, and the comments about the tender meat. In a half hour the meal was finished; there wasn't much said. Elizabeth cleaned the pan and dishes in the snow and they all crawled into bed. As Hans pulled the blankets up to his head, he thought to himself, a warm bed in the winter is the best place in the Yukon.

CHAPTER 17

Winter was setting in since Bert and Hans tracked down the gold thief. Hans told the Mounties the entire story. Sergeant Steel told him they would make a trip with the dog sled to pick up the unlucky Jack McGraw, the poor fellow Hans shot in the head.

The winter days were getting shorter and colder. This was the time of the year that was hard on the miners; they would get up in the dark and quit work in the dark. It was hard on the candle supply, and when winter came, the prices for them went up.

The partners hauled many pounds of gold to the bank and changed the gold into cash. There was always a good chance that the cabin would catch fire and burn up totally. They knew the gold would still be there, but now, since one thief had robbed them, they didn't want to take a chance. The bank book and money was kept in a can buried in the dirt floor.

In the gold fields, Wednesdays and Fridays were visiting nights. The miners would take turns going from cabin to cabin. In the long winter nights they had to have some entertainment. Most of the time they played cards and rummy was the game, either five card or seven card.

This part of the Yukon was not big snow country. They did get the occasional blizzard, but most of the time it was light snowfall. It was known for its miserable cold weather. Forty below zero was very common, and with most of the hills cleared of timber, the wind was always blowing.

They were getting into November. The hole under the adjacent room next to the cabin was busy six days a week. Underground, the two men had made many drifts in all directions, trying to follow the old creek bed. The production was good. All of the good looking pay dirt was piled outside, and this would be sluiced in the spring. Much of the excitement had worn off of the gold prospecting. Even with all the money from the gold, there just wasn't much these sourdoughs could buy. There were hardly any supplies in Dawson. It was cruel country and winter would last seven months. There probably wouldn't be a boat up the river until June.

Everybody in the gold field became protective and greedy when the snow started falling. There was uncertainty in the minds of the miners.

PANNING GOLD IN THE CABIN

To take away some of the drudgery from being in the small cabin without much to do on these long winter nights, Bert and Hans would take turns panning gold from the box they used to haul the gold up from the hole. It was always exciting to swish the water around the pan looking for the sparkling gold. About twice a week the boys took turns panning for gold. They had to keep a hole open in the creek or melt snow for the water to use in the pan.

Having a woman in the little cabin made things much easier. When Bert and Hans were by themselves, irritation between the two became much easier.

It was Friday night and the partners had been invited to Tom and Richard's cabin for a drink and some cards. On these weekly visits, the host would, as a rule, make some kind of bread rolls. If they were sweet, it was a night for celebration.

They walked through a roaring blizzard to get to Tom's cabin. It was a miserable night. All three had flour sacks wrapped around their faces to keep off the stinging cold. On this kind of night, frostbite was upon you before you knew it. When the face became numb, it was too late.

Before they arrived at the door, Bert hollered, "Open the door, we're coming in."

When they entered the cabin, the warm air felt great, though it did drive the cold into their coats and their bodies. Even though they would see each other about every week, they still hugged and shook hands. Friendship in the gold fields ran deep; they all had to depend on each other.

To Hans's surprise, Olive was at Tom and Richard's cabin. Hans threw his coat and hat on a bunk and walked over to Olive.

"Gee, it's good to see you again, Olive. You look great, I think you're putting on a little weight, not that that's anything bad. It makes you look better."

Hans got into a situation about Olive's weight, and he was having a hard time retreating.

"Well, thank you Hans, I think now that I only work three nights a week, I'm getting more rest and must be eating better. I've been eating Richard's baking and I think it shows on me."

This drew a laugh from the group. The wood stove was putting out some good heat; no one had to hug the stove; the entire cabin was warm.

When they stood up, they could really feel the heat near the ceiling. There were two candles burning in the cabin. Every so often a draft from somewhere would make the flames bend back and forth. Hans was curious about what was going on between Tom and McDougal, the owner of the Golden Nugget.

"Say Tom, have you been in the Golden Nugget since you poked him?"

"Yea, I've been in there a few times. Old Mike and I kind of keep our distance. He's mad as hell since Olive came out here to stay. She had a big fight with the woman she was sharing the cabin with, so we invited her to stay at our cabin".

"I would have thought with so many people pulling out of Dawson City this fall, there would be plenty of empty cabins," Hans replied.

Olive was quick to respond, "Many of the miners moved to town when winter started setting in. Either they don't give a damn about their claim or they have some men working on percentages."

Tom had a deck of cards in his hands he was thumbing, "Anyone want to play some rummy?"

Elizabeth was just taking a sip of brandy from her tin cup, "I think we should sit around here tonight and talk; it's a good time to catch up on the news in the gold fields and old Dawson City."

The cabin was small, the ceiling was low, and the two candles didn't give off very much light. The smoke from the pipes swirled from the candle heat to the stove heat. It seemed the smoke was always going somewhere. All the gossip and rumors were covered during the evening. The shootings in Dawson never had been a problem, but in the gold fields, tempers ran high, when things were going bad in some camps. Partnerships had many frictions, mostly about who was not doing his share of work in the mine and in the cabin.

Hans started telling their friends about the gold thief and all the details leading up the shooting.

Richard said in a loud voice, "You shot the guy right in the forehead, deader than a doornail?"

"Listen Richard, it was an accident, I was just trying to scare the S.O.B." He went on and told the rest of the story.

"By the way, on the way back down the river we shot a cow moose. You guys come over and by we'll give you a bunch of meat."

"Yahoo" yelled Richard, "Fresh meat again."

Around eight p.m. Richard brought out a pan of sweet rolls he had in their little oven. He had even made some frosting from sugar and condensed milk. He placed the pan in the center of the table. The group stared at the pan full of hot sweet rolls.

"Richard, you must be the best baker in the gold fields," Elizabeth commented as she picked up a knife on the table, and started cutting the rolls apart.

After they were cut, she held the pan in front of each person, and each pulled out a hot roll. Tom brought the coffee pot off the stove, and offered each person some in their cup.

There wasn't much said for a few minutes, this was a real treat in the primitive cabin in the middle of the wilderness. There were enough rolls, so each person had two. Each wanted to savor this treat, so the rolls were eaten very slowly. After they were gone, it was coffee sipping time.

Bert was the first to speak, "Richard, I think you're wasting your time here in the gold mines, I think you could have made just as much with a bakery in Dawson City."

Then the praise for Richard's baking came on strong.

"The next time we have you folks over, I'll bake some pies; that is if we can still find some dried fruit."

Hans rose from his chair, "This was a great evening, I really enjoyed being with all you people, you can't beat having friends to talk to on a cold winter evening. Now I think we should head for our camp. I suppose our fire is getting a little low. So thanks for everything Tom, Richard and Olive."

Bert and Elizabeth said their thanks. They put on their heavy woolen coats, wrapped their scarves around their heads and headed home. The cold blast of air after the warm cabin was miserable. With their heads down, Hans led the way. The strong wind was blowing out of the north; the snow on the exposed flesh stung the skin. The cold made their noses run almost constantly. For the men it froze on their beards, but for Elizabeth, it made her face even colder. She held her scarf against her nose to keep it warm.

It only took about ten minutes to arrive at their cabin. They rushed in and walked to the stove. The fire could be seen through the cracks in the stove. They removed their mittens to warm their hands. People in the Yukon always had this ritual, even if their hands weren't cold. They would either put their hands to the stove, or back their butts to it to feel the heat. This has been going on since man first built a wood fire.

The stove was stoked for the night; each partner went outside to do their duty before bed, hoping they could all last until morning. Elizabeth put on her long cotton night gown, crawled into her primitive bed with its moss mattress. As she snuggled on her side, she thought to herself, this is nice. I'm in a warm cabin and this warm bed is best of all. She pulled her blanket up over her head, keeping her nose in the open so she could breath. She closed her eyes. Now she could think about all the things she would like to have someday, when she returned to the United States. She had her socks on, but her feet were a little cold. She rubbed them together, to warm the toes; get them warm, and all would be okay.

Even though Hans and Elizabeth were fifteen feet apart, they were having many of the same thoughts. Hans, like most men in the Klondike, enjoyed his warm bed. It was the one part of the north woods, where he felt secure and comfortable. Hans' thoughts went to Olive, as they had over the past summer and fall. She came north to be with him, now she was living with one of his best friends. He didn't know if he should be upset with his friends, or upset with his past girl friend. He lay there in the comfort of his warm bed, thinking about what had happened during the last year. He thought to himself, I should be grateful. I came north with really no chance of becoming successful in this crazy gold venture. I've been in the Yukon about five months, and things have really been going good for me. I guess the only bad thing was losing Olive. Maybe if I would have been more aggressive when she first came north, she might still be my girl friend. Men can sure do some stupid things. I guess I don't want to keep looking back and see the mistakes I've made. When he lay in his bed, his mind was always going like a wild horse in a pasture. Maybe I should take advantage of what I have now, and forget about the past.

Bert and I own half of this claim, thanks to the kindness of Elizabeth.

He started thinking about her. She is truly a fine woman, good looking, very hard working, and a true friend. Maybe the good Lord has pointed my nose toward Elizabeth, and I don't know it. He lay there with her face very clearly in his mind. Maybe someday she will take a liking to me and I'll have found a woman I can love here in the north.

Soon he drifted off to sleep.

It was the middle of November and one day lead into the next. Each day was the same as the other, the only difference being the length of the day light. Now there were only a few hours of daylight each day.

Bert still wanted to work in the hole, Hans offered to change with him, but he always liked to be the one finding the nuggets among the black dirt.

One day turned into the next; digging for gold now became boring. Months ago, it was exciting. Now it was another just another day's work, the same food each day, and living in a small cabin with two other people became a test. This was a real test of friendship or companionship.

It was now the latter part of December and they were heading toward a new year. The pile of pay dirt outside the digging tent was growing fast, it was money in the bank, but they couldn't spend it. Bert had been working in the hole for months, and he had come up with an irritating cough, and it was telling on his partners. Most nights were spent playing cards, the weather outside was brutal. At 60 below zero, no one wanted to go visiting their neighbors. The three sat around the table in the dimly lit log cabin, playing seven card rummy. The cards were dealt, and then it was the wait for the first person to get their cards in order and make their play. Sometimes it would take forever for the first person to play. Whether it was the long hard winter or the fact that Bert had spent too many days down in the damp hole, he didn't seem to be in a very good mood most days.

"Bert, are you awake, or are you asleep?"

This would bring on an unfriendly look from Bert.

"Now do I look like I'm sleeping? Come on, Hans; don't talk to me like a jackass."

In turn, Elizabeth would interject, "Now boys, it's just a game of cards, no use getting upset."

It was bad when one person held cards for a long time, then laid them all down at one time. Elizabeth didn't seem to take this game too seriously, but when this happened to Hans or Bert, their faces became flush, and they were ready for some harsh words.

"Now, why the hell do you hold all those cards, and then lay them all down at one time? You should lay them down when you have a run or three of a kind."

When Bert made this comment, he seemed to really be upset with Hans.

"These are my cards, if I want to hold them until I can lay them all down; it's my business. Where did you learn to play this game?"

Elizabeth always jumped in and smoothed the rough waters between them. "Boys, it's only a card game, we're not playing for gold."

The days were dwindling by, each day was the same as the last, and it was hard to keep working hard every day when not seeing any end to the drudgery. Bert's condition wasn't getting any better. He had a bad cough, he looked haggard, and he spent many hours in his bed.

The daylight was almost gone, the nights were boring and everyone was getting on each others nerves. Bert could no longer work in the hole. So there was a transition in the camp. Hans had to go into the hole. He didn't really mind this job. The temperature was always around fifty degrees although it was damp, not a lot of light and you were always working in cramped positions. As the winter dragged on, Bert's illness seemed be getting serious. Most of the time he lay in bed, his appetite went down to almost nothing. Elizabeth spent most of her time taking care of him. The doctor came to their camp one night. After the check up, he told Elizabeth and Hans that Bert just has a bad cold.

CHAPTER 18

After a few days, Hans awoke one morning and the cabin was quite cold. Before Bert became sick, they used to take turns getting up in the morning to stoke up the fire. He crawled out of his bunk, fed the fire box; and with an open draft, the stove started heating up right away. He put the water on the stove for coffee.

"How do you feel this morning, Bert?"

He seemed to be sound asleep. Hans made up the coffee, poured a cup and sat down at the table. With one candle burning, the cabin was very dreary. As he sat at the table, he looked around at the walls. Every place he looked there was something hanging, if it wasn't pans, it was clothes or boots. It really looked like a rat's nest. He thought to himself, this is my last winter in this God forsaken country. I'm not going to spend another winter living like a rat in a hole. The gold be damned, there is more to this life than making money.

He poured a cup of coffee for Bert, and pulled a chair over to his bunk. "Here Bert, a little hot coffee will make you feel better, warm the cockles of your heart."

He appeared to be having a good sleep.

Hans put his hand on Bert's arm lying beside his head uncovered. "You must be really cold; your arm sure is cold."

He raised his arm, it was stiff. Quickly Hans felt for the big vein on Bert's neck; he knew then. Bert was dead. Damn, his best friend died during the night. Hans sat beside his friend, staring at his face, it was peaceful. He thought Bert had found a way to beat this Yukon winter. No more frozen fingers and toes, if everything went according to plan, he would now be in Paradise.

Hans walked over to Elizabeth's bunk, he knelt down beside her, "Elizabeth....Elizabeth, wake up."

Soon her large eyes opened slowly; it took her a second to focus on Hans. He put his hand on hers. "Elizabeth...I have something I hate to tell you. Our friend died during the night."

She sat up in her bunk, eyes wide open now, "Oh my God, you mean Bert is dead?"

Hans put his arms around her, held her tight. As they embraced, they both started to cry, they now needed each other more than ever.

For a few minutes they clung to each other, Elizabeth looked Hans straight in his eyes, "Dammit, I thought Bert was a little sick. Maybe I could have done more for him, I should have taken better care of him."

"Elizabeth, don't make it hard on yourself, we both loved the guy, we don't want to blame ourselves for his passing."

Hans went back to the table while Elizabeth dressed herself.

"I think I should go tell our friends about Bert, they would want to know."

"Don't be long."

He bundled up in his warm clothes, pushed the door open, and headed for Tom's cabin. He could see smoke coming from their chimney, so he knew they were up and about. He knocked a couple of times on the door.

"Come on in."

Hans walked over to the table, sat down, and pulled off his cap and scarf.

"I've got bad news."

"What the hell happened?" Tom asked.

"Bert died during the night"

"I thought he was just a little under the weather," commented Richard.

"He hasn't been feeling good for the past month or so, we thought he had a cold. That's what the doc said not long before he died."

Olive walked up to the table; put her arm on Hans' shoulder.

"It's a shame. You two were very good friends. I'm sure it's hard to loose a friend like Bert." She gave him a kiss on the cheek.

For a while it was quiet in the cabin, and then Richard spoke up. "Do you know anything about Bert's relatives?"

Hans looked at the group, "I really don't know much about that; in fact he never talked about his folks or anyone else. He came north from Idaho, worked on a ranch out in north central. I guess he never told me much. Bert was really a hell of a nice guy, he always pulled his share of the load, and he was a damn good partner."

Olive asked, "What do you intend to do with Bert's share of the gold?"

"I don't know what to do. I'm not sure what town he came from, he just never wanted to talk about his past. Maybe I can figure out something in the future. Now I have to get back to the cabin, Elizabeth told me, don't be long."

"Damn, it doesn't seem possible old Bert is gone, he was really quite a guy. We had some great times on the Chilkoot Trail. I'm goanna miss that guy." Tom said as he sat at the table with his head in his hands.

As Hans left the cabin he said" I'll keep you posted on the details."

Elizabeth and Hans also sat at their table; nothing was said for some time.

HANS AND ELIZABETH TAKE BERT TO TOWN

Hans spoke, "I think I'll load Bert on the sled and take him to town."

Elizabeth answered, "Good, I'll go with you, we should take care of him as soon as possible."

They loaded Bert on the sled, wrapped him up real good. There was a light snow coming down, it was sort of twilight, they could just make out the landmarks in the heavy overcast. The wind was bitter, the snow burned their faces. It was hard to walk with your face pointed toward the ground. The sled pulled easily on the hard packed snow.

They arrived at the undertaker's cabin. They knocked at the door; the tall, slender fellow came out. "You got another body for me?"

Hans could see the skinny fart was about half drunk.

"Yes sir, our friend died last night, we want you to take care of him."

"So you want me to take care of him? Now you know, there is no way in hell I can put your friend in the ground. It would take me a month to get a hole just deep enough to cover him. I'll tell you what I've told the others, I'll put him in the shed in the back with all the others. Come spring when the ground ain't so damn hard, I'll bury him."

"We owe you for the funeral?"

The undertaker took another drink from his bottle, "Ah that will be one hundred dollars for the wood casket and funeral, and I'll have to have another fifty dollars to store your friend until spring."

Hans paid him in full, and then said. "Would you give me a piece of paper, showing this bill has been paid in full?"

The undertaker cocked his head, looked up, "You don't trust me do you? You're one of those big time miners with all the damn money, and you don't trust anyone."

Hans replied, "Mister, I'm in no mood for pissing around with you, I just lost a good friend, and I don't want any shit out of you."

He got his receipt and they left without any more conversation. They walked toward town.

Elizabeth tugged on Hans' arm, "Let's stop and have a drink to our good friend Bert."

He nodded his head, and they walked toward the Golden Nugget. It felt good to get into the bar. It seemed like they always kept the bars warm, must have figured the men would drink more. There were about eight people standing at the bar, they must have been the everyday drunks. They either moved to town for the winter or were on their three day drunks. Elizabeth and Hans were at the end of the bar, talking quietly to each other. From out of no where Olive walked over to them.

"Olive, what are you doing here at this hour?"

"Mike wants me to come in one afternoon a week, he's trying to get more whiskey money out of the sourdoughs."

They talked for a while, then Mike came into the room from the back; he walked over to the three.

"Well if it ain't big Tom's buddy. Are you going to hit me when I'm not looking, like your friend?"

"Listen Mike, I have no quarrel with you, we just stopped in for a drink, and we don't want any trouble."

"Are you trying to weasel Mrs. Larson's claim from her, like your friend Tom did to old Jeb?"

Hans stood there staring at his drink; he certainly didn't need abuse at this time.

Then Elizabeth spoke up, "Mike, I think it's about time you mind your own business. Hans and I are partners in my claim, and as far as that goes, it's none of your damn business."

Hans had about all he could do to contain himself. It was bad enough that Mike was hacking about Tom, now he's getting Elizabeth involved. Hans took a drink of his whiskey, with his large fist around the small glass.

"Well, it sounds like you're one big happy family out there in the sticks."

Olive didn't like this kind of talk either. She said, "Mike, you shouldn't talk that way, you don't know what you're talking about."

"You keep out of this, don't forget who you're working for, maybe you should be living out there with these leeches."

"Maybe I'm already living out there, what do you think about that? In fact, I am living out there with Tom, and I don't want to work for you any longer. I quit."

Hans thought to himself, by golly, Olive does have some spunk, to tell Mike McDougal where to go.

"You listen to me Olive; you can't quit the Golden Nugget. When I hired you I told you it would be through the winter."

"That was your idea. I never said I was going to stay through the winter. You might be able to run some of this town, but you don't run me."

By now Big Mike was mad as hell; he took a large drink of whiskey, and slammed the glass down on the wooden counter.

"Olive, if you don't come to work when you're supposed to, I'll come and get you. No one treats Mike McDougal like that. If you think that coward that hit me can get away with this, you're crazy."

Hans thought to himself, I can't take much more of this shit from McDougal. Just then Big Mike, in a coward's way, threw a drink into Olive's face. In a spilt second, Hans slammed his big fist into McDougal's nose. When the large fist hit his nose, something went crack, blood spurted from Mike's nose and he fell into the wall behind the bar. Hans rushed behind the bar, just as Mike was on one knee. Hans brought his fist up along the other side of Big Mike's jaw. It was a brutal hit, Mike rolled to his right, slid under the bar, banged his head on the beer barrel.

Big Mike was out cold. Hans stood there waiting for him to get up. He laid there, blood oozing from his nose. Hans walked around to the other side of the bar; told the ladies, "It's time to leave."

He stopped after a few steps and said. "If any of you jaybirds thought I did wrong to Mike McDougal, and want a piece of me, step right up, I'm ready and willing."

It appeared Hans had made his point. Not one of the bar flies made any motion to come forward. It appeared Mike didn't have any loyal friends. Hans still had his fist clenched when he walked out the door.

As the three walked through the winter night, nothing was said. The snow creaked under foot, the wind was now at their backs, they moved along in single file. They came to Hans' cabin.

"Come in a minute before we go to Tom's. I want to put some wood in the stove."

Soon they arrived at Tom's cabin. Both Tom and Richard were having some beans and bacon.

Tom asked, "How come you're home, Olive?"

"I quit working for McDougal; we had some words at the bar. He was giving my friends a hard time, so I told Mike I quit. Then when I was standing there, the big ox threw a drink in my face."

Tom came off his chair like a shot, "What, he threw a drink in your face? I'll kill that son a bitch."

Elizabeth, said, "Hold it Tom, your friend here, came close to killing him. When we left, he was lying in a pool of blood under the bar."

"He really made me mad," Hans said, as he raised his fist above his head. "I was hoping the jackass would get up off the floor so I could punch him again."

"He's got a real bad hang up about our two camps," commented Elizabeth. "In fact, I don't think we have heard the last from Mike McDougal. He thinks he's some kind of big shot in Yukon. This winter he bought up many of the claims. I think he thought he would get Jeb's claim and he had his eye on my claim."

Quiet Richard raised his arm for attention, "I think we had better be on the watch for that McDougal guy; sure as hell, he's going to send some of his paid stooges out here to give us a hard time. He might even have killing on his mind. We should keep our 30:30's close at hand. I think he'll be back one of these days giving us a lot of trouble. I don't know why this guy has to act this way, he's going to cause us a lot of trouble in the future."

Hans picked up his coat, turned to the group and said, "I think we are dealing with a guy who has a loose screw in his head, so we better all be careful. I think Elizabeth and I'll head for our cabin. See you later on."

Hans and Elizabeth bucked the wind back to their cabin. When they entered, it was warm, it felt good.

Elizabeth asked, "How about some coffee?"

"Sounds good to me, maybe it will settle me down somewhat. This has been some kind of a crazy day."

They sat down at the dimly lit table; the stove was heating up with the familiar twining of the metal.

"Ah, this feels good, nothing like a warm cabin, a hot cup of coffee, just sitting here taking it easy."

"Hans, you have the right idea. I would like to talk about some things. Over the past few months, I became very fond of Bert. He was a kind and gentle man. He made me feel good when we talked; he really treated me like a lady. I'm not saying I was in love with him, but I was very fond of him."

"Elizabeth, over the past few weeks, I could see that you and Bert had something in common, or you had feelings for each other. I want to say something to you. Even though I was supposed to be close to Olive, I have more affection for you than I have toward her."

"Hans, I'm really surprised to hear this. I know you are a strong affectionate person, but I didn't really know you had any feelings toward me."

Everything now seemed so different for the two people living together. Before there was always another person to be considered, now it was just up to the two of them. Hans went over to bank the fire for the night; he said he was going to bed.

As he was getting ready for bed, Elizabeth said, "Good night Hans."

He answered. "Good night Elizabeth."

In the following days, the work schedule took on a different format. Hans was working in the hole and Elizabeth was working the crank on the windlass. One day turned into another. They had plenty of moose meat left from the fall; it was kept in the room where they had the windlass for the hole. Many of the cold Yukon evenings were spent playing cards at the dimly lit table.

As time went on they became closer. They were now the only team working on this mine and Elizabeth told Hans whatever they dug out of the ground would be half his. Hans always had a close place in his heart for Elizabeth, but as time went on he knew he was falling in love with her. Even though the wood heater kept the cabin fairly warm, it was as a rule, feast or famine, the cabin was either very warm or by morning very cold.

One night as they were sitting playing cards, Elizabeth surprised Hans by saying, "We should move our beds next to each other. That way we could keep each other warm. Two warm bodies next to each other would bring a lot of comfort during the night."

He was elated at her suggestion; he had never been in the same bed with a woman. That night as time drifted on and it was getting toward bedtime, Hans was very excited at the prospect of being able to be in the same bed with Elizabeth. She was truly a very pretty woman, and he had admired her for many months. Even though they were about to sleep in the same bed, every thing was still very proper. Elizabeth had on her full length nightgown and Hans had on his perpetual long johns.

The first part of the night, they were pretty much on their own side of the bed. As the cabin started cooling toward morning, they came closer together. By morning, Elizabeth was right next to Hans, to soak up the heat. When they both awoke in the morning they liked the feeling of having someone close by for companionship and warmth. As Hans lay there in his warm bunk, he really felt elated; he had never had this feeling before in his life. Maybe it was the time when he should have a woman at his side. He felt overjoyed with the new situation with Elizabeth, for sure this was a new day in his life.

"Hans, I'm glad we became partners, I don't know what I would have done if you and Bert hadn't been close by. I certainly couldn't have worked this claim by myself. I guess I could have hired some men to help me, but then they might have stolen me blind."

"I hope our friendship gets closer as time goes on, you're a very pretty woman."

She gave him a big hug.

After that night, Hans had a new outlook on his life and his future. Today was Sunday, so no work. Thank God for the Mounties, otherwise everybody would be working seven days a week.

After breakfast and clean up, Elizabeth told him, "I think today would be a good day to put the sourdough to work. I might as well make a week's worth of bread."

"Well, if you're going to be tied up baking for a while, I think I'll walk over to Tom's camp, and see what's going on."

It was a cool morning full of sunshine, there wasn't a trace of wind, there didn't seem to be much activity on the claims. The only thing moving about were the Canadian Jays, the miners referred to them as "camp robbers". If you left any food around, they were bound to pick it up. Hans had the birds eat right out of his hands as they hovered in flight.

As he walked along, he felt good, but it was sad to think that since Bert passed away, his life had improved immensely. He felt guilty about this. He thought about the saying 'Sometimes good things can come about from bad things.' He thought to himself, if Bert had lived, would he have had a chance to get this close to Elizabeth?

CHAPTER 19

As he walked through the snow his boots made a high pitch squeaking sound, the old timers said it had to be very cold for this to happen. As he turned the corner to head for Tom's cabin door, he saw three men coming over a far hill. The only thing he really took notice of was that one man was much larger than the other two.

He knocked, and hollered, "It's me, Hans"

A voice from inside, "Come on in."

Tom motioned for him to sit down at the table. They only had three chairs so Richard was sitting on his bunk.

Tom said, "Got your cup along for some coffee?"

Hans pulled his cup from his pocket, and set it on the table.

"Watch out, the coffee is hot as hell."

Just then they could hear footsteps squeaking in the snow.

Hans said, "I bet that's the men I saw coming over the hill."

There was a knock on the door, then, "We would like to come in and talk some business."

Through the door, the heavy voice couldn't be distinguished.

Tom said, "Who wants to talk some business?"

"This is Mike McDougal; I have something I want to show you.

Tom replied "Just a minute."

Tom whispered to Richard, "Take the 30:30 and get back in that dark corner. I don't trust this son a bitch. Come on in, the door is unlatched."

Olive was sitting on her bunk, Tom and Hans were standing by the table. McDougal and two of his stooges came through the door.

"Well, look what we have here, the two cowards that hit a man when he isn't looking."

Tom said, "McDougal, we don't want any of your shit, if you have something to say, say it or get the hell out."

Hans could see McDougal had a revolver strapped to his waist. With his coat jacket hung loosely over the stock, it was easy to see.

"You and your buddy, think you're so damn smart, but maybe you're not as smart as you think."

Tom, thought to himself, he thinks Hans is my buddy, he doesn't know Richard is my partner.

Again McDougal continued, "You see, you smart fellows, you didn't know Jeb signed over this mine to me in 1897. He was a little drunk, and was out of money, so I made him a deal he couldn't pass up. I gave him two thousand dollars and as of January 1, 1898, this mine is Mike McDougal's. "

Tom's face became very flush, for a second he didn't know what to say.

"You expect me to believe that bullshit? If Jeb had made a deal with you, he would have told us. Why would I ever believe you?"

McDougal pulled a paper from his pocket. "Take a look at this deed, it's all legal. You can see Jeb's signature at the bottom and he put the date in himself."

Tom said, "Let me see the so-called deed."

McDougal handed over the deed. "We "We made two of them so don't get any fancy ideas."

Tom sat down at the table, so he could make better use of the candle. As he read through the deed, it looked just as McDougal said. Damn, how could Jeb had done this to us? He looked at the bottom of the deed, where Jeb had signed and dated it.

"McDougal, this deed is pure bullshit, it's a fake and you're a crook."

"What the hell do you mean this deed is a fake? You can see it's all legal."

Tom held the deed toward McDougal, "You screwed up big shot, and I can prove it."

Now Big Mike McDougal was getting flushed in the face. "You show me where this deed is a fake."

Tom put the deed down on the table, directly in the candlelight.

"First of all, Jeb had very good hand writing, you probably didn't know Jeb came from Austria. In those days, they were taught to practice good penmanship. This signature looks like he made it riding on a horse but where you really screwed up is on the date."

"What's wrong with the date, big shot?"

"Lean over here and I'll show you, you see that 7, on the year 1897?"

"Ya I see it, what's wrong with it, it's a 7 isn't it?"

"Ya, it is a 7, but it's an American 7, the Austrians made a horizontal line on the top side of the stem, like this -7-."

BIG MIKE ACCUSES TOM

McDougal reached for his pistol, "If you bastards think you're going to cheat me out of my gold mine, you're full of shit."

Just then there was a tremendous explosion in the cabin. The dust settled from the ceiling; the burst of energy from the muzzle almost blew out the candle. Tom fell backwards. In an instant, Richard was sure Tom was dead. He pulled up the rifle to his waist and fired at McDougal. Another loud explosion followed. Olive put her hands over her ears. Big Mike McDougal sank to the ground like his legs went dead.

Richard came out of the dark, "You two yahoos, don't get any wise ideas, the first guy that moves his hands is going to get a bullet in his gut."

Tom fell to the floor of the cabin, Olive rushed to his side. Hans leaned over and put his hand under Tom's head. Then he could see blood on Tom's arm above the elbow. Hans ripped open his sleeve. The bullet had hit the outside of his arm, going through part of his muscle.

Tom said, "Damn that hurts like hell, where is McDougal?"

Hans said, "He's on the floor, Richard shot him, when he shot you."

One of the two men that came with McDougal spoke up for the first time. "You birds are in trouble now, I think you killed McDougal, you'll hang for this murder."

Hans walked over to where McDougal was lying in a cramped position on the floor. His eyes were rolled back.

Hans said to himself; damn, he does look like he's dead. He felt his pulse on his neck; nothing.

"I think he is dead, you two check to see if you can feel a pulse."

The two men knelt down alongside the body. After a couple of minutes, they stood up. "He's dead all right, I know some boys who are in big trouble."

Hans took a step toward them. "You're talking damn big with a gun pointed at you. Maybe we should just kill you two and stick you down the mine hole."

"Hey mister, we didn't do anything to you, we were just keeping McDougal company."

"Tell you what boys," said Hans, picking up the deed on the table. "I'm going to write down here what happened. McDougal shot first and the other man shot in self defense, and you two birds are going to sign the paper. Any questions? "

The two men leaned over the table, with hands shaking, and signed their crudely written names, under Hans' writing.

"And you date it too. Now I want you to go into Dawson City and find Sergeant Steel. Tell him the whole story, and don't leave anything out. You either tell him how to get out here or bring him out. Don't forget Dawson is a small place, you pull any bullshit on us, we'll find you."

They left without saying a word. By this time Olive had a cloth wrapped around Tom's arm.

He said, "Where is the whiskey? I need a shot bad, maybe that will kill the pain." When he sat down at the table, he looked like he had been through the mill. Olive said, "What are we going to do with McDougal's body?"

Hans replied, "We'll drag it outside, I'll get a shovel and some snow to soak up the blood."

After the body was dragged outside, Hans did get a shovel to soak up the blood. He then opened the door and pushed the blood soaked snow outside. He went back inside. Richard walked to where Hans was standing.

"After I fired the one shot at McDougal, I forgot to put another shell in the chamber. It's a good thing for me those guys didn't reach for their guns. I would have been up the creek."

Olive looked up from dressing the wound on Tom's arm. "I'll bet those two stooges of McDougal's will try to make this out like we murdered the big fat ass."

Hans followed with, "All we have to do is tell the truth, each person, tell exactly what they saw. If after we tell our story, and they think we are guilty, we'll go on from there."

Olive was making some good stout coffee; she thought everyone would need some to brace them up. Next they could hear footsteps on the crunching snow. The door opened, it was Elizabeth.

"Who the hell is the guy laying out there in the snow, I almost fell over him? Is he drunk or what?"

They all gathered around the table or near by. With the steaming hot coffee, the story about Mike McDougal was told to Elizabeth who listened intently.

"I guess I thought Mike was a crook of some sort, but I didn't think he would sink this low, to try to steal this claim from you fellows."

Hans pulled his pocket watch from his pocket, "Damn, it's been an hour and Mountie Steel still hasn't showed up. I think we should hustle into Dawson to find him, we have to get this matter settled."

Hans and Richard headed out of the cabin into the winter night. As they neared Dawson, they could see the glow of the town in the dim sky. It was close to twenty to thirty below, the air was bitter on the exposed skin. It burned so bad they had to walk backwards sometimes. When they were close to town, the smoke from the all the wood fires rose in a straight line about a hundred feet in the air. Then it moved in a line to the north toward the Yukon River. This was some crazy north wood's thing that always happened whenever the temperature was about thirty below zero.

They had to pass the Golden Nugget on the way to the Mounties' office. When they were about a hundred feet from the Golden Nugget's front door about fifteen men came out, all were talking.

At first there wasn't anything said between them; then one of the guys that had been with McDougal said, "There are the two sons a bitches who killed poor Mike."

Hans and Richard stopped opposite the mob, about fifteen feet away.

A big guy in the mob said. "Is that right, you two are from the cabin where Mike was shot?"

They stood in silence, not knowing what to do. The big guy took a couple steps toward them and said, "Hold" Hold on there fellows, we don't want any trouble."

Hans pointed toward McDougal's two stooges, "They were supposed to get Sergeant Steel and bring him to our cabin to settle this shooting."

The big brute said, "We'll settle this shooting right now."

He took another step toward Hans who pulled off the mitten on his right hand and stuck his hand into his coat pocket. He aimed something in his pocket toward the big guy. The big guy saw that Hans had a pistol in his pocket.

Hans said, "If you birds want some lead in your bellies like Big Mike, come and get me."

The big guy said, "You're going to be in big trouble when the Mounties find out you have a gun in Dawson, you know that's against the law."

"I suggest you boys go back into the Golden Nugget and have a drink, before some of you spill your blood on this new fallen snow."

They stood there. Hans said, "Now get."

They broke ranks and trudged off toward the Nugget. Hans turned and headed down the street, Richard came close behind.

"Where the hell did, you get the pistol?"

Hans pulled his big hand out of his coat pocket, his forefinger pointed straight out. "You son of a gun, you fooled the hell out of me. I thought you might shoot someone back there, man I was scared."

They bucked the wind to Sergeant Steel's office. They knocked on the door and soon there was a response.

Sergeant Steel came to the door. "Come in out of the cold, step over here by the stove, it's a hell of a night out there."

They shed their woolen coats, and moved over to the heavy wood stove.

"Can I get you men a cup of hot tea?"

Richard said, "That would be great, on a night like this, a hot cup of tea should warm me up."

Sergeant Steel invited them to sit down at the table. When they were all sitting, including Corporal Hutchinson, Sergeant Steel told the two guests, "Gentlemen, you came here for a reason, I think at this time we should hear you out."

Hans set his tea cup down, and then said, "I'm afraid Richard had a run in with Mike McDougal tonight."

After that he told the sergeant the entire story and he listened intently. He had a tablet on the table, and throughout the story, he was making notes.

When Hans finished, the head Mountie asked him, "Are you the one that tracked down the gold thief, and in turn shot him dead?"

Hans really hated to hear this conversation come up at this time.

Reluctantly, he said, "Yes, I was one of the two men that tracked down the thief who stole our gold and unfortunately he was killed when he opened fire on us."

"Now you have another case where your friend shot and killed a man, in what you call self defense," the Mountie replied.

"Sir, I know it doesn't sound good for us, but that is the case. If you would come to our camp, we have a signed statement by McDougal's two friends who came with him to our cabin. In fact, they were supposed to come and tell you about the shooting. I can see they must not want anything to do with the Northwest Mounted Police."

Sergeant Steel wrote some things on his pad, and then looked toward the two visitors. "We'll take a hike to your cabin in the claims. We'll bring along a sled to haul back McDougal's body."

CHAPTER 20

The four men bundled up for the cold and headed toward Richard and Tom's cabin. It was about a half an hour walk. By the time they arrived at the cabin, they were glad to get near the stove. The snow was now coming down in earnest. Sergeant Steel and the corporal sat down at the table. They read through the story that the two friends of Mikes had signed as witnesses.

"You understand, we'll have to have a formal hearing. I guess you don't intend on leaving Dawson real soon. We'll let you know about the outcome of the hearing."

With that, the two Mounties left the cabin, loaded Mike on their sled, and headed for Dawson.

"God, what a hell of a night! I'll be glad to get the hell out of this wilderness," commented Hans.

When Hans left Tom's cabin, he gave a few words of encouragement to his friends. When he and Elizabeth arrived at their cabin, the fire in the stove had died down. Hans loaded the stove and told Elizabeth to grab the bottle and their two cups. "I know we need a drink to settle down."

They sat there in silence for some time, mainly looking down at the brandy in their tin cups.

"Hans, these shootings are getting me down. In the past three months you have been involved more or less in two shootings, and now two men are dead. I don't really like this. I'm not used to being around killings like this." Even though she was right about the killings, it really wasn't his fault.

"Elizabeth, you have to understand one thing. These killings were brought on by the people who were killed. If they hadn't acted first, most likely no one would have been killed. I sure as hell don't like killing people, but when someone shoots at me, I don't think I have any other choice."

The remainder the night, the cabin conversation was at a minimum. Hans knew that when Elizabeth was in a somber mood, the less said the better. He picked up the cards on the table and started playing solitaire. He knew this would keep him out of a conversation with her. He had a soft spot in his heart for her, and he didn't want to make any waves between the two. Tomorrow was another day, and the conversation would change.

When morning arrived, the cabin was cool. Hans and Elizabeth were in the same warm bunk. The night before had been somewhat of a trial for their affection. Hans was the first to awake. He could hear Elizabeth was still in a deep sleep. As he lay there, he thought of their togetherness.

He realized that he was truly in love with this woman lying next to him.

He wondered to himself what he should say to her to convey his feelings. He remembered last night Elizabeth had been very upset with him for killing the man who stole their gold. Even though he knew the crook deserved what he finally got in the end.

He heard her stir, and thought she must be awake.

He whispered, "Elizabeth….and again, "Elizabeth." In the dark cold cabin, she woke up. "Hans, are you talking to me?"

"I wasn't sure if you were awake, I want to say something to you."

"What is it Hans?"

He hesitated, "I want to tell you, that you have made me feel so different in the past week. I have grown much closer to you since the passing of Bert. I don't know if I should say this, but I feel very close to you, if that means I love you, then I do. You have made me a different person, I feel I have a new purpose in life, and I want to take care of you."

She lay beside Hans in the warm bunk, and didn't know for sure how to answer his comment.

"Hans, we're in a very harsh country. I'm sure you're a lonely man, I have been a lonely woman. I hope and pray that you and I have found a common bond. I truly think I love you also, time will tell. It isn't hard in this country for a man to tell a woman, he loves her when the men outnumber the women, five hundred to one. I do believe you, Hans. We have been together for many months, and I do have the same feelings toward you."

Much of the excitement of digging for gold had dissipated. Now it was work, week after week, day after day; it was hard work, and it was getting boring. Hans spent most of the days in the hole. With the pick he chewed away at the frozen ground. It was cold and damp below ground, the work was very hard on the body. He had to lie on his back, picking away at the black dirt. The candles put out very little light. After all the hours he spent in the hole, he felt the chill in his bones. As time went on he started to hate the damn hole. At times he would think to himself, to hell with all the gold, we must have many thousands of dollars so far. How much do we need to go to the states and have a good life? Hans' thoughts came to Elizabeth. I wonder if she means what she says, does she really love me, and will we go to the states next spring?

Throughout the following winter months, Hans thought about Elizabeth and her feelings every day while he was in the mine. One evening after supper, they sat down at the table. The wood in the stove was making a crisp crackling sound; it was a peaceful evening after a long day's work. Tonight, they ate moose meat, which by now was getting very low since they had started sharing the meat with their friends. It didn't last as long as they had hoped. From now on it would be dried salmon or bacon. As they sat across the table, there was peace in this rustic log cabin. Elizabeth laid her hands on top of Hans' large right hand; a very warm feeling went into his hand and his body. They sat there looking at each other. He could see a gleam in her eyes he hadn't seen before. He placed his other hand on top of hers; the warmth was stronger than ever.

He looked into her eyes, and asked her, "Elizabeth, do you love me?"

At that time she squeezed his hand and said, "Yes, Hans, I do love you." He stretched his body to give her their first kiss.

Then he said, "Elizabeth, you have made me a very happy man. I have been in love with you for a very long time. When I first met you on your claim, your beauty overwhelmed me. You had a lady- like appearance I had never seen in a woman. I really think in many ways you are stronger than most men in the gold fields. I think this is one of the reasons I was so attracted to you. I truly hope we grow very old together, and have many happy years".

In the morning they brought the gold into the Canadian Bank of Commerce. After all the bags were brought in they watched the assayer determine the quality of the gold. Two hours passed before all the gold was assayed. Then another half an hour before the bank officer sat down to talked to the pair.

The first thing the officer said was, "You have a large amount of wealth in those bags. Just how do you want us to handle the gold?"

Elizabeth spoke up. "We want to convert the gold to cash. We want five hundred dollars in cash and the rest deposited in your bank for when we head south this spring. We also want a box in the bank to keep our deposit books. We don't want to loose the book in a fire or whatever. By the way, what did the gold come to in cash?"

The banker took his pencil, made a number of figures on his pad.

"Well…the total amount comes to one hundred twenty seven thousand dollars."

Elizabeth looked toward Hans, he was grinning from ear to ear. They signed the receipts, picked up their five hundred in cash, and left the bank. Outside they picked up their sled and started toward camp.

"Hans, we have to buy a bottle, no matter what the devil it costs. There isn't hardly any food left in Dawson to speak of, but there is always liquor. We better invite Olive, Tom and Richard; this is a time to be with our friends."

The group gathered at Hans' cabin for their gold cashing in celebration. They had a great time talking of what they intended to buy when they all arrived back in the states.

On May 1, 1899, spring came to the Klondike gold fields. The snow was starting to melt; the ground was still frozen, so the sea of mud hadn't arrived. The sky changed from the wispy high ice cirrus clouds to the lower puffy cumulus clouds, and the sky seemed to be a brighter blue.

All around the Yukon valley, small streams were making their way toward Eldorado and Bonanza Creeks, soon the sluicing would begin. The sourdoughs had waited from last September, until this day, to start working on the large pile of pay dirt they had removed from their holes. Soon, all through this rich valley, the miners will be working hard to separate the gold from the black mineral soil. This will be a far cry from the quiet, somber, seven months of bitter cold winter, when many of their friends died.

In a month or so, the first boat would come up from St. Michaels. With its arrival would be many desperately needed supplies; mainly food which was running very low with the miners. Recently, more and more miners had to trade or borrow food supplies from their neighbors. Flour was very low; most remaining in the camps was full of bugs which were easily removed with a strainer. Sugar had long since been depleted, coffee was in short supply, but miners have found spruce needles make a tolerable substitute.

The undertaker had his poor wood structure about full, with fifty seven miners who wouldn't be going back to the states with any gold in their pockets. The talk around the camp was that the undertaker most likely spent all the money for their burial on whiskey. Most figure with his dumb luck, he'd probably hit pay dirt when he digs the holes for these poor souls.

Hans and Elizabeth quit digging in the hole, all of their time is now spent picking away at the frozen pile of pay dirt. They use their pans and cold water to melt the dirt. The water is ice cold, soon the hands become numb, their fingers become so stiff they can't even pick a gold nugget from the pan.

Even though the temperature is above freezing, their hands are always in the water. Most miners have a fire built close to the pile to help melt the dirt, but mostly to warm their hands. By supper time Hans and Elizabeth are totally beat from the crouching down to pan the dirt; their knees and backs are so stiff they can hardly straighten up or walk.

Hans removed from a bag on the floor, their last remaining bottle of brandy. There was little left in Dawson, and the price was seventy five dollars a bottle. "Well Elizabeth, this is the last one, we haven't had a drop for a month. Since this back breaking work feels like it's wrecking my body, I say we numb the pain."

They both sat at the old crude wooden table, sipping their brandy. Elizabeth looked at her hands; she had cracks from the cold dry weather. "Hans, I have to get something on these dry hands, these cracks are driving me nuts, and they hurt like hell."

"How about some bacon grease to help your chapped hands, and then wrap them up at night? Maybe the grease will soak in and do some good."

"Hans, if we want to get the hell out of this wilderness by July or so, we may have to hire some help to clean up that large pile."

Hans sat there thinking about what she just said, "I never gave that a thought. If we could hire a couple men and pay them fifteen dollars a day, hell, that's only two ounces of gold a day. It wouldn't take them long to pay their wages each day. If we can keep them busy digging and panning, we'll get that pile wore down in a couple of months."

"I think you should go into Dawson tomorrow, and try to find a couple honest workers. You better stay away from the Golden Nugget; you might get killed in there."

After a couple stiff drinks, they ate the last of the salmon. Their choice of food was slim. There was still some moose meat left. Soon they would be down to the liver, heart, the neck and front legs and they would be eating a lot of soup.

Shortly after they ate they would go to bed. They were about out of candles and Dawson was also out. Life in the Klondike was getting worse, instead of better.

CHAPTER 21

Early the next morning, after breakfast, Hans headed for Dawson. He didn't really like the fact that he had to go into town and hire a couple of men. This time of year the town was full of bar flies and men who didn't get into the claims in time to find a good job.

He decided to go into Diamond Tooth Gerties. It was about nine thirty in the morning. He thought maybe I'm looking in the wrong place for a couple of hard working men. He had a cup of coffee; he sure didn't need a bracer, this time of the morning. As he stood at the bar, he glanced around the saloon. There wasn't much going on, a few guys were sitting around the tables, nursing a drink and the others were playing cards. This didn't look good at all; they looked like poor prospects for a work crew. He decided to take a walk around Dawson.

The sun was out; there was heat in the sun now. It really felt good; the air was still, not a bit of wind blowing. He walked past the butcher shop. As a rule, he would have plenty of meat hanging outside in the cool temperature, but today it looked like one mangy hind quarter of a moose hanging by itself.

Hans saw the livery stable at the end of the street. He thought to himself, I wonder if that horse we sent back from forty miles up the Yukon River ever made it back. He walked through the large double doors. As soon as he entered he could feel the heat from the horses. Old Zeke Miller started this stable the first part of ninety eight. He rented out teams to haul lumber for the mining operations. Hans walked in, saw a couple guys in the back loading manure into a wagon, and then he saw Zeke sitting in a little room by the wood stove.

The old guy must have been snoozing for when Hans said "Hello" old Zeke almost fell off of his chair.

"Come in mister and have a chair, if you want something, we can talk about it."

Hans sat down on the other side of the wood heater.

"Say, Zeke, last fall we had to track down some thief who stole some of our gold, he had one of your horses I think. The thief came to his end up by Stewart River. The next morning we hit the horse on his rump to send him back. Did he ever get back to your stable?"

Old Zeke sat there rubbing his chin, "You say that was in September?"

Hans said, "Yes, I I think about the middle of September, and I do believe it was a white horse. That thief was quite fat; he probably was a big load for the horse."

Zeke's eyes seemed to light up, "Yea, I remember that dude, he looked like a sneaky person, and I doubled the deposit on that bird. You say this guy dropped dead?"

"I guess you might say he dropped dead. He tried to steal our gold, and then he tried to do away with us up toward Stewart River. We wanted to talk to him, the next thing he started shooting at us. I fired one shot to get his attention, by golly if I didn't kill the son of a gun."

"You know I heard about that from the Mounties, they came by to rent a couple of horses to haul that big fellow back to Dawson."

Hans got up to leave, "I guess I was curious if your horse made it back. I think I'll mosey on."

Hans started through the barn, at the door he came upon the two workers. He stood looking at the two men for a second, he knew the two, but couldn't place them.

One of them said, "Hey, you're von of da guys that pulled our butts out of da virlpool at Canyon Rapids."

Hans stood there for a bit, and then said, "By God, if it isn't Olson and Johnson. We first met you guys at Tagish Lake. How come you're working here, and not in the gold fields?"

"Ve spent most of da vinter vorking fer some crook, last veek he fired us, said ve vere stealing from him."

"Did you?"

"Hell no, da old fart vas drunk every day, I tink da booze pickled his brain."

Hans asked, "What do you figure on doing next?"

"Da first boat dat docks here in da spring, ve're going to get on dot boat and get da hell out of here."

Hans looked them straight in the face, "You want some work? I'll pay you each fifteen dollars a day, and I'll give you your noon meal."

Olson said, "Let me talk to Zeke da minute."

Soon Olson was back, "Vhen do ve start? Zeke said ve could keep on staying here, den ve do some chores each day."

"Grab you rubber boots and work clothes, I'll take you to the claim."

On the way, Hans told the two he would have work for them for a good month. He then thought of Richard and their claim. "I just might have a friend needing some help."

The three walked at a brisk pace back to the claim. When they arrived at the cabin, Hans gave a knock to let Elizabeth know he was coming in.

"I found a couple of workers for us; I would like you to meet them."

The three walked into the log cabin.

"Elizabeth, I would like you to meet," then Hans stopped. "I forget your first names, I know you're Olson and Johnson, but I never heard your first names."

"Vell, I tell you vhat da first names are, dey call me Olaf Olson and my friend here, dey call Arns Johnson."

"Well, now we know. Elizabeth, you heard their names."

They all shook hands.

She said to their guests, "Would you like a cup of coffee?"

Arns spoke up first, "Yea I tink ve would like some coffee."

At the table, while drinking the coffee, Olson and Johnson told the story how their last employer accused them of stealing the gold and fired them.

"Now, I vant to tell you von ting, it vasn't us dat were da crooks, it vas the crook ve ver verking fer. Now, dat old geezer vas a slick feller, he sure made it look like ve stole from him." Olson commented.

Elizabeth hadn't said a word until now, "Hans has talked about you fellows back on Tagish Lake. I think a person should believe in others, until otherwise proven wrong. We're looking for a couple of hard workers; we won't even talk about the last guy you worked for. Now you will be working for us. One thing, what you hear at this camp and what you see at this camp, is our business, and no one else's business. So when you leave here at the end of your work day, forget everything you heard and saw. We'll pay you fifteen dollars a day, and if you work hard and the gold comes in, you will get a bonus."

Olaf answered Elizabeth, "By golly, you sound like da kind of person ve vould like to verk ver, right Arns?"

"Ya, dot sounds goot to me."

She continued, "We will pay you in cash every Saturday evening, and we expect to see you back here on Monday morning by eight a.m. It's about noon, so if you two want to start right now, and work until six p.m. we'll pay you for a day's work. What do you say about that?"

Olaf said, "Dot sounds like a goot deal to me, eh Arns?"

Arns nodded his head in approval.

Elizabeth told her new crew, "Stay sitting, I'll make you each a bacon sandwich that will take care of your bellies until evening."

So now they had four people working on the large pile of pay dirt. Hans and Elizabeth soon found out that they had hired two good workers, there never was a time they didn't see them working.

The days went by, the weather was holding up very well. Once in a while, a so called Alberta Clipper would come through and drop a few inches of snow on the ground. The work went on; Bonanza Creek was flowing better each day. The sluice was put to work. This made the separation of the gold and the pay dirt much easier. Now they could shovel the dirt from the pile into the sluice box and let the water do the work. The sun would melt the pile of dirt, but they still had to chip away with a pick. Fires were also built around the pile to speed the thawing.

Olaf and Arns were earning their fifteen dollars a day.

As the days passed, the sun rose higher in the sky, the temperature was also rising. The aspen on the distant hills were turning green and the birds were checking out the gold fields. For the past two weeks the Canadian honkers were seen heading north to their breeding grounds in the arctic. Hans and Elizabeth spent many hours talking about heading south to the states; it was planning ahead that made their miserable work days tolerable.

By the first of June, the pile was getting down in good shape. They could see that one of these first days, they would be free to leave the cabin for the last time. One evening, while having their supper, Elizabeth looked up at Hans. "I've been thinking."

He answered, "Here we go again."

"No Hans, I want to suggest something to you. Olaf and Arns work like dogs for us, we owe them a good bonus, and maybe we could do a favor for these two guys. We could deed them a half interest in the mine. I feel we could trust them. We have no idea what we could get for our claim."

Hans replied, "Let me think about this idea until morning."

The next morning at the table while Elizabeth was serving breakfast, she asked Hans, "Well, did you give some thought about what we might do with the claim?"

"I did, in some ways I would just as soon sell it and be gone. Then I think of Olson and Johnson, I really want to be fair to the two of them. Oh, I guess we could give them half of the claim. We'll make up a paper, have the boys sign it and give it to the banker."

By the nineteenth of June, the pile was depleted. This meant Hans and Elizabeth would be leaving the gold fields very soon. It was anticipated that the first paddle boat up from St. Michaels would be coming any day. They rented a horse and cart to haul the remainder of the gold to the bank. This time the bank took about four hours to complete the transaction. When they left, they had two thousand dollars in cash and a receipt for a bank draft to the Seattle Bank of Trust, in the amount of four hundred and twenty seven thousand dollars.

The first thing Elizabeth said as they left the bank, "Hans, what in hell are we going to do with all this money?"

"I don't really think I know. By the time we get back to Seattle, we might have some ideas."

They went back to the claim. Olaf and Arns were standing by the last hole

Hans had made in the ground.

He laid his hand on Olaf's shoulder, "Well boys, I think you're in charge now. We have staked out the claim boundaries; you can see where we have dug underground. Dig where you want, what ever comes out is half yours. When we leave the cabin, what we leave, is yours. Do you have any questions?"

Olaf spoke. "By golly, you two are nice people, ve hope ve can find you and us some of dot gold, maybe ve both get a little rich."

Hans and Elizabeth walked over to Tom and Richard's claim. They went into the cabin to join Olive and gathered around the table.

"Hans and I are taking the first boat down river. We are heading into Dawson tomorrow to buy some traveling clothes; and there is a place in town where they have large bath tubs. When we leave, we hope to smell good and look good."

Tom looked at Elizabeth, "I think Olive and I will be ready to leave at the same time. We cashed in the gold yesterday, so we don't have many loose ends to take care of. Richard will be holding down the claim, so we'll see him later on, about a year from now."

It was all set. One of these first days, they would all take one last look at this miserable, wonderful gold field, and try to remember only the best of times.

CHAPTER 22

The Yukon Queen docked on the twenty eighth of June, the first boat up from St. Michaels. As soon as the boat was tied up, a string of young and old men came off the boat; they appeared to be the new batch of sourdoughs. Their dreams of finding gold most likely would end with a sad trip next fall down the Yukon, with empty pockets. Then, in the end, who is to say who will strike it rich?

As soon as the boat came in, Tom and Hans purchased the tickets. This was one boat they didn't want to miss. On July first, eighteen hundred and ninety nine, the Yukon Queen backed away from the dock with a full load of wood, and a number of very happy people. It was a little after nine a.m., the weather couldn't have been better. As the captain backed upstream, then put the paddle wheel in the forward motion, he gave two blasts on the steam whistle. The black smoke belched from the wood boiler, the Cheechakoes were heading down river.

DOWN THE YUKON TO ST MICHAEL AND SEATTLE

The present story ends now, but we would like to tell you what happened in later years to the people in this story.

Hans and Elizabeth kept in touch with Olson and Johnson. Over the following three years Olson and Johnson sent them fifty three thousand dollars for their half of the gold taken from the claim. By this time their partners said they had all of the ground dug up.

Richard stayed in the Yukon for many years; you might say gold mining got into his blood. After he and Tom settled up the following year, Richard went on to acquire many more claims. By the time he left Dawson City in nineteen four, he was still single, but he left town with a great sum of money.

Tom and Olive traveled to Dubuque, Iowa, to look for Jeb's sister. They knew she was in a convent, so it really wasn't hard to find her. She was a saintly lady. You could see she truly loved her work. When Tom handed her a check for sixty seven thousand dollars, she almost fainted; in fact, she had to sit down to gather herself.

In later years Tom thought back about this time. It was one of the highlights in his life. On the way back west, Tom and Olive stopped over at Big Fork, Montana. They had heard there was good land in the area for sale and the price was right. They found thirty four hundred acres, which they bought. It was north of Big Fork, on the Big Timber River. It was beautiful, with a large ranch home and plenty of out buildings. In time, the ranch was running four hundred head of cows, along with some prime bulls.

Over the years Tom and Olive had six children, four boys and two girls. Since they were Olive's daughters, the girls could keep up working with the boys on the ranch.

Hans and Elizabeth had a hankering to head south from Seattle to southern California. Along the way they went into Idaho, looking for Bert's heirs. They spent a month, cris-crossing the state, looking for someone related to Bert Thompson. There were people who had known Bert years ago, but no one knew of any relatives. It was a dead end, they hated to give up, but there wasn't any choice.

When the two arrived in California, they still hadn't made up their minds about in what to invest. One day they rented a horse and buggy to look over the southern part of the state. The second day the road took them through Napa Valley.

HANS AND ELIZABETH FIND THEIR RANCH IN NAPA VALLEY

On one drive way, there was a 'For Sale' sign. The drive way followed a small creek back off the road a quarter of a mile. At the end of the lane were old wooden shacks and a few out buildings. When they stopped, an older fellow was sitting on the porch. He told them he owned twelve hundred acres. He said he was too old to take care of the land and wanted to sell.

It didn't take them long to make up their minds to buy the land.

This was the land on which they spent the rest of their lives. At that time, this part of California was quite remote. With Bert's part of the gold, it was decided to build a school in his name. When it was built, it was one of the finest in the state.

Throughout the years, they had four daughters, and in years to come, Hans and Elizabeth had four sons in law. Later the twelve hundred acres were turned into a vineyard, and in a few years, the winery was making a profit.

After all the hardships in the Yukon, Hans and Elizabeth now truly had the good life.

THE END

AUTHOR'S BIO

Gene Madsen has been an artist for over 50 years. His travels to Dawson City in *the* Yukon and the Chilkoot trail inspired him to write this story about the greatest gold rush in American history.

Gene drew the illustrations in the book, to help the reader better understand the story.

Gene was born and raised in Iowa. He joined the Air Force in 1950 served 3 years in the Korean War. He studied art for 4 years on the GI Bill in New York City. After 9 years they moved back to Iowa. In 1971 with 4 daughters the family moved to northern Minnesota where they went into the real estate business.

Gene now lives the good life, painting, writing when he isn't fishing.

Made in the USA